Shimmerdark
sarah mensinga

For Christine

Copyright © 2021 by Sarah Mensinga

All rights reserved. No part of this publication may be reproduced or transmitted in any form or by any means, electronic or mechanical, including photography, recording, or any information storage and retrieval system, without permission in writing from the author.

First Edition published by:
Chattersketch Press

Cover illustration and book design by Sarah Mensinga
www.sarahmensinga.com

Sunlight for the bright month,

shadows for the dark.

Count the days by moonlight,

while hunters roam the world.

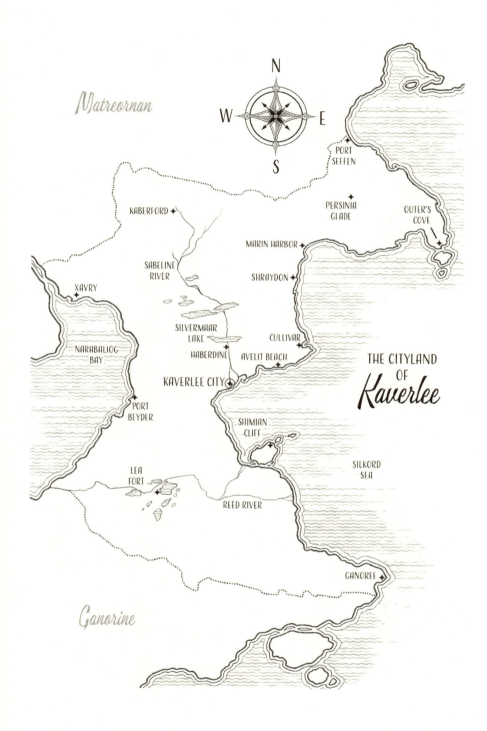

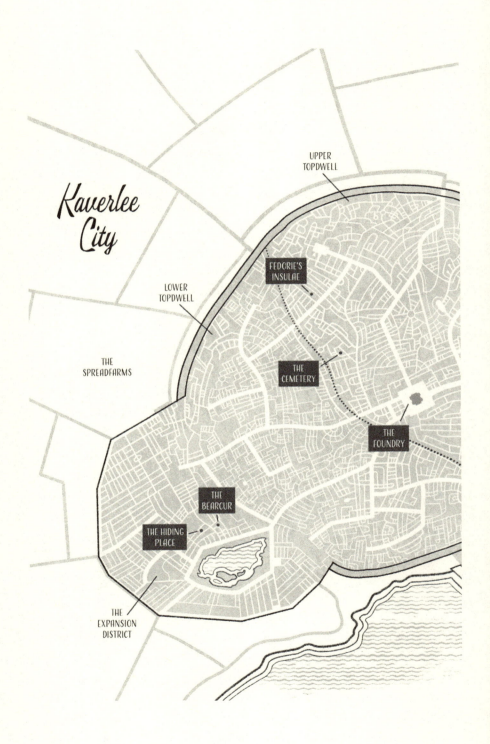

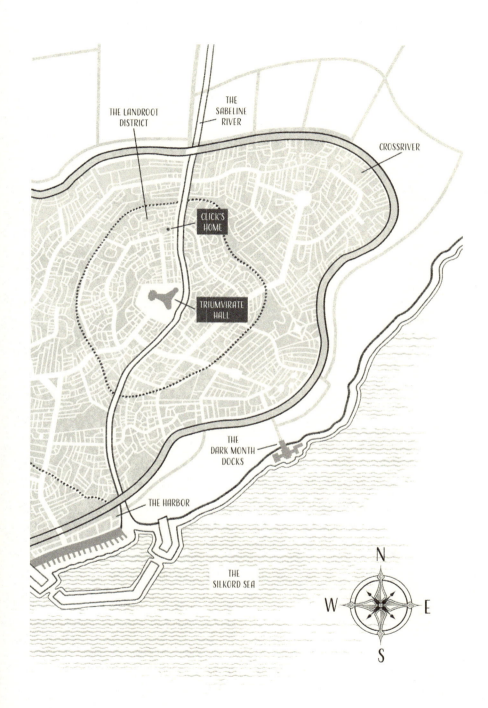

1

The Grimshore

They'll break in.

I'm sure of it.

The nocturnes will smash through the rock barrier and eat us. Me first, because I'll jump up and run, and then they'll devour everyone else. All that horror will surely happen in minutes too, which is strangely disappointing. It's not that I want a drawn-out, miserable death, but a quick, unceremonious end doesn't seem fair after surviving for this long either.

I should do something. I shouldn't just lie here listening to the beasts' overlapping snarls.

Maybe I can strengthen the barrier with shimmerlight—create some sort of energy blanket. But summoning that much cagic will temporarily blind me, and if the nocturnes still manage to force their way in, I'll be even more vulnerable.

I lift my head. Now I hear dry, raspy barking. It's surely wolievs.

I should wake someone else. I need help.

Tall and sturdy Fedorie lies next to me and Clicks snores beside her, but they're no use. I've tried to wake them during the Dark Month before, and when they lingersleep, they're completely unresponsive. Maybe it's because they're older; Fedorie is nearly forty, and Clicks is in his sixties. I might be able to wake Kary, though.

I create a small sphere of shimmerlight the size of a lemonelle, which hovers a few inches above my palm and casts pale blue light across our cave shelter. The floating ball of energy warms me too, which is comforting. There's probably snow outside.

I pull myself out of my itchy nest of a grass bed, and shivering in my ragged clothes, I walk around Fedorie and Clicks, over to where Kary sleeps. The rock beneath my feet feels like ice.

Kary's skin is just as cold, and he hardly seems to be breathing. Lingersleeping is so close to death, I thought everyone *was* dead the first time I woke mid-month.

"Kary," I whisper, shaking him. "Get up—please. I need you."

As for the nocturnes, they're getting louder. I hear nerve-twanging shrieks and angry snorts. Kary, though, doesn't move.

"Kary!" I push aside his ragged hair and pinch his neck just under his ear. Thank the source, he finally shifts and stretches.

It takes another few moments for him to open his bleary eyes and croak, "Xylia?" He hasn't used his voice for days, weeks. Not since the Bright Month.

"Do you hear them?" I whisper.

He props himself up on an elbow and looks sharply toward the cave entrance that we've sealed with boulders, mud, and moss. "Wolievs."

I nod.

Kary stands, brushes dry grass off his clothes, and together we creep across the uneven floor toward the jumble of rocks. After listening for another long moment, he makes a soft sound of despair. "If they find a way in..."

"I know." I touch his right arm, his shorter arm, the one missing a hand. "We can use the hollows." But I hate even thinking about the narrow pits that tunnel down at the back of the cave, formed by centuries of rain. The huge nocturnes wouldn't be able to follow us into them, but would we be able to wriggle back out? There are also only three shafts and four of us. One person would have to stand on someone else's shoulders, which would be a nightmarish position to be in if we got stuck. "I'll summon shimmerlight to distract them," I whisper. "It'll make me cagic-blind, though, so you'll have to lead me back there. We should also wake up Clicks and Fedorie."

"And they won't wake easily." Kary steps toward the pair, but then he turns back to the barrier and cocks his head to one side.

I hear it too. The sounds have changed from snarls and growls to whimpering.

"They're not trying to break in," Kary says. "They're just..."

"Fighting each other," I say with a soft, relieved laugh.

We wait a few more minutes to be certain, and then we return to our sparse bedding. My teeth chatter. Kary trembles too.

"Why don't you sleep here?" he whispers, lowering himself onto his thin, leafy palette. I usually sleep beside Fedorie but sharing my warmth with Kary is probably wise. Releasing the energy of my glowing shimmerlight globe, I wriggle in beside him and tuck loose grass and dried moss around us. Then he pulls me close with his left arm, his good arm.

It's surprisingly pleasant, curled up with Kary like this. His sweaty, briny boy smell is somehow comforting and so is the feel of his heartbeat.

Because I thought we might die a few minutes ago, fear still has its prongs in me, flooding me with urgent, unspent energy. I wonder if Kary feels the same way. He must.

A dreamlike sensation comes over me, full of anticipation and longing. I feel clear-eyed and purposeful in a way that only ever seems to happen in the dark. Without thinking, I lift my face to Kary's and press my lips against his.

He twitches, loosens his grip, and pulls away. "Xylia?"

The heady combination of loneliness and affection rushing through me quickly vanishes.

For an agonizing, embarrassing moment both of us are silent, and then Kary says, "Perhaps we should sleep back to back?"

What have I done? I know better. I'm a Predrae. I can't indulge my emotions. I have much more important responsibilities. "I should sleep in my usual place." I roll away from him.

"No, no, stay," Kary says. "I didn't mean… You'll be cold over there. I'm sorry, it's just…"

"Don't," I say sharply. My pride can't bear hearing him explain why my mistake was a mistake. "Don't say anything else." I then scurry back to my chilly spot beside Fedorie. At least now I have burning shame to keep me warm.

Fedorie runs towards us, bounding heavily across the rough ground as only she can. She's also yelling something, but the wind sweeps her low voice away.

Kary hurries forward, a chunk of driftwood under his arm. "What is it?"

I put down the fish I'm scaling and stand up. Fedorie doesn't look frightened or hurt, so why is she running?

She soon reaches us, but she's too breathless to speak.

"You look as if you've seen the Great Drae," I joke, and oh, if only that were true.

Fedorie waves her large hands at the shore. "Calvolin…" she gasps.

"Is he in trouble?" Kary asks, and that's likely. Ever since Clicks broke his glasses, he's been scraping his shins and stumbling into bogs.

Fedorie shakes her head, though, and at first I think she's grimacing, but then I realize she's smiling. "No, he's fine—he's just waiting with…" She spreads her arms. "A ship!"

"A ship," I echo. There can't be a ship. There has never been a ship. I must have heard her wrong.

But she nods. "Yes, indeed! A Kaverlee ship with all the flags and banners! She just dropped anchor, and a rowboat's heading to shore."

It's happening.

It's really happening. We're finally being rescued.

My heart floats up like a cagic spark. When we first dragged ourselves onto this miserable island, I didn't think we'd be here long. Surely Drae Devorla would search for me, her apprentice. But that was seven years ago. And what perfect timing—in another few years I'll wink out and lose my ability to summon shimmerlight. Now there's still time for Drae Devorla to teach me the secret of lifelong cagic; a technique she can only share with her Predrae.

"Hurry up!" Fedorie urges us. "You have to see it!" She's already running back to the shore.

I start to follow her, but then I realize Kary isn't moving.

"Aren't you coming?" I ask.

He gives me a strange look, and it's a look he's had ever since we woke up from our last lingersleep: part caution, part resolve, part thoughtful, and all very Kary.

"You go on," he says. "I'll cover the fish."

"Leave them. We'll soon have plenty to eat." Just thinking about home makes my mouth water. It's been so long since I've had anything cooked with spices and sauces. And there are so many other wonderful things we'll be returning to as well… clean clothes, cagic lighting, heaters, beds. Also, proper underclothes and books and windows that keep bugs away. We won't have to fatten ourselves up for lingersleeping either.

My hands go to my plump stomach. Will the Triumvirate Hall courtiers understand that we have to eat a lot to prepare for lingersleeping? They have strong walls and a star net to protect them during the Dark Month. They've never had to live like this.

"It really is a miracle," I say to Kary as he covers the fish with a basket and puts a rock on top to keep it from blowing away.

"I suppose so," he says, yet he doesn't sound happy. "You go on. I'll catch up."

Confused, I make my way across the rocky island that, years ago, Clicks nicknamed the Grimshore. Kary should be overjoyed.

We'll never be scratched by thorns again, we won't have to smell the swamps when they get hot and stinky mid-month, and we'll never be out in the rain for so long that our fingers and toes swell like bloated, dead fish.

Soon I reach the water, and then I see the ship. Its robust hull bobs almost impossibly high on the surface of the sea, reminding me of a fluffy bird on a tiny branch. A giddy tremble shivers through me too, for Fedorie was right; this vessel is definitely from Kaverlee. It's flying our cityland flags and has a Triumvirate banner. Because I'm used to being surrounded by broken, tattered, and faded things, and it's been so long since I've seen something beautifully made and properly maintained, I tear up. The boat's green and gold hull looks freshly painted, sailors have neatly furled its pristine, white sails, and the two energy reservoirs bolted to its upper deck gleam brightly in the sunlight. It's breathtaking.

Four unfamiliar people stand on the rocky beach too, talking to Fedorie and Clicks.

"There she is!" Fedorie waves me over.

It isn't easy to cross the sharp, slippery rocks, but I soon reach them. A tall man wearing a three-cornered captain's hat smiles at me. He's so wonderfully clean and so finely dressed, I'm tempted to lean over and smell him and then run my hands over the fine fabric of his palliumcoat.

"You must be the missing Shimmerling," he says.

I curtsy—awkwardly. It's something I haven't done in years. "Yes, I'm Predrae Xylia Amoreah Selvantez, Heir of the Great Drae."

The three other sailors exchange quick, uncertain looks.

"Is something wrong?" I ask.

"Everyone thought you were dead," the Captain says gently. "The Great Drae selected a new Predrae. You've been… ah… replaced."

2

Kaverlee

I've imagined returning home countless times, and for the most part, travelling from the Grimshore to Kaverlee satisfies my expectations. Because the *Duskrider* is a well-provisioned merchant ship, we're treated to warm baths, delicious food, and clean clothes.

But I struggle to enjoy any of it.

I've been replaced.

The Great Drae gave up on me.

I spend most of our journey feeling either seasick or heartsick. Yet at least I'm not alone; Kary seems just as miserable.

We spend most of our time sitting on the deck together, staring morosely at the Silkord Sea. Whenever I ask him why he's unhappy, I'm pretty sure he only gives me a small, sliver of the truth. He says things like, "I'll miss seeing you," and "I don't have a home to return to."

Fedorie takes him at his word though, and one evening while sailors are taming Kary's overgrown hair, she corners Clicks and me near the galley. "What are we going to do about our Kary?" she asks. "He's not from Kaverlee like us. His mother's dead, poor woman, and his father, well, he's not available either, is he?" She looks meaningfully down at us.

Kary's father is in prison, or at least he was when our ferry foundered.

"Then there's the..." Fedorie soberly holds out her arm.

Kary's never told us why he lost his hand, but it looked like a recent injury when we first met, all of us staggering sobbing and shocked onto the Grimshore. Like me, Kary was a child then, and I clearly remember the angry, bright pink skin covering his maimed wrist.

"He's welcome to live with me," Clicks says, lifting his bare chin, which is a part of him I'm not used to seeing. For the past seven years, a wiry, unkempt beard covered half of his face. The sailors helped him shave, and for the first time, I realize he must once have been a handsome man. "But the poor lad's from Matreornan," Clicks continues. "He doesn't have land justification for our city. That's a problem."

"A problem Xylia can solve." Fedorie gives me a firm smile. She was once my travel governess and guardian, and she sometimes still tries to boss me around. Although to be fair, she's just as forthright with Clicks and Kary. "You can ask the Great Drae to grant Kary land justification."

"Well... I'm not the Predrae anymore," I say, and a selfish, shameful part of me hopes that I'm reminding them that Kary isn't the only person who could use some sympathy and guidance.

Fedorie gives my shoulder a hearty squeeze. "That's not a problem. You're still a Shimmerling; You'll still live in Triumvirate Hall."

"I'll do my best," I say uncertainly.

I tell Kary about Fedorie's plan a few hours later. I find him where we usually sit, on the small triangle of deck in the prow of the ship. It seems to be the only place on the *Duskrider* where my stomach doesn't roil and churn. It's also a very beautiful spot right now. We're in the sunrise days, and the sky is a kaleidoscope of shifting colors and clouds.

"Your hair's so short!" I say, hitching up my trousers to kneel beside him. The sailor's outfit I'm wearing doesn't fit me properly, but it's still far better than the rags I wore before.

Kary leans back on his lone hand. "It's too short. I look like a woliev chewed on my head."

"Then you wouldn't have a head," I reason. Without his long, matted locks, his face seems to have new corners and angles. I still don't find him particularly good looking, but I can imagine someone else might.

"Ha, well, I *know* I look like woliev food because of this." He holds a shiny, flat object out to me —a handheld mirror. "I borrowed it from the crew. Are you curious?"

I feel like I'm picking up a venomous spider, but I do take the mirror and peer into it. An unfamiliar young woman stares back at me. She's not the round-cheeked little girl who once stood confidently at Drae Devorla's side. She resembles an agency worker who's spent too much time in a spreadfarm field. She has tan skin, thin black hair, scattered-grain freckles, and wary eyes. "I've changed so much." My voice shakes.

"You look the same to me," Kary says with a smile. But he also puts the mirror onto the deck shiny side down, hiding both of our reflections.

I tell him about Fedorie's plan then. How he'll live with Clicks, and how, after I plead his case, Drae Devorla will hopefully give him land justification so he can stay in Kaverlee. "What do you think?" I ask for his expression hasn't changed.

"It sounds like a good idea," Kary says lightly, although I hear a crinkle of hesitation in his voice. "What about you? What will you do?"

I don't have to think about my answer. I already know. "I'm going to make sure I become the Predrae again."

Kary nods. "Good."

After three lunar days, Kaverlee City emerges from a rosy fog. It's as grand as I remember, with countless buildings on sloping hills, all sparkling with cagic light. The protective walls surrounding the city look like stern, ancient arms, and workers are busy assembling the star net, stringing an immense wire lattice over the city. Once charged, the star net will keep flying nocturnes out of Kaverlee during the Dark Month.

It seems to take forever for the *Duskrider* to find a mooring place alongside the busy, concrete piers. Yet once the ship is secure, the captain won't let us disembark. He has us stay on board while he sends a messenger to Triumvirate Hall. "Her Imbued Eminence would be furious if I let someone so important wander the docks," he tells me.

I understand, but it's still an agonizing wait when we're so close to home. I stare hungrily out at the harbor, at the bustling, fragrant popinas, at the many chariots, coaches, and trailers, at the piles of cargo, and many ships. Even though it's late in the month and the harbor will soon empty, there are still so many people around.

In fact, rumor of my return must be spreading for Kaverleans begin gathering around the *Duskrider*. The attention sends fluttery, heart-thumping delight through me. Yet I wish this wasn't my first public appearance in seven years. I hardly look like the Predrae they would remember.

Four automatic chariots soon arrive, and several Shieldbearers join us on the *Duskrider's* deck. It's been so long since I've seen a Kaverlee guard, I'd forgotten how meticulously dressed they always are, with emerald green palliumcoats, silver shoulder clasps, and polished shockguns.

The Captain introduces us, starting with Sir Calvolin Nelvaso (Clicks's true name) and ending with me. "This is… Xylia Amoreah Selvantez."

Because he hesitated and didn't use my title, I clarify things. "I was once the Predrae."

The lead Shieldbearer, a man with a blocky mustache and rather flushed cheeks, says, "I'm afraid I must ask you to prove your identity."

My shoulders tighten. Not only have I lost my position, now people think I'm an imposter?

Fedorie snorts, clearly also offended. "Of course Xylia's the Predrae. I escorted her to Outer's Cove when she was a child, and I haven't left her side since."

The Shieldbearer frowns. "There have been pretenders in the past." He gives me an appraising look. "We simply need to see a demonstration of your cagic abilities."

Fedorie takes an angry step forward. "This is unacceptable. Xylia survived seven years in the wilderness. You should be—"

"It's fine," I say, putting my hand on her scarred, sunburnt arm. "I'll do it." I don't want to waste any more time here. So I summon shimmerlight and sculpt the glittering energy into a small, but not too small, replica of a nearby ship. Creating such a complex shape should be more than enough evidence that I'm the lost Predrae. My cagic control is why Drae Devorla selected me. Most Shimmerlings can only create small, simple shapes like spheres, pyramids, cones, and cubes. I can make much larger and more elaborate energy sculptures.

Several of the Shieldbearers breathe in sharply, impressed, and the crowd on the dock applauds.

"Now please take us to the palace," I say, and with a snap of my fingers, the glowing cagic ship bursts into a cascade of sparks.

The lead Shieldbearer nods and even awkwardly bows. "Yes, immediately. Although, I'm to bring only you to Triumvirate Hall. Your companions will be reunited with their families."

Fedorie makes a soft, pained sound. "I'm not leaving Xylia."

"It'll be all right," I tell her. "And this way you can see Markos."

Fedorie bends down and gives me a lung-crushing hug. "I'll write you, and as soon as they let me, I'll visit."

"Contact me if you need anything, my dear," Clicks tells me in his gentle way. "Anything at all."

Hugging him goodbye makes me realize just how skinny and frail he is. Our time on the Grimshore was surely hardest on him.

As for Kary, he takes my hand and whispers, "Be safe."

What a strange thing to say. "Of course I'll be safe," I assure him. "Triumvirate Hall is one of the safest places in the Connected Lands."

He and I briefly embrace too, but it feels like there's already distance between us. For the millionth time, I wish I hadn't tried to kiss him during the last Dark Month. That spoiled our friendship in a way I can't quite define.

When I'm finished saying goodbye, the Shieldbearers escort me down the gangway, through the crowd, and over to a cagic-powered palace chariot. Sitting inside is Matron Isme, the Maternal Superior of the Courtyard of Youth. I'm disappointed she's still in charge. We never got along.

"So it *is* you," she says as if she also suspected I was an impostor. She wears the traditional cowl and matching blue robes of a Maternal, and she has a lot more lines around her eyes than I remember. "Where were you all this time?"

I join her on the cream-colored chariot bench. "Captain Morrowmay found us on an island off the coast of Lowland Tilber."

"How unlikely." Matron Isme takes firm hold of the safety bar as our driver starts the chariot's cagic engine.

I grip the bar too, and soon the chariot is whirring through Lower Topdwell, past colorful shops, tall insulae housing, and crowded streets. We then drive through Upper Topdwell with its fine homes, lush gardens, and gilded coaches. My heart swells as I see familiar buildings. First there's the tall Foundry, where Kaverlee's energy is stored and refined. Then I spot the gleaming, copper roof of the Sabeline Tower, the tallest part of Triumvirate Hall—my home.

Home.

I'm truly home.

I'm so happy, tiny sparks of shimmerlight crackle down my arms.

Matron Isme gives me a sharp look. "I hope you haven't been wasting your gift."

"Of course I haven't," I say, willing the energy to fade.

For the rest of our brief trip, Matron Isme asks me questions about the Grimshore: what did I eat? How did I avoid the nocturnes? Who was with me and did they treat me well? And most mortifying of all; could I possibly be with child?

"Absolutely not!" I say.

When she finishes her interrogation, Matron Isme is quiet for a moment, and then says through pursed lips, "Lingersleeping; how clever." I think she's grudgingly impressed with me. Hopefully Drae Devorla will be even more amazed.

When we finally reach Triumvirate Hall, I tear up as our chariot rolls beneath the huge, brass gates and slows to a stop. A large crowd of courtiers, servants, and Shieldbearers has gathered to welcome me. I don't see any sign of Shimmerlings or the Great Drae, but they must be waiting inside. The people watching me now don't seem overjoyed by my arrival, but that's understandable. They're probably as confused as I am about what my return means. Perhaps they even expect to see a broken young woman stumble from the chariot. Well, I'm definitely not that, and as soon as the driver turns on the stabilizer, I stand up and give the crowd a confident wave. I'm pleased to hear scattered applause.

Triumvirate Hall is just as beautiful as I remember, with pale yellow marble walls, tall trees lining the plaza, and vibrantly colored flags representing the nine Citylands flapping along the roofline.

Head held high, I stride toward the steps that lead to the Gather Wing. Beyond that is the Three Crown Forum, and just beyond that is the—

"Slow down," Matron Isme calls. "I'm here to escort you, not chase after you."

So I stop and impatiently wait for her, and then we enter Triumvirate Hall together. Ah, it even smells the same—like velvet, waxed floorboards, and dried flowers. And of course, there's iron detailing everywhere. Nocturnes don't manifest near iron when the Dark Month begins, so it's used heavily in all settlements and shelters. We only had a few pieces of iron in our Grimshore cave, salvaged oarlocks and a medallion, and we always worried it wouldn't be enough to keep us safe.

Even though most of the palace's residents seemed to be at the front gates, we do pass a few servants and nobles, and they all greet me with stunned amazement.

"It is you; it really is!" one elderly woman says, clinging to my sleeve as if she pulled me out of the Silkord Sea herself. "I can't believe you survived! And you're so grown up!"

At the end of the central lobby, Matron Isme turns left instead of right, and I realize she's bringing me to the Courtyard of Youth, not to the Great Drae's apartment. It's possible Drae Devorla will greet me in the courtyard, but just to be sure, I say, "I must speak to the Great Drae immediately." The sooner I resolve my Predrae status the better.

Yet Matron Isme presses her thin lips into an even thinner smile. "That isn't up to you. The Great Drae is busy preparing for the Dark Month. She'll summon you when she's ready."

I frown. I know Drae Devorla has a lot to do during the sunset days: reservoir levels to check, gates to seal, periphery town reports to read, but surely seeing me would be just as important.

We soon reach the Courtyard of Youth, where I used to live. And as we cross the circular lawn surrounded by tall walls and protected by a domed, glass roof, Shimmerlings gather to gawk at me. Just like the crowd at the palace gates, they stare at me as if I might collapse in a fit of madness or reveal a gruesome scar from a nocturne attack. They are all so small and young—a few are little more than babies, wearing frilly gowns and clinging to the hands of blue-clad Maternals. As an eight-year-old, I fit in here. I was one of them. But now I'm nearly an adult, and it's clear I don't belong. There are only a couple of girls my age, and they're watching me closely, warily. They look familiar, but I can't recall their names. Even when I did live here, I spent most of my time in Drae Devorla's workshop.

Like the Shimmerlings, the courtyard is smaller than I remember but otherwise much the same. There are still a dozen colorful cottages, plenty of winding footpaths, a wading pool, and of course, the activity terrace. I only notice a few small differences; the amphitheater's seats are red instead of blue, the library has two stories now, and there's a small, charming building where the pastry tent used to be.

Thank the realms my Colossi are still here, although I don't like that they're sitting in flower beds. The Maternals used to keep them clean and oiled for me. Now the huge, metal figures might as well be oversized garden decorations.

I suppose their cagic-tempered bodies won't rust, but the soil still might damage their joints. At least this must mean no other Shimmerling can operate them—not even my rival.

"Where is she?" I ask Matron Isme. "Where is the new Predrae? I want to meet her."

"She's busy helping Her Eminence," Matron Isme says primly.

And of course she is. It's what I'd be doing.

"Perhaps you'd like something to eat, and…" Matron Isme eyes my stringy hair and baggy sailor's clothes. "You should also see to your appearance."

I bristle at that, but I do want to look like a Shimmerling again, so with a group of girls shadowing me, I head for the bathhouse, an elegant building decorated with wooden carvings of tropical fish.

And oh, it is glorious to sink into a huge pool of warm, perfumed water, and once I'm clean, it's just as delightful to wrap myself in a fluffy towel. After spending seven years carefully maintaining every scrap of fabric I possessed, it feels wonderfully extravagant to simply dry off with such a large piece of material.

I then enter the wardrobe room, where a Maternal shows me a selection of finely made stolas, underclothes, stockings, and shoes. I choose an impossibly soft, pale blue gown, and once I'm dressed, another Maternal ties up my hair, trims and paints my nails, and dusts color onto my cheeks and eyelids.

"Ah, there," the woman says, running a thin brush across my eyebrow. "I knew you were in there, Mistress Xylia."

And looking into a full-length mirror, I feel the same way. The haunted, ragged girl from the Grimshore is gone, and good riddance to her. My reflection is now polished and confident; the person I always imagine myself to be.

Freshly transformed, I make my way to the dining pavilion and claim a table beneath the latticed roof, leafy vines, and twinkling cagic lights. As curious Shimmerlings gather around me again, a Maternal brings me a large platter of food. And even though my meals on the *Duskrider* were far better than the endless fish and crab we ate on the Grimshore, these are the dishes I've been dreaming of: fresh cherrilynd relish, seed cheese, sauteed wild mushrooms, and briny tucker muscles. And in true Triumvirate Hall style, the spread is also pretty to look at, artfully arranged into a wreath and garnished with bright green mazeberries.

It's strange to eat with an audience, and I'm relieved when the girls start asking me questions. "Did you ever see nocturnes?" "What did you eat?" "Did you think you were going to die?" "Can you still summon cagic?"

"Of course I can," I say, although I struggle to answer the rest of their questions because I'm distracted; the lunar day is ending and there's still no sign of Drae Devorla. I'm more impatient than angry, but my impatience still coils up inside me, hot and anxious.

When I'm done eating, my Shimmerling inquisitors show me a fishpond, which I suppose is also new. And before long, a Maternal rings the sleeping chimes.

The girls scamper off to various cottages, and Matron Isme soon finds me. She's holding nightclothes and a small vial of cloudy, white liquid. "This will help you adjust to the lunar sleep cycle. No need to rest bimonthly anymore. I also expect you to generate cagic before heading to bed. You've missed seven years of contributions after all." She eyes me sourly as if I avoided donating energy on purpose.

I wish I could haughtily say I already visited the collection ports, but the truth is I haven't even thought about them. So I head to the nearest port and hold my hands over the brass donation tube. Energy sparkles and crackles down my arms as I summon seven spheres of shimmerlight and tuck each one into the opening, which hums with suction. Despite being irritated by Matron Isme, it is satisfying to do my part again. I've always liked knowing that our cagic protects and provides for others, flowing through the star net, reinforcing the city walls, and powering every home and shop. Our energy supports the periphery settlements too.

When I'm finished at the port, I instinctively turn to my old lavendrine-colored cottage, the one beside the library. But it doesn't belong to me anymore. "I suppose the new Predrae sleeps there," I say.

Matron Isme nods as she hands me the sleeping serum and nightclothes. "You'll be in cottage nine with Paislene and Auldora." She points to a pale green building on the far side of the lawn.

I recognize those names, although my memories of Paislene and Auldora are covered with years of dust. I remember Auldora always hanging off the Maternal's robes and Paislene often getting in trouble for sneaking out of the courtyard.

As I cross the neatly trimmed grass, I wonder how Fedorie, Clicks, and Kary are doing, and I feel slightly guilty that this is the first time I've thought about them since we parted. I hope Fedorie's husband was happy to see her. She told us so many stories about "her little Markos" that I feel like I know him. She especially enjoyed telling us how they met; she was a lonely Maternal who never quite fit in, and he was a Shieldbearer who told too many jokes. And even though their relationship was forbidden and they lost their jobs, Fedorie always insisted she'd "pay any price for love." Then there's poor Clicks. His wife died when the ferry sank, but he has two sons. I hope they've had a good reunion.

Finally, I think about Kary. I'm still certain there was something else bothering him about our return—something he didn't want to tell us. Hopefully I'll speak to Drae Devorla tomorrow, and hopefully she'll grant Kary land justification, and hopefully that will solve whatever's troubling him.

Auldora and Paislene are waiting for me in cottage nine's pastel-colored parlor.

"Welcome," Auldora says, smiling warmly. "Matron Isme told us you'd be staying here." She's thinner than I remember, and she's dyed her hair a rather decadent pink, but she still has the sad eyes and wilting presence of someone who'd follow Maternals around.

"I'm surprised you're not angry," says Paislene, picking her teeth. She's hardly changed, with her square body, long nose, and abundant curls. "Isme's being cruel, sending *you* to the Shimmerfade Cottage."

"The what?" I ask, although I'm not surprised that Matron Isme would find some subtle way to insult me.

Paislene lifts an eyebrow. "The Shimmerfade Cottage: where old Shimmerlings wither away—you know, Shimmerlings who are about to wink out, turn quench, dry up... however you want to say it."

But I shouldn't lose my powers yet, I'm only fifteen. I want to know more, but like everyone else, Auldora and Paislene also have questions: Where was I? How did I survive? Who found me? So I hastily tell them about the shipwreck and the Grimshore, and then I say, "But surely we won't wink out until we're nineteen. I'm only fifteen, and you two are what, sixteen?"

"Seventeen," Paislene says grimly. She stands up and crosses the room with short, impatient steps as if she's an animal examining the boundaries of a cage. "Shimmerlings wink out much earlier now, which isn't exactly surprising."

"What do you mean?" I ask.

Paislene pivots sharply and crosses the parlor again. "We donate energy five times a day. That's a lot of energy."

"It used to be three," I say, and now that I've pictured this cottage as a cage, I feel trapped too. "That's terrible."

Paislene gives me a sideways look. "But you don't have to worry. You haven't spent years filling energy reservoirs."

Yet fear still skitters through me. I may not have been visiting donation ports, but I have summoned a lot of cagic; I made plenty of shimmerlight shapes in order to move rocks and knock down trees on the Grimshore. I sometimes used cagic to heat the cave, and I regularly trapped crabs and small birds in shimmerlight cubes.

And because I might as well fret about everything, I ask who the new Predrae is.

"It's Tah Roli Miri," Auldora tells me.

I shift in my chair, a padded, teal piece of furniture that, like nearly everything in the Courtyard of Youth, looks like a child's toy. "I don't remember her."

"You might not," Paislene says. "She's younger than us, and well…"

They share a look, and then Auldora gently says, "She's not like you."

"Not like me how?" I ask.

Paislene tips her head back. "Hmm… how do I put it? Maybe think about it like this: you were a gamble, and she's a safe bet."

I look from Paislene to Auldora, still confused.

"The rumor is," Paislene adds, "you weren't easy to control. She is."

Again, I long to speak to the Great Drae.

Matron Isme's serum makes me sleep deeply and dreamlessly, and the next morning begins like they always used to; I wash and dress in the cottage, eat in the dining pavilion, and then visit a cagic collection port. Now that I've talked to Paislene and Auldora, though, I approach the port reluctantly and I'm tempted to tuck smaller spheres of shimmerlight into it. Who would notice? But then I feel ashamed. Kaverlee depends on the energy we summon.

As I send my final glowing orb into the humming tube, I have an idea. Forget waiting for Drae Devorla to remember me. I'm going to do something to get her attention. And I'm pretty sure the flashiest, most noticeable thing I could do is pull my metal Colossi out of their grubby flower beds.

It will mean using a lot of cagic, which suddenly seems very precious, but reminding the Great Drae that I'm here will be worth it. Besides, I should move the Colossi anyway. They shouldn't stay in the dirt.

I named them all long ago: Winch, Nibby, Goliah and Sevensy, and I walk over to Winch first for he sits directly below Drae Devorla's workshop windows.

"It's good to see you," I say softly, running my hand down his giant forearm, across hinged metal, leafy vines, and orderly lines of rivets. I briefly wonder what I'd be doing if I was still on the Grimshore. We'd probably be in the cave shelter by now, with Clicks neatly arranging our pitiful bedding and Fedorie bullying us into eating one last meal. As for Kary and me, we'd be checking the sealed entrance. I'd use a large shimmerlight wedge to tamp down any loose boulders, and because summoning that much energy temporarily blinds me, Kary would be my guide.

He was always the best shimmerlight assistant. Fedorie shouts too much, and Clicks is easily distracted. Kary, though, would rest his hand lightly on my elbow and patiently describe exactly how I should move each energy shape.

I wish I had his help now.

Instead, alone, I step back to get a good sense of Winch's long arms and legs, massive torso, and little head. Then I shake my hands—sending cagic dust glittering through the air—and I focus. Moving something this large takes effort.

I first pour energy into the small opening on Winch's chest, and as cagic fills the cavity in his torso, I reshape it with my thoughts, lengthening it into a crude skeleton.

My eyesight soon weakens, and a dark, blurry shadow seems to fall across the Courtyard of Youth.

I'm loosely aware of curious Shimmerlings gathering around me, but I don't pay attention to them—I concentrate on Winch.

When he's completely full of cagic and the energy's gleaming through his joints and glittering out of his glass eyes—I raise my arms and use his shimmerlight core to lift him out of the dirt and flowers.

His bolts grind and squeal as I coax him onto his feet. Vines also snap and leaves flutter down, but he's soon upright. Even though my vision is hazy, I think he looks much more impressive standing than he did sitting. He's taller than all the courtyard buildings, even the two-story library.

Drae Devorla found my metal giants in a storage room belonging to the long dead, Drae Myssariel. Drae Devorla thought the old Drae commissioned Kaverlee's tinker guild to build these huge, metal puppets, and she suspected Shimmerlings once fought nocturnes with them. It's an interesting theory, but I can't imagine anyone making the Colossi move quickly enough to be useful.

I long to glance at the workshop windows to see if Drae Devorla is watching me, but of course I must stay focused on Winch. I make him take several shuddering steps, and then I have him tug off the plants that still wind around his arms and legs. After that, I make him wave at me.

I wave back as if he's really alive—as if we're truly long-lost friends reunited.

Then carefully, making sure he doesn't crush anyone or anything, I guide Winch over to my temporary home, the green Shimmerfade Cottage. Each of his grinding, thudding steps shakes the courtyard, and although I can't see much, I hear Shimmerlings ooo and aaah. A few of them even clap, which warms my heart.

"Who are you?" a young girl asks.

I wouldn't have known what to say yesterday, but the answer blazes through me now. "I'm Xylia Amoreah Selvantez, the true Predrae of Kaverlee."

3

The Great Drae

I'm moving a second Colossus, Sevensy, when a young, filmy voice says, "Good moonlight, Xylia. The Great Drae would like to speak with you."

Wonderful. My performance did exactly what I hoped it would.

I carefully seat Sevensy on the lawn and then wait for my vision to clear. Once it does, I realize that it was a Shimmerling who spoke to me, not a Maternal. At first it seems odd that someone so young would bring me such an important message, but then I understand—this girl is no ordinary Shimmerling.

"You're her, aren't you?" I say. "The new Predrae."

She nods and blinks slowly as if she just woke up. "I'm glad you returned home safely." She eyes Sevensy. "I've never seen anyone move those metal men before. Perhaps you could teach me how to do that?"

"Perhaps," I say.

I expected Tah Roli Miri to be pretty or at least intimidating. But no, she seems timid and otherwise unremarkable with red-rimmed eyes and thin, drooping hair. And even though she's wearing an impeccably tailored stola, it's a dreary moss color with far too much black trim.

I suppose I should be relieved. With the Great Drae comparing me to someone underwhelming, hopefully it will be easier to impress her. And yet, it also stings that Drae Devorla felt this wispy girl could be my replacement.

"Do you remember the way to Her Imbued Eminence's apartments?" Tah Roli Miri asks as if she's not quite certain herself.

"Of course I do," I say, and then I set off across the lawn. Merciful light, I could find Drae Devorla's chambers if I were cagic-blind; follow the long corridor beneath the Maternals' dorm, climb the stairs lined with statues of former Great Draes, and finally pass beneath the bookshelf archway. I navigate the familiar route with ease, and soon I'm standing before doors with golden owleck handles—the entrance to Drae Devorla's chambers.

There, I hesitate.

I feel like I did seven years ago when a calm ferry trip suddenly became confusing, wet chaos—my future hinges on what happens next.

Taking a deep breath and reminding myself that Drae Devorla cherished me once so a part of her surely still must, I open the doors and step inside.

Oh, how I've missed this place. Her workshop is still full of intricate contraptions, partially built machines, and plenty of cagic reservoir tanks—some in use, others in various states of repair.

There are also shelves lined with tools and spare parts, as well as four large worktables crowded with smaller projects. I hear the familiar *tick, tick, tick* of machinery, and the air has a satisfying, oily smell.

Drae Devorla isn't like Kaverlee's past Great Draes or the Conduits from other citylands. She doesn't simply replenish and manage our energy supply. Instead, she tirelessly searches for ways to make our lives easier and safer.

Because of her hard work, the cagically charged barriers that protect Kaverlee City during the Dark Month are three times more efficient than they used to be, power reservoirs can hold more concentrated cagic, and she's made countless improvements to essential machines like chariots, heaters, cooking units, and scrubbers.

Yet where *is* Drae Devorla?

I circle the large room and finally find her working beneath what seems to be a subswimmer—a boat able to travel underwater.

"Your Imbued Eminence?" I call. "It's me, Xylia."

"Why of course it's you," she says, her voice muffled. She then wriggles out to greet me, and like her workshop, she's hardly changed. She has her frizzy, gray hair tied in a lopsided knot, she wears tinted safety-goggles, and she's holding a hammer in one gloved hand and a whirl-crank in the other. To my delight, she immediately embraces me and says, "You're alive! I was so happy to hear it! So very happy!"

"Did you look for me?" I say as she lets go, wishing it didn't sound like an accusation.

"Of course, I did." She pulls back her goggles and unbuckles her leather work apron. "I'm also sorry I didn't welcome you home sooner.

You wouldn't believe how many fuses I had to replace this month, and each time I fixed an energy projector, the lens cracked in another. It was maddening."

I smile. Those projectors infuriated her seven years ago too.

"Follow me. I need a break, and I want to hear about your adventures… or perhaps I should say, misadventures?" Drae Devorla leads me to the sun chamber, another room I know well. Located in the Sabeline Tower, it's a room where previous Great Draes entertained important guests. Paintings of waterfalls and lush gardens still hang on the walls, and a decorative window faces east, surely to showcase the sunrise days. Now, though, the sky is a deep, dusty blue. The sun has almost set.

The rest of the room is not very elegant, though. Because Drae Devorla values function over beauty, she's shoved all the original furniture—fine chairs and expensive tables—over to one wall and filled the space back up with storage chests, bookshelves, and a large drafting table buried in design sketches and hand-written notes.

After casually sending a few spheres of cagic energy into a wall-mounted donation port, Drae Devorla settles herself into a well-worn, leather chair, gestures at another chair, and looks at me expectantly. "So, Xylia, here you are. Trunks washed up in Ganorine, you know, but that's all we ever found of the Inlet Ferry. Please, tell me everything."

I try, yet my eagerness to ask about my Predrae status burns brightly in my thoughts, distracting me. I usually consider myself a good storyteller—at least Clicks says I am—but today there might as well be pebbles in my mouth. I forget to mention the most interesting parts of my story; like how Fedorie rowed us to safety with only one oar, or how we lost a sailor during the first Dark Month, and I often backtrack and repeat myself. I worry that I'm not making sense, and when I mention that Kary's from Matreornan and that he needs land justification paperwork, I catch the Great Drae eyeing a clock on the wall.

Merciful light, am I boring her?

After I finish my garbled account of surviving on the Grimshore, Drae Devorla assumes I'd like to hear about Kaverlee's past seven years.

I clench my jaw impatiently while she explains how King What's-his-name from Priffa died of a lung infection and that she's still having setbacks inventing a flying machine and how she'd like to make the Expansion District even larger. But when she starts outlining her plans for Kaverlee's underground power lines, I can't bear it anymore.

"Please," I interrupt, feeling suddenly very small. "May I be the Predrae again? All this time, I thought I was your apprentice."

Drae Devorla's expression becomes complicated. There's so much remorse and pity in it that I'm already devastated before she says, "I am afraid, dear Xylia, we selected a new Predrae."

"But you could change that," I say, hurt sharpening my words.

At least Drae Devorla doesn't insult me by pretending that isn't true. For although traditionally Kaverlee's Queen selects the Predrae, everyone knows it's the Great Drae who really chooses her apprentice. And of course, it should be her decision—a Predrae needs to be powerful, for one day she'll become a Great Drae who must manage all the energy in Kaverlee City and its surrounding lands.

"If you were significantly stronger than Tah Roli Miri, I'd step in," Drae Devorla says. "But… that's not the case."

Panic knots in my stomach, and I slide forward in my chair. "But Tah Roli Miri can't control cagic like I can. The Colossi were abandoned; I saw them. She obviously can't move them."

"You're right; she can't control the Colossi," Drae Devorla admits, eyeing the gray and gold tiles on the floor. "But she can do other things—things you can't."

"What things?" I say, my voice rising. "I can do *many* things. I moved some very big rocks on the Grimshore—"

"Hush, Xylia." The Great Drae holds up her hand. "I asked you here to discuss what will happen to you next—not argue about a decision I made years ago."

Next? I want to be the Predrae. How can she ask me to consider a different future? I've expected to be the next Great Drae ever since I was five years old.

"You'll wink out in a couple years," Drae Devorla says in a languid, relaxed way. "Then you'll have many options."

Just hearing the words "wink out" makes me feel sick. Waiting for my power to vanish will be like waiting for death.

And all that time, I'll have to keep donating cagic to the cityland—giving away the precious energy I have left. "I don't want to wink out," I say.

"No Shimmerling does." Drae Devorla leans back in her leather chair, rubbing her temples. "But at least in the meantime, you can relax and enjoy the Courtyard of Youth. I'm sure it's much nicer than the island you were trapped on."

I stand up because this feels like a conversation I should be on my feet for. The thought of being no better than any other Shimmerling—and eventually not even being that anymore—

clamors painfully through me. I need to say something clever, something impossible for her to argue with, but instead I blurt, "This isn't fair."

Sympathy flickers in Drae Devorla's eyes. I'm sure she hates that she lost me, and she also probably feels guilty that she's replaced me. "Once you wink out, you'll be free, you know. Freer than I'll ever be. You'll have plenty of marriage offers if you're interested in that. Former Shimmerlings often bear cagic generating children, which brings a lot of prestige to families."

I make a face. I don't want to be a wife. I want to be the Predrae.

"Or…" Drae Devorla says, smiling slightly. "You could become a scholar at Peremberie University or Polmores. You might even become a professor one day."

She looks out the window toward Polmores' jagged silhouette, and I suspect she's describing her dream. I bet she'd love to never have to think about cagic reservoir levels.

But being the Great Drae is my only dream, and if I can't change Drae Devorla's mind today, I'll have to try again. I suppose that means I need to make my cagic last as long as possible by avoiding daily energy donations. But how can I do that?

"You'll be academically delayed, of course," Drae Devorla continues, apparently still thinking about universities. "But I could hire a tutor—and I'm certain, given the circumstances, the universities will make an exception."

She's trying to be kind, but she's just upsetting me more. If she thinks the universities should bend the rules, why can't she?

"Does studying at St. Polmores or Peremberie interest you?" she asks.

I frantically try to think of another, better option. Who sees the Great Drae regularly but doesn't live in Triumvirate Hall? A solution occurs to me in a rush. "Let me search for new Shimmerlings. Let me become an Authenticator."

It's not a perfect solution, but it's better than nothing. Authenticators evaluate children with cagic gifts and then present the most talented ones to the Great Drae.

Drae Devorla looks at me with surprise. "I didn't know you were interested in authentication work. It's a worthy job but very challenging. I suppose once you wink out, I can contact—"

"No!" I cry so loudly my voice echoes off the high ceiling.

Drae Devorla blinks, shocked. No one shouts at her.

"I was just trapped on an island, please, *please* don't trap me in the palace." I drop to my knees, clasping my hands, not hesitating to beg for something so important. "I couldn't bear it! Please! The past seven years have been so hard!"

"Come now, Xylia…" Drae Devorla awkwardly pats my shoulder. "The courtyard is a lovely place… but I understand." She grimaces, and it's an expression I remember well. She often had that look when trying to unravel a complex engineering problem. "Your situation is unique. I suppose I could speak to the Chief Authenticator…" She looks deeply uncertain—as if she's about to change her mind.

But before she does, I scramble back onto my feet, saying, "Yes! Thank you! That would be wonderful, and I'm so grateful." And I am grateful. This way I won't have to donate what's left of my power, and I'll have time to figure out how to convince her that I'm the ideal Predrae before my cagic disappears forever.

Drae Devorla exhales, leaning against her drafting table. "Being an Authenticator isn't easy. Are you sure you want to do this? You'll have to travel to some very remote towns."

I nod because I will do anything, *anything* to become the Predrae again. Besides, the Periphery can't be worse than the Grimshore.

"Very well," Drae Devorla says warily as if she's already regretting her decision. "I'll contact the Department of Authentication."

"Thank you so very much," I say as I silently vow to find out what makes Tah Roli Miri so special. If she can do something amazing, I'll just have to learn how to do it too.

4

Outer's Cove

The next lunar day is gloomy; the sky is darker and rain splatters noisily on the courtyard's glass roof. I hover around the lavendrine cottage, waiting for Tah Roli Miri, and she finally appears around noon.

"Xylia," she says in her unhurried, almost befuddled way when she notices me. "It's nice to see you."

We briefly chat about the King and Queen, and then I steer our conversation over to cagic summoning.

"I was thinking," I say, smiling sweetly, "I'm known for my shimmerlight shapes, but what's your special talent?"

Tah Roli Miri blushes. "I can't control the Colossi like you can."

"What can you do, though?" I try to keep my voice light and casual, rather than intensely competitive.

Tah Roli Miri shyly tucks a lock of hair behind her ear. "It's nothing really. You'll probably just laugh."

"I won't." I put my hand on my heart. "I promise. I'm simply curious."

Tah Roli Miri contemplates my words for a long moment then nods. "All right then." She walks several paces across the lawn and creates a large, flat disc of shimmerlight. It's a simple shape and not that impressive; but then Tah Roli Miri steps onto it, and I've never seen anyone stand on cagic before. To my increasing astonishment, she then guides the energy upward and circles the courtyard using simple arm movements. At one point, she's nearly three stories above me. When she returns to the lawn, she blinks away her cagic-blindness and eyes me uncertainly. "The Great Drae calls it transference."

"Transference," I repeat, struggling to hide my shock. I know the term; it means moving cagic energy. Yet what Tah Roli Miri just did was much more advanced than any transference I've ever done or seen. She was essentially flying. Her airborne feats make my ability to move the Colossi seem childish. "You're very talented," I say, as my insides mimic her twists and turns. If I'm going to convince Drae Devorla that I should be her Predrae, I'm going to have to learn how to float around on shimmerlight—and how long will that take?

❦

As I wait to hear from the Authentication Office, the Dark Month slowly creeps by. I reluctantly donate more cagic, I play many card games with Paislene and Auldora, and I have a formal audience with the King Macreolar and Queen Naradara, who welcome me home but also won't restore my Predrae status. Worse, the other

Shimmerlings take a sudden interest in my Colossi; I suppose inspired by me. No girl can move them on her own, yet working together, a group of Shimmerlings make Sevensy take several clumsy steps across the courtyard.

When I'm alone in the Shimmerfade Cottage, I practice shimmerlight transference, but it doesn't go well. I start by trying to stand on a cagic cube about the size of a bread loaf. However, the energy either bursts under my weight, sending sparks skittering across the floor, or it shifts and is too wobbly to stand on.

Both Fedorie and Clicks send me letters. They want to know how I'm doing, and they either want to visit me or they want me to visit them. When I respond—which is challenging because I still write like an eight-year-old—I politely turn down their offers and invitations. I tell them it's because I must be ready to leave as soon as the Authentication Department gives me an assignment, and I tell myself that the Maternals don't want Shimmerlings leaving the courtyard or hosting guests. But deep down, the truth is that even if I could see Clicks and Fedorie, I don't want to. They obviously feel sorry for me. It's all over their letters: "Such a shame you aren't the Predrae anymore." "The Great Drae has made a mistake. You are so talented!" I could never endure that much pity in person.

One of Clicks's letters also brings troubling news: Kary's gone. He vanished as soon as his land justification papers arrived.

Clicks is clearly worried, and he frets that Kary's criminal father might have done something nefarious, but I'm sure Kary's just looking for work. He's proud, like me. He wouldn't want to be a burden, the same way I don't want to be a failure.

More time passes, and I begin to wonder if the Great Drae agreed to my Authentication plan simply to placate me. But when the Dark Month is nearly over, Matron Isme finds me in the dining pavilion and hands me an envelope.

"Congratulations," she says without any fanfare. "You've been assigned to an Authentication team."

When I was shipwrecked, Drae Devorla was busy building new subtrains. Kaverlee had a transportation system already, but these new trains would be able to leave the city during the Dark Month on protected tracks. I remember Matron Isme saying they would forever change Kaverlee, for now the periphery towns and villages wouldn't be so isolated.

I was often with Drae Devorla while she inspected the various construction sites. She wanted to make sure the entire subtrain system was safe with strong gates partitioning the stations, sturdy tunnels, and impenetrable train carriages. I was more interested in what everything looked like, so Drae Devorla let me pick out the fabric that would cover the carriage benches. I remember spending hours sifting through colorful textile samples and ultimately choosing a crimson brocade with gold stripes.

Because I was shipwrecked before the new train system opened, it still feels new to me. As I stand on the Landroot Station Platform, it's very strange to be surrounded by sedate, disinterested people as a sleek, silver train glides toward us. It seems like everyone should be gasping in delight or applauding, instead of looking mildly bored.

As for me, though, I'm amazed. The train is beautiful and elegant, and just as Drae Devorla promised, it's very quiet. As it slows to a stop, all I hear is a gust of wind and the faint crackle of cagic sparks. My dark pallacoat dances around my yellow skirt, but my hair stays put, twisted up in a tight coil.

I wanted to travel with a large selection of fine stolas, but the seamstress helping me pack thought I should mostly bring practical traveling clothes. I knew she was right, but because I'd been wanting to wear palace fashions for so long, it was hard to leave my decadent gowns behind.

But the same seamstress showed me that subdued clothes can be stylish and interesting too. She arranged a more appropriate wardrobe for me, and I do really like it, especially the dark mauve pallacoat I'm wearing now. It has pleats in strategic, flattering places, and the hem is covered in tiny silver grommets, which looks a lot like a starry sky.

I step into the subtrain, and there it is: the crimson and gold upholstery fabric I chose seven years ago. It's a bit threadbare now, but it still looks elegant covering the seats. I wonder if Drae Devorla would ask for my opinion on important projects these days. Probably not, which makes me sad, and I feel even glummer when a loudspeaker reminds me where I'm going; this train follows the Periphery's northeastern coast to Outer's Cove.

Because my Authentication mentors are currently in a remote settlement with no subtrain station, I'll have to wait for them in that lonesome village.

Yet it's not really Outer's Cove that bothers me, it's who lives there.

"Your family will surely be pleased to see you," Matron Isme said when she gave me my subtrain tickets. "You used to visit them each year, didn't you?"

I nodded, trying to keep my expression serene and blank, for the truth is, I hated those visits. Because I was authenticated at a very young age and never knew my family, it was like being forced to visit strangers. And in the end, I was right to resent those trips; I was shipwrecked while returning from Outer's Cove.

Now, I sit across from the train's sliding doors and think about my parents' confounding decision. When Periphery children are authenticated, their family is offered an allowance and land justification in Kaverlee City. But my parents gave up a life of privilege and safety in exchange for annual visits with me. I still don't understand why. Shimmerling parents who move to Kaverlee can visit their children on Connection Day, so it's not like they wouldn't have ever seen me.

The subtrain leaves the brightly lit station with a confident whoosh and speeds into the dark tunnels. The windows reflect the train's bright interior, yet every so often, pillars flicker by or I glimpse a wire cage that protects the above ground tracks. I occasionally even see a gleam of moonlight on the Silkord Sea.

Someone left a newsreader on the opposite bench, and I pick it up. Newsreaders weren't allowed in the Courtyard of Youth, and so I find it slightly thrilling to hold something forbidden. On the first page is a drawing of me walking down the Duskrider's gangway with a headline that reads: *Former Predrae Survives Harrowing Ordeal*. What follows is a fairly accurate account of my time on the Grimshore. Whoever wrote it must have spoken to Fedorie or Clicks. I wish they had drawn me the way I look now, though. The girl in the newsreader seems defeated and broken, and although things aren't exactly going my way, I certainly haven't given up.

The subtrain first stops in Avelit Beach, pulling into a dimly lit station and waiting as passengers disembark. It passes through Cullivar next and then Shraydon, and by the time we reach Marin Harbor, my train carriage is almost empty. I suppose I'm not surprised. Not many people want to leave Kaverlee City during the Dark Month.

I buy a small meal in the dining carriage—sliced fruit, bland dumplings, and spiced tea. After I eat, I spend the next few hours planning a training regimen for myself so I can master Tah Roli Miri's fancy transference, and I also doze a bit, resting my head on a padded seat back.

I try not to think about my family, but I do anyway. Will my mother still constantly ask to braid my hair? Will my father still tell dull stories about the Hidden Gods? Will Fifsa still pester me to play dolls? Will Osren still put dead mice in my bed?

Now when I look through the subtrain's windows, all I see is a blur of gray, blue, and black, and even if I put my face against the glass and curl my hands around my eyes, I still see nothing. Although there is one moment, when we cross a deep gorge in a protected bridge, that I notice the shaggy shapes of nocturnes climbing over snowy rocks below—wolievs probably.

At last, the subtrain eases into Outer's Cove station with a soft hiss that almost seems like a polite, put-upon sigh. The doors slide open, and I step out onto a tiled platform, where I pull an envelope from my handbag. Matron Isme wrote down important information for me, such as my Authenticator trainee number, the subtrain schedule, and directions to my family's Dark Month shelter: *Follow the central tunnel, climb the third flight of stairs, and enter the first enclosure on the left. The door is an empty grain bag.*

It's absurd to see "empty grain bag" written in Matron Isme's prim, curly handwriting on expensive palace stationary, and I almost laugh out loud. Instead, though, I tuck the note back into my handbag and wait for my traveling chest.

After a few moments, a voice crackles through the loudspeaker on the wall. "Outer's Cove! End of the line!"

Although this place is smaller and humbler than the stations in Kaverlee, it's still clean and functional like all Drae Devorla's projects. The pearly tiles covering the walls have an appealing simplicity, and aside from a prudent use of iron to keep nocturnes from manifesting, there's no unnecessary decorations or showy architecture.

"Ah! Here you are!"

I turn to see a young woman walking toward me. She must be my older sister Fifsa.

As soon as she's within arm's reach, she hugs me so tightly I yelp. She then inspects my face, running her hands along my jaw.

I'd forgotten this about my family—how they handle me like I'm a prized trinket.

"Just look at you!" Fifsa squeezes my pallacoat sleeves. In comparison, her cloak is frayed and has a large, old-fashioned collar. "We might as well be twins, wouldn't you say?"

With her pointy chin, dark brown hair, and scattered moles, I suppose Fifsa does resemble the young woman I saw in Kary's handheld mirror. But now that I've dyed my hair a gleaming blue-green and I cover my moles with opaque cream, I don't see a similarity. I also don't wear spectacles like Fifsa does.

The station porter finally trundles over with my traveling chest, but then he heaves it off his dolly and *walks away.*

"Excuse me sir," I call after him. "I'd like assistance with my bags. This isn't my final destination."

"Didn't think you lived in a subtrain station," he says, smirking. "You'll have to take it from here, miss. I've got other duties."

I'm stunned by his rudeness. The Kaverlee porters picked up my luggage from Triumvirate Hall. I can't carry this chest on my own.

"Oh, it's not so bad," Fifsa says, grabbing one of the trunk's hinged handles. "I'll help."

"Well, I'm going to file a complaint," I say, gripping the other handle with both hands. I suppose if I survived on the Grimshore, I can haul my belongings a short distance. But what poor service. I bet Tah Roli Miri could move this trunk on floating shimmerlight. I wish I could too.

"Osren would have come to meet you as well," Fifsa tells me as we stagger through the station like two dockworkers, "but he's on nocturne patrol. And of course, Mother's making far too much food. You know how she gets."

I don't know how she gets, but I keep that thought to myself.

We haul my traveling chest out of the clean, spacious subtrain station and into the much older Outer's Cove shelter, a dank space full of tents and crude shacks and far too many people. I immediately feel claustrophobic, and I have the odd sense that I've traveled from modern, bright Kaverlee to the farthest corner of the periphery lands in a single stride.

It will all be worth it, I remind myself. I no longer have to donate cagic, and I'll have plenty of time to practice transference.

"Will I see Father today?" I ask, and if I wasn't carrying my trunk, I'd cover my nose. The shelter reeks of sweat, mildew, and animals. I understand that farmers don't want to risk their livestock because nocturnes will devour anything, but I wish they'd build a separate shelter for them or at least have better ventilation.

Fifsa hasn't answered my question so I ask it again. "What about Father? Will I see him today?"

"Ah…" She adjusts her grip on the heavy chest and then looks up sadly. "I guess no one told you, but… Father's dead."

"Oh." I feel a pang of loss, which I suppose is natural, but it still surprises me because I hardly knew him.

"It happened two years ago," Fifsa explains. "A molzer tunneled into the shelter."

"How terrible," I say. Molzers are a very rare species of nocturne.

She nods and lifts her spectacles to brush aside tears. "Three other people died too. I'm so sorry you had to hear about it from me. That's a pitiful welcome home, isn't it?"

All I can remember about my father is that he was a wiry man who smelled like incense, often talked about the Hidden Gods, and called me Xye-Xye whether I liked it or not.

"How are you doing? Do you need to rest?" Fifsa asks before we descend a crooked flight of stairs.

"I'm fine," I lie, wishing I hadn't brought so many outfits. My trunk probably weighs as much as I do, and the handle's pulling painfully on my palms.

53

To make matters worse, I stumble at the bottom of the stairs, and I drop my side of the trunk onto my foot. I wail, and it's more a cry of frustration than pain.

"I'm so sorry," Fifsa says. "I'm moving too fast, aren't I?"

"No, no, it's not that." I hoist the trunk back up. "It's just so dark; I didn't see the last step." I glance up at a flickering cagic light bolted to the concrete ceiling. It's covered in rust and must be several decades old. "This shelter need better lighting."

"True, but it's not just the lights," Fifsa says. "We only get a small amount of cagic from Kaverlee, so we have to ration it."

"The Great Drae does her best," I say, feeling defensive.

"I'm sure she does," Fifsa says, and I'm not sure if she's being sarcastic or not.

We follow a narrow path between shacks, lean-tos, and jagged cave walls. Now and then, we squeeze past villagers and some of them stare at me. I suppose even in my subdued traveling clothes, it's obvious I don't belong here. A few people seem to recognize me too, and I don't understand why, but I hear them muttering angrily about Shimmerlings and the Great Drae. An old woman then steps into our path, blocking us, and I think she's upset with me.

Yet she turns to Fifsa. "Tury's still missing."

"Oh, I know. I heard." Fifsa puts her hand on the woman's shoulder. "At least it's almost dawn. I'm sure he'll show up then."

"I hope so." The woman presses a hand to her mouth.

"I *know* so," Fifsa assures her. "He's probably in the animal pens again. You know how he hates crowds."

The woman nods. "I hope you're right," she says, and once she shuffles off, Fifsa and I keep moving.

"I've been friends with Tury since we were small," Fifsa tells me. "This is the third time he's vanished during the Dark Month. Usually, though, we've found him by now."

"You don't think…" I shiver, horrified, imagining someone trapped outside of the shelter.

Fifsa shakes her head. "No… I'm sure he's down here somewhere. This is a big place."

We then climb a daunting flight of stairs, and once we're gasping and slouching at the top, Fifsa says, "Well, here we are! Or I suppose I should say, here *you* are. I live somewhere else." Her cheeks turn pink as if she's made a special announcement and she looks at me expectantly.

I'm not sure how to respond.

"I live with my husband's family," she adds. "I'm married!"

I nearly say, "Already?" but I swallow the comment. It's just that people rarely marry when they're seventeen in Kaverlee. Fedorie married Markos when she was twenty-six, and Clicks married his wife when he was thirty.

"My husband Gefro can't wait to meet you," Fifsa gushes, her cheeks still rosy. "But he's working in the deep cellars today." She turns to the nearest shack. "Mother! Xylia's here!"

I feel a chilly rush of something, trepidation maybe, as my mother appears. Unlike Fifsa, who transformed from a doll-loving child into a too-perky young woman, Mother has barely changed. Her hair is slightly grayer, and her face has a few more lines, but otherwise she's the same frail-looking woman who gave me an unwanted kiss goodbye seven years ago.

"Xylia!" she says in her thin, fragile voice, and then even though she looks weak, she pulls me into a surprisingly tight embrace. "I never thought I'd hold you again, my dear, darling daughter!"

"Whose fault is that?" I want to say, but I don't.

Mother lets go of me, but then she strokes my hair like I'm an expensive Landroot dog. "I'm so glad you've come to visit us. I really am—even if it's just for a short while. You're welcome to stay longer, though… If you like."

I glance at Mother's patched stola and the mismatched walls of her shelter. "I don't believe this is where I'm meant to be," I say gently.

Mother bobs her head. "Of course, of course. Just know that you're always welcome." She brings her hands together. "Well, come on in. I have soup simmering, and as soon as Osren returns, we'll eat."

Mother's hut has only one room and no proper beds. She lends me a hammock, though, and shows me how to draw the privacy curtain. "We can't use mattresses in the caves," she explains. "It's hard enough to keep mold out of our clothes. I am sorry, though. I'm sure a hammock isn't what you're used to."

"I went without a bed for seven years," I remind her. "A hammock's fine." I take off my pallacoat, but I'm not sure where to put it. It's so new and pristine, setting it down anywhere in Outer's Cove might ruin it. After a few moments of uncertainty, I drape it across my trunk.

"My poor daughter." Mother's voice quavers. "You've faced so many challenges."

I don't like the way she's looking at me—it's as if she wants something from me. Forgiveness maybe? Love? Whatever she's searching for, I don't think I'm capable of offering it.

When Osren arrives, he says, "Take a look at this," instead of offering a conventional greeting, and he thrusts a battered shockgun into my hands. "It's over twenty years old and holds only one-point-four paraunits of cagic, and Father still killed a nocturne with it. Could Kaverlee's precious Shimmerlings do that?"

The correct answer is "no," for Shimmerlings don't need to shoot nocturnes. With cagic barriers and a star net protecting the city, we don't even have to use Dark Month shelters.

Besides, no one can kill a nocturne with a single shockgun blast. If my father killed a nocturne with such an antique weapon, the creature was either already injured or very old. But I don't want to get into an argument with Osren, so instead I say, "It's nice to see you again."

Osren, though, doesn't seem to be listening, and as Mother ladles soup into tin cups, he keeps badgering me. "The thing is, cagic energy isn't distributed fairly. Everyone knows Kaverlee gets more than its share, and it isn't right. Periphery towns are more vulnerable."

I know I shouldn't get drawn into his rant, but I can't resist. "Look, the city needs more energy because more people live there. Besides, Drae Devorla thinks of Kaverlee City as the beating heart of our cityland. If Kaverlee is healthy and stable, it can support smaller settlements like this one."

Osren exhales noisily. "But that's not what happens, is it? The Great Drae keeps making Kaverlee grander and gaudier, while the rest of us in the Periphery suffer." Osren folds his arms. With his dark hair and brown eyes, he looks like a male version of Fifsa, which I suppose means he also looks like me. I wish he didn't.

"You're not being fair," I say, "I traveled here on a subtrain that Drae Devorla built for you." Another memory comes to me.

"Besides, before I was shipwrecked, she planned to construct cagic barriers and star nets in the Periphery to protect settlements like yours."

"We don't want barrier walls. I know how 'safe' those are." Osren stands so he can loom over the rest of us. "Besides, the Great Drae only lavishes attention on rich settlements with big ports."

I also stand. "I assure you, Drae Devorla is a wise and fair leader. No one knows her better than me."

Osren looks smug. "The new Predrae does."

"Osren!" Fifsa exclaims. "That's going too far."

And I'm so offended, I'm speechless. I feel like I've gulped in too much air and now it's trapped painfully near my heart.

"Both of you, please sit down," Mother begs.

Neither of us do, and Osren keeps staring intensely at me. "So why aren't you the Predrae anymore, huh? I think it's because Drae Devorla knows us Selvantezes are smart. We notice things, and she was worried you'd soon see how flawed she is, how corrupt."

"You're wrong," I say, pressing my hand against my chest. The cagic always simmering inside me feels hotter than usual.

"Be nice, Osren," Fifsa hisses.

He ignores her and stays fixated on me. "Admit it, Drae Devorla got rid of you on purpose."

"She would never do that," I insist. "She loves me." Or at least she once did. I'm sure of it. Maybe that's why being replaced hurts so much. I was once Drae Devorla's surrogate daughter, and now… I'm nothing.

Osren finally doesn't have a retort, but now everyone's watching me, and they look frightened.

It's only then that I realize cagic sparks are zipping around my arms like angry wasps.

I take a deep breath and will the energy to fade. But how unusual. I've never had a shimmerlight manifestation while angry—it's only ever happened when I'm happy. Is this a sign that I'm winking out early?

"Eat, darling." Mother nudges my bowl closer to me. "We're all just hungry—anxious and hungry."

I sip the soup. It's salty and citrusy, and although it has an odd gritty texture, it tastes good.

At least there are only two more lunar days until the Bright Month dawns. I wouldn't be able to survive here any longer.

5
Family

I have trouble sleeping that night, for the Outer's Cove shelter is no quiet, peaceful Courtyard of Youth. Hundreds of people surround me, many of them snoring, whispering, soothing crying babies, or simply clanging around their rickety compartments.

I get up once to use the communal lavatory, which to my disgust consists of smelly, partitioned pits at the bottom of the giant steps—I almost miss our trench on the Grimshore. And when I finally do drift into a peaceful dream, Mother's clock interrupts it with a jangling ting-ting-ting-ting!

I keep my eyes closed and pretend to sleep as Mother and Osren climb out of their hammocks and groggily follow their morning routine. Both of them have work shifts today.

Someone, Mother probably, clatters a kettle onto their small cagic stove, and I soon hear the steady whine of steam.

"I haven't seen my youngest child in seven years," Mother whispers. "Now I must spend hours shelling peas in the deep cellars? It's unbearable. I wonder if Gressa would give me the day off."

"She won't and don't ask," Osren says. "If you get on Gressa's bad side, she might transfer you to a different village or put you in a traveling labor camp."

"That won't happen," Mother whispers. "Gressa likes my tin bakes."

Osren scoffs. "It could easily happen. You've sold too many of your hours."

Mother sighs.

Once they're gone, I swing down from my hammock and pull on stockings, a black wool skirt, and a cloudy blue blouse with frilly sleeves. After that, I eat the breakfast Mother left out for me—berry jam on a slice of chewy seed cake with a strong, floral-smelling tea.

Since I hardly know my family—it feels wrong to be alone in their home eating their food. It also makes me feel obligated to them, so to get rid of that uncomfortable feeling, I meticulously wash all the breakfast dishes. I also roll up the hammocks, fold the blankets, and sweep the floor.

Then, at last, I'm free to practice transference.

I start by creating a small shimmerlight disc about the size of a dinner plate, which I then try to stand on. I make it hover just above the concrete floor, gingerly place a foot on the cagic, and then gently ease my weight onto the shaped energy. It feels a bit like stepping on a firm, warm sponge. When I feel stable enough, I slowly, ever so slowly, lift my back foot. My vision darkens and blurs, and I hang onto Mother's table to keep my balance, but I soon have both feet on the shimmerlight disc. Progress!

I spend another hour carefully stepping on and off different, simple shimmerlight shapes: a cube, a flat square, a flat diamond. Eventually, I try to will the energy platform upward and because sometimes thoughts aren't enough, I also gently wave my hand. The cagic shape rises faster than I expect, and alarmed, I lose control. The energy shatters into bright, snapping sparks, and I crash to the floor, cracking my elbow. Sitting up, I tentatively probe the joint with my fingers and find a tender spot that will surely become an ugly bruise.

After a few more painful falls, I take a break from practicing. I'm not sure when Mother and Osren will return, and because I don't want to be a burden, I decide to make dinner. Maybe a nice meal will convince Osren I'm no spoiled Shimmerling.

Mother stores food in covered baskets, and most of her stash is unfamiliar, but if I can roast fish and boil crab over an open flame, I'm sure I can cobble something together. Another challenge is that most of Mother's food is in tins, and I don't know how to open those. I pick up one of the shiny canisters and hold it up to the feeble shelter light. Maybe it has a latch somewhere that I can twist or lift or…

"Knock, knock!" someone says.

I turn and see Fifsa pulling aside the empty grain bag door. She's not alone either; a curly-haired young man with round cheeks and a pronounced neck follows her into the hut. He must be her husband Gefro, and realms, he also looks too young to be married.

"Good moonlight," I say, surprised. "I thought everyone was at work."

"Geffy's on his way to the deep cellars," Fifsa tells me. "But I switched my shift to a mid-lunar one so we can visit."

"Mid-lunar?" I say. "Won't you be tired tomorrow?"

"That's what I said." Gefro sits down on a chair, and Fifsa settles onto his lap even though there's a perfectly good bench nearby. "Fifsy's so stubborn, though." He gives her braid a playful tug.

Fifsy—*Fifsa*, I mean—giggles. "It's no big deal. I can always find time to sleep. I can't always see my little sister."

"So Xylia," Gefro says. "How did you survive all those Dark Months?"

I look at the floor, wishing he wasn't massaging my sister's back. "We lingerslept, but—"

"Wait, wait, what's lingersleeping again?" Gefro asks.

Fifsa pipes up. "It's when you sleep for the entire Dark Month and stay awake during the Bright Month—like animals do." She flushes. "Not that I'm comparing you to an animal, Xylia."

I cringe.

Gefro stares at me, amazed. "You really did that? I can't imagine staying awake for that long."

"You get used to it," I say, although the truth is, I never really did. I often woke up during the freezing, pitch-black Dark Month, and my dreams were always the wild, vivid sort that only happen when I'm not sleeping deeply. "We survived much like you do here; we sheltered in a cave when the sun went down."

"That sounds so scary." Gefro pulls Fifsa close, and she sneaks him a smile. "Did anyone die?"

"One man, but... it was right after we were shipwrecked, so I don't remember it well." And thank the realms. I've always suspected

Kary remembers more about that tragedy than I do. He had a lot of nightmares during our first year on the Grimshore.

"How'd he die?" Gefro leans forward.

"He thought a different cave would be a better shelter," I say. "He was wrong."

Fifsa pales.

I manage to politely answer or dodge Gefro's other inane questions, such as: "Have you ever driven a cagic chariot? What are King Macreolar and Queen Naradara like? Is Parade Day fun?" Finally, he gives my sister a lengthy, far too intimate kiss and heads off to work.

"Oh hurray, now it's just us!" Fifsa says cheerfully.

"You don't have to stay for long," I say, feeling strangely trapped.

Fifsa gives me an exasperated-yet-friendly smile. "Of *course* I do! You're my sister, and now we can finally spend time together. I wish it wasn't such a short visit, though. And why are you holding a can of smelties? Were you going to cook Mother dinner? That's so sweet! I'll help of course. Mother will cry when she discovers her daughters have made her a meal—just you wait."

Mercy and light, Fifsa's talkative. I hand her the tin. "Do you know how to open this? We have… a different type of tin in Kaverlee."

"Really!" Fifsa says with interest as she rummages through the storage baskets, selects two different cans, and then pulls out a winding gadget. She hooks it on the edge of the tin, cranks it several times, and slices off the top.

So that's how you open them.

As we stir, chop, and boil, Fifsa chatters about how sweet Gefro is and how they hope to have five children.

"Or six—as long as none are like Osren," she laughs.

I laugh too, and for a brief moment, it doesn't seem so bad to have a sister.

Thanks to Fifsa's expertise, we soon have a stew pot bubbling away full of dried tartberries, tinned fish, yellow rice, and soft white beans. It doesn't look good, but it smells delicious.

Fifsa sets the lid at an angle so steam can escape. Then before I can stop her, she opens my traveling chest. "I just adore Kaverlee fashions. I bet you have some gems in here."

"Please don't go through my things," I say. My family's habit of handling me whenever they please apparently extends to my belongings too.

"Don't worry, I'll put everything back." Fifsa shakes the ruffles out of an orange and fuchsia palace stola. She then holds the gown against her chest and twirls, making the bright fabric flare outward. "You know, I've always wondered what things would be like if I'd been the Shimmerling and you'd been the Quench. Can't you see me in a gown like this? I suppose that would make you the married sister."

I've never dreamed of being someone's wife—probably because I always knew I was going to be the Great Drae and Cityland Conduits can't marry. Refilling the huge cagic reservoirs, tending to the barriers, and caring for the Shimmerlings are all-consuming tasks.

Fifsa eyes me sideways, grinning slyly. "Have you ever kissed anyone?"

My thoughts rush to Kary, and what I refuse to say out loud burns a blush into my cheeks. I can feel it.

Fifsa laughs in the same airy way she did when Gefro was here. "Oh, I see! I don't think we're all that different, you and I."

Perhaps a part of me is like Fifsa—a buried, stifled part—and perhaps that version of me would love to marry and live in a Periphery village. I wanted to kiss Kary, after all. That longing was there—is there. But since I've spent most of my life expecting to eventually become the Great Drae, I suspect any other future would always feel like a consolation prize.

After admiring a few other outfits and trying on my hats, Fifsa offers to give me a tour of the Outer's Cove shelter. Since that will get her out of my trunk, I accept. We ask Mother's neighbor to check on the stew, and then we head off into the underground passages. Fifsa first shows me the massive shelter's entrance doors, which are made of iron and covered with charged, cagic wires. Then she shows me the spring-fed, freshwater reservoir, the baths, and the modest forum. Finally, we walk through the cramped work caverns where villagers toil for various labor agencies. Fifsa tells me that most of the contracts in Outer's Cove are for tinned food that's then sold to other shelters.

"It's hard work," Fifsa tells me over a cacophony of canning machines and meat grinders.

Just as Fifsa predicted, Mother weeps when she discovers we made dinner. Since the recipe was Fifsa's doing, I give each serving some city flair by arranging seeds and dried tartberries into a dragonfly shape on the stew's surface.

"It's supper, not art," Osren says, immediately stirring his food. The dragonfly in his bowl vanishes.

But Mother carefully eats around her dragonfly and doesn't disturb it until she absolutely has too.

At the end of the meal, Fifsa scoops up Osren's shockgun. "Time for my shift!"

"You're on nocturne patrol?" I ask, stunned. I assumed she'd head down to the work caverns. "You're so…" Small, I think, and fragile. "Er, it just seems like an unusual job for you," I conclude rather lamely.

"A shockgun is deadly no matter who pulls the trigger." Fifsa smiles brightly. "Do you want to join me?"

"Yes," I say, surprising myself. I am curious to see Outer's Cove's defenses, though.

"Wonderful!" Fifsa says. "Mother, Xylia will need to borrow some warm clothes."

"I have a pallacoat," I say.

Osren snorts. "You'll turn to ice in that flimsy thing. Might as well wear a spiderweb."

"The Dark Month is just as cold in Kaverlee City." I give him a sharp look. "And because we don't hide underground, I'm used to it."

I pull on my silver-spattered pallacoat, fuzzy scarf, wool cap, and gloves. Then we head to Gefro's family compartment, and there Fifsa puts on grubby outerwear that seems decades old. After that, with the antique shockgun slung over her shoulder, my sister leads me through several tunnels and up a wet, spiral staircase. The air becomes icy, stiffening my lungs as we reach a small chamber carved into the rock. Inside it, sitting on a bench beneath a small window, is a boy holding a shockgun.

"Thanks for switching shifts with me," Fifsa says.

The boy stands and stretches. "No problem. This your kid sister? The lost Shimmerling?"

Both Fifsa and I nod.

The boy, who's surely only about ten or twelve years old, looks me over skeptically. "There's no way you survived in the wild. Your clothes are too nice."

Fifsa sighs. "She's changed clothes since, you dummy."

"'Spose she could have," the boy says, not sounding convinced.

As he saunters away, I look out the window. I mostly see flat, snowy spreadfarms and a silvery patch of the Silkord Sea, but there is a group of buildings off to the left. That must be where most of the village lives during the Bright Month. The shelter entrance is directly below, Fifsa tells me, and there are two other watch-windows, one on either side of us.

"The nocturnes'll start vanishing soon," she says, sitting on the lone bench. She rests Father's shockgun against her knee and doesn't even bother to turn on the charger. "Usually a group of sharecks lurks around down there, but we probably won't see any today."

The sun isn't visible yet, but the horizon's glowing misty pink. By tomorrow, it will be light, and in two days, it will be safe to leave the shelter. Even better, my authentication mentors—the mysterious Golly and Theandra Shalvo—will be able to travel.

Warmer weather will be nice too. Right now, Fifsa and I are exhaling tiny clouds of vapor, and although I certainly won't tell Osren, I'm jealous of her ugly, padded palliumcoat. My pallacoat, although lovely, is definitely only intended for short trips from heated houses to heated chariots, not for sitting in frigid caverns for hours.

Even though I should conserve my cagic, I'm too miserable, and so I create a block of shimmerlight to warm us up.

"How nice," Fifsa says, leaning toward it. Then, only a few minutes later, she grabs my arm and points a mittened hand. "Look!"

The jagged shape of a nocturne lumbers over a distant ridge. It must be a shareck because of the fins lining its spine. It's moving slowly too and will probably vanish soon, returning to the unknown realm where nocturnes live during the Bright Month. Fedorie would love to see this. She was obsessed with nocturnes and had memorized all sorts of facts about them. Just seeing one of the monsters makes me shiver, though.

"Don't worry, we're safe up here." Fifsa wraps her arm around my shoulders, and I find her touch slightly more tolerable than before. "I've missed you so much," she adds. "When you were trapped out there on that island, did you miss us?"

"I missed home," I say, trying to be gently honest rather than bluntly honest.

Surely Fifsa knows what I mean, though. My home is Triumvirate Hall. It isn't here. She lets go of me and sighs. "When I was young, I used to tell people that the Great Drae kidnapped my sister. Sometimes it still feels like that's what happened."

"Don't be ridiculous," I say. "I'm a Shimmerling, and Shimmerlings belong in Kaverlee. The palace protects us, and we have to be there to provide energy for the cityland. Can you imagine what life would be like if there wasn't any cagic? You wouldn't be able to charge your shockgun or use a stove and your shelter gates would be useless."

Fifsa is quiet for a moment, and then she says, "That doesn't change the fact that strangers took my baby sister. I remember it, you know. I remember Mother and Father crying. I remember Osren telling the Authenticators that if they wanted you so badly, they'd have to fight him. He was only seven."

That makes me chuckle softly. I can't imagine Osren fighting for me now.

Fifsa warms her hands in the shimmerlight cube's soft, blue glow. "I'll probably have children soon, and what if they're like you... cagic-touched? What if I lose them?"

I'm sure she doesn't realize how insulting she's being, so I try not to get upset. Fifsa just doesn't understand what being a Conduit means; Drae Devorla lives a life of service and sacrifice. Yet Fifsa's probably never visited Kaverlee City and rarely left Outer's Cove. It's not her fault her perspective's limited. "I was treated well in Kaverlee," I tell her. "I liked living in the palace."

Fifsa's nostrils flare. "But you were young—*so* young. What if you hadn't been authenticated at that age? What they'd taken you at seven or eight?"

I don't understand what she's trying to say. "My cagic powers are very strong. There's no way I would have been authenticated later."

"I'm not talking about cagic." Fifsa gives me an impatient look. "What I mean is, if you were authenticated as an older child, you would remember that you didn't want to leave us. You would remember that you once loved us as much as we love you. But now you never can; they warped your mind in the palace. I thought being shipwrecked might help you see things differently—but it didn't."

"No one warped my mind," I sputter. To think I was beginning to enjoy Fifsa's company. Still, I think I know why she's truly upset. "You know it's not my fault Mother and Father didn't move to the city. I'm sure you missed out on many opportunities because they stayed here. If it had been up to me, I would have insisted my family move to Kaverlee proper. If you had, Father would probably still be alive."

I expect Fifsa will continue arguing, but instead she sighs and gazes through the crude window. "The nocturne's gone," she says flatly.

It is, and soon—so soon—I'll leave too.

Yet in the lunar morning, Mother hands me a letter that says otherwise.

"A postgirl just brought it round," she says. "It came through the code office."

I tear open the brown envelope and pull out a sheet of lined paper. Chunky black handwriting reads:

Dear Ms. Selvantez.

Delayed. Traveling north to Port Seffen for important possible authen. Will collect you before next Dark Month. Stay where you are.

Sincerely,

Golly Shalvo, C.A.

My hands shake as I reread the letter. Maybe I misunderstood something. But no, the worst has happened. I'm trapped in Outer's Cove—with my family—most likely for the entire Bright Month.

I squeeze my fingers together, and oddly, the cagic always flowing through me feels wrong.

My drinking glass suddenly explodes in a burst of strange energy.

Mother screams in shock, and so do I. I've never seen cagic like that before. It looked like a splash of ink surrounded by glittering blue sparks.

It wasn't shimmerlight—not at all.

Is there such a thing as shimmerdark?

6

Horselets

The Bright Month arrives with blushing light, frosty grass, and thankfully, no dawn storms.

Mother's obviously pleased I'm trapped in Outer's Cove and maybe even a bit gleeful. Her steps are bouncy, she picks everything up with unnecessary flourishes, and she even attempts to tell a few jokes: "Did you hear the one about the woliev who ate too many pies?"

Well, if she thinks my extended visit means I'm staying forever, I need to quickly correct her assumption.

So as Mother, Osren, and I move our belongings from the underground shelter to their Bright Month cottage, I say, "Thank you for letting me stay with you. And don't worry, I'll be on my way as soon as the Authenticators arrive."

Osren grunts dismissively, either because doesn't care or because he wishes I'd leave sooner.

Yet Mother says, "Of course, Xylia," and there is an indulgent sweetness to her words. It's as if she's a Maternal telling Shimmerlings that the flying wish dolphin really does exist. "Whatever you decide," she adds, "I'll support your decision."

"I have decided," I say slowly and loudly to make sure she's really listening. "I'm leaving Outer's Cove to become an Authenticator."

"And *if* you do, I'll respect your choice," Mother says far too cheerfully.

"I've already made my choice." I frown as I adjust a basket of linens in the barrow I'm pushing. It was about to topple out. "I can't stay here."

Mother smiles. "We're saying the same thing, dear."

We're definitely not, but at least I've tried.

After easing our barrows down a steep, bumpy road and through a grove of short, hunched trees, we reach the Selvantez cottage. My family may have aged and changed, but the little house nestled by the sea is exactly the same. Its sloping roof still has warped, mossy shingles, and Father's Hidden God trinkets still decorate the walls inside. The porch door even makes the same grumpy sound when it swings shut.

I carry crates and baskets into the kitchen while Mother bustles about, opening the heavy Dark Month shutters to let in the chilly, dawn air.

"No sign of nocturnes!" she says proudly. "I keep telling Marsa to scrub her floors with citrus oil before sheltering, but she never listens. Her front door has been smashed in twice by nocturnes, and ours never has."

"Where do you want these?" I ask, holding up some blankets.

"Actually, take this, Xylia." Mother hands me a heavy pitcher, but before she tells me where to put it, we hear Osren wail.

"It's ruined! All ruined!"

"What's ruined?" I ask as Mother rushes outside.

I put down the pitcher and follow her around to the back of the cottage. There, we find my brother stomping around a heap of splintered wood. It might once have been a small shed. He snatches up particularly jagged planks and hurls them into the long grass, shouting things like, "Stupid!" and "Waste of time!" and "Bile-guzzling nocturnes!"

Mother gasps. "Osren!"

Wishing I wasn't related to him, I say, "A tantrum won't solve anything."

Osren looks tempted to throw splintered wood at me. "Nobody wants your city opinions." He then pouts at Mother. "Why do they keep destroying it? Is it the smell? I can't afford to rebuild it over and over, but I like to keep"—he eyes me suspiciously—"our *investments* here rather than at Bernan's. I'm better with them."

Mother shakes her head. "I'm sorry, Ozzie. Maybe this is a sign that your little project isn't a good idea. If the labor agents file a complaint, you'll lose everything."

"What are you talking about?" I ask. "What project?"

Osren glares at me. "Stop pretending you care."

I suppose he's right, I don't care, but I am curious. "If you need help rebuilding, let me know."

Osren spits out a puff of air. "You? Help me?"

"Yes." I nudge the wreckage with my foot. "I did all sorts of hard work on the island."

"So you say." Osren narrows his eyes. "Or maybe there never was any shipwreck. Maybe you just didn't want to visit us anymore. You obviously hated Outer's Cove, and you still do."

"Osren!" Mother cries. "That's enough."

But I don't get angry—not this time. I certainly don't want that strange shimmerdark appearing again, and perhaps it's better to show Osren that I'm not spoiled. So I take a deep breath, smile, and turn to Mother. "We have time for another trip to the shelter before supper. Let's get the barrows."

It takes two lunar days to fully move Mother and Osren from the shelter to the cottage, and then we spend a third day helping Fifsa's in-laws move too. During our final trip to the shelter, I wryly think of how frustrated I was carrying my trunk through the subtrain station. Little did I know I'd soon spend hours hauling all sorts of belongings.

I must admit it's nice being in the cottage, though. I settle into Fifsa's old room over the porch, and something about the crisp sea air and watery dawn light gives me hope; maybe it's a good thing that the Authenticators aren't here yet. Now I have plenty of time to practice transference.

Mother and Osren resume their work for a local labor agency, and while they weed the nearby fields, I take advantage of being alone. I wake when Mother and Osren do, put on my warmest clothes, and eat a quick breakfast—usually sliced pearettes and bread. Then I wade through the long grass to the shore, where the land seems to tear away like ripped fabric. And there, in the briny, frosty air, I try to improve.

I quickly learn that kneeling is easier than standing on shimmerlight discs, and once I figure that out, I'm able to travel short distances before my eyes darken with cagic-blindness.

Sometimes I lose my nerve and the energy softens and dissipates beneath me, other times I move the cagic discs too quickly and I fall off, but after a week of hard work and several painful crashes, I can travel ten feet in any direction clear-eyed. Such simple movement won't impress the Great Drae, but it's encouraging progress.

When it's too rainy to practice transference, I read. Father had several volumes of Hidden God folktales, Osren seems to enjoy murder mysteries, and then there's Mother's scrapbook. I pretended I wasn't interested in it when she first showed me her collection of newsreader clippings about me, but later, when I was alone in the cottage, I flipped through the stiff pages. She's saved stories about my Predrae selection, which are less interesting than I expect. But there are also stories about the shipwreck. I scour those for signs that the Great Drae was sad or worried about me, and all I find are impersonal statements like, "Triumvirate Hall considers the loss of Predrae Xylia Amoreah Selvantez deeply regrettable."

Some of the articles mention Clicks and his wife Bermy too, referring to them by their proper names, Lord Calvolin and Lady Bermilia Nelvaso. But only one article includes Fedorie: "The Predrae's travel governess was also lost." And there's no mention of Kary at all.

Thinking about Bermy always makes me sad. Clicks rarely talked about his wife when we were on the Grimshore, but Fedorie once told me that Bermy refused to climb into the rowboat we used to escape the ferry—she panicked. To save at least some of us, Clicks had to leave her behind.

Mother also kept a story about Tah Roli Miri's official Predrae Induction, and that irks me a little. The writer mostly unenthusiastically describes what the new Predrae wore to the many official ceremonies. Yet at the end of the clipping is a quote that gives me hope: "I believe Tah Roli Miri will be a dependable asset to Kaverlee," says the Great Drae. "But no one will ever replace Xylia."

No one will ever replace Xylia.

I carefully peel the clipping out of Mother's scrapbook, an easy task because the glue is brittle and dry, and then I hide the scrap of paper in my trunk.

At the end of the day, when the moon sinks down to the horizon, I often help Mother in her garden. She's growing fast crops there: crisscross squash, stretcher beans, and snowflake berries. It seems unfair that she can't have a larger garden and grow heartier slow crops—she certainly has room for one—but the labor agencies have harvest rights for certain plants. Some evenings, though, I walk to the village market with Fifsa or help her search the grasslands for her friend, Tury. He's still missing, although a lot of people think he crept onto a subtrain and ran away. Apparently, the Authenticators coming to meet me were also planning to evaluate him, and he was dreading it.

That surprises me for several reasons. Why would anyone not want to be evaluated? Also, it's rare for boys to be cagically gifted. Even though in Midnith most Shimmerlings are boys, girls are usually more talented. There were only two male Shimmerlings at Triumvirate Hall when I was young, and they didn't live in the Courtyard of Youth. And if Tury is the same age as Fifsa, he'll be winking out soon. Why would the Authenticators even bother?

"If he died in the wild during the Dark Month, you won't find a body," Osren tells us. "The nocturnes eat people whole, you know. One gulp and gone."

As for Osren, if I'm feeling extremely patient, I help him rebuild his stable. Osren is very exacting about its construction, and whenever I do something wrong, he clucks his tongue and says, "Just as I expected."

Ever so slowly the Bright Month passes. The lunar days grow warm and then unbearably hot as the sun climbs to the top of the sky. Bugs endlessly rattle and buzz, shadows shrink, and we end each day with a swim in the ocean. To preserve my traveling clothes, I borrow outfits from Fifsa. Her stolas and cloth hats aren't flattering, but at least they're comfortable in the stifling, mid-month heat.

On one airless, sticky day, I have the horrible realization that I've been in Outer's Cove for three weeks, and if the Authenticators are going to collect me, they'd better arrive soon. At this time of year, the Bright Month is only five weeks long.

The thought of spending an entire Dark Month in Outer's Cove makes me so gloomy I can't focus on transference. So instead, I spend the morning giving Osren's hutch a final coat of paint while he's at work.

When Osren comes home, he doesn't say thank you, but the next morning he appears on the bluffs where I'm practicing.

"I need to talk to you," he shouts over the nearby waves, surprising me.

The cagic disc I'm sitting on dissipates in a spray of blue-green sparks, and I tumble to the ground.

"Talk to me about what?" I say crossly, blinking my vision clear and brushing blades of grass off Fifsa's stola. I expect him to criticize my painting.

But instead, Osren nods at something he's cradling in his woolen palliumcoat.

As I walk over to him, a narrow, triangular head noses its way out of the fabric.

"Is that... a tiny pony?" I say softly, for the question seems too ridiculous to ask at a normal volume.

"It's not a pony," Osren says as if I'm an idiot. "It's a horselet. The stable we rebuilt is for my herd."

"A horselet," I say, shocked that my off-putting brother could own something so sweet. "May I hold it?"

"Only if you're careful," Osren says.

I take the small animal into my arms, and it feels like I'm holding a bundle of warm sticks wrapped in a velvet blanket. The creature certainly is horse-like, but its tummy is rounder, and its eyes and pointy ears are overly large. And just when I don't think it could be any cuter, the little animal makes a high-pitched neighing noise. "It's... it's adorable."

"Of course *you'd* say that." Osren rolls his eyes.

His hard tone makes me think about how we had to eat everything we caught on the Grimshore no matter how appealing it was. And although horse meat isn't common in Kaverlee, it is in some citylands. "You're not selling these for food, are you?" I ask.

Osren scoffs. "Don't be stupid. They're too valuable. The Mighty Sharn bred them, and they're popular pets across the Silkord Sea. My friend Bernan and I bought four from a smuggler, and once we have a big enough herd, we'll sell them in Kaverlee City."

The Mighty Sharn is Highland Tilber's cagic conduit, just like the Great Drae is ours. I know she experiments with the natural world because Drae Devorla used to complain that her creations were reckless.

"These horselets must have been expensive," I say. "Where did you get the money?"

I expect Osren to say it's none of my business, but his mouth slides sideways and he says, "Triumvirate Hall gave Mother and Father some sesterii when you were shipwrecked. Compensation, I suppose. Too little too late, I say. Anyway, after Father died, Mother invested in my business."

I hope she hasn't wasted her money. "I think he wants to be put down." The horselet is squirming in my arms. "Will he run away?"

"*She's* a mare, and of course not," Osren says. "She's well-trained."

So I put the horselet into the grass. She prances around us on her tiny hooves and sometimes nibbles on wildflowers, but Osren's right, she doesn't wander off.

Maybe when I'm the Predrae again, I'll buy one of these little animals from him. I don't think Osren's ever smiled at me, but I bet if I paraded a horselet around Kaverlee and told everyone where I purchased it, he would.

7

Tury

A few days later, I'm sweeping out the cottage when I hear Mother frantically calling for help.

Since Fifsa lives with Gefro's family and Osren's working late, it's just me who races toward Mother's gasping cries. I scramble down an embankment and hurry across the rocky beach. If Mother's injured, how will I bring her home? Could I carry her on a shimmerlight disc? I'm not sure I have enough control.

I soon see Mother ahead, standing in an inlet, apparently unharmed. Yet just beyond her are the remains of *something*.

Feeling queasy, like something's stuck in my throat, I keep moving forward.

Mother has her back to me, and she's still calling out, "Xylia! Xylia! Come quickly!"

I rest my fingers lightly on her arm, and it's as if my touch steals her voice. She falls silent for a long moment and then whispers, "Tury."

I find it hard, so hard, to look at what's strewn across the rocks, but when I do, I realize I'm not just looking at a dead person. There are much larger bones there too—nocturne bones.

Animals have gotten to both bodies, and what little flesh remains is swollen and gray and surrounded by flies. I want to run. I don't want to keep looking at this. But I can't leave Mother. "Come," I say. "Let's get help."

Mother sways when I tug on her arm, but otherwise she doesn't move. "If a nocturne killed Tury, then what killed the nocturne?"

It's a good question—and a troubling one. I reluctantly examine the beach again, and this time, I notice a cave halfway up the cliff. A rumpled blanket spills out of its mouth. Was Tury trying to lingersleep in there?

I take a hesitant step forward. Judging by the nocturne's long skull, it must have been a woliev. Even though it's dead, its massive claws, barbed quills, and serrated teeth are still frightening.

It's somewhat like a wolf, its namesake, but it's also a bit like a huge, nightmarish porcupine.

How did this monster die, though? I suppose I can't expect to see obvious wounds now that it's been lying here for so long. Yet when I walk around the scattered bones, I notice dark spiderwebs of scorch marks on them. I'm pretty sure those are cagic burns.

"Someone else must have been here too," I say, covering my nose. There's not much left of the bodies, but they still smell. "That woliev was killed with a shockgun."

Mother's lips twitch. "Maybe Tury had a shockgun."

I nod. I suppose they could have killed each other. Yet if that's the case, where's the shockgun now?

I look at the scorch marks again. The only time I saw a severe cagic burn was when Drae Devorla overfilled a reservoir at the Foundry. When the excess shimmerlight crackled out, it seared through the floor and nearly caused an explosion. Compressed cagic is very hot and highly combustible.

I glance at Tury's curled hand—the most recognizable part of him. Mercy and light, this is sad.

"I liked Tury," Mother says, her words soft and barely audible over the noisy surf. "He was shy and quiet—so different from the other children in the village. I sometimes read him stories."

Even though it's sunny and hot, I shiver as we return to the cottage, and I still don't understand why the Authenticators would evaluate a seventeen-year-old. Did his powers manifest recently? Did he hide his abilities?

Mother's still trembling, and after she stumbles twice, I take her arm.

"Fifsa told me Tury didn't want to be evaluated," I say. "Why?"

I suspect it's because he didn't want to leave his family, but Mother says, "He was probably afraid of downleveling."

"Downleveling?" I say, confused. "What does that mean?"

Mother looks surprised. "You don't know? It happens a lot. It happened to me."

That's still not an explanation. "I've never heard that word," I say, mildly annoyed that Mother knows something I don't.

She pushes open the porch door. "Surely you realize Authenticators don't take every cagic-touched child to Kaverlee."

"Of course," I say. "They're looking for the most powerful children."

"But what about the others?" Mother walks over to the kitchen table and sits down wearily. "What about the ones who aren't powerful enough?"

I've never thought much about those children. I suppose if I had, I would have assumed they went on living unremarkable lives, able to produce harmless cagic sparks and eventually winking out. Mother, though, seems to be hinting at a grimmer fate.

"They're downleveled," Mother says in a hushed voice as if someone might be listening. "Drained of cagic."

"Drained?" Is that even possible? "How?"

"I believe the Authenticators use machines." Mother shudders. "You can surely ask your mentors when they arrive."

Now I feel even more sorry for Tury. He thought the Authenticators were going to take his cagic. Of course he ran away. "And you say this… downleveling… happened to you?"

"Yes." Mother rests her arms on the table and slumps. "I was never that powerful, but when I was a baby my nose sparkled when I cried."

I struggle to listen, for the ugly term *downleveled* is filling every corner of my mind. "Did it hurt when they drained you?"

"I don't remember." Mother shrugs. "I was so small. But I've heard it's painful, yes." She looks at the door. "We can't just leave them there, Tury and that monster. I should call for someone." She starts to stand.

I reach for the table. "No. You stay. I'll go."

She nods, looking grateful, and so I jog back out into the sunshine, which now seems unrelenting and harsh. I hurry over to Gefro's house first, but he and Fifsa are still working on the spreadfarms. His mother tears up, though, when I tell her the sad news, and she promises to send my sister and her husband over as soon as possible. I then sprint along the gravel road to the small village center, where the market, bathhouse, and forum are. The battered, wooden buildings stand just south of the shelter entrance, and I head for a noisy popina. When I enter the smoky, crowded place, I'm not sure who to talk to, so I simply shout, "Tury's dead!"

Chairs scrape, mugs slam, and I even hear some Hidden God oaths. Moments later, I'm leading two dozen laborers back to the Selvantez cottage. Osren's among them. It seems he was having a drink before heading home.

"Don't tell Mother," he says, and he's morbidly interested in our discovery. As we walk, he asks me all sorts of questions about the bodies, and when he isn't grilling me, he shouts instructions to everyone else. "Don't touch anything until I say so and follow my lead."

As Osren and the other workers climb down to the beach, I head back inside the cottage. I hope Fifsa will have already arrived, but Mother is still alone. She also doesn't seem to have moved while I was gone. Her hands are even in the same positions, the left one gripping a tea towel and the right spread flat on the table.

If Fifsa was here, I'm sure she'd be trying to comfort Mother, so I ask, "Are you hungry or thirsty?" We usually eat supper around now.

Mother's head jerks up as if suddenly realizing I've returned. "No, I'm fine. Sit with me, Xylia, won't you?"

I join her on the bench, although I sit on the opposite end. She slides closer to me anyway and puts an arm around my shoulders. I long to shake her off, but I don't want to upset her even more. Thank the source, her embrace doesn't last long.

"Why don't you ever hug back?" she asks, releasing me.

"I will if you want me to."

"What I want is..." Mother trails off and then quietly folds the small towel she'd been twisting.

As she smooths the linen, I think about downleveling again. I wonder why the Great Drae never told me that a person's cagic ability could be removed. I suppose if I hadn't been lost at sea, I'd probably know more.

"I wish they'd never taken you away," Mother murmurs.

"I wish I was never shipwrecked," I say. "Why didn't you and Father accept city justification and move to Kaverlee? If you had, I wouldn't have been on that ferry. I'd still be the Predrae." Over Mother's slim shoulder, I see men carrying a bundle up from the beach—it must be Tury. I also smell smoke. Osren and the villagers must be burning the nocturne.

Mother sighs. "If we'd moved to the city, we wouldn't have seen you anymore. I couldn't bear that, and neither could your father."

I stare at her—stunned. "But parents *can* visit their Shimmerling children. Connection Day is every other Bright Month." Did my parents make their fateful decision because of a misunderstanding? It's so cruel it's almost funny. "Did no one tell you about Connection Day? There are picnics and shimmerlight shows, and I was always sad that I never had a guest."

Mother meets my eyes but not with her usual timid gaze; it's a harder look. "Only one of us could have seen you on those days and only with palace approval and only for a highly supervised couple of hours. We would have been strangers to you."

You're strangers to me anyway, I think, although I gently say, "I'm sure we would have had better visits. Coming here always felt like a punishment. You would have had an easier life in Kaverlee too, you and Fifsa and Osren. I never understood your decision, and I still don't."

"I couldn't give you up." Mother's eyes shine. "You were only two years old—just a baby. You still slept in my bed, and you'd cry when you couldn't see me or your Pa. And you surely can't remember leaving, which is a blessing, but you were crying like your heart was being torn out. We all were. I even... I even tried to convince the Authenticators to downlevel you, but I couldn't fool them. Your cagic gift was too strong."

"You what?" I'm still struggling to accept that permanently removing cagic is possible, and now I learn my own Mother tried to strip away my talents. "You would have destroyed my greatest gift just so I'd stay here? That's so... so selfish!"

"It wasn't like that," Mother whispers. "Xylia... if you had lost your cagic, you could have kept your family."

It's probably wrong to be so angry, but just thinking about downleveling is unleashing my most vicious thoughts. I feel unable, or maybe just unwilling, to keep them inside. "You're so possessive," I say, and although that's not the right word, I'm too upset to speak carefully. "Because you forced me to come here every year, I was on that doomed ferry. I lost *seven years* of my life, I lost my position, and now I'm in danger of winking out. It's your fault I'm not the Predrae anymore—yours and Father's."

Mother winces as if I've hit her. Her eyes glisten and her lips tremble.

I start feeling sorry for her, and I don't want that, so I leave, slamming the porch door so hard it doesn't groan grumpily like usual. It squeals and strikes the cottage so forcefully the heavy shutters shake.

8

The Authenticators

Mercifully, the Shalvos arrive two days later.

Osren tells me by bursting into Gefro's family home, where I'm now staying, and shouting, "Time to pack your fancy clothes. The Authenticators are here, and I told them you'd come right away."

Thank all the powers that churn and spark in the Hidden Realms, I'm finally leaving Outer's Cove. "Where are they?" I put down the book I was reading: a rather gossipy account of the royal family.

"They're with their... well, it's called a seg-ment-ed-coach," Osren speaks in a slow, exaggerated way as if I might not know what a seg-coach is. "They've parked it in the middle of the village."

Fifsa emerges from the cellar, a basket of infyroots in her arms. "We have to tell Mother." She shoots me a sharp look. "If you leave without saying goodbye, she'll be inconsolable. And should I invite the Authenticators over for a meal? It's not as if you have to rush off today. The sun won't set for another week."

She's right. The shadows are long, but the sky is still an unflinching blue.

Because Fifsa insists on informing Mother, we first go to the Selvantez Cottage. We find her gardening in a droopy hat that makes her look even more forlorn. And when Fifsa tells her that my mentors have arrived, Mother nods sadly and doesn't even look at me. Osren vanishes for a moment and then reappears with one of his horselets on a lead. We then all walk to the village, and at first I'm not sure why Osren's bringing the animal, for when it comes to his horselets, he's usually very secretive. But as I watch the little pony prance alongside us, I think I understand; Osren hopes the Shalvos will buy it.

Since I'm not eager to talk to Mother, she seems too downcast to speak to me, and Osren is distracted by his horselet, Fifsa chatters for all of us. "I can't believe you're already leaving, Xylia! And I've decided I will invite the Authenticators over to eat. Although Gefro's family might not like that. So let's invite them to your cottage, Mother. What sorts of food do you think they'd enjoy? I make a delicious baked fish, but maybe that's too simple…"

The Authenticator's seg-coach is huge and battered, with tough, chunky tires and two trailers. It must have a powerful cagic motor hidden under its steel exterior.

We find the Shalvos nearby, speaking to parents who believe their children are cagic-touched. As for the children, they try to pet Osren's horselet.

He nudges them away with his foot. "Stop that. No. Don't touch."

Golly and Theandra Shalvo are a mismatched pair. He's tall and covered in soft, saggy bulk as if he was once very muscular. She is petite, stern-looking, and very pregnant. Both Shalvos wear bland, gray uniforms, brimmed sun hats, and shiny Authenticator pins.

As soon as we arrive, Osren steps forward and rather theatrically says, "Allow me to introduce Xylia Amoreah Selvantez, the former Predrae of Kaverlee."

I look at him, surprised that he's almost being nice. I suppose he's trying to impress the Shalvos so they'll buy a horselet.

"I'm glad you're here," I say honestly. It's almost like being rescued from the Grimshore all over again.

"And it's wonderful to meet you," Golly says, reaching out to shake my hand. His big palm looks like a nocturne paw compared to mine. "You're a famous Shimmerling, you know. First, you're one of the youngest Predraes ever selected, then you survived in the wild for seven years, and now you choose to leave your comfortable palace life to help our noble cause? You're very self-sacrificing."

I hadn't thought about myself that way, but I'm pleased Golly has. I want to impress the Authenticators, and after my stressful visit to Outer's Cove, I hope we get along.

He then introduces me to Theandra, and all this hand shaking makes me feel nostalgic. I used to greet foreign Conduits and dignitaries like this when I was the Predrae. "I hope you didn't have a difficult journey," I say.

"The roads were muddy, but we're used to that." For such a small person, Theandra's voice is surprisingly deep and raspy. "I'm sorry we didn't arrive sooner. We had an unexpected detour—an evaluation in Persinia Glade. Now we're heading south again, I'd like to reach Marin

Harbor before the next Dark Month. We have several children to evaluate there, and it has good rooms to rent in its shelter."

Fifsa steps forward, surely to invite the Shalvos to dinner. Yet before she can, Osren asks the Authenticators if they've ever seen a miniature horse. "The captivating creatures can be trained like dogs," he explains, holding out the little animal. "They are docile and extremely clever and"—Osren eyes Theandra's huge belly—"excellent with children."

"How charming," Theandra gives the horselet a stiff, disinterested smile.

"They are indeed charming." Osren looks offended by her lack of interest.

"You must be hungry and tired," Fifsa tries again. "I'm Xylia's sister. Would you like to join us for dinner?"

"We'd be honored to accept your invitation." Golly smiles broadly. "A home-cooked meal sounds delightful."

So we temporarily part ways with the Shalvos, and Fifsa takes charge. "Just a few hours to whip up something delicious? It's a challenge, but not impossible. Mother, Osren, go ready the house. Xylia and I will run to the market and meet you there."

The next few hours are hectic. Yet even though Osren tries to pick fights with me and Mother gives me long, injured looks, we still make an impressive meal of spiced crab with marinated rice and stretcher beans.

When the Authenticators arrive, though, they seem more interested in me than the food. Golly immediately corners me on the porch and tells me about his favorite evaluation techniques.

"I use a three-step approach; initiate, investigate, and assess." He holds up three fingers. "The Great Drae has made incredible improvements to the devices that measure cagic in children. But as you can imagine, convincing our young subjects to sit still for an accurate reading is another matter altogether." He chuckles.

He also seems pleased that I haven't winked out yet. "Most people in the Periph have never seen a true Shimmerling and have all sorts of misguided ideas. Parents often beg us to evaluate children who can barely produce cagic sparks. Things can become tense when we tell them that their family won't be moving to Kaverlee City any time soon. It's a matter of education and exposure, you see."

I assume that Golly is the more talkative of the two Shalvos, yet at dinner, Theandra also has a lot to say. As we eat, she tells me that they've evaluated fourteen potential Shimmerlings recently and only authenticated one. "In the past four years," she adds, "we've located twelve children powerful enough to present to the Great Drae, yet she's only accepted seven."

Theandra also tells me she plans to move to Kaverlee City when her baby is born. "I'll stay there until the child is able to travel, which will hopefully only take a solar cycle or two, but during those months, Golly will depend on you. It's essential that you're fully trained by then. I hope you're a quick study."

They are telling me everything but what I really want to know. "When are we leaving?"

Fifsa glowers at me, while Mother stares miserably at her plate.

Theandra doesn't seem to notice their reactions. "We'll be on our way in the morning. With the unfortunate death of the boy we were planning to evaluate here, we have no reason to stay long. Will you be ready?"

Mercy and light, that's good news. I nod and say, "I've already packed."

As soon as Mother's clock rings the next lunar day, I pull off my eye mask and spring out of bed. I've been sleeping on a simple palette of blankets in a corner of Gefro's family kitchen, and after I wash up, I dress in their pantry. Then with Fifsa's help, I carry my traveling chest to the seg-coach, which is still parked in the village. Mother and Osren arrive moments after we do. Mother is already dabbing her eyes with a handkerchief, while Osren is optimistically holding another horselet. This one is glossy black with bright, intelligent eyes; it's the prettiest horselet I've seen so far.

Before we leave, it seems I must officially join the authentication team. Theandra gives me paperwork to sign, and as she does, I spot a letter from Drae Devorla in my file. I wonder what it says. Yet Theandra must notice me eyeing the message because she tucks it beneath other documents. "Sign the top three papers," she instructs. "The first is a vow to protect children, the second is a promise to report all findings, and the third is a safety declaration."

As I sign the documents in my embarrassing, childish scrawl, Golly hauls my trunk into the second seg-coach trailer. It looks like a metal house on wheels, complete with windows.

There are two tiny cabins inside, and Golly wrestles my trunk into the left one. There's a narrow set of bunkbeds in there, and I suppose I'll be sleeping on the top bunk because Golly heaves my trunk onto the lower bed. There's no room for it on the floor.

"Theandra and I sleep in the cabdwell in the main coach," Golly tells me. "And we usually house potential Shimmerlings in the first trailer—although we don't have anyone traveling with us right now. Therefore, unless we suddenly have many children to transport, you'll have this trailer to yourself. We use the other cabin for storage. Don't go in there, though. Theandra has an intricate filing system."

"I won't, and thank you," I say, eyeing my bed. The mattress looks thin, but like Mother's hammock, it will be more comfortable than Grimshore bedding so I'll manage. I'm also pleased to have the whole trailer to myself.

Golly lumbers back outside. As he descends the folding metal steps, he says, "It's a marvelous vehicle, isn't it? Drae Devorla designed these coaches years ago, and they've held up. Built like sharecks! The other Authentication teams use them too."

Two-year-old me must have traveled to Kaverlee in a seg-coach like this. There's nothing familiar about it, though, but that's not surprising. I don't remember anything about my authentication.

As I say my final goodbyes, Mother soaks her handkerchief with tears and tells me she loves me.

I hug her loosely, not sure how to respond honestly while also being kind. I settle on, "I'm glad your health is good."

Fifsa then hugs me with a tight, whether-you-like-this-or-not embrace. She's so aggressive, I almost expect her to search my pockets for coins. "Now swear you'll come back and visit. It will destroy Mother if you don't."

"I'll do my best," I say vaguely.

"You'd better," Fifsa says, jabbing me with a finger.

Osren doesn't hug me, although he puts his hand on my shoulder in an odd spot—too close to my neck. "It was good to see you again, sis. If you have any family loyalty, you'll tell your city friends about my horselets."

"I'll think about it," I say, and Osren rolls his eyes. If he could get me to sign some sort of advertising contract, I'm sure he would. But the truth is, I probably will tell people about his horselets. They are delightful, and when I'm back in my lavendrine cottage, I'd love to own one. Maybe the black horselet he has with him now.

Then we're off!

Golly drives the coach, while Theandra and I ride in the back, in the cabdwell. The clean, cozy space reminds me of a compact, well-kept home. A small kitchen lines one wall, while a table partially surrounded by padded benches stands against the other. Woven rugs cover the metal floor, and there's also a small lavatory with an equally small bathing alcove. When I ask Theandra where she and Golly sleep, she explains that the table lowers so that it's level with the benches. The bench cushions can then be arranged into a bed. "It's comfortable enough," she tells me.

She also immediately puts me to work.

"Please sort through these wire messages." Theandra slides a stack of cards across the table. "I'll be filling out paperwork about the young man we weren't able to evaluate. There are a lot of detailed forms to complete: cessation of evaluation, a cause-of-death survey, a family records alteration request." She grimaces—or maybe smiles? With her sharp features, it's tough to tell, and she seems like a person who enjoys complicated paperwork.

Flipping through the message cards, I glance at her. Theandra's not ugly, just angular, as if her skull is too large for her face. Her bony features also clash with her firm, round, ball of a belly.

She looks over at me too. "You'll have to go faster than that, and once you've sorted the messages by location, order them by date."

I stiffen. I hate being told what to do—who does? But I also remind myself that I'm here for a reason; this job will give me regular access to the Great Drae so I can become the Predrae again. I begin organizing the cards into neat piles: Port Beyder, Shimian Cliff, Lea Fort, Avelit Beach, Marin Harbor…

"Your work will help us plan our route efficiently," Theandra explains.

I nod and continue sorting. Yet I'm not used to traveling by seg-coach, and soon its jolting and jostling makes my insides feel like frothing floodwater.

Pressing the back of my hand to my mouth, I look helplessly at Theandra. The bouncing cabdwell doesn't seem to bother her at all. She's primly filling out a form with a mechanical pen. She has another pen in her mouth, a red one, and she occasionally uses it to check boxes.

Oh, I feel sick, and although I should probably tell Theandra, I'm afraid to speak—it might not be words that come out. Feeling as if I'm taking an immense risk, I quickly blurt, "Theandra!"

Her eyes flick over at me, and with an understanding nod, she turns to the midpassage, which leads to the guidebox. "Golly," she calls. "We need to make an emergency stop."

The seg-coach and its two trailers lurch to a halt, and I manage to clamor out of the cabdwell just in time to vomit on some unlucky bushes. As I stagger away from the brush, I see that it's no wonder I felt ill; the road is in terrible shape. It's dented with potholes and cracks, and roots are pushing up through the pavement too. Drae Devorla should know about this. If she cares about anything, it's infrastructure.

"I'm sorry," I murmur to Theandra as she climbs down from the seg-coach to bring me a cup of water.

"Don't worry about it," she says while I rinse out my mouth. "It takes time to get used to riding in the seg. Why don't you sit with Golly? Riding up front often helps the children travelling with us."

Still shaking, I allow Golly to help me into the guidebox where the coach's controls are. He easily hoists me up over the truck's big tires, reminding me of a giant in a children's story. Come to think of it, he even looks like a giant, with his saggy features and wide, almost fish-like mouth. I try not to imagine what the child in Theandra's belly will look like.

Golly starts the cagic engine, and it makes a confident *whirr-whump* sound. For a while we travel in silence. I gaze out the windows at a landscape that's sometimes barren and rocky and other times covered with green spreadfarms. I let my mind wander from small things, like how unpleasantly firm my seat is, to larger questions, like where do nocturnes go during the Bright Month? They vanish when the sun rises, but that's all we know.

I'd prefer to quietly watch Kaverlee's Periphery roll past, but Golly strikes up a conversation.

"I think you'll find it interesting to see how people respond to us," he says loudly over the seg-coach's thrumming motor. "Lots of folk think we're a free ticket to a luxurious life in the city, and they'll try to push children with feeble—sometimes phony—powers on us. Other parents have heard misleading things about the Courtyard of Youth. They don't trust us, so they downplay their children's abilities. Ultimately, we must protect the children and Kaverlee's natural resources. Now did I mention that Theandra and I take a three-step approach? It involves interviewing the children and the parents, performing a practical evaluation using a variety of cagic barometers... and perhaps you should be taking notes?"

"If I write, I'll be sick again," I say. Besides, I don't have a pen and paper here in the guidebox.

"It's fine. I teach using repetition. We'll talk about this many times." Golly then launches into a detailed explanation of the seven levels of cagic power and how to differentiate between them. After that, he gives me a lengthy rundown of the five different categories of cagic manifestation: shimmerlight volume, shimmerlight shape complexity, shimmerlight density, horizontal transference, and vertical transference.

"I'll always remember when they found you," Golly says with an impressed whistle. "I wasn't on the authentication team, no, but we all heard about it. Your score was seven, seven, four, five, five. One seven is rare. Two sevens are unheard of. We talked about it for years."

I feel miffed that I didn't get more sevens. And why is my weakest score in density? I've always made very solid cagic shapes. It also seems unfair that vertical transference and horizontal transference are considered two separate skills, when they are really the same ability— moving energy. I wonder what Tah Roli Miri's scores were, and I wonder what Drae Devorla's scores were too. I never see her summon or shape shimmerlight other than when she donates energy.

It's also strangely depressing to have my talents reduced to a series of numbers. It's as if Golly's taken something I've always considered too wondrous and beautiful to fully understand and boxed it up in dull, inflexible statistics. Somehow the rich mystery of cagic is diminished by those numbers. I've always thought shimmerlight was wild and limitless. Defining it seems to tame it, and there's something deeply disappointing about that.

Feeling grumpy, I fidget on the wide, upholstered bench. I have less patience with Golly, too, as he drones on about what a Shimmerling expert he is. I *am* a Shimmerling. If anyone's an expert, it's me.

"You're lucky you're on our team," he says. "I've got twenty years of experience and Theandra has seventeen. You'll learn a great deal from us."

"And maybe you'll learn something from me," I say.

Golly laughs. He must think I'm joking. "Wouldn't that be a surprise! Just be ready to listen, learn, and… *absorb*. Study everything Theandra and I do. We're at the top of our game."

I stifle the disagreeable things I'd like to say because I don't want to be on Golly's bad side. I'd still rather be here than in the Courtyard of Youth, regularly donating cagic. I need to swallow my pride, cooperate, and continue to practice transference whenever possible.

Yet my willingness to cooperate is immediately tested when we arrive in a small labor agency camp.

"You'll need to change your clothes," Golly tells me as he turns off the seg-coach. Its motor powers down with a low whine and a series of clicks.

"Change? Why?" I glance at my green stola-suit, stockings, and dressy-yet-practical boots. There's nothing wrong with my outfit.

Golly flicks a few switches. "But surely you brought some fancy stolas with you."

"I have two, yes." I follow Golly into the midpassage; a short corridor connecting the guidebox to the cabdwell's living area. "But those gowns are too nice for a place like this."

"That's exactly it, though." Golly turns, trapping me in the small space. "You're a real flesh and blood Shimmerling. You represent the glory of Kaverlee City and the elegant life these people aspire to. You—more than Theandra or I—can inspire trust. So I want you to dazzle and sparkle like you just stepped out of the Courtyard of Youth. Do you understand?"

I don't like being cornered in this narrow walkway by over-sized Golly. "So I'm just a prop?" My voice sounds meeker than I'd like and unpleasantly reminds me of my mother's. "With my cagic powers, I can do more than just—"

Golly raises one of his big hands to silence me. "If you are a diligent student and prove that you understand my methods, yes, in time I'll allow you to do more. Right now, though, you need to wear your frilly stolas and summon shimmerlight whenever I tell you to."

9

Downleveling

For seven years I longed for my palace stolas. I ached to feel dense ruffles and crinolines swishing around my knees, and I so badly wanted to bury my hands in brightly colored lace. On the Grimshore, I would sometimes even pretend to stretch stockings over my legs and tie them in place with invisible ribbons.

Putting on a lavish stola now, though, in a hot, cramped cabin is like eating a berry pastry when I'm not hungry.

I wonder if I'm mostly miserable because I don't have any Maternals here to help drape my gown, apply my cosmetics, or tie back my hair. It's certainly challenging to do it all myself. It's also unpleasant to know Golly and Theandra are waiting just outside.

But when I finally step out of the seg-coach's second trailer and face a crowd of curious laborers, I finally realize why wearing a frilly palace stola seems so wrong. My traveling clothes made me feel professional. In this stola, with its three layers of satin, I feel out of place and foolish. It's as if I'm wearing a costume to a party I thought was a masquerade—but isn't.

"Presenting Xylia Selvantez, former Predrae of Kaverlee," Golly says as if he's an auctioneer and I'm on sale.

The laborers stare at me, either awed or unimpressed. It's surprisingly difficult to tell.

Theandra then asks them where to find the children we've come to evaluate. As a man points across the field, Golly leans toward me saying, "You look perfect, but the next time I introduce you, put on a bit of a show—summon some shimmerlight."

He's trying to train me like I'm one of Osren's horselets. I manage to stifle my anger, but I'm too irritated to reply.

"It's about making an impression," Golly adds. "Trust me, my methods always work."

The twins we're here to evaluate live on the far side of the labor camp and seem to share a cabin with at least two other families. Many dusty adults and children pour out of the rickety building as we approach.

Like the other laborers, these people stare at me, even the babies. I steadily return their gaze as Golly introduces me again and gives me a pointed look. I grudgingly raise my hands to summon cagic. Yet before any shimmerlight appears, I suddenly dread that I'll accidentally attract that inky energy again—the strange shimmerdark. Fortunately, only brilliant blue light crackles out of my fingertips. I effortlessly shape the energy into a large, bright snowflake. After it rotates several times, I snap my fingers and it bursts into a shower of sparks.

My audience murmurs and a few people clap. Then a ragged man wearing a large straw hat pushes a boy and girl forward. The children hold hands and are probably about six years old.

"Caught 'em playing catch with some sparks," the man says, "and I thought, now that ain't right." He gives the children an odd, focused look. It's as if he expects them to impress us and also believes they've done something wrong. "They're my sister-in-law's kids, and since she died, I took 'em in. That means me and the rest of my kin get to move to Kaverlee, right? And no labor agency will own our hours no more?"

He turns to the children, grabs the boy's upper arm and shakes him. "Go on, show 'em, Bilvy. Make those sparkles and make 'em nice and bright."

"That's not necessary, sir," Theandra says, rearranging the papers on her clipboard. "We will complete a thorough evaluation of the children."

"Of course, of course. You lot do your jobs." The man adjusts his sun hat. "I ain't gonna stand in the way."

It's clear that the man yearns to live in Kaverlee City, and his grasping eagerness is off-putting. Yet, looking at his bony, underfed body and considering the bleak settlement where he lives, I understand his desperation. He's fighting for his future just like I'm fighting for mine.

"Now remember," Theandra tells him. "Few children are gifted enough to meet the Great Drae, and she selects an even smaller number of children to serve in Triumvirate Hall. It's far more likely that these two are either passing summoners, which means having weak power, or pulse summoners, which means they are powerful but their cagic is unstable and therefore useless. Don't get your hopes up."

The man's eyes widen. "I'm telling you, these two got some high quality cagic. They're the real thing. Some folks were trying to hide 'em, but I reported 'em, I did. My name's Jesper Trent, by the way. Jesper with a J. Not Chesper. People sometimes make that mistake." He grabs Bilvy again—this time by the elbow. "Now you do what these folks say or you'll wish you had."

Bilvy looks like he might cry.

"That's enough, Mr. Trent." Golly steps forward. "We don't need assistance, and I assure you our evaluation will be accurate."

He then leads the children into the seg-coach's cabdwell, leaving Jesper—not Chesper—standing outside with his arms crossed.

"We usually work in village forums," Theandra tells me as she climbs into the seg-coach too. "But in camps like these, we make do with our coach."

I follow her, bunching up my stola's many layers just so I can fit through the seg-coach door.

Now that we're all inside, Golly invites the children to sit at the table, while Theandra arranges several charts on a clipboard.

"Evaluation forms," she whispers to me. "It's best for one person to observe and record, while the other performs the evaluation. I'll teach you how to fill these out so you can assist Golly after I have the baby."

I glance at the blank lines and tiny boxes and try not to sigh. Hopefully it won't take me too long to impress the Great Drae and return to Triumvirate Hall.

Golly doesn't start by questioning the children or demanding cagic demonstrations. Instead, he offers them a wooden toy, cups of juice, and several snap biscuits.

The children snatch up the food and drinks, hastily mumbling thank-yous between slurps and bites.

"We want our subjects to feel comfortable," Theandra whispers to me. "The evaluation won't be accurate if they are frightened or defensive."

Once the juice and biscuits are gone, the children eye the wooden toy, looking both suspicious and curious. Golly shows them how it works, winding a crank on the side. When he sets the small box back on the table, it plays tinkling music and a sweet-looking shareck figurine appears in an arched opening. The boy tentatively picks the toy up, and as he and his sister inspect it, Golly asks them questions.

The boy, we learn, is not called Bilvy—his name is Vonnet. "Jesper forgets," he murmurs. "He ain't our relation, neither. He just wants to live in the city."

The girl's name is Rutholyn, and I think both names are too big and unwieldy for such frail-looking children.

They aren't twins either. Rutholyn is seven years old, while Vonnet is nine. He's just very short. I wonder if his height has something to do with how skinny he is. I also wonder if Drae Devorla knows how hard life is for laborers. I'll have to tell her the next time I see her.

Golly talks to the children for nearly an hour, asking them about their diet, health, and the health of the people they live with. He also asks them if they work on the spreadfarms, if they've ever had significant injuries, where they were born, and so on. Theandra hastily scribbles down the children's responses while also whispering additional information to me. "Listen for the truth *behind* the answers. Youngsters rarely know facts about their early life. Sometimes parents or other family members can give us clear information, but sometimes no one can be trusted. See how Golly asks indirect questions and never pushes for a response? Temperament and personality are also important, so I like to make notes about that in this section on the second page. And see this column? We only fill that in if we're evaluating children south of the Reed River. Some of them are Ganorine immigrants, therefore the Vazor of Ganorine has primary claim rights on their cagic abilities." And so on and so on.

Authenticating is far duller than I ever imagined, yet also somehow more complicated. At least all this dreariness is making me feel very motivated to work on my transference. Hopefully, I'll be able to practice again soon.

Yet the evaluation becomes interesting when the children show us their cagic abilities. It seems they've invented a simple game of passing a tiny shimmerlight spark back and forth. The boy creates it, letting the focused, blue energy slide down his finger like a sunlit water drop. He flicks it over to the girl, who catches it in her little hands and then sends it back.

"That's an interesting pastime." Golly gives Theandra a meaningful look.

Theandra nods in return, muttering, "Very interesting."

The children's shimmerlight isn't that bright, but they have good control. I'm impressed, and I hope Drae Devorla will be too. Let these siblings be the rare children who become Shimmerlings.

Let them leave this terrible place and live happily in the Courtyard of Youth. I smile encouragingly at them.

The girl, Rutholyn, returns my smile, and perhaps feeling more confident, she sends the cagic spark back to her brother along a curling, corkscrew path.

For some reason, though, Vonnet grimaces. He then turns to Golly and softly asks, "Can we have more food, sir?"

"Certainly!" Golly booms. "Let's take a break."

Theandra produces a tray of toasted pile-ups—enough for all of us—and I'm pleased to see she's given them some Kaverlee flair. She's cut pine-tree-shaped holes in the flatbread and filled them with vibrant green, pickle-pepper sauce.

Rutholyn is staring at me, so I say, "Do you have any questions about the Courtyard of Youth?"

Golly stiffens, and maybe he doesn't want me speaking to the children. Yet Theandra squeezes his shoulder, and he seems to relax.

"I don't know if I have something to ask," Rutholyn says, looking at me with huge gray eyes. She'd be a pretty child if she wasn't so dirty.

"Would you like to live in Triumvirate Hall?" I ask.

Her eyebrows furrow with concern, and she turns to her brother. "I think I only want to live there if Vonnet's livin' there too."

Vonnet shakes his head. "That's not gonna happen."

"It could," I say. "Your evaluation isn't finished yet."

"Actually, he's probably right," Golly says. "Boys manifest cagic differently than girls. Their power is rarely stable enough to be palace Shimmerlings."

"I suppose that's true," I say. "But Midnith has male Shimmerlings."

Golly shrugs. "Midnith processes cagic differently than we do."

I think about Fifsa's friend Tury and shudder. Did he have unstable cagic? Is that why he liked being alone? I wish I knew what he looked like when he was alive because thinking about him makes me picture his remains on the beach. I wish I could replace that grisly image with something else.

Rutholyn makes a snuffling noise. Her cheeks are pink, and her eyes shine with tears. "But I don't think…" she says. "I don't want to go to the city by myself! I want to stay with Vonnet!"

Vonnet takes an angry bite of his pile-up. "You don't get to choose, Ruthie. If they pick you, you gotta go."

"Let's not worry about what hasn't happened yet and may never happen." Theandra holds out another tray. "Who likes chocolate foam?"

Nearly everyone it seems, and the decadent treat cheers up Rutholyn. I'm the only one who doesn't take a small bowl, for I can't risk staining my stola.

When the children are done eating, Golly pulls three latched, leather cases out from under the cushioned bench. He opens them, revealing metal devices. He then spends the next few hours using the machines to test Rutholyn and Vonnet. He attaches wired cuffs to their wrists, sensors to their temples, and at one point, he even places a mesh helmet on Rutholyn's black curls.

Theandra stands beside me at the door, softly describing everything Golly does. "Now this is called the Phlebmetric. It measures the passive cagic in a person's blood. It's very, very accurate, but only if the test subject sits still—which is of course challenging for little ones." She also frequently reminds me that,

"No machine can ever replace a carefully executed practical examination."

As the devices click, whir, and hum, Vonnet and Rutholyn sometimes wince and whimper, but they are also clearly doing their best to cooperate. Perhaps they hope Golly and Theandra will give them more food, or perhaps they fear their so-called relative, Jesper, who's still lurking outside.

While I watch Golly fiddle with the machine's various knobs and switches, I wonder what my cagic levels are. I certainly hope they aren't lower than they used to be, and if they are, do I want to know? I might lose faith in my Predrae plan, and I'm not ready to give up on that just yet.

Vonnet and Rutholyn's evaluation continues late into the lunar evening. Then Theandra sends the tired children outside to impatient Jesper so she and Golly can review the test results.

"The girl's a gem," Golly says as we sit around the cabdwell table. "Look at these Chromatic Examiner readings. She's very strong."

Theandra nods. "She'd be a great asset for Triumvirate Hall."

"Vonnet scored just as high," I say, wondering why they aren't talking about him.

Golly laughs. "I need to keep reminding myself that you're new to this."

Theandra chuckles too. "Boys often test well, Xylia, but we have to judge them differently. Their cagic is rarely stable, remember?"

"But…" I stare at the evaluation forms, wishing I'd paid more attention when Theandra explained what each section meant. "Does this mean he'll be sent somewhere to be downleveled?"

The Shalvos exchange knowing looks, and Golly says, "An Authenticator has many responsibilities, Xylia. They aren't always pleasant."

"You mean *we* downlevel him?" I feel queasy as I think about Vonnet's joyful-yet-cautious expression as he let the cagic spark slide down his finger. I know that feeling. I know how wonderful it is to have energy bloom on my skin. "But his cagic belongs to him. Taking it away is… stealing."

"It would be illegal not to take it," Theandra says gently.

Who made these terrible laws? And why? I wish I wasn't so far away from Triumvirate Hall. I have so many, many questions for Drae Devorla. "Could we at least bring both Rutholyn and Vonnet to Kaverlee City? See what the Great Drae thinks?" A nervous shiver runs through me. I'm not ready to show off my transference skills, but the fate of these children is more important.

Golly shakes his head. "I already know Her Imbued Eminence won't be interested in the boy." He then stands to stretch his oversized, sloping shoulders. "The Great Drae's policy is that unless a boy scores a seven, not to present him for review. Were there many boys in the palace when you were there?"

"Only two," I say, wishing I'd paid more attention to the imbalance.

"Evaluating boys is more of a formality." Theandra taps her many papers into neat piles and tucks them into moss green folders. "Hopeful parents would be unhappy if we blindly downleveled all boys."

"It still doesn't seem fair," I say. There's so much I didn't notice as a young Shimmerling, and when I was on the Grimshore, I should have asked more questions. Instead, I avoided talking about the Courtyard of Youth because it made me homesick.

"Don't think about Authentication in terms of fair or unfair." Golly thuds down on the bench so heavily the entire seg-coach sways. "Our job is like a treasure hunt, and some treasure is more valuable than others. Xylia, what do you think would happen if we didn't downlevel passing summoners? There are bad actors out there—evil people who'd use those children as cheap, vulnerable power sources. You're used to beautiful gardens and donation ports, but there are other ways to collect cagic, cruel ways."

"It still doesn't seem right," I say.

"I hope you won't question all of our methods," Golly says, and there's a warning in his tone.

"Now dear." Theandra takes Golly's hand. "Remember this is a lot of information for Xylia to take in, and some of it may be hard to hear." She turns to me. "I have a Matreornan evaluation manual I think you should read. It will answer many of your questions."

She gives me a small, musty-smelling book, and I take it back to my cabin. It's written in an old-fashioned, overly formal tone, and after struggling through it, I'm still confused. I suppose it's mildly reassuring, though, that these gender-based theories have been around for a long time.

Yet I'm still angry that Vonnet will be downleveled. It seems unnecessarily final. He's so young, and his cagic is surely harmless. Why take away something that makes him special—makes him happy?

In the morning, Vonnet doesn't seem surprised when the Shalvos tell him he'll be downleveled. He nods in a tired, resigned way.

Rutholyn cries, though, and I think her sobs are mostly because she doesn't want to travel to Kaverlee City without her brother.

"It's normal to feel nervous," Golly tells her, "but this is an exciting opportunity."

"I think I'm sure I want to stay with Von!" She clings to her brother.

As conflicted as I feel, I try to help. "If you become a Shimmerling, Triumvirate Hall will give Vonnet city justification. They'll buy his work hours, and he can live in either Topdwell or Crossriver, which are both wonderful neighborhoods. He'll also have a monthly allowance, and he can visit you on Connection Day."

"But I don't know anyone in the city," Vonnet says.

"That doesn't matter." I feel like I'm trying to reassure myself too. "The palace has a special task force dedicated to welcoming—"

"We'll discuss all that later," Golly says. "Please remember that I would like you to quietly observe."

I press my lips together.

"Very well," Theandra says cheerfully. "Let's eat before we do anything else. I have a light breakfast ready inside." She leads the children into the seg-coach.

I'm about to follow them, when Golly holds up a finger. "One more thing, Xylia. From now on, every evening, I'll approve your outfit for the next day."

"Is that really necessary?" I ask. He must be saying this because I'm not wearing a frilly stola this morning. But surely he doesn't expect me to wear the same two gowns over and over and especially not in such a dusty place.

"If I tell you to do something, then yes, it's necessary." Golly gives me a stern look before heading into the seg-coach to eat. I stay outside. I'm hungry, but I don't feel like sharing a table with him right now.

The Shalvos spend the rest of the morning giving Rutholyn transference tests, and then after lunch, it's time to downlevel Vonnet. Theandra takes Rutholyn for a walk and invites me along, but I ask to stay with a somewhat lame excuse that I'd like to learn about every aspect of Authentication work. I'm not sure why I really want to stay, though. Maybe it's because I hope the process won't be as cruel as I expect. Or maybe it's because I don't want Vonnet to have to go through something so awful alone.

Golly leads Vonnet into the cabdwell, has him put on a simple gray robe and then tells him to lie down on a thick mat spread across the limited floor space. Vonnet trembles as Golly buckles leather cuffs around his wrists and ankles, and then fits a metal halo onto his head. Wires connect the cuffs and halos to a machine that looks a lot like the evaluation devices he used yesterday. It's larger, though, and has two glass cagic reservoirs. One of the reservoirs is already full of bright, swirling cagic energy. The other one is empty.

"How does this work exactly?" I ask.

"Think of it like a cagic rinse." Golly tilts his head toward the full reservoir. "Cagic is attracted to cagic—so if we flush high amounts of it through a person several times, we draw out their energy. Once there is no longer any residual cagic in Vonnet, he'll stop generating energy."

I'd like to hold Vonnet's hand while he's being downleveled, but I probably shouldn't touch him while the machine's running. What if it rinses away my cagic too? I'm a little nervous that even being in the cabdwell during the procedure will sap my power.

Golly places a wooden rod between Vonnet's teeth—so that he doesn't bite his tongue—and tells him to relax. After that, Golly winds a crank on the side of the downleveling machine and flips a switch. The metal box begins to rumble and vibrate, but nothing seems to happen to Vonnet. He is wide-eyed, though, watching the glass reservoirs anxiously. The sound of the machine grows louder and louder until it hurts my ears. Golly shouts something that I can't hear and then flips another switch. Vonnet's little body suddenly arches off the mat and his eyes roll backward. Small threads of cagic light skitter across his skin toward the wrist cuffs and the halo of metal strapped to his head. Spit dribbles out of the corners of his mouth. I also smell the sour combination urine and cagic burns.

I wish I hadn't asked to stay. I want to leave. It's as if Golly is cutting a healthy hand or foot off this child. It's sickening. How can Drae Devorla condone this? Maybe she's never witnessed a downleveling and doesn't know how terrible it really is.

I realize Golly's watching me. He probably expects me to cringe or be sick. I do feel ill, but I try not to let it show.

The machine runs for an agonizingly long fifteen minutes—marked by a slowly rotating dial. When it finally shuts off, Vonnet lies limp and still on the mat with his eyes closed. I see dark scorch marks on his wrists, ankles, and forehead. His hair is singed too and patches of it are missing.

Now I'm desperate to leave, but Golly tells me to stay with Vonnet until he wakes up. "Offer him water and clean him up with that sponge and basin over there. Help him dress, and when he can walk, take him home. Don't worry if he has trouble speaking.

Children often have slurred speech for a week or two after a cagic rinse, but it usually goes away."

Usually goes away? So it sometimes is permanent? I nearly cry and only my resolve to not look weak in front of Golly stops me.

Vonnet sleeps for an hour. While I wait for him to wake up, I sit quietly at the table and think about Tury. His flight makes more sense now. He didn't want to be downleveled, and now that I've seen a downleveling, I don't blame him. I also think about my mother—she was a baby when this horrible thing was done to her.

When Vonnet finally opens his eyes, there's a deep sadness in them. His cagic ability was precious—something I'm sure he cherished—and now it's gone forever.

In a small way, I can relate. I loved being the Predrae, and that's not who I am anymore. I still have my cagic powers, but I will wink out soon. Cagic has always sparked and prickled in my lungs, heart, and mind. Even now I feel it humming through my bones.

Soon it won't be there.

That will be a sort of death.

"I'm so sorry," I whisper, steadying Vonnet as he sits up.

He stares at me and says nothing. I want to help him in a real way, not just clean him up and walk him home, but how?

He's silent as I gently sponge his small body clean and help him back into his ragged clothes. I then find scissors and trim away his burnt hair. Sweeping the floor afterward, I have an idea.

"There's a good chance your sister will become a palace Shimmerling," I say, "If she does, then when you arrive in Kaverlee, find Sir Calvolin Nelvaso and Fedorie Straechos. Tell them Xylia sent you. They'll help you get settled, and you can trust them, I promise. They took care of me and... loved me for many years."

They did love me, didn't they? I've never thought of it like that. I feel guilty that I've only exchanged a few letters with them since our rescue, and as for Kary, I should write to Clicks and ask if he's reappeared.

Vonnet tries to respond but can't manage it. Instead, he nods weakly.

I take one of Theandra's blank evaluation forms and write Clicks and Fedorie's names on the back, and then I fold the paper up and give it to Vonnet. He doesn't seem to know what to do with it, so I tuck it into his pocket.

I still feel heartsick as I help him stagger back to his hut, but at least he might escape a life of manual labor and poverty. Instead, hopefully he'll spend a lot of time playing dashball with Fedorie and attending academic parties with Clicks. Vonnet's life will be different, but it won't be ruined.

As for me, though, I don't want a different life. I just want my old life back, and I hate that it keeps drifting farther and farther out of reach.

10

The Blue Folder

Rutholyn leaves the labor agency settlement with us, and we travel through the next lunar day, hoping to reach Marin Harbor by the evening. The sunset days have arrived. Outside the cabdwell windows, the sky glows orange and red and is often striped with slow moving, purple clouds. The temperature is also gradually dropping, and it's hard to believe that in only three days, it will be time to shelter again.

I still find it strange that I'm not rushing around on the Grimshore, preparing to lingersleep. Usually I'd spend the last Bright Month days eating a lot and making sure our cave shelter is secure. Instead, I'm now sitting in the jouncing cabdwell, helping Theandra duplicate evaluation forms.

We arrive in Marin Harbor as the moon sets, and it's a pretty town with brick buildings circling a sandy bay. As we climb out of the segcoach, I see that even though it's late, the townspeople are still busy preparing for the Dark Month. They're leading livestock through huge shelter doors, scrubbing all traces of food out of their homes, and covering their windows with heavy shutters and boards. And even though it's moonset, small children play in the cobblestone streets, throwing felted balls and flier kites. I suppose if I were a parent and my children were about to be cooped up for a month, I wouldn't care about bedtime either. The boys and girls are well-bundled because it's now very chilly, and they look so comical in their thick, wool cloaks, pointed knit hats, and mittens with fuzzy baubles.

After parking the seg-coach beside the statue of an ancient Great Drae—Drae Phillaberah I think—Golly sets out to rent a room in a nearby cauponium. Before leaving, he tells me, "It's too early to enter the shelter, but Theandra needs a softer bed. The seg-truck is an uncomfortable home for a mother-to-be." He mimes himself an imaginary swollen belly. "You'll stay here with Rutholyn."

I wouldn't expect him to rent me a room too, but it still feels like a punishment. Golly's made it clear he thinks I interfered in Rutholyn and Vonnet's evaluation. He's given me two lectures on "living up to my potential" since we left the labor camp, and I get another as he replaces one of the coach's large cagic reservoirs.

"It's not that I don't value your contributions," he says while reaching under the coach to unlatch a steel canister. "It's a matter of respect. You must respect Theandra and me. You also must respect the longstanding traditions of Authentication, the children we evaluate, and above all..." He straightens and gives me a probing look. "I *beseech* you to respect yourself, Xylia."

He's using far too many words to make a simple point, which I'm sure is, "do what I tell you." But I nod, and even though something about him always makes me want to clench my teeth, maybe he's right. Maybe I should trust the Shalvos more. They do have a lot of experience, and this is important work. Yet if Golly's going to demand my respect, I wish he'd show me some. I don't say this out loud, though, because I want the lectures to end.

Grunting with effort, Golly locks a full cagic reservoir into place and hauls the empty one out from under the coach. "Don't feel too discouraged, though," he adds. "I have a treat for you—something you'll really like."

I'm immediately skeptical because I doubt Golly knows what I like. Surely he won't surprise me with a fine Kaverlee meal, a visit to the theater, or the thing I long for most of all: news that Drae Devorla has changed her mind and named me Predrae again.

Sure enough, his treat is not a treat at all. It's a disorganized pile of handwritten notes.

He smiles indulgently, though, as he places them on the cabdwell table. He acts like he's presenting me with the key to Triumvirate Hall's treasury.

"Thank you," I say, trying to sound grateful rather than baffled. The first page simply says, *Replace with portrait of Golly.*

Theandra enters the cabdwell just then with Rutholyn trailing after her. They must be coming from the public baths, for the little girl's hair is damp and she's wearing a clean stola that's much nicer than the rags she had on before. I suspect the Shalvos travel with plenty of children's clothes.

"I hope you realize how lucky you are." Golly lovingly pats the jumble of paper. "You'll be the first to read my masterpiece, aside from Theandra, of course, my editor. And keep this manuscript to yourself, lots of trade secrets in there. Once it's published, it will surely be required reading for all new Authenticators."

When I pick up the manuscript, Theandra gives me a glowing look as if simply touching Golly's writing is an accomplishment I should be proud of. "It *is* an excellent book," she says.

Back in my cabin, I try to read a few pages before falling asleep, but Golly's writing is even drier than the Matreornan manual. The first chapter has a lot of disconnected stories and constantly mentions what Golly calls the "Five Signs of Authentic Authentication."

Yet I'd probably struggle to read anything right now, for I can hear Rutholyn crying in the neighboring trailer. I wish Theandra was here to comfort the girl, but she's at the cauponium, so I guess it's up to me. The trouble is, I don't know much about children. For a while, I simply wait, hoping Rutholyn will cry herself to sleep, but her shuddering gasps go on for an hour. Finally, I climb down from my bunk, venture out into the cold, golden light, and climb into her trailer. She's in a cabin identical to mine, lying on the lower bunk with her back to the door.

"Are you alright?" I ask, even though the answer is clearly no.

She doesn't respond, and worse, she cries even louder.

Ugh, what do I do? I think I remember Maternals bringing me milk-spice tea when I was small and couldn't sleep. I'm also pretty sure a palace musician once played me a relaxing lullaby. But I don't have comforting drinks to offer this child, and I don't sing well. Fedorie used to rub my back when too much cagic crackled through me, so I try that. Sitting beside Rutholyn, I gently stroke her bony rib cage.

At first she clenches up, but after a few moments, she softens. And although she doesn't turn to face me, she wiggles closer.

"I would like to ask if there's candy in the palace," she whispers.

"There is," I say. "There's even a bakery where you can order anything you want."

"I'd ask for a brightberry muffin."

"They'll make you a dozen," I say. "Once I ordered a cake, and the palace bakers decorated it with real, sugared flowers. It was delicious and so big I had to share it."

Rutholyn rolls over and looks at me. Her eyes are red, and her round cheeks are splotchy. "I just want one muffin. I don't want to share it."

"I suppose I wouldn't want to share a single muffin either," I say.

Rutholyn's mouth curves into a tiny, reluctant smile.

And she's no longer crying, so I must be doing something right. I pull up her blankets, and I keep rubbing her back until she closes her eyes. When I'm pretty sure she's sleeping, I creep back to my trailer, feeling strangely elated. I might not be a certified Authenticator yet, but successfully calming Rutholyn must be a step in the right direction. I feel like I've earned a checkmark on one of Theandra's many charts.

When the town's lunar morning chimes sound, I test Golly's patience by putting on a wool suitwrap. It's his fault he forgot to approve today's outfit.

As soon as Golly and Theandra return from the cauponium, they summon Rutholyn and I to the cabdwell for breakfast.

"I have good news," Theandra announces, while awkwardly maneuvering her large belly around the small kitchen. "We discussed you two and made a decision."

"You have?" I say, suspicious of decisions reached without my input.

Golly joins us at the table, taking up an entire side of the wraparound bench. "Usually Theandra and I personally bring potential Shimmerlings to the Great Drae. However, we still have several children to evaluate here, and we'd like to finish those evaluations before our little man arrives."

"Or our little miss." Theandra gives Golly a twinkly smile. She then turns to me. "There's a subtrain station here, therefore Xylia, you will bring Rutholyn to Triumvirate Hall."

Golly raises one of his bushy eyebrows. "Does escorting the child sound like something you can handle?"

"Of course," I say, wishing he had more faith in me.

"Perfect," Theandra says. "You'll also deliver paperwork to the Authentication Office for us. I'll need a few days to prepare it, though."

That doesn't leave me with much time to practice transference before seeing Drae Devorla. I can't waste a moment, so how will I avoid the mundane chores Theandra always assigns me?

With a troubled sigh, I drape my hand over my forehead. "Merciful realms... I'm not feeling good. Seg-coach travel still doesn't agree with me."

Golly frowns. "Theandra hasn't been sleeping well, and you don't hear her complaining."

Theandra also gives me a skeptical look, but after touching my brow, she says, "She does feel warm, Golly. Maybe she should rest. She can't bring Rutholyn to Kaverlee if she's sick."

I put on a show for a few more minutes, picking at my breakfast, then I feebly say, "I'm going to lie down." Yet as soon as I'm alone in my trailer, I pull on warm clothes and sneak back outside. It's now misting rain, but hopefully that will make it easier to find an isolated place to practice. Thankfully, I soon come across an empty spreadfarm field on the far side of Marin Harbor.

I'll still have to be careful, though. When it's overcast, nocturnes sometimes manifest early. At least I can see a sentry tower in the foggy distance, and nocturnes usually appear near open water. If the sirens start wailing, I should have plenty of time to run to safety.

Finding a flat stretch of grass, I experiment with a different type of transference—creating a bar of cagic energy and hanging onto it while it moves.

Since transference is easier when I have momentum, I jog across the soft ground holding up a bar of shimmerlight. Then still clinging to the energy that's spitting and crackling in the rain, I tuck my legs up. Thank the realms, I keep gliding forward.

My second attempt is even better. Not only do I move forward, I also will myself upward through the misty raindrops. Yet I struggle to control my descent, and I land hard on my side.

"If Tah Roli Miri can do this, I can too," I tell myself.

So I get up and try again. I splash through the intensifying rainstorm, picturing Triumvirate Hall, my true home. And as icy rain pelts my clothes and numbs my skin, I imagine I'm the Predrae again: important, valued, and best of all, able to keep my cagic powers for the rest of my life. Finally, as I launch myself upward, I think about how badly I want to be Great Drae Xylia.

Again, I reach an impressive height, streaking upward with my clothes flapping behind me like a wet flag. As my vision dims with the inevitable cagic-blindness, I take a massive risk. I release the bar of energy I'm hanging onto and attempt to land on a new shape, a disc of shimmerlight, midair. So what if I break my neck? My neck is useless if I'm not the Predrae. I must push myself.

Yet the cagic always simmering in my chest suddenly feels hotter than usual, and I lose my focus. My disc of shimmerlight disintegrates, and I plummet to the ground, landing flat on my back. Air gusts out of my lungs, leaving a hollow of frustration. I probably should have broken some bones, but the soft, muddy earth saved me.

I lie there for a while, sore and tired and waiting for my vision to clear. It's strange because what I'm trying to do, this aerial transference, feels so possible. It almost seems like something I'm meant to do, but there's also something holding me back. An invisible thread seems to tie me to the ground, and I don't know how to break free.

Fat raindrops smack my arms and legs as I pull myself out of the mud, and then I try transference again.

And again.

And again.

Sometimes I fly high, but I can't land safely. Sometimes I travel far, but I'm just grazing the ground. Once, while cagic-blind, I accidentally ride a shimmerlight disc into a tree. That's certainly my most painful mistake. Snapped branches tear my pallacoat and scratch my arms, stomach, and thighs.

Yet I don't give up, and I'm sure my Grimshore friends would be proud of me. If Clicks was here, he'd probably tell me about some accomplished genius who failed many times before succeeding. As for Fedorie, she'd urge me to "beat my fear into submission," and Kary would simply say something like, "Xylia, *of course* you can do this. Don't doubt yourself."

I practice for eight long hours, and by the end, I feel hopeful. I'm much better at transference than I was yesterday, and hopefully my new skills combined with my old ones will impress the Great Drae.

Thunder rumbles above and lightning jabs at distant trees. I should probably head back to the seg-coach. If I was on the Grimshore, we'd be entering our cave shelter early.

So I trudge back toward Marin Harbor, attempting to avoid the soggiest parts of the field, and when I reach the town, I see I'm not the only one who's worried. Families hurry past, carrying suitcases and little children, while civilian guards patrol in groups, their shockguns charged and glowing.

I hurry over to the seg-coach. There I find the Shalvos also hastily preparing to enter the shelter.

"Where have you been?" Theandra gives me an exasperated look as she struggles to carry an evaluation machine. "You said you were resting, but I couldn't find you. Now you're covered in mud?"

Golly appears behind her, lugging an even larger machine. "You're hardly worth the trouble, aren't you? We've been toiling away, while you were off playing in the rain."

"I'm sorry." I should probably offer more of an explanation, but I struggle to think of one. "It seemed like fresh air might help me feel better, and then…" I gesture at my muddy clothes. "I fell."

"It was foolish to leave without telling us," Theandra says as I help her lift the evaluation machine into a nearby cart. "And to be honest, I think you're lying. You're filthy from head to toe. You can't have merely fallen. But we can discuss your misbehavior another time. Hurry and get your things. Marin Harbor's tucking under early. The shelter gates shut in a half hour."

"But I need to change." I look down at my grimy, soaked clothes.

"You'll have to do that in the shelter," Golly shouts. "Go on! Get your trunk, or you'll have nothing to wear."

Splashing back to the second trailer, I climb inside. My muddy boots make a smeary mess on the metal floor, which I'm sure I'll hear about later.

Well, the Shalvos make mistakes too. Someone left a light on in the cabin opposite mine, the one used for storage. A blue, glowing line gleams beneath the narrow door. If that light stays on for the entire Dark Month, it'll drain the seg-coach's energy reservoirs. Golly will probably do a final check before locking up, but if he doesn't notice the light, I'm sure he'll blame me.

So I try to turn it off. Yet when I open the storage room door, a crate tips over. Numerous moss green folders spill into the hall. Drat. The filing crate must have been leaning against the door.

"No!" I moan.

Why wasn't it secured better? The seg-coach is constantly driving over bumpy roads, and I know how meticulous and organized Theandra is.

It's probably Golly's fault. He must have dumped it in here while he and Theandra were rushing to pack up. He surely left the light on too.

I quickly gather folders and shove them into the crate, not bothering to put them in any particular order. Soon I've put them all back— or wait… maybe not. There's another folder beneath the lower bunk.

I'm not sure why a lone folder would have slid farther into the cabin while the others scattered in the opposite direction, yet that doesn't matter. It's not in the filing crate and it should be. I strain for it, and as I'm stretching my fingertips out to the far, dusty corner, I hear an odd whining wail—a siren.

Deepest realms, nothing is going my way.

I pinch a corner of the folder.

Someone must have seen a nocturne. I need to move. There's no longer time to haul my trunk to the shelter either. I'll just grab an outfit or two.

I toss the folder on top of the others and reach for the lid. But before I close the crate, I notice that the new folder isn't moss green like the others—it's dark blue. It doesn't go in this crate. It must have already been under the cot.

Strange.

The sirens howl louder.

"Xylia?" Golly bangs on the outside of the trailer. "It's time to go!"

"Coming!" I cry, yet I stay where I am, kneeling on the floor. Should I put the mystery folder back under the bed? I flip it open.

And freeze.

I was expecting evaluation forms or maybe a forgotten report written in Theandra's prim, decisive hand. That's not what this is.

The sirens keep blaring.

And the trailer shudders as Golly thumps up the metal steps.

There are drawings in the folder—awful, crude drawings.

I stare at sketches of girls in frilly palace stolas, some of them young—all of them gruesomely injured. Some of them have been decapitated, stabbed, and worse. One of them even looks like me. And there's a man hurting the girl who looks like me. And that man is obviously Golly.

These are his drawings.

I feel like I can't breathe. And when I do breathe, my lungs feel oily as if something unwanted slithers through me.

The sirens are so loud now; it's almost as if they are inside the trailer.

The cagic in my chest crackles hot again, just like it did in the fields, and this time it hurts. I press a fist against my ribs.

"Xylia!" Golly's shouting even though he's right behind me. "Aren't you listening? Can't you hear the sirens? Nocturne's are manifesting. We have to go!"

I should have closed the vile folder when I heard his footsteps. I should have flung it under the bed and scrubbed all thoughts of it from my mind. Instead, I'm still stupidly holding it open.

"Xylia! For realm's sake, you—" Golly abruptly stops talking, and I don't have to turn around to know he sees what I'm holding.

"Give me that," he says, his voice high and strained.

I don't move. I can't move.

"Golly!" Theandra shrieks somewhere outside. "Golly! We have to go! We have to go now, and I can't find Rutholyn!"

I twist to look up at him, and I'm not sure what to say. "Theandra…" I start uncertainly. "She… she has to get to the shelter. She's expecting."

Golly squeezes farther into the narrow space between the cabins, blocking the door. "I said give that to me." His voice is now low and ragged at the edges. He leans forward, but the space is so cramped, he still can't reach the folder. Instead, he grabs my shoulder and squeezes. My bones grind together as more cagic sears its way through my rib cage.

I try to stand, even though I'm not sure how that will help. Should I give him the drawings? Should I refuse? Should I push past him and drag Theandra and Rutholyn to the shelter?

But Golly must think I'm trying to fight back. Without letting me go, he turns slightly, and then—oh realms; he *throws* me, hurling me into the storage cabin. I crash into the crates, which are all painful corners and sharp wooden edges. And I can't help it; I summon cagic in defense. It fills me, fierce and hot, and there's so much of it. Odd, skittering sensations dance down my arms and legs, and I feel overwhelmed with energy. It's changing and churning inside me.

Golly's finally able to grab the folder, and he raises his other, massive hand, his fingers curling into a fist.

He's going to punch me.

Yet before his blow crunches into my nose and teeth, the cagic saturating my body bursts free. A torrent of energy—dark energy—streams out of my chest and fingers and, like an otherworldly scream, my mouth.

I'm not cagic-blind either. Clear-eyed, I watch the deluge of energy smash Golly back through the passage, through my cabin, and then through the *wall*, leaving a jagged hole.

I gasp, straightening. I was already stunned by Golly's drawings, but now I'm astounded. I've never summoned that much energy—has anyone? It was the strange cagic again too, the shimmerdark. I didn't even know it was possible to bash someone through a metal wall. I also don't feel drained. Instead, a huge amount of energy still pulses through me—prickly and eager.

But what have I done?

Frigid Dark Month air rushes in through the hole in the trailer and so does the deafening blare of sirens.

Is… is Golly dead?

I move forward, shimmerdark sparks drifting around me as I peer out the jagged gash. Golly lies on the roadway below, splayed and bleeding on the wet cobblestones and beside him is the despicable folder. I hear a scream—Theandra—and seconds later, I see her, splashing up to Golly and dropping to her knees. "Darling! Darling, say something!"

His fingers twitch, and he groans.

I'm surprised he's alive.

"What happened—what happened?" Theandra cries. "Did a cagic reservoir explode?" She then gazes up at the trailer's damaged side and me. Her face contracts with confusion.

"She…" Golly gasps. "Attacked…"

Theandra's uncertainty sharpens into fear, and now she looks at me as if I'm a salivating, growling nocturne. "Corruption! Cagic corruption!" she cries, her voice breaking. "HELP! HELP! THIS SHIMMERLING'S CORRUPTED! SHE'S AN ILLEGAL CONDUIT!"

"No!" I say, and strangely effortlessly, I ride a shimmerdark disc down to Theandra's side. I then scoop up the folder of awful drawings and press it into her hands. "I didn't mean to lose control. I swear I didn't. But…I found these. Golly… he drew them…"

She tries to push the folder away. "That doesn't matter, you—"

"Look at them," I insist.

So Theandra opens the folder and stares at the sketches. At first her lips and eyebrows curl in disgust, but then she shrieks "HELP!" again. She also starts tearing up the drawings page by page, stomping the ragged, white scraps onto the wet street. "A corrupted Shimmerling tried to kill my husband! HELP!"

"No, I didn't!" I say, and now several civilian guards are running toward us, their shockguns raised.

"Don't move!" one of them shouts.

"It was an accident!" I cry, realizing I probably look dangerous. My hair's tugging on my scalp, and it feels like the cagic suffusing me has spread my muddy locks up and out like the branches of a tree. Glittering flecks of shimmerdark also keep flying off my skin like floating, still burning ash.

The civilian guards' eyes dart between me and fallen Golly as they stumble to a halt.

Theandra reaches into her dripping rain cover and yanks out her bronze pin. "Theandra Shalvo," she sputters. "Authentication Officer, serial number six-zero-eight. With the authority of the Great Drae, I order you to kill this corrupt Shimmerling."

I really must look terrifying because the guards don't hesitate. They raise their gleaming shockguns, preparing to fire.

Again, I react without thinking, creating a ring of shimmerdark that expands out from me like a ripple. It's much less energy than I bashed Golly with, but the thin loop still knocks everyone down, including pregnant Theandra. A few shockguns fire wildly up into the rainy sky.

But the civilian guards are soon scrambling back onto their feet. I need to get out of here. Whatever changed inside me—whatever's making me so powerful—it surely won't last. So creating another disc of shimmerdark, I throw myself onto it, and clinging to the edge, I transfer myself up and away.

It's cold comfort that at least right now, I'm definitely more powerful than Tah Roli Miri.

11

Cattern

I sail over Marin Harbor's shuttered brick homes and land hard, rolling to a stop in the same lonesome field I was practicing in earlier.

What just happened to me? Or I suppose, what *is* happening to me?

I stretch my hands out and watch in terrified wonder as an inky shape forms between my fingers—a wavering oval. It looks like a solid shadow wrapped in shimmery gauze. Summoning more energy, I make the shape bigger until it's as large as a chariot. The energy is so easy to manipulate, and incredibly, my vision's clear.

I need to experiment more with this strange power, but there's no time.

The sirens are still screaming.

My life is still in danger; I should be in a shelter by now. So I release the shimmerdark, and the energy scatters like black, sparkling snow.

Legs trembling, I run back toward Marin Harbor. What will Drae Devorla think of Golly's injuries? What will she think of my shimmerdark? It's all too much to make sense of. I feel like Theandra ripped my thoughts up along with Golly's drawings.

And as for Theandra, how should I feel about her? Even with proof of Golly's awfulness, she still sided with him, and she didn't just tell those civilian guards to arrest me, she told them to kill me.

As I near the town, one of the distant streetlamps briefly vanishes and then reappears. Something just passed between me and it, momentarily blocking the light. I breathe in cold, damp air. That something must be a nocturne.

Three uneven breaths later, I see it: a cattern crossing the field.

Oh realms, an actual cattern.

I've seen a dead one before, stuffed in the Triumvirate Museum. But this is entirely different; black fur covers tight rolls of muscle, four yellow eyes watch me, and back spikes roll in mesmerizing waves as he slinks forward. I think I hear a purring growl too, but it's hard to tell with the sirens still blaring.

I'm going to die unless I do something. Should I use transference? Maybe. Yet Fedorie says catterns can spring up and snatch birds out of the air.

The strange, feline beast continues to undulate toward me, looking like slippery, murky oil and smelling like death. He's less than a coach-length away now.

What do I do? *What do I do?*

I could bash him with solid shimmerdark, the way I attacked Golly, or I could dazzle him with bright shimmerlight and try to escape while he's distracted. Although, can I even summon shimmerlight anymore?

My fear is like another nocturne, prowling around inside my mind, making it impossible to think clearly.

With a curdled yowl, the cattern lunges forward, and still not sure what to do, I try to run. Yet the nocturne's long claws catch the trailing hem of my pallacoat, and I thump to the ground.

I have seconds to live—seconds.

The cattern swipes at me, so I attempt to repeat my Golly attack. I stretch out my arms and send a rush of blue-edged shimmerdark at the beast. I shape it like a cube this time, for simple shapes are easier to manipulate. And just like when I knocked Golly out of the trailer, using this much energy doesn't blind me.

But curse high-quality Kaverlee fabric. Instead of tearing away, my pallacoat stays stubbornly caught on the cattern's claws. Not only is he knocked across the field, I'm dragged after him. The cattern hits the ground first, and I crash into his flank spikes.

Ugh, pain, pain, pain.

I try to take off my pallacoat, but the cattern leaps up so quickly, I'm whipped back down to the ground. He then snaps at me, and I frantically throw up a hand. Because my slim bones and thin flesh can't stop such huge teeth, I wrap my arm in shimmerdark. And again, I'm shocked by how powerful the new energy is. When the cattern's jaws clamp onto my wrist, my skin doesn't split and my bones don't break. The unfamiliar energy protects me completely. I widen the shimmerdark sleeve and pull my arm out. I then tug my cloak free as the cattern chomps in frustration on the energy filling his mouth.

It occurs to me that if I expand the tube, I'll shatter the creature's jaw. That would be a cruel but effective way to maim him, although I probably wouldn't kill him. Yet before I decide what to do, the cattern swipes at me again. I'm forced to let the tube of energy dissipate so that I can summon a shimmerdark shield instead.

It seems I can only control one shape at a time—just like when I summon shimmerlight.

With a frustrated snarl, the cattern darts over my shield—he's so quick! I react instinctively, sending a fist-sized ball of energy into his foreleg. I hear bones crunch, and the cattern rolls backward, yowling and screeching.

I'm still alive. I can hardly believe it.

My heart beats drum roll fast as I stumble away from the nocturne, and of course, he limps after me. I can outrun him, but not for long. Could I strike him with something more powerful than what I hit Golly with? Gasping for breath, I cross the squelching mud and sleeping crops. I also summon a flat diamond of shimmerdark, making it hover in front of me as I run. I'm not sure what to do with it, though. I could climb on it and transfer myself away. Yet, I also think about how cagic behaves. Pressurized cagic is dangerously hot and volatile, which could be a powerful weapon. Feeling reckless, I summon more energy into the diamond shape while forcing it to stay the same size.

As I hoped, the cagic heats up. Not only do I soon feel warmth radiating from it, the light dancing along the energy's edge changes from blue to green and then yellow to orange. Soon the shimmerdark diamond is laced with fiery red light and sparks are streaming off it. I've created my weapon just in time too, for I hear panting and snarling behind me. The cattern's caught up. Planting my feet in the wet muck, I spin and send the blazing hot energy flying toward him. The shimmerdark strikes true, slicing through the monster. I stare in shock as the cattern drops in two sizzling pieces on the wet field.

I flinch away and nearly retch. I didn't think compressed cagic would work *that* well.

Yet as revolting as that was, I just killed a nocturne.

All by myself.

I don't even use a shockgun.

In a triumphant daze, I set out for Marin Harbor again. Although now I realize there aren't any twinkling lights where the town should be, and I can't hear sirens anymore either.

Everyone must be in the shelter.

I should be there too.

At least I can get there quickly. I create a square of dark energy, making it hover like a tabletop. Then kneeling on it and wrapping my fingers around an edge, I send it racing toward the dark, barely visible town. Even transference is different with shimmerdark; it's so much easier to control the hovering energy.

Soon I'm passing boarded-up houses, the town's forum, the segcoach, and then the cauponium where Golly and Theandra rented their room. And as I continue traveling in my unconventional way, I realize it's no longer raining. It's as if whoever turned off the sirens turned off the clouds too.

Finally, I spot the shelter doors and seeing them shut tight sends an icy jolt of panic through me.

"Let me in!" I call as I reach them. Surely someone's on watch. I see lookout windows over the shelter's entrance, much like the ones in Outer's Cove.

I expect to hear locks unlatching, hinges groaning, and voices urging me inside, but nothing happens.

"Let me in!" I call again, climbing off my shimmerdark square and releasing the unusual energy. I don't want to alarm whoever's peering out at me.

Yet the two-story tall doors remain silently, stubbornly closed.

I hug my torn sleeves to my chest as a chilling thought takes vice-like hold of me: if Theandra can order civilian guards to kill me, she can also order them to keep me out of the shelter. Deepest realms, would she really do that? I suddenly find it hard to breathe.

I can't survive out here during the Dark Month, exposed and alone.

I may have defeated one cattern, but it was a harrowing cliff's-edge victory. Also, if the nocturnes don't kill me, the cold will.

I desperately examine the lookout windows. They are small and barred, so I wouldn't be able to climb through them. But maybe I can convince the person on watch to let me in.

I summon shimmerdark again, and kneeling on the circular disc of glimmering black energy, I rise upward. Yet as soon as I'm level with the lookout window, I'm greeted by a bearded man aiming a shockgun at me. "You can't come in," he says. "The Authenticator said so."

"But I'm not dangerous," I say. "She's lying."

"She said you'd say that, and even I can see you're calling on some kind of demon energy." He eyes my cagic disc as he cranks a lever on his shockgun. I hear the ominous whine of the weapon's turbine. "I also saw what you did to that other Authen," he adds.

Ducking, I quickly lower myself back down to the road. This is even worse than being shipwrecked because at least on the Grimshore I wasn't alone.

But I can't waste time being upset. More nocturnes will find me. I need shelter and a house won't do. Nocturnes have an excellent sense of smell, and they can easily break through doors and walls. A cave with a small entrance would be best, but I don't know this area. It could take me several days to find an ideal cavern—if I find one at all—and by then it would be too late. I also haven't eaten enough to survive lingersleeping.

I frantically look around and spot the seg-coach. Golly said it could withstand nocturne attacks, so the armored vehicle will have to do until I think of something better. I ride a shimmerdark disc back the way I came, toward the coach which glows faintly. After all the trouble I went through, the light is still on in the second trailer. As I draw nearer, I see one of the Shalvos' precious evaluating machines lies forgotten in a puddle too, so I suppose when Theandra rushed into the shelter, she was thinking about Golly, not closing up the seg-coach. I'm sure she was also busy taking care of Rutholyn.

And ugh, Rutholyn—I feel sick just thinking about her. I hope Golly's injuries didn't frighten her too much. I also hope she's safe with Theandra who I now don't trust at all.

The seg-coach isn't locked, probably because the Shalvos left so hastily, so I climb into the cabdwell and bolt the door. Realms, what gut-deep relief. For the first time since finding Golly's awful drawings, I'm not in immediate danger. I lean against the wall and take several deep breaths.

It's still hard to believe that Theandra wants me dead, and is my shimmerdark truly corrupt shimmerlight?

If so, then I shouldn't be able to summon shimmerlight anymore. Yet stretching out my hand, I easily create a globe of bright energy. Huh.

Maybe the drawings were the real reason Theandra wanted to get rid of me. Some people don't handle emergencies well, like Clicks's poor wife. Maybe an irrational part of Theandra hoped that if I vanished along with the despicable sketches, it would be like they never existed.

I look around the Shalvos' small living space, at the cabinets, the little kitchen, and the convertible table-bed. Maybe it's good that I came here. The Great Drae should know what just happened, and I don't want her to hear Theandra's version of the story first. If this shimmerdark doesn't fade, it's clear proof that I should be her Predrae.

I turn to the mid-passage, which leads to the guidebox. I bet I could drive to Kaverlee City. I wouldn't even have to worry about running low on energy; I can charge the coach's reservoirs myself.

First, though, I need to get my luggage and unhook the trailers; there's no point pulling extra weight.

Before I venture back outside, I look out all the windows, and thank the source, no nocturnes are nearby. It still takes a lot of courage to open the cabdwell door and retrieve my trunk. I move it lightning fast too, transferring it on a square of shimmerdark. It's harder to detach the trailers, though. Sturdy, steel couplers secure them to ball hitches, and there are tangles of chains and thick cables too. By the time I unlatch and unhook and unravel everything, two sharecks are nosing around a nearby market stand.

Slipping down to the wet ground, I creep back through the cabdwell door, and then—hardly breathing—I ease it shut.

Realms, I should get moving.

I clamor up to the guidebox. Because I spent so much time sitting beside Golly, I think I understand steering and breaking. Yet, how do I turn the seg-coach on? It has so many switches and dials.

And darker realms, the sharecks have noticed me. They're shambling toward the coach like fat sharks on stubby limbs with too many fins. I slide into Golly's seat, and ugh, it has a depression shaped like his backside. I try not to think about it as I flip, turn, and push random controls. I almost wish Golly were here. At least he knows how to start this dumb vehicle.

Nothing happens.

I glance out the window at the sharecks. They glare back with beady eyes.

Trying to ignore my fluttering anxiety, I wonder what Theandra would do. I don't think she knew how to drive the coach—but I bet she wrote instructions down somewhere. I'm sure she'd want to be able to operate it in an emergency.

Or maybe, and this would be even better, the seg-coach has a manual.

I jump up and rush back to the cabdwell. If there is a manual, I bet Theandra kept it with her many books.

I fling open cabinet door after cabinet door. In one, I find neatly stacked books but no manual. In another, I find folded rain covers—one of those would have been helpful while I was practicing transference. Then I find canned goods, pots and pans, a tool set, and some scissors.

The coach rocks as something scrapes against its side.

"Go away," I mutter, yanking out drawers now. I'm sure the coach's windows are strong, but I doubt Drae Devorla tested the glass with real nocturnes.

The seg-coach sways again, and I hear more terrible noises. It's as if the monsters are trying to claw their way in.

Argh, Theandra! Where would you keep a manual?

Not sure where else to look, I return to the guidebox, and desperate to get rid of the monsters, I hit the center of the steering wheel. A loud, blaring sound rings out, and thankfully, I hear scrambling and snorting outside. I then see both sharecks lumber away. They don't go far, but I hope they'll give me a few moments of peace. However, the larger one immediately charges the coach. He slams into the front so forcefully the vehicle skids backward several paces and the engine hood buckles. "Don't you dare break anything important!" I shout.

Yet now that I'm back in the guidebox, I have a sudden idea. If Theandra owns a seg-coach manual, she'd probably store it in a useful spot, such as near the driver. I probably would have thought of that sooner if I wasn't so scared. Crouching, I search through the many small compartments and storage nooks beneath the coach's controls.

And wonderful, here it is! A booklet with a drawing of a seg-coach on the cover. I also find some other helpful items: a tin of medical supplies, a small cagic-powered lamp, a map, and two blankets. Even better, someone—probably Theandra—flagged what must be important pages of the manual with colorful paper markers.

The big shareck looks like he's going to charge the coach again. His gray mouth retracts, showing his teeth, and oh, he has so many. I pound the steering wheel again, sounding another off-key *BLEEEEEERT*.

The nocturne hesitates, snarling.

Yet I'm sure honking won't intimidate him for much longer.

"Come on. Come on." I scan the manual while continuing to slam my left fist onto the horn. *BLEEERT! BLEEEEEERT! BLEERT!*

Ugh, why are these instructions so complicated? So *there's* the starter button, but what's all this about shifting between gear mode and acceleration mode?

The coach shudders, and I'm pretty sure the smaller shareck is biting a wheel.

I suppose I'll have to figure out the finer details of driving later. I jab the starter button, which should really be labeled and in a more logical place, and how sparking, the controls light up and the cagic engine rumbles. The whole guidebox then begins vibrating as if something badly balanced spins beneath it. Taking a deep breath, I step on the largest pedal.

The engine protests with a metallic yowl and crackles of blue cagic flare up between the floor panels. That's not right. But at least the seg-coach lurches forward.

The sharecks dash off, and oh… no, I hit a house. Bricks fly, pillars topple, and I flip a switch that I think controls the heater. Instead, bright guide-lights turn on, illuminating the dark town. Even better.

I wobble and bounce the big coach down Marin Harbor's main street, passing two more sharecks near the shelter gates.

Oh realms, I just knocked a brass statue out of a garden, and now I'm demolishing a fence, but at least I haven't hit more buildings.

Maybe I'm getting the hang of this.

Yet unseen mechanical parts are still grinding loudly and angrily under my feet, and something smells burnt and acidic. As soon as it's safe, I'll stop and read the entire manual. I can't afford to damage the seg-coach. I need it.

I swerve to the right and careen down a thin lane lined with warehouses. The coach then bumps and heaves itself over something big... maybe farming equipment? And I seem to be heading into the labor agency fields. I grab a lever I remember Golly often moving and yank it back and forth. Each time I move it, the seg-coach's engine whines less, until miraculously, the big machine runs smoothly. I also twist a mysterious knob and warm air blasts my knees—so that's how I turn on the heater.

I suspect the seg-coach is carving twin paths of destruction through the sleeping crops, but I'm soon able to steer the rolling monstrosity onto a raised, gravel-covered road—maybe the same one we traveled on yesterday. I should probably look at that map I found, but there's a compass among the glowing controls and Kaverlee City is to the south, so I'll just drive that way for a while. No need to stop this thing after working so hard to start it.

If I wasn't so shaken, I think I might even enjoy operating the seg-coach. It's a little like moving my Colossi around the Courtyard of Youth, and I find it oddly satisfying to control something so much bigger than myself.

I'm also glad that, at least for now, I'm safe. That seems worth celebrating. So even though I'm alone, I let out a triumphant cheer.

"Shimmerlady? Is that you?" a small voice says.

12
Rutholyn

I bring the seg-coach to a jerking halt. "Rutholyn?"

"Yes?"

"Where are you?"

She's briefly silent and then says, "Hiding."

I find her moments later in the seg-coach's lavatory, huddled between the tiny latrine and tiny shower.

"You should be in the shelter," I say, frustration weighing down my words.

"I know that, but there was too much danger." Rutholyn smears tears onto the backs of her little hands as I help her out of the cramped space. "I didn't know what to do, 'an then I was in here."

"Theandra didn't look for you?" I ask.

"Maybe… and I don't know," she whispers.

Theandra was so distracted by Golly's injuries she left cagic equipment in a puddle. I could see her forgetting about Rutholyn too.

But what now? Do I take this child back to Marin Harbor? Holding her hand, I lead her into the guidebox. "Why didn't you say something sooner?" She must have been terrified while I was honking at the sharecks and driving wildly away from the town.

"I wasn't sure it was you," she says softly. "I thought you might be a bad person instead of you."

I'm glad she doesn't think I'm a bad person, but that must mean she didn't see me attack Golly.

"I have to take you back." I sit down heavily and hug my knees to my chest.

Rutholyn sits down too and tilts her head, looking thoughtful. "But also, where are you going?"

I might as well be honest with her. "Kaverlee City, but only because I couldn't get into the Marin Harbor shelter."

"Why?"

"Some people think I'm dangerous—but I'm not. It's complicated."

Rutholyn is quiet for a while and then says, "I might decide to come with you."

"No, no, absolutely not," I say. "You're safer with Theandra."

Rutholyn shakes her head so quickly it's almost a shiver. "Theandra told people to shoot you. Theandra's a bad person."

So she did see what happened or at least part of it.

I sigh and rub my eyes, exhausted. Even if I brought Rutholyn back to Marin Harbor, would they open the shelter doors for her? There would be even more nocturnes in the streets by now, and it would be extremely risky to let anyone in.

So I say, "Fine," and start driving again. This time, I get the segcoach moving without as many shrill metallic squeals.

I hope I'm doing the right thing. I did tell the Shalvos I'd take Rutholyn to meet Drae Devorla, so in a way, I'm keeping my word.

As I guide the seg-coach through the wet darkness, Rutholyn curls up on her seat and closes her eyes. It is lunar night, I realize—her bedtime.

While Rutholyn rests, I think about shimmerdark, and I wonder if anyone else has summoned it before. Maybe I'm just experiencing an unusual burst of energy before winking out, the way some people have sudden clarity before death. But if this is a phenomenon connected to winking out, my strength doesn't seem to be fading. If anything, I feel stronger. It's as if my cagic talents were half-asleep and ever since I faced Golly, they're fully awake.

How Conduit apprentices like Predraes avoid winking out has always been a great secret. Is it possible that my argument with Golly somehow triggered that mysterious change in me?

Maybe I now have a power that'll last for the rest of my life.

The thought sends a ripple of hope through me.

And if my power has become permanent, surely Drae Devorla will make me her Predrae again.

I glance at Rutholyn. She's closed her eyes and slumped against the door, and she looks even younger now that she's sleeping. I hope Vonnet is safe in a shelter. I also hope he's recovered from his downleveling.

I still don't understand why such a cruel procedure is necessary. Who cares if a few children create sparks in the Periph? I can't see what trouble it would cause.

I pass several roads that branch off from the one I'm following, and I hope they aren't important. I don't want to stop and check the map.

It might disturb Rutholyn, and according to the compass, we're still heading in the right direction.

I do see a few nocturnes as I drive—bearcurs judging by their humped backs and curled horns. They watch us pass by but don't attack. I suppose they have no idea that this rolling metal box has two tasty humans inside.

After three hours, the road splits. Each path continues south, although one veers slightly to the right and the other to the left. This time I do stop and look at the map.

Fortunately, Rutholyn doesn't wake as I ease the seg-coach to a halt. Fighting weariness, I unfold the map I found earlier. It takes me a while to find Marin Harbor on the creased paper, and it takes me even longer to figure out which road we're on. It's definitely not the one Theandra's covered with pencil notations, which traces the Silkord's curving eastern shoreline and passes through many small villages and labor agency camps. I haven't seen any buildings since we left Marin Harbor or any sign of the sea. After careful scrutiny, I figure out we're in an empty, forested area near the Sabeline River. But if I turn right, we'll soon reach Haberdine, and if I remember correctly, that's a large town known for making high-quality furniture.

Well, good. Rutholyn and I have enough food to last a few more lunar days, and then the fine carpenters of Haberdine will hopefully let us into their shelter.

I suppose Theandra might have sent a wire message warning them about me, though.

That likelihood dangles ominously over me for a few moments. But even if we aren't welcome in Haberdine, Rutholyn and I can still raid storehouses. I can't believe I'm considering stealing, but I'll be sure to repay my debts when I reach Triumvirate Hall.

So I start the coach back up, turn slightly right, and keep driving.

After a while, Rutholyn opens her eyes. "Did you know that I'm hungry?" she says.

"I didn't," I say, and I'm hungry too. Well, traveling by seg-coach has been safe so far. It's probably safe to stop for a short while.

Bringing the big coach to a halt and asking Rutholyn to keep watch in the guidebox, I climb through the midpassage to the cabdwell. I'm not sure how to use the Shalvos' cagic stove, so instead I heat a small shimmerdark disc and put a can of beans on it. I also find a bottle of pink cheremy juice, which I pour into two cups.

When I call Rutholyn to the table, she appears with a wrinkled nose. "You didn't know that I don't like beans."

"We can't be picky right now," I say. "We need to eat something."

That doesn't convince Rutholyn. She drinks the juice and ignores the beans.

When it's time to wash up, I realize Golly and Theandra hadn't refilled the seg-coach's water supply. I suppose that's something they would have done after the Dark Month. There are dozens of glass bottles in the storage area below the table-bed's benches, and all but two of them are empty.

I carefully wet a dishcloth and wipe everything off. When I'm done, I rinse the cloth. Yet despite trying to conserve water, I still empty half a bottle.

"I would like to tell you that I'm still hungry," Rutholyn says faintly as I hang the cloth on a hook.

"There are still some beans," I offer.

"But can you find me crackers?"

Evidently, I can. She's lucky.

I start to head back to the guidebox, but then I slow to a stop and yawn. Maybe I should rest instead. I'm extremely tired, and no wonder; I spent hours practicing transference, then I faced Golly, then I battled a cattern, then I escaped Marin Harbor in the segcoach.

I need to sleep.

So I send Rutholyn and her cracker tin back to the guidebox, and I ask her to keep watch again.

"But I don't think I like being alone," Rutholyn says, her little voice laced with fear. "Sometimes there might be owlecks out there and sometimes wolievs and sometimes rattatears."

Plenty of monsters are probably nearby, but we're in a sturdy segcoach. "You'll be fine, and you're not alone. I'm only resting, and you can wake me at any time." I then turn the engine back on so that the heater will run. It's surprising and mildly alarming how quickly the coach cooled off.

"But I really don't want to be all the way alone!" Rutholyn says, her voice rising, and how do I calm her down? I'm too sleepy to be patient.

I wish I could give her a toy. The music box Golly had during the evaluation would be perfect. I don't know where it is, though, and I didn't see it when I was searching earlier. Maybe a creative cagic shape will cheer her up. It's worth a try.

I sit in the driver's seat again, and I summon shimmerdark into my hands. The most charming creatures I can think of are Osren's horselets, so I use them as inspiration. Manipulating the energy like clay, I first shape a triangular head, then I add a round belly, four legs, a mane, and a tail. I think I make the horselet's eyes too large and the tail too long, but Rutholyn won't know the difference. I look up, and I'm pleased to find her smiling.

I gently place my cagic sculpture on the driver's seat. I must say, it's some of my finest conjuring, and I wish Drae Devorla could see it. I also wonder how long it will last. Shimmerlight fades after an hour if it isn't properly stored in a reservoir, but shimmerdark seems different.

"Do you like it?" I ask Rutholyn.

She nods, her eyes crinkling with delight.

"Perfect. It will keep you company while I sleep."

First, though, I use the lavatory, and I'm glad there's a lever that empties the cistern onto the road—I wouldn't want to have to go outside to dispose of anything. I then attempt to convert the table into a bed. It's thankfully not too difficult; I just remove part of the support pole. Once the table is as low as the benches, I rearrange the seat cushions to form a mattress. I try not to think of the Shalvos tangled up on the bed—she is expecting after all—yet covering the seat cushions with a blanket makes me feel a little better. After wrapping another blanket around myself, I quickly fall deeply asleep.

Rutholyn soon interrupts my dreams, and it's not because she's shaking me and telling me that nocturnes have found us.

Instead, oddly, I wake to the joyful sound of her laughter.

13

Glowy Pony

At first I'm disorientated, and it takes me a moment to figure out where I am.

But once I remember all the terrible things that happened in Marin Harbor, hearing Rutholyn giggle seems very wrong. It's almost more frightening than if she were screaming.

Pushing my blanket aside, I climb off the table-bed and hurry to the guidebox. What I find there... well... it utterly stuns me. Rutholyn is floating a tiny shimmerlight spark around the guidebox and the horselet is chasing it.

The horselet.

The shimmerdark sculpture I made her, the thing that was a motionless statue of energy and has no business being anything else.

It's still deep black with blue sparkles glimmering on its surface, but otherwise it's trotting around like a living, breathing animal.

It's even tossing its dark mane and bouncing Rutholyn's shimmerlight sparks off its nose.

How can this be?

My abilities have changed, yes, but I doubt I can create life.

Could Rutholyn be moving the sculpture? Perhaps she's manipulating it in the same way I control the Colossi. "How are you doing this?" I ask.

She turns, apparently surprised that I'm awake. I guess with the cagic heater whirring, she didn't hear me walk through the midpassage. "I'm only just playing with him," she says.

I feel like I'm trying to swallow wood chips. "Is that thing moving on its own?"

She gives me an "of course" nod.

Impossible.

It is impossible, isn't it?

Now that Rutholyn is no longer making her cagic spark dance around, the shimmerdark horselet wanders toward me, blinking its luminous, starry eyes.

There's clearly something alive in the cagic, and whatever it is, I don't like it. Well, if I gave this creature a form, I can take it away. With growing worry that the longer this thing exists, the more permanent its presence will be, I try to release its shimmerdark.

Yet although the strange horselet shivers and briefly dims, the blue sparks glittering on its dark body promptly brighten again. It then tilts its head, and is it annoyed? Hopefully, I'm imagining that.

So I create a new shimmerdark shape, a globe the size of my fist. I can't control two shapes at once, and whenever I create a second energy shape, the first always vanishes. But that doesn't work either. The shining horselet is still standing on the guidebox floor staring at me.

What sort of creature is this then? I don't like that it appeared in the middle of a dark forest either. Has some sinister spirit put on my horselet sculpture like clothes?

"Rutholyn, go hide in the cabdwell," I say.

But Rutholyn, foolish girl, lifts the bright horselet to her chest and hugs it. "I don't like that you're being upset." She looks out the dark navigation window. "What's wrong?"

Oh, I wish she wouldn't touch it. "What's wrong is that I don't know what you're holding. Please, Rutholyn, put that down. It could be dangerous."

"But you're the one who made him," Rutholyn says, still clinging to the mysterious thing. "Also, he's nice."

Again, the shiny horselet looks directly at me, and I have the unsettling sense it's following the conversation.

"I made a shimmerdark shape to cheer you up," I tell Rutholyn. "But my cagic shapes don't move on their own. Whatever that is, we need to get rid of it." I have no idea how, though, because it seems I can't dispel its energy. Maybe I could push it out of the seg-coach or trap it in a cagic reservoir.

But Rutholyn doesn't let go of the shimmerdark horselet. She also lowers her eyebrows. "I won't let you hurt Glowy Pony."

Oh realms, she's named it. I suppose it's my fault for making such a sweet-looking sculpture, or maybe it's Osren's fault for showing me horselets in the first place.

I hear something outside. It might be wind moving through the trees, but it also might be nocturnes. I need to start driving again.

"Alright, alright… let me think." I take a deep breath. It seems crazy to talk directly to the gleaming thing in Rutholyn's arms, but I'm not sure what else to do. Crouching down, I look into its shiny eyes. "Do you understand me?"

Deepest realms, it nods.

I shudder. "Did I make you—like this?"

The cagic horselet shakes its head no, which is both interesting and unnerving. Gathering up my courage, I touch it, and unsurprisingly, I feel the warm, staticky dryness of cagic. Its body feels like all my shimmerdark shapes do, firm and prickly—almost like a tightly wound ball of twine.

The pony doesn't seem to be able to talk, and that's a relief. A strange voice is the last thing I want to hear in the middle of a monster-infested forest.

Yet what am I communicating with? Just like we don't know where nocturnes come from, we also don't know much about cagic. Long ago, people believed the energy was a gift from the Hidden Gods. Now we're taught that some of us are born with the ability to summon energy, the same way some of us are randomly born with freckles.

Maybe shimmerdark isn't the only new thing I can summon. "Did I bring you here?"

The horselet blinks and doesn't answer. Maybe it doesn't understand my question, or maybe the answer is more complicated than a simple yes or no.

"Will you hurt us?" I ask.

The thing shakes its head, and Rutholyn huffs, "I know that he's good because I can feel his goodness."

I have no idea what to do. Since I can't seem to get rid of this thing, worrying is my only option, and I suppose I can worry and drive at the same time.

"Well, sit down then," I tell Rutholyn, and I slide behind the wheel and flick the guidelights back on. The endless trees reappear as well as the narrow road dented with potholes and gashes. No wonder Theandra preferred the seaside route. Again, I wonder if Drae Devorla knows what a bad state these Periphery roads are in. I'll be sure to let her know when we reach Kaverlee City. The seg-coach rocks from side-to-side as I drive, and it makes all sorts of creaking noises. But we've come so far now, we might as well press on to Haberdine.

I glance at the glimmering horselet-thing again. It's perched beside Rutholyn, and after turning in circles, it flops down like a sleepy dog. It does seem harmless, but it must be here for a reason, and I can't imagine it's here to help us.

Feeling anxious, I try to focus on the certain danger outside the seg-coach rather than the potential danger inside. We're in a hilly pine forest now, one full of tall, ancient trees. Here and there, drooping branches bristle with needles, and there are a lot of mossy trunks and sparse underbrush. I wish I knew what time it was in the lunar day, but I've lost track. I can't see the sky well enough to spot the moon, and if there's a clock in the seg-coach, I don't know where it is. With my terrible luck, it's probably one of the few items that made it into the shelter with the Shalvos.

We drive for what feels like hours. The forest stretches on and on, and the glowing horselet continues to mysteriously exist. At times, it stands alertly in the navigation window as if expecting trouble. Other times, it watches me, which is worse. I try to ignore it and keep my eyes on the bumpy road, but I can't stop wondering what it is and what it wants... or I suppose, what he is and what he wants; Rutholyn refers to him as if he's male, so I guess I will too. When she falls asleep again, I softly ask our unusual visitor more questions.

"Do you know who the Great Drae is?"

He peers at me for a long while and then nods. Huh. Interesting.

"Are there more of you?"

He nods again.

There are? I tremble. "Are they nearby?"

No answer, which is unsettling. Although honestly, all of this is unsettling.

When Rutholyn wakes up, I stop the seg-coach again and assemble another bland meal, this time of tinned fish, leftover beans, and crackers. Unsurprisingly, Rutholyn only eats the crackers. After I wash up, and there's only half a bottle of water left.

"I think I'm now thirsty," Rutholyn tells me while still nibbling on a cracker.

"Me too," I say. "But we have to save this."

I drive a little further, and we enter what seems to be an abandoned labor agency camp. Maybe we can find water here. It seems strange, though, that such a tumble-down place would be on the road leading to a large town. The camp doesn't seem to have been used in years. The place is choked with weeds, the road sometimes disappears like a poorly drawn line, and if there's a well, it's not in an obvious spot.

I also can't find where the road continues to head south, even though I drive around the caved-in cottages and sagging warehouses several times. At one point, I even accidentally start driving back the way I came until I notice the compass pointing north.

With no moonlight, the buildings appear and vanish in the guidelights like phantoms. And even though some of the structures are falling apart because of neglect, nocturnes have clearly smashed in a lot of them too.

"I'm still thirsty inside," Rutholyn murmurs.

"Fine, have some water," I say. "But don't drink a lot, and whatever you do, don't spill it." The coach's energy gauge is also at *low*, but that's easier to deal with. I can charge the reservoirs—I can't summon water.

"There has to be a road leading out of here," I say the fourth time we pass the same sentry tower. "It's on the map!"

"Glowy Pony, will you help us?" Rutholyn whispers.

I shake my head. "No, no, not that—" But too late, the glittering horselet leaps up to the navigation window and amazingly, bizarrely, shivers through the glass. He then trots across the shareck-dented engine hood and jumps down into the tall weeds.

"Go on; go after him," Rutholyn urges as the horselet cantors off to the right. Since he's made of inky energy and it's so dark out, he looks like a translucent blue ghost.

I wonder if he wants us to find the road or if he'd rather we lose our way. But without a better option, I turn the steering wheel and follow him.

The sparkling horselet does seem to know where he's going. He confidently prances around stone steps that are no longer attached to buildings and passes through the crumbled ruins of a barn. Then all of a sudden, something huge drops down from the sky and lands on him.

Both Rutholyn and I scream.

Purple-brown wings gleam in the coach's guidelights, and I briefly see a massive, triangular body, round eyes, and a curved beak covered with barbs.

An owleck!

Seconds later, the monster's flapping upward again and our strange horselet guide is gone.

"No, no, no!" Rutholyn pounds on the navigation window. "I don't want Glowy Pony to be dead! No!"

But with a flickering shimmer, the horselet reappears in the guidelights. He tilts his dark head toward us apologetically as if to say, "I hope I didn't worry you."

"Oh good, he's alive now." Rutholyn sinks down into her seat. "He's back alive."

But I'm not relieved. If the shimmerdark horselet isn't troubled by nocturnes, can anything harm it?

"You should keep following him," Rutholyn suggests.

Against my better judgment, I do.

Glowy Pony leads us past three more old buildings, two made of wood and one of stone, and then the shiny horselet does something completely confusing; he hops into a thicket of saplings.

"He wants us to go inside there." Rutholyn points at the leaves.

I don't like this. I still don't see any sign of a road, and if I drive through those saplings, anything could happen. We might even plunge into a ravine. Very reluctantly, I follow the horselet, crushing young trees beneath the seg-coach's tires.

But a few minutes later… we're back on a worn, dented road.

"He knew this was here?" I say. "How?"

"He's helpful," Rutholyn says as if that explains everything.

I hear a cagic pop and there's a strange, staleness to the air, and then the gleaming horselet reappears beside Rutholyn.

"I think you are a very good pony!" she gushes, patting his head.

Feeling more baffled than ever, I keep driving, coaxing the seg-coach's rugged tires over fallen trees. Travelers mustn't use this road anymore. I wish Theandra had written that on her map. There were other roads approaching Haberdine from the east and west. They must be more popular.

"Augh!" I cry as a shaggy bearcur lopes across the road. As if the seg-coach is frightened too, it stops. The engine falls silent, the heat fan turns off, and the guidelights fade away.

We must be out of cagic.

Well, great. I don't want to face the savage nocturne version of a bear, so hopefully I can refill the reservoirs from inside the seg-coach.

Summoning shimmerlight, I head to the cabdwell and roll back the rugs. Good, there are access panels in the floor, and the always organized Theandra has even labeled them.

Pulling up a handle marked "Reservoirs," I drag aside the largest panel. A rush of icy Dark Month air floods the cabin, making me shiver, and the roadway seems surprisingly close below. If I wanted to, I could touch the gravel. And between those little rocks and me, are the steel canisters Golly replaced.

The reservoirs are too big for me to pull inside the cabdwell—they probably hold seventy paraunits of energy each. So reaching down, I unplug the power cables and put my hands near a reservoir port. I first summon a small globe of shimmerdark, but the reservoir won't accept it. The energy sphere bursts when I try to force it into the canister. Odd. So instead I summon shimmerlight and that works fine.

Both Rutholyn and Glowy Pony watch me work. Rutholyn sits patiently on the table-bed, which I've left in the sleeping position, while Glowy Pony trots around, agitated. After a few moments, he climbs onto the kitchen counter and bats small objects onto me—an egg timer, a spice shaker, a spoon.

"Stop that," I say, my hands still on the reservoir.

I wonder how Drae Devorla will react to him. Perhaps Glowy Pony's appearance is a sign that my cagic is corrupt.

"Ow!" I cry as a coaster bounces off the back of my neck, and I glare at him. "Stop it or I'll…" I'll what? If an owleck can't carry him off, there's not much I can do.

Therefore enduring a mostly harmless barrage, I fill only one of the two reservoirs so I can quickly get moving. I then replace the floor panel and spread the red and maroon rug back over it. As soon as I return to the guidebox, I turn the heater on and start driving again. I can't wait to get out of these woods.

Yet as we continue to travel, the road gets worse and worse. There seems to be a path through the trees, but I'm often just using the compass.

"Should I ask Glowy Pony to guide us again?" Rutholyn suggests.

"No," I say because it might be Glowy Pony's fault we're lost.

But only a few moments later, the forest thins, and I see a glistening, flat expanse in front of us. "A lake!" I cry. I think there's a lake north of Haberdine on the map. A lake also means we can refill our water supply.

"Also, there's a bridge!" Rutholyn points out the passenger window.

She's right. Even though I guess we did lose the road, we were still near it. A straight, flat bridge stretches across the water. It's made of stone and brick, and it looks strong enough to support the seg-coach.

I check the map. This must be Silvermaar Lake, and yes, Haberdine's on the other side. What a relief.

"We'll stop in the middle for water," I tell Rutholyn. "It will be easier to see nocturnes there."

She nods as I ease the seg-coach onto the bridge. It's much smoother than the bumpy hills we've been driving on, so for the first time in hours, Rutholyn and I aren't bouncing on the seats.

When I think we're about halfway across, I stop the coach and head to the cabdwell. There, I pull on my pallacoat—still muddy from fighting the cattern—and put six bottles into a canvas laundry bag. One of Golly's stiff socks is bunched up at the bottom—gross.

"I'll look for nocturnes," Rutholyn says, wrapping a blanket around her shoulders, apparently willing to go outside.

"No, *no*, you're staying in here," I say. "Look out the windows and sound the horn if you see anything."

"But then I can't see all the ways at the same time." She juts out her little chin. "There might be flying monsters too."

She's right. The seg-coach doesn't have that many windows, and I do need someone to warn me about nocturnes.

I suppose I shouldn't leave her cooped up with the mysterious shimmerdark horselet either. "Fine," I say, "but listen closely. Keep the passenger door open and stand on the mud cover. Don't stand on the bridge. If there's any trouble—anything at all—jump in the guidebox and lock the door. I'll take care of myself."

Rutholyn nods solemnly.

I climb out the passenger door with the laundry sack slung over my shoulder and the bottles clinking inside. Even though I expect it to be cold, the freezing temperature is still bee-sting startling. I'm surprised it isn't snowing.

It's also eerily quiet without the coach's motor running. There's only the whispering hush of wind in the distant trees and the soft lap of water on the bridge pilings. The air smells like algae and tangy pines, and clouds hover above me like gawking onlookers, waiting to see if I'll survive.

"I'll be right back," I tell Rutholyn as I walk to the nearest bridge support.

She nods and shivers, and for better or worse, Glowy Pony stands beside her, perched on the engine hood.

I peer over the railing at the rippling water that's about ten feet below the bridge. I then create a shimmerdark panel the size of a doormat and climb onto it. Again, I marvel at how easy it is to control this new energy for I glide effortlessly over the railing and down toward the inky lake.

Rutholyn's little voice wafts after me. "Shimmerlady, be careful!"

"I will," I call back, wondering if any aqua nocturnes are nearby. There's a reason we seal off Kaverlee's harbor during the Dark Month. Sharecks can swim, and there are octovipers and daggerfish too.

Hovering over the waves, I open a bottle and dip it into the icy lake. My hand aches as I hold it underwater, making air glug up and out. It seems to take ages for the bubbles to stop.

"Shimmerlady?" Rutholyn calls.

"Hang on!" I say, trying to close the dripping bottle. The lid's attached with a wire hinge that's hard to manipulate now that my hands are useless frozen claws.

"Shimmerlady!" Rutholyn cries again. "Something's on the bridge!"

14

Wolievs

"Get in the coach!" I shout, finally capping the bottle with a clumsy combination of chin, teeth, and thumb.

"I think there's many monsters," Rutholyn calls. "I think they're wolievs."

"Get in the coach *now!*" As I raise my energy platform, I hear the ominous sounds of claws scraping stone and raspy heavy breathing. My cagic perch is soon level with the bridge, and the wolievs are closer than I thought—so close I can see the blend of quills and grimy fur covering their stocky bodies.

I aim the shimmerdark I'm kneeling on at the open guidebox door, but I'm a split-second too slow. A woliev rams into me.

Darkest realms, it's like being hit by a seg-coach. The impact swats the water bottle out of my hand and sends me flying. I come to a rolling stop as the other bottles shatter beneath me. Jagged glass pokes through the canvas laundry bag and my pallacoat.

Is this it?

Is this how I die?

I look up just as a woliev lunges, his gaping mouth full of pointy, yellow teeth and vinegary-smelling saliva. Wailing and hardly thinking, I hurl a globe of shimmerdark at him, but the woliev dodges and the energy only singes his quills.

Somewhere behind me, Rutholyn screams.

The seg's door! Blazing realms, it's still open!

More wolievs scramble toward me. Since I'm still on the ground, I create a long bar of energy, wrap my arms and legs around it, and slide myself sideways. I'm like a knife spreading butter. As I hope, the low, swift movement keeps me clear of swiping claws and snapping teeth.

I then spring to my feet and turn toward Rutholyn's shrieks. A nocturne's jammed itself in the seg-coach's door, trying to reach her. I need to do something.

But the other wolievs are charging me again, muscles churning, eyes blazing.

"Get to the cabdwell!" I shriek at Rutholyn as I run from the wolievs, fighting to untangle myself from the bag of broken glass. Hopefully she's already in the back of the coach. She'll be safer there, harder to reach. Finally able to tear off the laundry bag, I send a whip-like crescent of cagic at the wolievs. It knocks them down, but only temporarily.

I moan in frustration. Creating a bar of shimmerdark overhead, I hang onto it and whisk myself down the bridge. Even though I killed a nocturne in Marin Harbor, there are at least a dozen wolievs chasing me. I can't fight them all.

Seconds after I land, a woliev pounces on me, teeth snapping and claws raking. I fall hard on the bridge and just barely shield myself with energy shaped like a turtle's shell. More wolievs join the attack, and since I made the shield so quickly, it's translucent and not that strong. It's as if I'm wrapped in a thick blanket that only softens their blows.

Groaning, I struggle to focus, to survive. First, I strengthen the shield, and then I make it larger, hopefully pushing the beasts away. Huddled beneath this overturned, black bowl of energy, I can only see my folded arms and legs and the damp flagstones.

Maybe I should fight these wolievs the same way I fought the cattern: compressing shimmerdark until it's searing hot.

I can only create one shape at a time, though, and I can't heat my shield or I'll roast myself.

But I also can't keep hiding. Rutholyn needs me.

Listening to the wolievs angrily snuffling around my temporary shelter, I get an idea. If shimmerdark heats up when I force more energy into a shape, then surely shrinking a large amount of cagic and crushing its energy into a smaller area will have the same effect.

Taking a deep breath, I expand my shimmerdark shield, adding cagic until it's the size of a small house. I then quickly crunch all that energy into a thin hoop surrounding me. As I hoped, it radiates heat and red sparks dance on its surface.

The wolievs seem briefly confused, but then they attack again. Yet the first beast to throw himself on the energy ring dies with a splurching gasp and sizzle of burnt flesh. Unfortunately, his momentum sends his heavy corpse bashing into me. I fall backward, releasing the red-rimmed shimmerdark so that I don't eviscerate myself. *Wham,* I hit the bridge, and ugh, the dead nocturne lands on me. Before I can feel either victorious—one down, so many to go—or horrified, teeth lock onto my right ankle. I scream in pain as a different woliev drags me out of the gory mess.

I'm in agony, but I keep my wits and cover my trapped foot with energy. I then splay my fingers, expanding the cagic and forcing the woliev's mouth open. I pull myself free and immediately create another shield, for I'm still surrounded by monsters. This time, I shape the shimmerdark into a giant bell so I can stand up beneath it. I then limp down the bridge, my ankle aching as if it's full of shredded metal. It's hard to think clearly while I'm this uncomfortable, but I still need to come up with a plan. If I were alone, I'd escape with transference—sail off on a shimmerdark disc. Yet Rutholyn's still trapped in the coach.

Lifting my bell-shaped barrier a finger's width, I peer out from under it. At least in my confusion, I hobbled closer to the coach. The wolievs are also prowling around my shield, snarling and surely eager to attack again.

It's hard to leave my energy shell, for a part of me wants to hide forever. But when I do, I send a large crescent of shimmerdark flying toward the nocturnes. It's not compressed and hot, so not deadly, but it still hits them hard. Two nocturnes stumble and fall, while others yelp in pain. My attack also knocks the seg-coach sideways, and the front bumper crumples against the bridge's guardrail. That's not good. I can't damage the seg-coach—I need it.

But maybe it's lost already. The woliev trying to get into the guidebox has shredded the passenger seat. I see bits of fabric and padding hanging out the door. I'm sure he's broken the coach's controls too.

The nocturnes surround me again, and it still seems impossible to defeat them all. If only I could just frighten them off.

"Go away!" I shout as I shape an expanding ring of shimmerdark that spreads out from me on all sides. It's how I knocked down the civilian guards, but even though the nocturnes are shoved back, yelping and snarling, they stay standing. My cagic also strikes the seg-coach again, chipping its gray paint.

I wish I knew Rutholyn was alright in there.

A dark, shaggy nocturne barks at me, and I shout wordlessly in return, trying to sound as ferocious as possible. Maybe I can trick these monsters into thinking I'm more vicious and bloodthirsty than they are.

But of course they aren't intimidated by me. The pack presses closer, drowning out my pitiful roar with far louder howls.

I wonder if they were tracking us, waiting for a tender human to leave the safety of the coach. Fedorie always said that wolievs relentlessly chase their prey, exhausting it, and maybe that's what they're trying to do to me. It might even be working because when I send out another wave of shimmerdark, it's thinner and weaker. The wolievs hunch and wince as the cagic passes over them, but that's all. Surely sensing my fatigue, two of the larger nocturnes lunge at me—the shaggy one again and a brute missing an ear.

I try to dodge their attacks by creating a bar of shimmerdark, grabbing onto it, and transferring away, but I'm not quick enough. The shaggy woliev leaps up and her jaws clamp onto my pallacoat, forcing me to let go. I crash painfully down onto the roof of the seg-coach.

But at least I hear a "Help!" from below, and although I hate that Rutholyn's voice comes from the vulnerable guidebox rather than the safer cabdwell, I'm glad she's alive.

As I stumble across the top of the coach, the shaggy woliev springs up to join me on the roof.

I pull a shield of shimmerdark around me like a cape—but I've made it hastily so it's not that thick. The woliev clamps her jaws around my upper arm and then shakes me violently. My shoulder bends to its limits, and my arm feels like it might rip off. Desperately, I use my free hand to summon a ball of energy and crack it against the woliev's head.

With a yowl, the beast whips me sideways and releases me. Screaming feebly, I spin off into the frigid Dark Month air, out over the cold lake. The spiraling motion is confusing, but I'm able to wrap a belt of shimmerdark around my middle, and I both slow myself down and stop myself from plunging into the water. But oh, being held up by my waist alone is extremely uncomfortable. I quickly carry myself back to the bridge, and although I'd love to land far away from the wolievs, I still have to help Rutholyn. So I aim for the segcoach roof, and as soon as I land, I send a massive cube of energy at the shaggy woliev still hunched there.

As if I struck her with a giant mallet, she careens off into the darkness, and seconds later, I hear a splash. Then as quickly as possible, I create a shimmerdark triangle and shatter the driver's side window with it. After that, stunned that I'm still somehow breathing, still able to do anything, I create a hovering ramp and use it to slide in through the open window.

"Shimmerlady!" Rutholyn shrieks as I land awkwardly in the driver's seat. She's huddled behind the steering wheel, which the nocturne wedged in the passenger door must have snapped off. The metal circle is now jammed near the floor pedals, keeping Rutholyn just out of reach of the monster's claws. Glowy Pony stands loyally, although uselessly, beside her.

Oh, I'm so glad she's not hurt. I'm also thankful that the passenger door isn't any larger.

I send a ball of shimmerdark at the trapped woliev, attempting to knock him out onto the bridge. But although the energy crackles forcefully against his head and shoulders, it doesn't dislodge him. He roars furiously and swipes at me, so I turn my back. The guidebox is too cramped for me to quickly shape a shimmerdark shield, so the monster slashes my pallacoat and gouges my skin and muscle.

I scream in pain. Calling on as much energy as I can, I fling out a forceful, expanding bubble of shimmerdark. This second wallop of energy bashes the trapped nocturne free. It also shoves away the wolievs teaming at the driver's side door, shatters the navigation window, and makes Glowy Pony fizzle, vanish, and then reappear.

But oh no. The energy must have also struck Rutholyn, for she's slumped over. The force of my cagic probably slammed her head against the control panel. Is she unconscious? Dead?

Scooping her up, I carry her down the midpassage and into the cabdwell—the safest place in the seg-coach.

Looking over my shoulder, I see Glowy Pony following us as more wolievs try to climb into the damaged guidebox. They'll find it easier to get in now that the navigation window's gone.

Nearly crying with weariness after letting so much energy course through me, I drop Rutholyn onto the table-bed, and since there's no door between the guidebox and cabdwell, I create one with a panel of shimmerdark.

I then turn to Rutholyn, and merciful light, her chest rises. She's breathing. Realms, what a relief.

Glowy Pony appears at her side, and the seg-coach shakes and shudders. Those wolievs just will not give up. They are still trying to force their way in. I hear claws scraping against the roof and walls, and they also seem to be thumping their massive bodies against the cabdwell's rear door. Somehow, they know it's an entrance. How intelligent are they?

At least I have a moment to catch my breath, although it's also a moment to realize how injured I am. My ankle—the one the nocturne dragged me with—is swollen and stiff. My arm is bruised and punctured, and my slashed back stings and pulses in a way that means I'm probably bleeding heavily.

I hear more barking and snarling, as well as groaning steel and snapping wood. A woliev must have made it into the guidebox and is now squeezing down the midpassage. I hear the lavatory walls and storage cabinets buckling and bending.

I think my shimmerdark door will hold, but as long as it's there, I can't create any other cagic shapes.

I need to get rid of these monsters; I need to destroy them all—but how?

Rutholyn's eyes flutter open.

I wish I had good news for her, but instead I say, "The seg-coach can't protect us for much longer."

"What do you think we're going to do?" Rutholyn whispers.

"Maybe we can ride a shimmerdark disc into the forest and hide there," I suggest. But that's not a great plan either. The woods also have monsters.

Rutholyn shakes her head, wide-eyed. "But I don't like that. We need the coach, and we need crackers and a place to stay warm. Also, we need walls…"

And even if I transfer us away from the bridge, the wolievs will probably follow us, track us. We're trapped. The realization feels like a hand on my throat.

I hear the midpassage walls creaking and breaking, and I suppose I can at least kill the woliev crawling through it. I'll use my best trick—creating hot shimmerdark by crushing the energy of a large shape into a smaller one.

"Don't look," I tell Rutholyn.

She covers her eyes.

I then shrink the cagic door, revealing the woliev wriggling through the midpassage—a spotted beast with a broken tooth. I have to compress the door's energy into a very small cube before the edges glow red. But as soon as it's hot, I thrust my arms forward, sending the tiny-yet-lethal weapon into the woliev's skull. I then expand the shape again. The monster's eyes bulge, something wet seeps out of its nose and mouth, and it slumps dead, blocking the passage.

Rutholyn peeks at the fallen nocturne for a second and then turns away, wincing.

I wish it was the only beast we had to destroy. The coach rocks violently as wolievs continue to bash themselves against the cabdwell's back door. The hinges squeak and the once secure handle rattles. I wonder how long we have before it breaks.

I need to get Rutholyn out of here. I don't know where we'll go after that, but the seg-coach clearly won't keep us safe much longer.

At least there's another way in and out of the cabdwell.

I kneel, push the rug aside, and open the panel covering the cagic reservoirs. I'm pretty sure the coach is too low to the ground for wolievs to crawl beneath it—yet Rutholyn and I can fit down there.

"What are you doing?" Rutholyn asks, rubbing what must be a sore spot on the back of her head.

"I'm not sure yet," I say.

I can't squeeze past the cagic reservoirs, and even Rutholyn isn't small enough for that, so I'll have to remove at least one of the shiny tanks. Unfortunately, the latches Golly used are beneath the canisters and out of reach. I suppose I'll have to cut the tanks free with shimmerdark.

First, I unplug the cables, then I focus cagic into my hands, and after heating a small square of shimmerdark, I use it to melt one of the joints. It takes a while, and does it ever smell, but eventually the metal snaps.

"They are coming in where we don't want them too," Rutholyn whispers, pointing at the cabdwell's exterior door.

She's right. The wolievs have bent back the top corner of the door, and part of its frame is also loose. Claws scratch through the gaps, and the monster's yipping, hungry snarls are so loud Rutholyn covers her ears.

I focus on freeing the reservoir to clear our escape route. Two more metal bands break apart, each with a sharp *ping*.

"I'm all the way scared." Rutholyn moves to my side, and Glowy Pony trots closer too.

"It'll be fine!" I say, not sure I believe myself. But at last, yes! Finally! The reservoir clatters down onto the bridge with a muffled clang.

"Follow me!" I squeeze through the opening, carefully avoiding the ragged, hot metal.

But Rutholyn doesn't move. "I think we will get eaten out there."

Even Glowy Pony won't join me, which is ridiculous because the nocturnes can't hurt him. If only he could fight like I do. With a little more firepower, I might be able to defeat these monsters.

Yet that gives me an idea. If it's just extra power I need, I have it. A fully charged cagic reservoir lies beside me.

"I've changed my mind," I call up to Rutholyn. "Stay where you are." I then reach for the canister I refilled only a few hours ago.

A woliev peers under the seg-coach and growls. Another appears and then another. I curl up to stay out of reach. Now they know where I am, which isn't great, but it might stop them from battering the cabdwell door.

The reservoir is heavy, so I push it with a cube of shimmerdark, rolling it out from under the coach. If my plan works, it'll cause a lot of destruction, so I need to move the reservoir as far away from the seg-coach as I can.

I then create a mat of shimmerdark and squirm onto it. Clinging to the edge, I swiftly carry myself out from beneath the coach, startling the wolievs as I streak past them. As I hoped, the wolievs chase after me, and I see there's still about ten of them left. When they've nearly caught up to me, I change directions, clinging tightly to my energy mat as it swerves. I then return to the cagic reservoir. Once there, I have a few short seconds to roll the cannister farther down the bridge before the wolievs close in again. When the monsters are almost close enough to attack, I create a bar of shimmerdark, hang onto it, and hover away. Again, I land farther along the bridge, tempting the wolievs to chase me.

I play my perilous game with them several times—transferring myself along the bridge using shimmerdark and then doubling back to roll the energy canister away from the seg-coach.

I hope Rutholyn's alright, and I'm sure she's watching me through the cabdwell window.

Once I've moved the reservoir five bridge supports north, I don't leave when the wolievs close in—instead I lift myself upward, crouching on a shimmerdark disc.

As ten sets of yellow-gray eyes watch me float up into the dark sky, I struggle to both control my levitation and expand the disc I'm sitting on.

My shimmerdark soon spreads out like a black pool edged in dancing blue light. It's so large I can no longer see the wolievs or the seg-coach, just Silvermaar Lake, stretching out dark and vast.

When I have the trembling sense that I'll lose control if I summon any more energy, I walk to the edge of the disc. Now I'm not above the bridge anymore; I'm standing over the lake.

I'm also about to be so cold—and oh, this had better work.

I take a short, sharp breath to gather my courage, and then I jump. At the same time, I crush the vast disc of cagic into a small, blazing hot sphere of shimmerdark, and I send that sphere streaking down toward the reservoir. As it drops, I do too, plummeting toward the frigid lake.

The canister explodes, just like I hoped it would, and for a glorious, satisfying second, I see a rainbow of sparks and flames blossom up from the bridge. Then I splash into the water.

Eeeeergh, it's brutally, painfully cold.

So cold I think my heart might stop.

If I want to live, I have to get out of the lake immediately.

It takes me a long, shapeless moment to gather my wits. I feel as if the seg-coach has rolled over me several times. I try to create an energy disc to lift myself upward, but nothing happens.

I suppose I can't summon cagic underwater.

I have to get to the surface.

Frantically kicking and paddling, I try not to think about what might be lurking in the icy darkness. And although I'm thankful I know how to swim; I've never been in such frigid water and never swam fully clothed. When the ferry sank, I was in a lifeboat.

Finally, my head breaks the surface. I gasp in frosty air and reach up to create a shimmerdark bar.

It sizzles and crackles under my wet fingers and feels like a mass of sharp pins. I lengthen it and grab on with my other hand. Then I haul my drenched self back onto the bridge.

At first, all I can do is collapse onto the stone, shivering and sopping. But I'm still alive. Realms, I'm relieved.

I also see that the exploding canister made a huge hole in the bridge and surrounding it are smoldering woliev parts.

I did it.

I saved us.

"Rutholyn!" I shout, limping back to the seg-coach.

She unbolts the cabdwell door, and I tumble inside, my wet clothes slapping onto the rug. I vaguely notice that Rutholyn managed to shove the floor panel back.

"You need to be dry," she says, and I hear her shut and bolt the door.

"I know," I mumble.

But I can't see to my own needs just yet. I still have to protect her. Standing up wearily, I shove the dead woliev out of the midpassage with a shimmerdark cube. Once I've flopped its body onto the bridge, I climb back into the damaged vehicle and block the midpassage with a new shimmerdark panel. To kill two birds with one stone, I fill the door with extra energy, heating it until the edges glow a cozy orange. Now we'll be safe and warm.

I have just enough strength left to strip off my wet clothes—an agonizing ordeal—and then I pull on the first outfit I find in my trunk, a long, sleeping gown. Once dressed, I wrap myself in a blanket and fall onto the table-bed. Rutholyn curls up beside me.

"Keep watch," I mumble, and I'm not sure who I'm talking to, Rutholyn or Glowy Pony. After that, I fuzzily consider how impressed Drae Devorla is going to be with me, and then I succumb to a deep, dreamless sleep.

15

Haberdine

I wake to stinging pain, the odd sensation of small fingers prodding my back, and the *plink, plink, plink* of rain on the metal roof. I'm also cold. Blinking my eyes open, I see that my shimmerdark panel still blocks the midpassage, but the sparks skittering across it are no longer orange. Instead, they're a greenish-blue. I suppose hot shimmerdark eventually cools off.

I blearily roll over and find Glowy Pony and Rutholyn sitting beside me. She's wrapped herself in a heavy blanket, and she's also wearing a simple, glimmering tiara of shimmerlight. I think she's using it to see—how clever.

"There's still blood coming out of you," she tells me.

That explains why I feel so weak. "How much?"

Rutholyn holds up a red-soaked rag. "This much. I couldn't find any bandages. I only found that." She nods at what seems to be a tin of medicinal balm. It smells pleasantly like pineflower oil.

"There are more medical supplies in the guidebox," I say before realizing they probably aren't there anymore. And thinking about the damaged guidebox with its shattered windows, broken steering wheel, and shredded seats is sobering. When I was fighting the wolievs, my only goal was survival. Now that the battle's over, I wish I'd tried harder to protect the seg-coach.

Rutholyn touches my shoulder. "Also there are rattatears out there."

The dead wolievs must be attracting scavengers. I should have expected that and pushed their bodies off the bridge.

"I don't think rattatears will bother us." I try to remember what Fedorie used to say about them. "They aren't hunters."

I summon more cagic into the shimmerdark door to warm up the cabdwell, and then I take off my gown so Rutholyn can more easily tend to my injuries. Oh, I am a mess. Shallow cuts and ugly purple bruises cover my arms, and my back feels like... well, it feels like I just fought a pack of wolievs. "Should my cuts be sewn closed?"

"Maybe... I don't know." Rutholyn presses a damp cloth against my torn skin and then smears some balm on the wounds.

The pain around my spine brightens, and I wince.

I didn't see any sewing supplies in the seg-coach anyway, so I suppose we might as well just cover my wounds.

I help Rutholyn make bandages out of clean kitchen rags, which we secure with laces pulled out of Golly's boots. Once my injuries are well wrapped, Rutholyn asks, "What should we do now?" And I'm sure she's really asking, "How will we survive?"

With the seg-coach broken, we don't have many options. "We'll have to walk to Haberdine... or maybe ride on an energy disc. At least we're close."

Rutholyn strokes Glowy Pony's dark head and frowns. "Do you think you can stop nocturnes from always trying to eat us?"

"I hope so," I say, and then realizing a child might need more reassurance, I add, "We just killed a pack of wolievs, so the nocturnes should really be afraid of us."

Rutholyn smiles, and then in the soft glow of her shimmerlight crown and my shimmerdark door, we prepare to leave. I first change into warmer clothes, and since most of my outfits are for hot Bright Month weather, I put on both of my densely ruffled stolas, two sets of leggings, a vest, and a pair of Golly's woolen socks. And oh, how I long to bathe. I smell like woliev breath and lake water.

Once Rutholyn is also warmly dressed, wearing several of Theandra's coziest outfits, we take the remaining downleveling equipment out of their storage cases. We then repack those cases with two empty bottles, a few tins of food and a wind-up can-opener, a big kitchen knife, the remaining crackers, the medicinal balm, and a pair of blankets.

"Look at what Glowy Pony wants us to have," Rutholyn says, holding up a basket of hats and mittens.

"What do you mean, Glowy Pony wants us to have these?" I ask.

Rutholyn looks blankly at me. "I don't know. He went to that drawer, and I opened it, and there was this basket."

I give Glowy Pony a suspicious look. "How did you know that was in there?"

The shimmerdark horselet blinks innocently, and then he trots over to a different drawer and touches it with his nose.

I open it and find two canvas rain covers. How strange, but also, how helpful. "Thank you," I say. One of the rain covers is huge and surely Golly's. The other is about my size and must fit Theandra. Taking scissors, I chop the bottom off both, that way Rutholyn can wear Theandra's and I can wear Golly's.

Footwear is also a challenge. Rutholyn's wearing thin canvas shoes with flimsy soles, and although I have several pairs of boots, none of them are sturdy enough to hike in. Besides, my right foot is still swollen and might not fit into a shoe. Yet other than Golly's far too big boots, I can't find much.

I cautiously ask Glowy Pony for help. "Are there other shoes here?"

The horselet shakes his head, *no*, and I believe him, which makes me feel like I'm losing my mind a little.

"We'll find better shoes in Haberdine," I tell Rutholyn, easing my injured foot into one of my boots and lacing it loosely.

I also want the map and compass from the guidebox, and I hope I can get them without upsetting the rattatears. The compass will be especially challenging to take because it's built into the control panel. I'll have to pry it free.

"Are you ready to go?" I ask Rutholyn.

"Maybe," she murmurs, looking very small in her grown-up clothes. "I'm scared that something will want to eat us."

"Me too," I say, and it does seem reckless to leave the seg-coach. Even though it's badly damaged, it's still a shelter full of useful supplies. And now if I fight nocturnes, I'll have to protect Rutholyn at the same time.

But it would be just as risky to stay here. The Dark Month's only beginning, and we'd quickly run out of food. So I release the cagic door, and we creep down the cold midpassage to the guidebox.

Rain's now splattering in through the broken navigation window and everything's drenched. Outside, I see five rattatears gnawing on the dead woliev I pushed out of the seg-coach. The grimy rodents aren't as large as most nocturnes, only about as big as dogs, yet they still look frightening with their scruffy bodies and ropy, forked tails. At least they seem more interested in the dead woliev than us. Yet if a hungry owleck spots them, it might snatch up Rutholyn or me instead.

Theandra's map is gone except for a few soggy fragments stuck to the floor. Thankfully, though, the compass is in good shape, and I'm able to twist it out.

"Stay close," I whisper to Rutholyn as I climb down the big coach wheel. I then reach up and help her follow me. A rattatear hisses at us but doesn't attack, and the others don't even look up as we quietly creep away from the seg-coach.

"I think this will be a long walk," Rutholyn says, watching Glowy Pony canter soundlessly ahead.

"I think so too," I say, limping beside her, glad the broken section of the bridge isn't in the direction we need to go. If I remember the map correctly, we'll reach Haberdine as long as we keep heading south. I very much hope the road ahead will be easier to follow than the one behind us.

Once we are well away from the rattatears, I decide to attempt to use transference to carry us to Haberdine. I'm ambitious at first, creating a hollow globe of shimmerdark with a circular opening. It looks like a big egg, is roomy enough for Rutholyn and I to sit inside, and will provide warmth and shelter from both the nocturnes and the weather. Yet because of its complex shape and large size, I'm only able to make it float a hand's span above the bridge and move at a snail's pace. We could walk faster.

So I try a simpler shape, creating a round disc of shimmerdark as wide as my outstretched arms. I then climb onto it, pull Rutholyn into my lap, cover our legs with a blanket, and hang our leather cases on my back. We still don't travel fast, for I don't want to topple off or get too cold, but we move somewhere between a walking and running pace, and it's much easier on my ankle. Because I might have to suddenly release the disc to defend us, we hover no higher than chest height.

It occurs to me that the glowing shimmerdark might attract flying nocturnes, and only seconds later, Glowy Pony abruptly stops and looks skyward.

I look up too, and at first, I can't see anything. Yet after a few seconds, I glimpse the triangular, stocky outline of an owleck.

Rutholyn shrieks and presses closer. Fear whips through me too, but I push it away. I fought a pack of wolievs. I can handle one owleck.

I abandon the disc beneath us so I can create a shimmerdark shield, and we fall to the bridge, landing in a jumble. Rutholyn yelps indignantly but then falls silent as owleck talons scrabble against my shield. Cagic crackles brightly, and then the monstrous bird sails off into the darkness with an offended screech. By the time the nocturne circles around again, I've had time to create and heat a flat, thin length of shimmerdark. I send the sizzling energy upward, and it stabs through the huge bird with a wet, crackling sound. The dead owleck drops into the lake, and a spray of cold water splatters onto the bridge.

"I think you did a good job," Rutholyn says in her overly serious way.

"Thanks," I say, helping her to her feet and feeling more confident as I reshape our transference disc. I learned from my fight with the wolievs, and hopefully I learned enough to keep us alive.

Glowy Pony has also been surprisingly useful. Not only did he find those mittens and rain covers, he noticed the owleck before I did, giving me precious time to react.

"You helped us," I say to him. "Thank you."

Glowy Pony looks up at me, blinking his bright eyes. He still makes me uneasy, but I'm also kind of glad he's here.

We soon reach the far shore, which has a sandy beach rather than a rocky one. Rutholyn and I climb off the shimmerdark disc, and I fill our bottles. Nothing attacks us, but I ready a hot disc of shimmerdark just in case.

I then use that disc to purify our water by setting the bottles on it until the water boils. After the bottles have cooled, Rutholyn and I drink our fill, and then I repeat the process, refilling the bottles and boiling the water. Yet this time, when we can comfortably handle the glass, we tuck the bottles inside our clothes and hug their warmth to our chests. No longer shivering, we climb back on a glittering shimmerdark disc and continue along the road.

There aren't as many trees on this side of the lake, and I'm not sure how I feel about that. It will be easier for nocturnes to find us, but I suppose it will also be easier for me to see them. The road is still in terrible shape, though, which makes no sense. Surely it should get better the nearer we are to Haberdine. Doesn't anybody there travel north?

As our disc glides forward, the landscape becomes hilly. The rain keeps falling too, sizzling and popping when it strikes the shimmerdark, and the higher we go, the windier it gets. It's soon so cold, my fingers and toes ache, my face stings, and my nose is constantly running. Every now and then, I stop to warm our water bottles, but it barely helps. At least no nocturnes trouble us for a while. But as we pass a frozen creek, a shareck bursts out of the forest. I have just enough time to dump us on the ground and compress our transference disc into a small, hot dart of energy. Yet because of the monster's loping, uneven gait, I miss, and instead of quickly killing the beast, all I do is severely slice its leg.

How horrifying. With a cry, Rutholyn ducks behind me as the shareck slides down the wet rocks, bleeding and shrieking. I scramble to summon and heat more cagic, and then I behead it, which is disgusting, but at least it's dead. "I'm so sorry," I say to Rutholyn, and really to the monster too.

I suppose that's silly, though; that shareck was about to happily disembowel us. Yet as deadly as nocturnes are, the Dark Month is their domain. Rutholyn and I are intruders, invaders.

"At least it wasn't a senneck," Rutholyn whispers.

I nod. Sennecks are the most dangerous nocturnes, at least in this part of the Connected Lands. In the eastern arm, people are afraid of tigrons and waspers.

I make a new transference disc so we can keep traveling, and although it's finally stopped raining, a thick fog has settled. We don't see any more sharecks, but a rattatear jumps on our transference disc and bites Rutholyn through her mitten. An owleck also carries me high into the air before I'm able twist free and kill it, and then a slow, surely ancient tortrussor crosses our path. He's huge—the size of the seg-coach at least—and covered in mossy spines and small plants.

Yet aside from glaring at us for a moment, he keeps lumbering forward, and thank the realms. I don't want to battle something so massive and well-armored.

After seeing the tortrussor, though, I wonder if I could make Glowy Pony larger to protect us. When I explain the idea to him, he shakes his head. But I say, "At least let me try."

However Glowy Pony was right, it is bad idea. By the time he's waist high, he seems unable to maintain his cagic form. Energy sheds off of him, and his crisp horselet shape softens and droops.

"Fine, fine," I say. "Hold still." And thankfully, it doesn't take me long to return him to his original size and shape.

Soon after that, we reach another bridge that stretches across a deep ravine. It's much shorter than the lake bridge and made of timber thick enough to support a subtrain. On the far side, I see the hazy, angular silhouettes of buildings.

"Haberdine! We made it!" I cry, and I lower our shimmerdark disc so we can walk the rest of the way.

"Now we're here!" Rutholyn hugs me as Glowy Pony prances in a happy circle around us.

High over the buildings, poles support a star net that looks a lot like a fishing net draped over the town. I thought Kaverlee was the only place in our cityland with aboveground cagic protection during the Dark Month. I suppose Drae Devorla must have installed barriers here while I was on the Grimshore.

I look around, and sure enough, I see the same cagic projection towers that shield Kaverlee's Expansion District.

I remember Drae Devorla talking about building a barrier system in Port Beyder. She hoped that one day everyone in the Periph would live like we do in Kaverlee City: able to stay home during the Dark Month, rather than hiding in underground shelters.

But why isn't the barrier system here working? Shimmerlight walls should stretch from tower to tower, and the star net should glow bright blue.

Perhaps it's still being built.

Yet on the other side of the ravine, a sign reads: "No Trespassing. Looters will be fined." The buildings here aren't boarded up for the Dark Month either. I see broken windows, missing shingles, debris in the streets. The terrible roads north of town now make heartbreaking sense. "No one lives here," I say.

It's a crushing realization in so many ways. Nobody is here to feed or protect us. There are probably no fresh supplies to be found.

"But why?" Rutholyn asks, her voice trembling. She's also cradling her hand, the one that the rattatear bit.

"I don't know," I say. "But let's look for the town's shelter anyway. If we can find a way in, we'll be safe there." I try to reassure myself that everything will still be alright. At least now I won't have to hide Glowy Pony or explain why we're outside during the Dark Month. Maybe I can even leave Rutholyn inside the shelter and go hunting. I've cleaned and cooked small animals before—I hate doing it, but I know how. And if I find enough food, maybe Rutholyn and I can lingersleep through the rest of the Dark Month.

"Oh!" Rutholyn peeps happily as she holds out her uninjured hand to catch a snowflake.

I've seen plenty of snow in Kaverlee, but Rutholyn has probably spent all her Dark Months underground.

"It is the most beautiful thing that ever was," she whispers, examining the tiny flake.

The snow is pretty, and it somehow softens our gloomy surroundings, making it easier for me to believe we're going to survive. It also helps me imagine what the mountain town was once like. I notice the wooden trim on roof lines, carvings on pillars, and colorful glass in the occasional unbroken window. Haberdine was probably a lot like Kaverlee's Crossriver District; older, charming, and full of stories.

As we walk down a quiet street, it occurs to me that there might no longer be a shelter here. Once they had barriers, the townspeople might have filled it in. Thankfully, though, that doesn't seem to be the case. We soon find the shelter entrance, and like other towns, the huge double doors are in a central, easy-to-reach place. It's also built into a hillside and flanked by massive, fortified towers.

The doors are closed, though, and seem to be bolted from the inside. When I try to force them open with a cube of shimmerdark, they won't budge. I suppose I could heat cagic and cut the hinges, but that would take a while and then the doors would be useless. As eerie as this abandoned town is, I would still like to use its shelter.

"Where did Glowy Pony go?" Rutholyn asks.

And that's a good question. He was at my feet a moment ago. I look around and eventually spot him perched precariously near the shelter doors. He seems to be climbing up the rocky cliff.

Rutholyn tugs on my sleeve. "I think he wants us to be following him."

"We're staying here," I say.

"He's always right, though," Rutholyn says through purple lips.

I suppose Glowy Pony did help us find the road in the abandoned settlement. Maybe he can help us find a way into the shelter. "Do you know how to get inside?" I ask the glimmering creature.

He nods.

So rather than climb up after him and risk slipping on the rocks, Rutholyn and I ride up on a shimmerdark disc. Glowy Pony stops on a rocky ledge where he hops a few times on a low, concrete structure jutting up from the ground.

Moving closer, I realize he's showing us a fortified air vent that surely connects to the shelter below—it's a way in.

"How did you know this was here?" I ask the horselet. It wasn't visible below.

Like usual, all he does is look at me, cock his head, and blink.

I climb off the shimmerdark disc and peer through the metal grate covering the vent. A ladder made of angled, rectangular notches descends into darkness within. I'll have to use cagic to cut through the grate… or maybe not. There's a latch. After some fiddling with numb fingers, I manage to pry the vent open. I then reluctantly send Rutholyn down the shaft first so I can close things up behind us. Only rattatears would be small enough to enter this way, but I still don't want to share the shelter with anyone.

As Rutholyn climbs down the ladder, she wears another shimmerlight tiara.

"Good idea," I call softly as I shape a square of shimmerdark to carry us the rest of the way down.

For a while, we descend a narrow shaft, then it widens, and then we reach a flagstone floor. It's still cold but not nearly as bitter, and after a moment, Glowy Pony appears beside us with a crackling pop.

So I can see where we are, I send a globe of shimmerlight into the air. The pale, blue cagic illuminates rows of dusty, neatly parked chariots and coaches, and stacked wooden crates. Something shifts uneasily inside me. If Haberdine's empty, why are these vehicles still here? Many of them look expensive.

I'm kind of glad they're here, though. I can't wait to sit down or even better, lie down, and the covered chariots are probably clean inside, with padded seats.

Yet Glowy Pony is still prancing around impatiently. He clearly wants to lead us farther into the shelter, so we follow him down a few sets of wide stairs. This whole shelter looks like the inside of an old castle. Unlike the sparse functionality of the Outer's Cove shelter, someone designed this compound to be a pleasing place to spend the Dark Month. The walls are made of gray and pink granite blocks arranged in patterns, and here and there are mosaics of sunlit fields and glades.

We walk through another storage hall and then pass arched doorways with brass numerals on them. These must be the apartments Haberdine families sheltered in. Eventually, Glowy Pony stops at a door marked forty-seven and taps his nose against it. I guess this is where he thinks we should rest.

Yet when I try to open the door, it won't move. It's locked.

"You're absolutely sure we should go in here?" I ask.

Glowy Pony nods and puts his front hooves on the door.

Maybe there's something useful inside, like code office equipment. It would be wonderful to find a way to contact Drae Devorla.

Telling Rutholyn to stand back, I use a thin, hot shard of shimmerdark to slice through the door's bolt. I work slowly because I don't want to harm anything on the other side.

Several moments later the door swings open with a squeaky, metallic groan.

Glowy Pony confidently trots into the dark space, and Rutholyn and I cautiously follow him.

This doesn't look like a code office. This looks like a dwelling.

It's a strange home, though. Not only are there tables, chairs, and rugs—there's also a disorganized hoard of artwork. Fine paintings lean against the walls and sculptures rest on nearly every surface. There are even extravagantly odd items, such as a stuffed rattatear wearing comical silver armor and holding a bag of crumpled printed money. Stranger still, in the middle of this jumble of finery are jars of water and jars of what might be pickled fish and vegetables. I also see a few piles of rumpled clothes, and I smell sweat and stale air.

As we move farther into the room, Rutholyn's shimmerlight tiara reveals a bed.

And in that bed is a person.

16

Aerro

I step farther into the room, wishing I hadn't ruined the door and feeling like a vandal. But who is this? He seems to be lingersleeping. And how old is he? His skin is soft and spotted with pimples, but he also has a short, scruffy beard.

The man's eyelids flutter, and oh no, the noise I made cutting the bolt must have disturbed him.

We should leave.

But we also need help, and he's probably harmless. Even if he isn't, I've been fighting nocturnes; I have no reason to fear an isolated human.

Glowy Pony seems to agree, for he leaps onto the bed.

"No," I hiss at the horselet.

He glances at me—insolently, I swear—and then jumps on the stranger's belly.

The man groans.

Rutholyn presses herself nervously against my side, and we both step backward.

"Do you think we should run away now?" Rutholyn asks.

"Maybe," I whisper.

The man rolls over and blearily opens his eyes. Noticing us, he shakes his head, possibly in disbelief. He then pushes his blankets aside and sits up. "Who… who are you?" he croaks.

"I'm Xylia," I say, not adding the "Amoreah Selvantez, former Predrae" part.

He rubs his eyes as he lowers his feet to the floor. "But… why are you here? Nobody comes here. Didn't you see the signs?" He's wearing a threadbare, mismatched combination of formerly elegant clothes. His worn outfit reminds me of my Grimshore rags, although it isn't quite as tattered. And now that he's sitting up, I see his hair is long and hangs in tangled, elbow-length clumps. It looks like he hasn't brushed or trimmed it in years. "Is it still the Dark Month then?" he says. "And… and…" He examines Glowy Pony with a mild expression. "How did you get in here?"

I find it odd that he isn't alarmed by Glowy Pony, and I'm not sure how much of our story I should share. "There was a misunderstanding. We were locked out of the Marin Harbor shelter, so we came here."

"That's a long trip." The young man narrows his eyes and stands up. His movements are stiff and jerky, and I don't think it's just because he was lingersleeping. There's something peculiar about him. "How did you survive?" he asks.

"It wasn't easy," I say, being both honest and vague.

He nods, eyeing the broken bolt. "You have cagic power, though? A lot of it?" He says it casually, as if discussing a book we've both read.

I suppose it's clear that I melted the door, so I say, "Yes."

"And you can also summon shadow energy," he says softly. "And you're never cagic-blind anymore?"

"How do you know all this?" I ask, feeling more confused than ever.

Tears glimmer in his eyes as he holds out his hand. Dark sparks swirl in his palm, coalescing into an applen-sized sphere of shimmerdark. "I thought I was the only one."

He's like me. Merciful light, is that even possible? Beneath my awe, though, is a knot of frustration. My powers aren't special or rare if the first person I meet has them too.

He releases his cagic and walks—or rather springs—toward us. He's shorter than me, and even though he's lingersleep pudgy, he's still a small person.

"This is… this is unbelievable," he says, and at least he seems equally surprised. "I hoped that something would change here and end my monotonous existence, but I never imagined this! How did you find me?" He smiles brightly. "Or were you looking for me?" His voice is raspy, and I get the sense that he hasn't talked this much in a long time.

I point at Glowy Pony. "He led me here."

The young man nods. "Of course, or course. They are good at finding things, aren't they?" He turns. "Flutter? Flutter, where are you?"

A glittering shimmerdark butterfly dips out of the darkness and lands on his shoulder.

"That's the same as Glowy Pony," Rutholyn whispers. "But also a butterfly."

"What are these creatures?" I ask.

The ragged young man shrugs. "I *wish* I knew. But no, I have no idea. You're the first people I've seen here in years! Flutter showed up after everything went wrong. She didn't have that shape at first, no, no. She was just a cloud of dark energy following me around. So I gave her a shape, and now she helps me find things and warns me if I'm in danger. She's a good friend—my only friend."

I look at Glowy Pony. I suppose I gave him his shape too, although I didn't mean to. I turn back to the young man. "You were cagic-touched… but not downleveled? And you didn't wink out either. Why?" Realms, I have a lot of questions. "And what happened to Haberdine? Why is it empty?"

"Ah yes, I *do* know about that," the young man says, and although his joyful tears are gone, his eyes still gleam intensely. "But first, you both look tired, and are you hurt? I've never had guests. Do you want anything to eat or drink? I hardly remember how to be a good host. Would you like to rest… or lingersleep? Do you know what lingersleeping is?"

"I know," I say, and although I want to keep talking to this curious person, Rutholyn is leaning more heavily against me. She's surely exhausted. I slept after the woliev battle, but she didn't. I should get her settled before I do anything else. "I don't need to sleep yet, but my friend does."

"She can use my bed, of course." He gestures loosely at it. "I'm such an idiot too; I haven't introduced myself. I'm Aerro. You're Xylia, yes? And you are…?"

Rutholyn swallows. "I'm Rutholyn."

I look at Aerro's bed. I can't imagine it's clean. This whole place smells like grime and sleep, yet hygiene isn't really my highest priority right now. "Come Rutholyn, let's get you settled."

"Oh, and here, allow me." Aerro darts across the room, and thankfully pulls off the blankets and replaces them. The new ones are hopefully fresher, but since they were heaped in a corner, who's to say.

I help Rutholyn pull off her rain cover as well as some of her other layers. Her rattatear bite doesn't look as bad as I thought it might—only a few superficial scratches. We can deal with it later. As soon as I've tucked her into bed, Glowy Pony hops up next to her and lies down too. Does he sleep? I'm not sure.

"Good moonlight," I whisper to her, feeling a swell of pride because I did the impossible; I fought nocturnes and kept us alive, and now here we are in a much safer place.

Rutholyn curls up, looking content, so leaving her to rest, I follow Aerro through a passage into another room. He leads the way with a glittering ball of shimmerlight that casts a familiar blue glow. The second room is as cramped and cluttered as the first with more paintings, sculptures, and various luxury items such as ceramic lamps and polished jewelry boxes.

I pull off my rain cover, and then I heat a shimmerdark sphere to warm the small room. That seems to amaze Aerro. Maybe compressed shimmerdark isn't something he's figured out.

"You must be thirsty," he says and pours dark liquid into a ridiculously extravagant gold goblet. As I sip what tastes like vinegary wine, Aerro arranges a plate of dried meat and what looks like pickled cabbage for us to share.

This is so strange, sitting on a beautiful sofa across from a ragged young man surrounded by treasure. "Why are you alone?" I ask.

"I'm surprised you don't already know," Aerro says, folding his legs. He's sitting in a luxurious-yet-faded armchair. "I mean, a whole town... gone! Don't people talk about it?"

"They might," I say. "I was away from Kaverlee for many years. So what happened here?"

Aerro blows out a breath of disbelief. "Isn't it obvious? The barriers failed."

Something solid and certain inside me tips over. "That's impossible."

"Oh, believe me, it happened." A frown worries the corners of Aerro's mouth. "The barriers worked perfectly for two years, and then one day..." He snaps his fingers. "They turned off—no warning, no siren, no nothing. My parents thought the Great Drae would save us, but she didn't. Some people made it to the shelter but not many, and because they were scared, they locked it before everyone else could get in. People were pounding on the doors, screaming, begging, and then... dying."

I put my goblet on the floor because my hands are shaking. "Deepest realms, that's terrible."

"My family didn't make it in," Aerro adds, rocking slightly. "When we reached the shelter, the doors were shut, and nocturnes were everywhere. But since there was plenty of"—he drops his head—"*food* to be had, we made it back home. My Father, he..." Aerro wipes his eyes on the embroidered trim of what was probably once a very fine tago. "I'm sorry, I've never told anyone about this."

"It's alright," I say, already dreading the unhappy ending his story must have.

He rocks quietly for a moment and then continues. "Father thought we should hide in our cellar. He hoped the nocturnes would eat their fill and go away."

I nod as I try not to imagine the attack too vividly.

"But a cattern found us, and we were trapped." Aerro's voice drops to a paper-thin whisper. "I'd always been able to summon cagic, so I tried to save my family with shimmerlight, but it wasn't enough. Yet when the monster tried to kill me, a strange dark energy appeared—and I realized I could control it. I used it to kill the cattern, but it was too late to save anyone else." Aerro stretches out his hand and ashy sparks dance around his overgrown fingernails. "I didn't know what to do, so I ran. I took food from a grocer's and I hid in the Forum basement. Somehow, down there, wrapped in shadow energy, I survived that first Dark Month."

Aerro gives me a long, bewildered look as if he's almost forgotten who I am. "When the sunrise days finally came, I heard voices—maybe the sound of survivors or Shieldbearers, I wasn't sure—but I kept hiding. I already knew Triumvirate Hall didn't want male Shimmerlings, which is why my parents never reported me, so I was sure Drae Devorla would hate what I'd become. I couldn't let anyone know what had happened."

"Kaverlee does have male Shimmerlings," I say. "It's just boys rarely have stable cagic so there aren't that many." I don't like that I'm repeating something the Shalvos taught me.

Aerro's guarded expression seems to put on even more armor. "If Drae Devorla knew about me, she'd downlevel me—I'm sure of it—and downleveling might as well be an execution."

I think of Vonnet's thrashing in the cabdwell and struggle to push the memory aside. "My mother was downleveled, and she's fine."

Aerro frowns. "My brother was downleveled, and he wasn't. That's why my parents never reported me."

"What happened to him?" I ask, not sure I want to know.

"When he was young, he was very bright." Aerro picks up a piece of dried meat. "But not after they downleveled him. He acted like a small child from then on. It was terrible."

I feel like I should be surprised, but I'm not. Golly did mention that downleveling sometimes causes permanent harm. My thoughts turn to why Aerro's cagic changed. "The dark cagic appeared when the nocturne attacked you?"

Aerro nods.

I was facing Golly, not a nocturne, when I first summoned shimmerdark, but like Aerro, I was afraid. That must be the connection.

I then think about Fifsa's friend Tury. I thought a shockgun blast killed the nocturne near him, but maybe Tury's cagic changed—maybe he and the woliev killed each other.

Yet Rutholyn's been in great danger, and she can't summon shimmerdark. Is it because she's too young? It must be.

Drae Devorla will want to know about all of this. I quiver with excitement and even my thoughts feel cagically charged. "Come with us to Kaverlee," I say to Aerro. I don't want to share the attention I'll get for being unique, but this is too important. Shimmerdark might be the greatest discovery of the century, and Aerro's a part of it. "The Great Drae will be amazed by both of us."

Yet Aerro tightens his grip on his armrest. "The Great Drae? I don't want to see her. She killed my family and murdered this town."

I try to be patient. "That was surely an accident."

Aerro digs his fingernails into the plush fabric of his chair. "It's still her fault. Her barrier failed, and she didn't help us."

"Maybe there was nothing she could do." It was nearly impossible for me to defeat a dozen wolievs. I can't imagine trying to save an entire town. "Look, I know Drae Devorla, and I know she cares deeply about everyone in Kaverlee City and the Periph."

Aerro leaps up, nearly spilling his goblet of wine. "What do you mean, you *know* her? Why are you really here? Who are you? Did you come here to find me? Capture me?"

"No, no, *no*," I say quickly. "Nothing like that. I had no idea you were here. I only know Drae Devorla because I was her Predrae."

Aerro's glare intensifies. "So you're *that* Xylia. Aren't you supposed to be dead?"

"People thought so," I say. "But I survived the shipwreck… just like you survived here."

"Now there's a new Predrae." Aerro eases back in his chair. "Drae Devorla betrayed you too."

"She didn't betray me—she didn't know I was alive." Feeling defensive, I swirl the rest of my wine into a little whirlpool. "Anyway, can Rutholyn and I stay here for the rest of the Dark Month? As soon as the sun rises, we'll be on our way."

He nods and starts rocking again. "You're welcome to stay, absolutely, but why bother returning to Kaverlee at all?"

That's an easy question to answer. "Because it's my home. Besides, when Drae Devorla sees how powerful I am, I believe she'll make me her Predrae again."

Aerro looks skeptically at the ceiling, and I understand why he doesn't trust Drae Devorla, but he's also never met her. He's never seen her obsessing over barrier wall schematics or seen her spending hours repairing cagic compressors. I suppose we'll be here for a few weeks, maybe I can change his mind before we leave.

And although he usually lingersleeps through the Dark Month, Aerro does decide to stay awake. "It's so nice to have people around," he tells us the next day, and I'm sure he's been lonely.

Once we've eaten breakfast—an odd combination of dried berries and smoked rabbit meat—Aerro proudly takes us on a tour of the shelter. We've already seen his art treasures, the paintings and sculptures, but he also has large stores of clothes, blankets, tools, books, and even several dozen shockguns.

"Why do you have these?" I ask, for it's chilling to see so many weapons in one place.

Aerro looks at me as if I should already know. "I'm going to spend the rest of my life here, so I need to be prepared for anything."

Anything, I suspect, doesn't just include nocturnes.

Aerro doesn't have a lot of food, but he has enough to share. During Bright Months, he tells us, he tends sleeping crops. "I have several vegetable plots in the forest. I try to make the plants look like they're growing wild, though, in case anyone finds them." He keeps some of what he harvests in a cellar, infyroots, crisscross squash, and the like; the rest he dries or pickles.

As for entertainment, Aerro proudly shows us a wardrobe full of games. He has card games, toss games, and notion games that use tiles, beads, and figurines. "I've had to make up new rules for all of them," he says. "That way I can play alone."

The most useful items Aerro's hoarded, though, are bandages, pain pills, and medicinal creams. My foot's getting better, but my back still burns with infection. And even though Aerro's medicine stash is probably no longer very potent, it's still better than nothing. Rutholyn helps me clean and tend my wounds, and I put a fresh bandage on her hand. The two of us also bathe in the shelter's baths. Aerro knows how to charge the old heating equipment, and once the water's warm, it's really very pleasant. Afterward, we dress in outfits from Aerro's hoard and wash our clothes.

Strangely, Aerro's life reminds me of the Grimshore; he's isolated and has to take care of himself. Yet while he has many supplies and luxuries, I had company, and company, I realize, is far better.

Because he's been alone for so long, Aerro spends the next few days constantly with us, constantly talking to us. It's honestly a bit exhausting, although I am interested when he explains how he uses shimmerdark, which he calls "shadow cagic."

"I mostly hunt with it," he says, demonstrating how he creates a loop of energy around an animal's neck, which he then tightens. "I only hunt during the Bright Month, though."

He also has excellent balance while riding shimmerdark discs, which makes me jealous. Standing transference surely looks much more impressive than my sitting and kneeling.

Yet he doesn't know how to compress and heat shimmerdark, and I realize I don't want to teach him. I suppose I'm being selfish, but if he does return to Triumvirate Hall with us, I still want to be the obvious choice for Predrae.

While trying to sleep at night, I often think about Shimmerlings and our relationship to cagic. Under the right circumstances, could any Shimmerling wield shimmerdark? Both Aerro and I first summoned it when our lives were in danger. But most Shimmerlings live in the Courtyard of Youth, where they never face any peril.

I have so much to tell Drae Devorla when I return and so many questions to ask.

I wish I didn't have to spend the rest of the Dark Month in Haberdine, though. I'm giving Theandra weeks to spread wire-message rumors about me, and if Golly's dead, I'm sure those rumors will be vicious. The sooner I reach Kaverlee City the better.

I begin to wonder if I should travel home alone. I'm sure I'd make it if I didn't need to protect Rutholyn. I could leave her here, and then return for her during the Bright Month. I'd need a good map of the area, though. Glowy Pony might be able to lead me home with his knack for finding things, but I'm not sure how powerful he is. And I might also be able to follow the Sabeline River, but that might not be the most direct route. Yet when I ask Aerro for a map, he claims he doesn't have one.

"But you have everything else," I say.

He shrugs his skinny shoulders. "Why would I need a map? I'm not planning to go anywhere."

I look for maps anyway, searching the chariots and coaches parked in the shelter. Their guideboxes are all empty though, and they also seem to have been recently ransacked. There are fresh handprints on their dusty doors. Does Aerro want us to stay?

My suspicions are confirmed during our third day in the shelter. As we share a meal of dried venison and pickled bird's eggs, Aerro says, "You'll love it here when the Bright Month comes. I can show you the library and the old temple. Last month, I found tortrussor eggshells in the amphitheater."

"We saw a tortrussor on the road!" Rutholyn exclaims, turning to me. "It would be nice to stay here if Vonnet could be here too."

"You're more than welcome to stay," Aerro says, sounding hopeful.

But I'm not even slightly tempted to stay. I don't want to be stuck on another Grimshore. "Rutholyn, I promised I'd bring you to the Great Drae, and I also need to tell her about shimmerdark."

I can almost feel Aerro's frustration. It seems to make the air prickly. "When you return to Kaverlee, you can't tell Drae Devorla I'm here. If she finds me, I'll lose everything, and I'll be downleveled."

We're sitting around a silver gilt table in the inner chamber of his apartment. I look across the shiny surface, and I wish I knew how to soothe the sticky fears that keep him trapped here. "I won't say anything," I promise. "But I swear on all the realms, Drae Devorla would never hurt you."

"She already has," Aerro says quietly. "And she's hurt you too. You just refuse to see it."

Once we're done eating, I put Rutholyn to bed. Yet I don't feel sleepy. Since I also don't feel like spending any time with Aerro, I tell him I'm going for a walk.

"A walk?" he says, frowning. "A walk to where?"

"Just around the shelter," I say. "Don't worry, I'm not leaving." So I bundle myself up in warm clothes and head out into the chilly shelter. Unsurprisingly, Glowy Pony follows me.

"I feel sorry for Aerro," I tell the small cagic horse. "But he's also being really stubborn and stupid."

I feel silly talking to Glowy Pony as if he's a friend, yet our one-sided conversation gives me an idea. "You're good at finding things. Can you find me a map?"

Glowy Pony tilts his head—thoughtfully, it seems—and then he trots confidently off into the darkness.

I follow.

The glittering horselet leads me into an area of the shelter I've never been to before. It's newer, with smooth concrete walls and undamaged tile floors. It's also dustier than the corridors around Aerro's apartment. He mustn't come here much.

Glowy Pony canters down a staircase lined with modern lights that are of course dark because the shelter has no power. At the bottom of the stairs, he stops.

"Are the maps here?" I ask, and we seem to be in a huge chamber for my voice echoes.

All I can see is Glowy Pony, who hops a few times. What's he trying to tell me?

I fill my hands with cagic, and as light pools around us, I suck in a sudden, surprised breath.

We're on a subtrain platform.

I didn't know Haberdine had a station. Although I suppose, there's no reason I would have known. The station was surely closed after nocturnes destroyed the town, and I was gone during that time. It looks like this station was still being built, too. Sending my shimmerlight around the large space, I see palettes of unused tiles and train tracks only run halfway down the lengthy chamber. Yet a tunnel stretches off into the darkness, and if no nocturnes have entered the shelter, it must be well sealed. If I'm lucky, the passage might connect the station to Kaverlee City. I can't think of any other towns nearby.

I smile at Glowy Pony. "This is *so* much better than a map."

He nods.

I hurry back to Aerro's apartment, where I find him playing a notion game that involves balancing tiny chariots on small bridges. Rutholyn's still sleeping.

Aerro looks up. "Do you want to play?"

"No, I'm tired." I sit in the chair opposite him. "I was thinking though… many shelters have subtrain stations. A protected tunnel would be a safe way for Rutholyn and I to reach Kaverlee. Does Haberdine have a station?"

Without hesitating, Aerro says, "No. Of course not." It sounds like honesty, but the look in his eyes is more complex.

He surely knows about the station. He's lived here for years.

Well then.

He says I can't trust Drae Devorla, but clearly, I can't trust him.

17
The Tunnel

I crawl in bed beside Rutholyn and wait for Aerro to go to sleep. Eventually the blue shimmerlight glow in the other room fades, the sofa creaks as Aerro stretches out, and then I hear his raspy, steady snoring.

I stay still and silent for what feels like an hour, making sure he's truly asleep, and then I push back the coverlet and lower my feet to the floor.

It's time to continue our journey.

I silently find everything Rutholyn and I brought with us, and I also take some preserved food from Aerro's supply. I arrange our belongings elsewhere in the shelter, in what might once have been a communal kitchen, and then I return to Aerro's apartment. With a globe of shimmerlight hovering at my shoulder, I gently shake Rutholyn awake. As soon as her eyes open, I press a finger to her lips and whisper, "We're leaving. Follow me."

Rutholyn frowns, maybe unhappy that I woke her. Yet after yawning and stretching her short arms, she stumbles after me. When we reach the communal kitchen, I explain my plan. "Glowy Pony found a subtrain station. There's no train, but the tunnel surely leads to Kaverlee City."

"But why do we have to go now?" Rutholyn leans sleepily against a cupboard.

"Well, because…" I'm not sure how honest to be. "Because Aerro will be sad we're leaving, and he might try to stop us."

Rutholyn still looks confused. "But how can I say goodbye to him?"

"Don't worry about that." I hand her the lighter of the two leather cases, the ones that used to hold Authentication equipment. "Just think about Vonnet. If the Great Drae chooses you, the Maternals will send for him."

Rutholyn smiles when I mention her brother. So even though I don't want to raise her hopes too high, I tell her cheerful stories about the Courtyard of Youth as Glowy Pony leads us to the subtrain station. I describe the musicians that often perform in Triumvirate Hall and the special trips Shimmerlings take to the Harbor Playhouse, the Crossriver Parks, and during the Bright Months, to the spreadfarms just outside the city.

When we reach the subtrain platform, Rutholyn stares at the curved, tiled walls in amazement. "I'll like Kaverlee City if it looks like this."

"It's even more impressive," I say as I lift her off the platform and into the channel of incomplete tracks with me. Because my injured foot feels better, I decide not to create a shimmerdark disc for us to ride on just yet.

We start out at a good pace but soon slow down. It's the middle of the lunar night so we're both sleepy, and the tunnel is unchanging and monotonous.

Hoping conversation will keep us awake, I ask, "What was your life like in that labor camp?"

"I don't always know," Rutholyn murmurs.

I take her hand. "What sort of work did you do?"

She yawns. "I sometimes mucked out the pens, and I sometimes helped in the kitchens, and I sometimes pulled up weeds."

"What about your parents?" As soon as I ask the question, I realize they may be dead, so I hastily add, "Never mind. You don't have to answer that."

But she does. "Momma went all the way to the realms 'cause she was sick, and Papa was so sad he went there too. Vonnet promised to always take care of me, and now you're the one doing that." She lifts her small chin and smiles.

"I'm trying to," I say, my heart twinging. If I do become the Great Drae, I'm going to insist that the King and Queen investigate the labor agencies. No one should own children's work hours.

"Where are your momma and papa?" Rutholyn asks.

"My father died," I say, and for the first time ever, I wish I knew more about him. Why was he so fascinated with the Hidden Gods? Everyone knows they're only myths. I should have asked more about him. And as for Mother, she mentioned growing up in a labor agency orphanage. I suppose she was a lot like Rutholyn. I wished I'd asked her about that too. How did she meet my father? Why did they settle in Outer's Cove? There's so much about my family that I don't know.

"I always miss my momma and papa," Rutholyn says, her voice echoing off the rounded brick walls.

Even when I considered traveling to Kaverlee alone, I didn't like the idea of leaving Rutholyn behind. I suppose it must have been even harder for my parents to give me to the Authenticators, to strangers. It's odd to have something in common with them. I also realize that although I've always blamed my family for trapping me on the Grimshore, it's also kind of good that I was there. Without my cagic to move boulders, catch small prey, and provide warmth, it would have been harder—probably impossible—for Fedorie, Clicks, and Kary to survive. What a strange shift in my perspective.

"I hope I get to be a momma," Rutholyn says just as a faint blue-green light flashes in the corner of my eye. I turn quickly.

There are two patches of light behind us in the tunnel, one small and high and the other larger and low. They're both moving closer, and I'm pretty sure I'm looking at Aerro's transference disc and his shimmerdark companion, Flutter.

"Aerro?" I call, but no one answers as the approaching lights grow brighter and brighter. The faint glow that must be Flutter moves in erratic zigzags, while the other light is level and steady.

At last, I hear Aerro say, "So this is how it is; you pretend to be my friend and then you betray me."

I still can't see his face, but the shimmerdark he's standing on illuminates his laced boots and wrinkled breeches. Flutter's shape is clearer now too. Did she wake him up? Did she lead him to us?

"I'm sorry," I say, as Rutholyn worries her mitten-covered hand into mine.

"You're only sorry you've been caught," he snaps, and I can finally see all of him. He wears a heavily embroidered palliumcoat over his rumpled sleeping tago.

"I was stupid to trust you," he continues. "You—the acolyte of my greatest enemy."

Rutholyn tightens her grip.

"Don't be…" I nearly say "ridiculous," but I'm sure that would only provoke him, so instead I say, "Why did you lie about the subtrain station? You know I need to return to Kaverlee as quickly as possible."

He stops his glimmering shimmerdark disc about eight paces away from us, and with an ease I wish I had, he steps down onto the concrete floor. "I want you to stay—obviously. It's for your own good."

"You don't know that," I say. "Did you hide all the maps too?"

With his pale hair sticking out in all directions, Aerro looks like a yet-to-be-discovered nocturne. "I didn't hide the maps," he says. "I burnt them."

"You burnt them?" I echo.

"Don't you see, I'm trying to protect you. The Great Drae is evil. Look what happened in Haberdine because of her! And she'll hate—*hate*—that you can summon such powerful cagic. She doesn't want competition. And as for you…" Aerro turns to Rutholyn. "Do you really want to be cooped up forever in that gilded cage? Forced to give your energy to spoiled people who will never be satisfied and will always just want more and more?"

"I don't want to be here," Rutholyn says softly.

I don't either. If only I'd taken the coastal route on Theandra's map. I would have avoided the bridge with the wolievs, and I wouldn't be arguing with an unstable person now. "Aerro, please, I understand you're angry with Drae Devorla for making a few mistakes, but—"

"A *few* mistakes?" Aerro shouts in such a shrill way, I grit my teeth. "You make it sound like she spilled a drink. No. She's responsible for *hundreds* of deaths. You have no idea what I saw—or heard. Those people… My own parents. My brother. There was so much suffering… brutal suffering, and you don't even care. I always thought if I told someone about that day… they'd understand." Tears gleam on his face, reflecting Flutter's blue-green light.

"I do care," I say, of course I do—but Aerro doesn't know Drae Devorla. He's never met her in person. He's never spent hours with her adjusting reservoirs, fixing energy compressors, and checking conductors. I'm sure she was devastated by what happened in Haberdine. Keeping our cityland safe is her life's purpose.

"You know what I did during that first Bright Month?" Aerro says, wiping away tears. "I dragged bodies out of the shelter. Not everyone survived lingersleeping—I guess they hadn't eaten enough or drunk enough. I don't know." He swallows. "I dragged at least twenty corpses out of there—all on my own. I was only sixteen years old. Do you know how terrible that was?"

"I can't imagine," I say softly.

He looks down at the gravel-strewn tunnel floor. "I just want things to go back to the way they were."

"Come with us then," I say. "Please. You have an incredible gift. You could help people."

Aerro shakes his head. "No."

I look at him for a long moment, at his folded, skinny arms and mismatched clothes, and I feel so sorry for him. But I also can't force him to see reason, so I put my arm around Rutholyn's shoulders, and we turn away.

"Wait," Aerro says.

I glance back to see him making a strange movement with his hand, rolling his wrist. He's summoning shimmerdark—I'm sure of it. But why?

Rutholyn suddenly yelps, and I see a hoop of dark energy circling her upper body. It tightens, pinning her arms to her sides.

"No!" I shout as Aerro makes Rutholyn stumble toward him. "Stop it!" I try to disperse his shimmerdark ring, but since I didn't summon the energy, I can't seem to control it. Shimmerlight doesn't work that way.

"I won't hurt her," Aerro calls. "I'm just taking her back to Haberdine where she'll be safe—where you'll both be safe. I know you won't leave without her."

Of course I won't. Frustrated, I drop my leather case and charge toward him, painfully aware that I have no plan. When I fought the nocturnes, my attacks were lethal. But I'm only exasperated with Aerro, and I don't want to kill or maim him.

"I'm just trying to help you," Aerro says, retreating down the tunnel and making Rutholyn trail after him. "I'm also protecting myself. If you return to Kaverlee, you'll tell the Great Drae about me. I know you will."

I feel helpless. Can you change someone's mind when they're this deeply confused? "Aerro, please. I won't tell Drae Devorla or anyone about you; I promise." Unable to think of a better solution, I encase his foot in a cagic cube, trapping him and forcing him to stop.

He hisses in irritation. "It's going to be like that, is it?"

A prickling band of shimmerdark forms around my neck. I suck in a breath and dig my fingers between the ring of energy and my skin, fighting to disperse it. Yet just like before, because I didn't summon the energy, I can't manipulate it. "You don't want to do this," I croak.

"Let her go!" Rutholyn pulls on Aerro's arms. Now that he's wrapped shimmerdark around my throat, she's free. Glowy Pony also trots frantically around me.

"You're right; I don't want to hurt anyone!" Aerro's pointy jaw stiffens, and his eyes widen. "But I will if I have to. Don't make me. Swear you'll stay."

How can I promise anything when I can't breathe? A dark, fuzzy blanket seems to cover my thoughts, yet even now, it still seems wrong to kill Aerro. If I don't do something, though, I soon won't be able to do anything.

Maybe that's the answer—I need to make sure Aerro can't do anything.

I knocked Rutholyn unconscious in the guidebox while fighting the wolievs. Surely, I can do something similar to Aerro.

My strength fading, I create a large cube of shimmerdark behind his head. And as my aching lungs seem to shrivel, I smack the cagic shape against the back of his skull. His head whips forward, and when it recoils, his eyes roll back too. And oh, thank the realms, the shimmerdark band around my throat loosens.

Aerro collapses to the tunnel floor.

And I fall to my knees, gasping in frigid tunnel air and feeling tremendously lucky.

Rutholyn throws her arms around me. "You're all the way fine!"

"I am," I say, and now that Aerro isn't actively controlling the shimmerdark around my neck, I'm able to wave it away.

I look over at Aerro. He's now lying crumpled on the dusty tunnel floor. His arms and legs bend awkwardly to one side, and thankfully, his chest still rises and falls. I hope he'll recover, but I'm not going to wait around to make sure he does. I stand up, feeling dizzy.

"I don't like what just happened," Rutholyn says, watching Flutter land on Aerro's shoulder.

"Me neither," I say, picking up my leather case and creating a disc of shimmerdark for us to ride on—the faster we leave, the better. We climb onto the warm energy, and then I move us swiftly down the tunnel. Glowy Pony gallops along beneath us, and it takes me a long time to stop shaking.

I expected Aerro to be upset when we left, but I didn't think he'd become violent. And even though I'm furious he tried to strangle me, I'm also sad he thought that was his only option.

I look back to make sure he isn't staggering after us, but all I see is darkness.

Every now and then, our gliding disc of shimmerdark passes bolted maintenance doors; they must lead to the surface. I'm almost tempted to leave the tunnel to put more distance between us and Aerro. Yet I'd rather risk another fight with him than battle nocturnes.

A few hours pass, maybe three or four, and Aerro doesn't reappear. I suppose he still might be lying in the tunnel slowly freezing to death, but I hope he's simply come to his senses and is letting us go.

Every so often, Rutholyn and I stop to stretch our legs, and the third time we take a break, I notice the tunnel looks different.

Instead of plain gray stone, we're surrounded by a checkered pattern of orange and red bricks. I hope that means we're close to the city. I finally let myself imagine what I'll do when we arrive: travel directly to Triumvirate Hall to speak to Drae Devorla, and also bathe and put on fresh clothes. Then I'll take Rutholyn to the Dining Pavilion and feed her something wonderfully decadent, like syrup pockets with cracklings.

But not long after I notice the brick walls, the tunnel suddenly ends. I'm so surprised, I barely stop our transference disc in time. Both Rutholyn and I tumble off.

"No…" I say, helping Rutholyn to her feet. "No, no, no!" This tunnel should connect to Kaverlee's subtrain system. I was prepared to deal with a sealed gate, but not solid dirt. The tunnel was never finished. It must have been abandoned after Haberdine's disaster.

Realms, we must be close!

"What should we do now?" Rutholyn asks, and her little voice echoes off the curved walls.

"We keep going—outside," I say, closing my eyes and trying not to feel too disheartened. We almost avoided facing more nocturnes, but here we go again.

I turn to Glowy Pony. "Are we at least near the city?"

He nods.

That's a relief. "How do we get out of this tunnel then?"

Glowy Pony trots off into the darkness and Rutholyn and I follow him. After backtracking a short distance, we come to one of the access doors. Several wooden ramps cover a set of concrete stairs and two old barrows stand nearby. This must have been where labor agency workers hauled dirt out of the tunnel. What an exhausting task.

I climb up the ramps and attempt to open the door. Unsurprisingly, the handle won't budge. Either I'm too weak or it's too rusty. I suppose I could melt the latch with hot shimmerdark, but as furious as I am with Aerro, I'm not going to let nocturnes into his shelter. So instead I create a shimmerdark mallet and bang on the latch until, squealing, it finally turns.

After that, I use a large block of energy to shove the door open, for the hinges are stiff too, and then Rutholyn and I enter another brick-lined tunnel. This one is smaller and slopes upward, and I see a pale circle of moonlight at the far end.

Again, Glowy Pony leads the way. As he climbs out into the snow, sparks pop and sizzle at his feet.

After shutting the door behind us, I lumber out into a knee-high snowdrift and Rutholyn follows in my trampled wake.

I hate being out in the open again.

But at least I can see Kaverlee City. It's just beyond a rocky plain and several spreadfarm buildings, perched on a sloping hill beside the Silkord Sea.

"Is that your home?" Rutholyn asks, pointing with her mitten.

Is Kaverlee City my home anymore? The word home doesn't feel right. I suppose I'd like it to be my home again, and it is comforting to see those strong walls topped with a glowing star net. Even more cagic blazes on the far side of Kaverlee, in the Expansion District. There, the city outgrew its stone walls, so the barriers are made of projected shimmerlight. They're exactly like the walls that failed in Haberdine.

I've never seen Kaverlee from the outside during the Dark Month, and it's beautiful. I notice movement at the base of the walls, though, which must be nocturnes attracted by the sounds and smells of the city. I'm not sure how we'll get past them.

"What was that?" Rutholyn says, her voice trembling.

"What was what?" There doesn't seem to be anything around us aside from quiet snow. Yet I summon a shimmerdark shield just in case. "Did you see an owleck?"

Rutholyn shakes her head. "No... something's near me."

"Glowy Pony, do you see anything?" I ask.

But even though Glowy Pony's usually excellent at locating things, he seems distracted by the deep snow. He picks his way toward us as if each step is uncomfortable. I suppose cagic and water don't mix, so cagic and ice must be a bad combination too.

I examine the low mounds of white surrounding us. Maybe Rutholyn is imagining things. She is tired after all.

But then a nearby snowdrift ripples, almost like a saucer of milk, and seconds later, Rutholyn screams.

18

The Barrier

"No!" I snatch at Rutholyn's arm as she sinks into the icy white, catching her by the wrist.

She wails in pain.

Flustered and not sure what else has grabbed onto her, I slam my shimmerdark shield down into the snow.

Icy white sparks spray outward, and the edge of the cagic shape connects with something solid. Then a massive, ribbon-like nocturne whips up out of the snow, and realms, it's a senneck. It's also still clinging to Rutholyn's foot with a ring of needle-like teeth, and it waves many spiky legs as it tries to tug her from my grip.

"Let go!" I yell. I always thought the name senneck came from snake, but this thing looks more like a centipede. It's also completely white, so it must be able to mimic its surroundings. No wonder I didn't see it.

"Help me! Oh help!" Rutholyn screams.

"I'm trying!" I bash the monster with my energy shield again, and I can hit it harder now that it's no longer cushioned by snow.

The creature whinges and screeches and slithers backward, releasing Rutholyn.

Bright red blood soaks her stocking and shines wetly on her left boot, but I'm happy to see that she still has two feet.

"Run!" I tell her, pulling her upright and shoving her toward the city. "I'll catch up. Glowy Pony, keep her safe!" I suppose he can't do much, but at least she won't be alone. I then take two precious seconds to unstrap my leather case and toss it aside.

The senneck lunges at me. I shape shimmerdark into a sharp, flat diamond and attempt to heat it up. But the nocturne moves so quickly, I don't have enough time.

I leap sideways into a snowdrift, away from the senneck's toothy, round mouth.

I also quickly glance at Rutholyn. She's limping toward the city, good, and Glowy Pony's at her side, weightlessly trotting across the snow. I don't like that he's visible, but it probably doesn't matter. At this distance any Shieldbearers on watch will surely assume he's a black cat or dog.

The senneck dives toward me again, and this time, I create a bar of energy in the air. Grabbing onto it with my gloved hands, I sail away.

I need to be on the attack, not on the run. So when the senneck streaks toward me a third time, I stand my ground and send a large cube of shimmerdark into the fleshiest part of what must be its face.

The senneck's bulbous head flops backward, shuddering. I feel momentarily triumphant, but then the creature darts toward me again, knotting its long body around me, trapping me.

"No, *no!*" I yelp, and I look around for Rutholyn, afraid that an owleck will carry her off. Thankfully, she's still trudging through the snow. Yet she's moving so slowly, too slowly.

And while I'm distracted, the senneck tries to bite off my head.

Yelping, I cover my face and hair with shimmerdark, and just as quickly, I extend the edges of the energy down around my body. I'm essentially surrounding myself in a sleeve of cagic, forcing the senneck to loosen its grip. I then expand the shape so the nocturne must either unravel or be torn apart. After that, I release the shimmerdark tube, replacing it with a cagic bar, and holding onto that, I whisk myself up and away. Hastily, I search the white landscape for Rutholyn, and I spot her on a distant hill. But she's down on her knees now. What's wrong with her? Surely she's not that tired.

With a whistling shriek, the senneck races after me, slicing a curving line through the snow. Again, I don't have enough time to heat any shimmerdark.

Wailing with frustration, I create a large, flat wall of energy in the monster's path instead. The senneck crashes into it with a wet crunch.

And Rutholyn—she's lying down and Glowy Pony's darting frantically around her.

Something's wrong. I wish I could be beside her rather than here.

But I can't do anything helpful until this nocturne's dead.

Leaping onto an energy disc and clinging to it, I transfer myself backward, narrowly avoiding the writhing senneck as it tries to coil around me again. Well, I can attack like that too. Reminded of Aerro's cagic hunting tactics, I jump off my energy disc and create a large hoop of shimmerdark between myself and the senneck. As soon as the monster slithers partway through it, I shrink the loop, pinching the creature around the middle. The senneck makes a horrible sucking sound, and it wriggles as if it's fallen into boiling water. Wincing, I shrink the energy, squeezing it tighter and tighter as the nocturne flails its long body, straining to escape.

But then—ugh—the senneck's middle bursts with a gloppy spray of dark sludge, and the two separated halves fall twitching into the discolored snow.

I don't wait until they lie still. I quickly form another energy disc and throw myself onto it. I then glide over the cold, white ground to Rutholyn.

When I reach her, she's trembling violently, and her skin is ashy and gray.

"Rutholyn." I push her dark curls out of her face and try to sit her up. "What's the matter? What's wrong?"

Her eyelids flutter and she murmurs, "Xylia… Shimmerlady." Then her head slumps forward.

Poison. There must be venom in senneck bites—I had no idea. She needs a doctor. "Hang on. Kaverlee is so close. People there can help you."

I unclasp her traveling case to make her lighter, and then drawing a horizontal circle in the air, I create another disc of shimmerdark.

Glowy Pony nudges my leg, either impatient or concerned, but it just makes me realize how frustrated I am with him.

"Why didn't you warn us about the senneck?" I struggle to pick up Rutholyn. "You always know where everything is; why not that?"

Glowy Pony backs away from me looking hurt as I place Rutholyn onto the shimmerdark disc. Then clamoring onto it myself, I whisk the two of us toward Kaverlee as fast as I can. I hope the Shieldbearers will realize we're harmless, but then what? They can't risk unsealing a gate with so many nocturnes surrounding the city. And how will I get past those monsters? I have no idea.

"Stay awake Rutholyn," I plead with her as we hurtle forward. Snowflakes streak past us on all sides. Both our knit hats fly free and my eyes sting.

"Just a little farther," I say, huddling over her, trying to shield her from the bitter wind. We pass farm buildings that are only used during the Bright Month, and then we're sailing over the nocturnes: bearcurs, wolievs, catterns.

I still don't know how we're going to enter the city.

Rutholyn moans.

"We're almost there," I say. If transference didn't require such intense focus, I'd tell her that Kaverlee has excellent hospitals and soon skilled doctors will be taking care of her. I'd also let her know that I'm incredibly proud of her. She's been so brave and resilient, and I finally understand why Great Draes are devoted to their Predraes, and why mothers—

OOOF.

Something knocks me sideways. With a yelp, I tighten my grip on Rutholyn, and together we tumble into the snow.

A carrow's black wings flash overhead.

Screaming and hardly thinking, I raise my hands, summoning a shield of shimmerdark that I quickly expand into a glittering, black dome that covers us.

"Rutholyn! *Rutholyn!*" I cry in the cold, protected space. Sparks skitter and flash where the dome meets the snow, so I can see her. But she isn't moving, and merciful light, I can't fail her now. Pulling her out of the cold snow and onto my folded legs, I listen to the carrow scratching and pecking at the energy dome, unable to break through.

Maybe this dome is how we can enter Kaverlee.

The vast stone walls surrounding most of the city are impenetrable, but if I'm shielded by energy, I might be able to walk through the cagic barriers protecting the Expansion District.

"We're even closer now," I breathe in Rutholyn's ear, and making the dome taller, I stand and pick her up.

She says something, but her voice is too faint to understand.

"What was that?" I ask, hoisting her onto my hip so that her head rests on my shoulder.

"All the way tired," she whispers.

"So am I," I say, glad that she's still talking.

It's not easy, I quickly realize, to carry a seven-year-old child through deep snow, but I grit my teeth and move as fast as I can.

Every dozen or so steps, I create a small opening in my energy shield to make sure I'm heading in the right direction, and then I seal it again. Even small openings make the shimmerdark shape more complex and therefore harder to maintain and move.

It's frightening to walk in complete darkness, though, unable to see the nocturnes but having to listen to them snuffle, growl, and often fight each other only paces away.

Hopefully someone will tell Drae Devorla about the strange cagic shape nearing the Expansion District, and she'll realize I created it and come to help.

I walk and I walk, my legs burning and my arms shaking. Rutholyn is limp and heavy and so hard to hold onto. I have to save her, though, so somehow, I keep going.

Realms, this is taking forever.

I feel like I've been trudging for hours even though it may have only been minutes. My lower legs are so cold and stiff, I feel like I'm wearing concrete boots. At first, I'm simply wading through snow—seemingly endless snow—but then a rocky path appears beneath my feet and then an icy road.

Every time I make tiny openings in the dome, I see that I'm a little closer to the projected cagic walls, but I also see more nocturnes swarming around me. After a while, though, I hear muffled voices. They must belong to the Shieldbearers guarding the projection towers. I'm almost there. I've almost saved Rutholyn. I wish I could release my shimmerdark dome and tell the Shieldbearers to prepare a chariot to rush Rutholyn to the nearest hospital. But I'll have to do that once we're safely inside the city.

The next time I create a tiny opening in the dome, I only see blazing blue shimmerlight—we've reached the barrier.

All I can do now is hope my cagic shield will protect us, allowing us to pass through the energy field unharmed. Shimmerdark is stronger than shimmerlight, isn't it?

"We're there!" I tell Rutholyn, and then I walk forward.

A rainbow of light erupts around us, and my hair floats up. We're still covered by the shimmerdark dome, but colorful bolts of energy flash across its surface, loudly snapping and popping. The dome also wavers and squirms in my grip. I probably only need to take a few more steps, though, and then we'll be inside. We'll be safe.

Finally, the multicolored light vanishes, the energy stops crackling, and I don't hear the Shieldbearers shouting anymore. We must be through.

With a deep sigh of relief, I release the shimmerdark dome.

And a Shieldbearer shoots me in the head.

Healing

There's a soft cloth on my brow, I'm warm, and I have the fuzzy sense that although I'm hurt, something unnatural is dulling how much I care about the pain.

I blink my swollen eyes open. I'm in a dark place that has the puzzle-piece shape of a room wedged between two more significant rooms. I see a window, the shadowy outline of a chair, a lamp on a low table, and a chest of drawers.

I try to sit up but I'm too weak, and even small movements make my pain feel fresh and bright.

At first my memories seem to be hiding from me—shy things I try to beckon closer. I remember a bright light and a bursting, stinging in my forehead, and I remember Rutholyn, limp and heavy on my chest.

Where is she?

I collapse back onto linens that smell like lavendrops and lemonelle, my heart thudding.

Time passes, I'm not sure how much, and then I hear a soft, metallic click, the sound of a well-oiled doorknob. After that, a line of light appears on the far wall, and I watch the gleaming stripe widen to frame the shadowy outline of a person.

Someone's looking into my room, looking at me probably, but I can't see them because I'm facing the wrong way. I try to turn toward the door, but because I'm moving so slowly, by the time I can see it, whoever was there has gone.

Yet only a few moments later, I hear sturdy shoes crossing floorboards and the rhythmic clink of a tool belt. I know who's approaching—the Great Drae.

Yet even though I longed to see her before, I don't want to see her now, and I'm not sure why.

The door opens again, and because this time I'm facing it, I watch Drae Devorla enter the room. She's so comfortingly familiar: frizzy hair, leather apron, warm eyes. "Oh good," she says. "Tah Roli Miri said you were awake."

So that's who checked on me. I open my mouth and find it surprisingly hard to speak. "Is… Rutha… ded?" My words are garbled. Concentrating, I try again. "Isssshe dead?"

"Xylia," Drae Devorla says gently.

"Is sshe?" I feel like I'm pleading. Somehow whether Rutholyn is alive or not seems like a decision Drae Devorla can make right now.

The Great Drae doesn't answer, but the terrible truth is in her sagging expression and slumped shoulders.

No, Rutholyn can't be dead.

I squeeze my eyes shut and a sound comes out of me that's part wail, part whimper.

Drae Devorla lets me cry, and then she says, "I'm very sorry. I had no idea you'd risk traveling during the Dark Month, and I never imagined you'd have a child with you. You also clearly aren't in the violent state Theandra described. I'm afraid I told the Shieldbearers that if you reached the city, they weren't to let you in unless I was present. When you breached the wall, they considered it an invasion. They thought you were dangerous."

So they shot me.

Drae Devorla looks down at the floor. "And the little girl... the Shieldbearers didn't realize she had a senneck bite until it was too late."

If I hadn't been shot, I could have told them.

I sniff back tears, which makes my head throb. I want to be angry with Drae Devorla, but she didn't know what truly happened. All she knew was that I attacked a well-respected Authenticator using strange energy. Of course I seemed dangerous. Of course she had to take precautions to protect the city.

But, what a devastating misunderstanding.

When my tears slow, Drae Devorla says, "What I don't understand is, where did the little girl come from?"

Didn't Theandra tell her?

"She was"—I take a deep breath to steady my voice—"a potential Shimmerling the Shalvos found."

Drae Devorla's mouth flattens. "Theandra didn't mention that. It seems there's a lot she didn't tell me." Crossing the room, she turns on the lamp. "I heard how you entered the city. Your cagic has changed." She doesn't sound interested in or excited about my shimmerdark, which is strange, but I'm finding it hard to follow the conversation with my clattering headache, and well, broken heart.

"My cagic has changed, yes," I say, my lips and tongue being more cooperative.

Drae Devorla pulls back the drapes. Outside, the star net shimmers against the dark sky. She then sits in the chair and momentarily rests her head in her hands. When she looks up again, there are tears in her eyes. "I should have warned you this could happen. When a mature Shimmerling is in danger, there's always a risk they might become a Shimmercaster."

"Shimmercaster?" I whisper. "What's that?"

Drae Devorla leans back in the chair. "I'm a Shimmercaster and so are the Conduits protecting the other Connected Lands. A Shimmercaster is someone who's cagic has evolved instead of winking out. We can summon vast amounts of energy."

Then I'm as powerful as she is. But why is that bad?

"The trouble is," Drae Devorla continues, answering my unspoken question, "the Connected Lands' Treaty permits only one Shimmercaster and one apprentice per city, and Kaverlee already has ours. You cannot keep these powers."

"You mean I'll be downleveled?" Another layer of misery engulfs me. "No! Please, *please* no."

She nods and sighs and looks as if she'd much rather be repairing an energy reservoir than sitting with me. "I am sorry. But these laws exist for many reasons. And let's be honest, it sounds like you've already summoned a lot of corrupt energy."

What does she mean, corrupt energy? Is she talking about shimmerdark?

I must look confused because Drae Devorla says, "The black cagic you used to enter the city is unstable and extremely dangerous.

It's easy to summon, yes, and easy to control, but it will also damage your mind, causing deterioration."

"I didn't know," I say, and how frightening. Poor Aerro, too. He's been using shimmerdark for years. No wonder he behaved the way he did. My sorrow deepens. Here I thought shimmerdark made me special, but no, it's more like an illness. Warm tears slide down my cheeks. I don't want to be downleveled, but what choice do I have?

Also, maybe this is what I deserve. I should have stayed calm when Golly found me with his drawings. I should have pretended I hadn't seen them. Then I could have safely entered the shelter, brought Rutholyn to Kaverlee by subtrain, and reported Golly to the Great Drae. Or going back even further, if I'd just accepted that I wasn't the Predrae anymore, none of this would have happened.

"I can see you're blaming yourself—don't." Drae Devorla walks over to my bed and takes my hand. "This is my fault and my fault alone. I should have kept you in the Courtyard of Youth until you winked out. I took a risk and you and that child paid a devastating price. Again, I'm so very sorry."

She holds my hand for a while longer. Pain still radiates through me, but her touch helps.

Eventually she says, "I want to hear more about your journey, but first, I think you should rest."

I nod. I am tired, and I also want to grieve alone. Once I start crying in earnest about Rutholyn, it'll be hard to stop.

Drae Devorla lets go of my hand. "Come find me when you're feeling better. You're in my apartments, of course. The Shieldbearers wanted to lock you in the palace prisons, but I wouldn't hear of it.

You may not be my Predrae anymore, but you're still one of my Shimmerlings. I'll always look out for you. I hope you know that."

She then leaves, and I'm alone with my overwhelming sadness. I vaguely wonder where Glowy Pony is. I yelled at him out there in the snow, didn't I? I wish I hadn't.

Maybe he isn't here because he was connected to Rutholyn and now that she's gone, he's gone too. Or maybe he isn't here because he's upset with me. If that's the case, I don't blame him.

✦

The next day, we have a simple funeral for Rutholyn. A Maternal brings me to the ceremony in a wheeled-chair because I'm too weak to walk, and I spend the next hour wishing I had the strength to run away. I can hardly bear to look at Rutholyn's little body resting in its coffin. Because I didn't see her die, it's hard to comprehend that she's truly gone. I have the fuzzy sense we've both been cheated, and if I could try to save her again, I'd succeed.

After Matron Isme recites a poem in the palace library, Shieldbearers carry Rutholyn to the Shimmerling mausoleum. The rest of us follow in a subdued procession. At least the mausoleum is pretty. Rutholyn would like that. It's a small building in the Triumvirate Hall gardens surrounded by willow trees and, during the Bright Month, colorful iriserines and daislets. Right now, though, the flower beds are buried beneath ice and snow.

As I wait with the Maternals, I notice Queen Naradara has joined us. I don't make eye contact with the elegant, silver-haired woman, and I wonder if I ever mattered to her. She and King

Macreolar represent Kaverlee in matters of policy, trade, and economics, not cagic.

I spend the next day napping fitfully in my pocket of a room, my thoughts miserable and just as restless. I should have stayed on the Grimshore. If I'd become a Shimmercaster there, no one would be trying to downlevel me. Then there's Vonnet—he still thinks his sister's alive. He trusted us to take care of her.

Oh Rutholyn.

You were so courageous and sweet, and I failed you.

I've never felt regret so intensely, so completely. I feel like I'm drowning in it.

Every few hours, a medical Maternal visits me. She replaces my bandages and checks my injuries. Shockgun blasts are usually deadly, she says, and I suspect being a Shimmercaster able to channel large amounts of cagic saved me.

Sometimes I find the strength to stagger to the lavatory next to my room, but it's a slow, painful trip. The rest of the time, I lie as still as possible, and I try not to cry because it makes my constant headache worse.

After three lunar days, at least I think it's three, the red welts on my face fade to ugly purple bruises, my headache becomes just an irritating pang, and I'm able to hobble short distances. So I go looking for Drae Devorla. I dread being downleveled, but I still want to know when and where it will happen.

The Great Drae is easy to find, perched on a large reservoir in her workroom. As I limp toward her, I hear her calling out measurements to Tah Roli Miri who stands nearby, holding a pencil and clipboard.

"Seven even by six-point-two-five," Drae Devorla says. "And below the hinge, it's eleven-point-five by ten-point-two."

Tah Roli Miri notices me first. "Xylia," she says, sounding like she always does, as if I'm interrupting a daydream. "I'm so glad you're alright."

She seems happy to see me, which makes me feel badly about how I've treated her. I was so determined to become the Predrae again, I didn't care if it meant stealing her position. I'm sure she's proud of being the Predrae, just like I was, and also eager to avoid winking out.

"Ah, Xylia, I'm so glad you're up and moving around." Drae Devorla peers down from the reservoir, pulling back her protective goggles. She must have been wearing them for a while because they leave pink imprints around her eyes. "How are you feeling?" she asks.

"Stronger," I say, which is more accurate than saying better. I'm still miserable—but my head no longer feels like it's being held in someone's clenched fist and I haven't cried in a few hours.

Drae Devorla climbs down a ladder, peels off her work gloves, and unties her leather apron. "Tah, would you mind eating your midday meal in the Courtyard of Youth? Now that Xylia's here, I need to speak to her."

Tah Roli Miri nods, and before she drifts out of the room, she tries to hug me.

I dodge the embrace. "No, please," I say. I don't deserve empathy from anyone.

"Come Xylia," Drae Devorla says. "There's food in the dining room."

I'm not hungry, and I haven't been since Rutholyn died, but I limp after her. My body feels heavy and clumsy, like I've become a Colossus.

I miss my metal giants too. I can see them from the workshop windows overlooking the Courtyard of Youth. When I peered down yesterday, I saw Shimmerlings working together to move Sevensy and Goliah. They seemed to be having a very slow race with them, and although their control was impressive, I watched them sourly. I felt like a child seeing other children play with my toys. I tried to shake off my petulant feelings, for at least the huge figures weren't sitting in flower beds anymore, but it wasn't easy. And last night, I dreamed I walked them into the Silkord Sea and let them sink to the bottom.

The Great Drae's dining room is an elegant space that was surely decorated by a previous Drae. A glossy wood table and chairs dominates the room. Larger-than-life portraits hang on three of the walls and a huge window fills the fourth.

"You're uncomfortable, aren't you?" Drae Devorla says as she rounds the table. "Should I call for a medical Maternal? Do you need pain suppressants?"

"I'm fine," I say, trying not to wince as I ease myself into a chair.

A servant wearing a sleek gray tago steps out of the shadows to ladle soup into bowls for us.

"What truly happened with the Shalvos?" Drae Devorla asks. "It's obvious Theandra lied to me. She said you lost your wits and were dangerous."

I want to tell her the truth, but it's hard to think about Golly's drawings so it's even harder to talk about them. I do it, though. I tell Drae Devorla about finding the blue folder, and examining my spoon handle rather than looking at her somehow makes the conversation bearable. I remember those sketches far too vividly.

Drae Devorla listens quietly, and when I finish talking, all she says is, "Then what happened?"

So I tell her how Golly threw me against the filing crates and that he was about to hit me when my shimmerdark appeared. "I didn't mean to hurt him," I say. "I just… I wanted him to go away. I was scared."

"Of course you were." Drae Devorla's wrinkles deepen, especially the ones in the corners of her mouth and nestled between her eyebrows. "Did you show Theandra the drawings?"

"Yes," I say. "But she ripped them up, and then she told the guards to kill me. She wouldn't let me in the Marin Harbor shelter either."

Drae Devorla frowns. "And what about the child? How did she end up with you?"

It's even harder to think about Rutholyn. Every time I do, I feel a wave of pain and sadness. "She hid in the seg-coach. I didn't know she was there until I'd left Marin Harbor." I stare at my soup. It's some sort of brothy something, and I still have no appetite. Drae Devorla isn't eating either. "I probably should have turned around and tried to get her into the shelter." Why didn't I? It's hard to remember all the reasons now.

I should have done so many things differently.

"Is Golly dead?" I ask.

Drae Devorla nods, and I'm not surprised. Golly was severely injured when I last saw him. "And rest assured," she adds, "the Chief Authenticator and I will thoroughly investigate Theandra's role in this."

I suppose that's a small relief. Drae Devorla stirs her soup and eats some of it, and when her bowl is nearly empty, I ask, "When will it happen—my downleveling?"

Drae Devorla dabs her mouth with a napkin. "Not for another few days—maybe a week."

"Why not now?" I ask.

She pushes away her soup bowl. "There are cityland treaties that must be honored. Your downleveling will generate a lot of energy, and that energy must be shared with the Connected Lands. I've already wired messages to the other Conduits. They have a right to attend your downleveling and collect a share of the harvest."

The harvest? That's an awful way to put it. I also don't like that my downleveling will have an audience—and not just any spectators either, the highest-ranking dignitaries in the Connected Lands. Vonnet urinated during his downleveling. What if I do that? Please no.

"I can tell you're worried." Drae Devorla puts down her spoon. "Try not to think too much about it. Focus on resting and healing, and would you like your family here for support? Or perhaps Sir Calvolin Nelvaso and Madame Straechos?"

I shake my head. I created this mess on my own, and I want to suffer the consequences on my own.

20
Auldora

I spend a few more days in a medicated fog, loosely aware that Drae Devorla's often leaving Triumvirate Hall to welcome other Conduits. They've begun to arrive in armored boats at the protected dock—the only safe way to travel between citylands during the Dark Month.

I haven't asked the Great Drae about Haberdine yet, or even about Glowy Pony, and I'm not quite sure why. But late one evening, while she's off greeting the Vazor of Ganorine, I decide to see what Tah Roli Miri knows. I find her in the Great Drae's workshop, dutifully copying a technical drawing.

"Do you need something?" Tah Roli Miri asks in her languid way as I limp across the room. "Should I call for a Maternal? Are you in pain?"

"No, no, I'm fine," I assure her. "I just want to talk to you."

She slowly puts her pencil down and looks at me with concern.

"Have you ever heard of Haberdine?" I ask.

"Oh… oh yes. Haberdine." She glances at her hands, seeming troubled. "Such a tragedy."

"What happened?" I pull over a stool so I can sit beside her. Other than the bright light on the table, the room is dark. "Why did the barriers fail?"

Tah Roli Miri shakes her head. "An official was illegally selling the town's cagic rations, so they ran out of energy."

I'm surprised by how relieved I am. The projection towers weren't faulty. Drae Devorla wasn't to blame. Aerro was wrong. "Are you sure?" I ask.

Tah Roli Miri nods. "It was in all the newsreaders. The Great Drae is still upset about it." For a few moments, we sit quietly, and then she says, "I hope your downleveling goes well. I'm sure you'll survive."

"Survive?" I echo. I didn't realize downleveling could be deadly. Yet I suppose if my experience is anything like Vonnet's, having my cagic removed will be painful and invasive. And because I can summon far more energy than Vonnet could, the Conduits will have to remove a huge amount before I stop regenerating it.

I don't really want to talk about my downleveling, though, because I don't want to think about it, so I ask my other question. "Have you ever heard of living cagic? As in, creatures made of energy that can move and think on their own?"

"No." Tah Roli Miri looks mildly alarmed, which for her probably means she's quite shocked. "If you've seen something like that, you need to tell the Great Drae."

"No… it's just…" Maybe I shouldn't have brought this up. "I had a dream about it. I thought it might mean something."

Tah Roli Miri's gaze softens and drifts off. "Sometimes if I think about cagic too much, about everything we don't know… I get scared. What else is out there?"

When I return to my room, I think about Haberdine again. How could the town's energy reserves get so low without anyone noticing? And aren't most towns able to transfer more cagic from Kaverlee City during an emergency? Something about Tah Roli Miri's story doesn't quite add up; I really should ask Drae Devorla herself. So when I hear her voice a few hours later, I climb out of bed. I'm pretty sure Tah Roli Miri has left, so she must be talking to a servant.

Yet when I step into her workroom, I see her standing with Matron Isme, the Maternal Superior. "I'm sorry you had to wait," Drae Devorla says. "The Vazor of Ganorine is so talkative."

"It's fine," Matron Isme says. "Auldora's ready."

Ready for what? Neither woman seems to have noticed me, so I quietly step back into the shadowy doorway and continue listening.

Drae Devorla pushes a few frizzy gray curls out of her eyes and yawns. "Very well, let's get this over with."

Deeply confused, I watch Matron Isme pick up a small cagic lantern, and then she and Drae Devorla leave the workshop.

I follow them. I don't even think about it. If they're doing something that involves a Shimmerling, then it involves me too. And even though I shouldn't risk summoning more shimmerdark, it's an excellent way to move silently. After I ease the workroom door closed, I create a round disc of energy. Then kneeling on its warm, prickly surface, I hover behind Drae Devorla and Matron Isme as they descend the stairs.

They walk along the corridor that passes beneath the Maternals' dorm, and then they use an unremarkable door I've never paid much attention to. Yet the door won't open for me. They must have locked it behind them.

If I heat cagic and cut through the bolt, Drae Devorla will eventually realize I followed her.

I hesitate. She believed me when I told her about the Shalvos. She didn't have to. She could have accused me of murdering Golly. She gave me the benefit of the doubt, and maybe I should do the same thing now.

Yet I'm also about to be downleveled, about to make a huge sacrifice. It's only fair that I fully understand everything that happens in Triumvirate Hall.

Pushing aside my guilty feelings, I heat a small shimmerdark panel and use it to slice through the lock. With a soft noise, the door opens, revealing a dimly lit passage much humbler than the elegant parts of the palace I'm usually in.

I can't see Drae Devorla or Matron Isme ahead of me, yet gliding soundlessly forward on my shimmerdark disc, I soon spot them. They walk down several windowless corridors, descend two more long staircases, and then enter a much darker passage. Here, Matron Isme switches on her cagic lantern. The floors are rough stone and the walls are damp. The air is unpleasantly warm too, and when I hear a rhythmic thumping and feel my internal cagic vibrate, I know where we're headed: the palace's energy reservoirs.

Sure enough, the women soon enter a cavernous space full of large storage canisters. The shiny, steel containers stretch up to the vaulted ceiling, and shimmerlight gleams through thick glass windows in their smooth sides. Sweat trickles down my neck as I climb off my energy disc and let the cagic vanish. I don't have to worry about being quiet anymore. The rhythmic hiss and smack of the compression pumps will hide my footsteps.

Drae Devorla and Matron Isme fan their faces as they duck under the brackets holding the huge tanks upright, crossing the hall. It's strange to think that this vast underground chamber is only Kaverlee's second largest storage facility. Most of the city's energy is processed and contained in the Foundry, which stands on the border of Upper and Lower Topdwell.

I follow Drae Devorla and Matron Isme around a particularly huge tank and nearly scream.

Realms, what a horrible sight.

Auldora lies on a metal table, unconscious. Wired cuffs circle her wrists and ankles, and a copper halo wraps around her head. I also see downleveling equipment nearby, which doesn't make any sense. She's seventeen. She's about to wink out. Why would anyone downlevel her?

Yet with quiet efficiency, as if they've done this hundreds of times, Drae Devorla and Matron Isme begin adjusting dials, connecting cords, and tightening Auldora's various bindings. They also put a mask over her mouth and nose for a few moments. A tube connects the mask to a small machine that makes a wet, squelching sound. Something in the mask must be keeping her asleep.

Drae Devorla says, "Are you ready?"

Matron Isme nods.

But I'm not. With no plan and no idea what I'm interrupting, I rush forward. "No! Stop!"

The women stare at me, their hands still resting on switches and knobs.

And in a rush of horrified comprehension, I understand how the Connected Lands work. It's a vast, heartbreaking realization. "No one winks out," I say.

"Xylia." Drae Devorla moves cautiously toward me like I've become so unpredictable I might scratch or bite. "You shouldn't be here."

"No one *ever* winks out?" Now I'm shouting, and my voice echoes around the reservoirs. "You downlevel everyone," I say in a softer voice, gathering my scattered thoughts. "You downlevel all Shimmerlings before they turn into Shimmercasters—before they become truly powerful. But not me because I transformed earlier than you expected. I'm only fifteen."

Matron Isme looks flustered, frantic, but Drae Devorla watches me with a brittle, flat expression that has something unpleasant stirring beneath it.

"That's why even children who are barely cagic-touched have to be downleveled," I continue. "If they kept their powers… they might become like me."

Or like Aerro or Tury.

Drae Devorla abruptly breathes in, her nostrils flaring. "Yes, Xylia, yes. If their cagic isn't removed, Shimmerlings turn into Shimmercasters. Now calm down and think about what that means. You know how much power you have and how tempting it is to summon corrupt energy. Downleveling is the only way to keep everyone safe; the only way to use our natural resources efficiently and safely." She shakes her head. "I wish you hadn't followed us."

My head wound had been feeling better, but now it throbs. Thinking clearly suddenly takes an immense amount of effort. "So... I would have been downleveled even if I hadn't become a Shimmercaster?"

"Eventually, yes," Drae Devorla says quietly. "It would have been easier, though. You wouldn't have as much energy to remove, and it could have been done peacefully... like this." She gestures at motionless Auldora.

"It still seems wasteful," I say. "If there were more Shimmercasters, they could fill more reservoirs and help you protect the city. You wouldn't have to do everything on your own."

"You're right," the Great Drae says, her upper lip curling. "In a perfect world, we'd have more Shimmercasters. All the realms know I could use help. But more Shimmercasters would also mean more corrupt cagic—which by the way, can't power anything. And what if those Shimmercasters hurt others? I'd no longer have more power to stop them. Because of those concerns, Xylia, the Connected Lands have rules that regulate cagic use—rules I must obey..." She takes a step toward me. "And enforce."

"I still don't understand," I say, eyeing Auldora. No, I do understand; I just don't agree.

Drae Devorla rubs her forehead with her fingertips, as Matron Isme mutters, "Her curiosity has always been problematic." And there's something sinister in the way Drae Devorla looks at her that makes me think about Osren's claim: *Drae Devorla got rid of you on purpose.*

I have to know. "Was my shipwreck an accident?"

Drae Devorla's silver-flecked eyebrows crumple. "Probably."

Which isn't the definite "yes" I wanted to hear. I walk to the table and put my hand on Auldora's limp arm. She's the only person here on my side. "And what really happened in Haberdine? Did you destroy the town?"

"No, of course not." Her voice tightens. "A town official was stealing cagic." She doesn't say it with much conviction, though. Her words tremble and waver.

"Why was that possible?" I ask. "You know, I've been there. I've seen the shelter."

"And what exactly did you see?" she says sharply. But after wiping sweat off her brow, she changes her approach. "Forgive me, it's just you're right—it shouldn't have happened. I should have installed more alarms and made sure the reservoirs couldn't be tampered with. I should have made sure the backup reservoirs turned on automatically. I should have... I don't know, done things differently—built things differently." She looks at me intently. "This job, the position you so desperately want, is hard. One broken connector or one misread gauge? People die." Tears gleam on her cheeks, something I've never seen before. "I do try, you know. I'm always searching for better ways to compress energy and trying to make downleveling less painful and trying to invent better cagic distribution systems. I'm also always, *always* trying to make us safer with stronger barriers and more powerful shockguns. I try and try and try, and it's never enough. I feel like I'm always just a few steps away from failure."

I stare at her, feeling furious but also conflicted. I once thought she was entirely good, someone to admire and emulate. Now, if I thought she was completely evil, I could hate her and fight against her, but this is more complicated. She's supporting a terrible system because she believes she has no other choice, no better option. It's a murky, messy situation.

"People never say thank you either," Drae Devorla adds with a half-smile. "No, they just want their heaters, scrubbers, and ice chests. They want faster chariots, brighter signs, and more and more land that's completely protected from nocturnes." She exhales, suddenly looking drained and frail.

I pity her. I do. But I also can't let her downlevel Auldora, so I say, "I am sorry." Then I create a large ball of shimmerdark.

Yet before I'm able to smash the nearest downleveling machine, Drae Devorla surprises me and summons shimmerdark too. And not only does she shape the energy lightning-fast, she wraps it around my eyes, creating a blindfold. She then uses her cagic grip on my head to twist me sideways and disorient me. Pain flares in my already injured brow, and like Aerro's cagic, because I didn't summon this energy, I can't manipulate it. I also can't destroy the downleveling machines now that I can't see; I might hit Auldora or worse, rupture a storage tank. Frustrated, I let the shimmerdark I summoned dissipate.

"I thought you didn't use corrupt energy," I say, tugging on the cagic covering my eyes.

"I only use it when I must," the Great Drae says, putting a firm hand on my shoulder. "No Conduit can prevent accidental Shimmercasters—no matter how vigilant they are. Therefore, every so often we Conduits help each other capture illegal Shimmercasters."

"Should I call for the Shieldbearers?" Matron Isme asks.

"No, no," Drae Devorla says, keeping a tight cagic hold on me. "I can handle this."

But can she? She may have captured Shimmercasters, but I bet she's never fought wolievs or catterns or sennecks. Because I'm pretty sure she's standing behind me and slightly to my left, I send a fist-sized ball of shimmerdark at what I hope is her stomach.

Drae Devorla cries out, and I feel briefly triumphant, but then the cagic blindfold thuds me down onto the ground. My already tender forehead cracks against the concrete and pain rips through me, unbearable and overpowering.

Fingers touch my back, feathery and gentle. "Stop fighting, Xylia. I don't want to hurt you but believe me—I can."

"I'll stop," I whimper, stunned. The Great Drae I know would never get into a physical fight—or rather, the Great Drae I thought I knew.

She helps me up, but she also keeps me blindfolded. The world seems to sway, and again pain simmers, outraged, through my skull.

"The shipwreck wasn't my doing," Drae Devorla says, taking my hand and leading me to the right. "Another cityland conduit may have sabotaged your ferry, though."

"What?" A shudder runs through me, along with a ripple of painful memories: the flooded boat, the angry black water, the terrified people.

She takes a deep breath. "I'd told several of them that I thought I might have selected the wrong Predrae."

Wrong Predrae? Even then, she didn't want me. I feel like I'm trapped in a slowly collapsing building.

"You were powerful, yes," Drae Devorla says. "But you were also proud and rebellious. That's not the right personality for a Conduit.

The others suggested I dispose of you in a staged accident, and I wouldn't—couldn't, but a few months later, the Inlet Ferry sank."

So Osren was right, in a way. Drae Devorla didn't try to kill me, but one of the other Conduits—the Great Drae, so to speak, of another cityland—did.

"Be careful here," she says as I crunch my foot into what I realize is a flight of stairs.

"I was furious," Drae Devorla says, linking her arm through mine and leading me upward. "I truly was. I loved you, and I wish I hadn't told anyone I doubted you. I was so relieved when you were found, and I hoped that since you weren't the Predrae anymore, you'd be safe."

"There were a lot of other people on that ferry," I say, thinking of Bermy, Clicks's wife. "So many people died."

"Sixty-three," Drae Devorla says. "I did try to find you. I swear it."

I probably shouldn't believe her, but I do. "You're still going to downlevel Auldora, though, aren't you?"

Drae Devorla doesn't answer until we reach the top of the staircase. Then she says, "Auldora's lucky, you know. She's in a drugged sleep because at her age, the trauma of downleveling could turn her into a Shimmercaster. It also means she'll never remember the procedure. She'll simply wake up tomorrow and think she's winked out."

As far as downleveling goes, it does sound gentle. "Why don't you drug the children in the Periph?" Vonnet suffered so much. "It would be far more merciful."

"It would," Drae Devorla agrees. "Unfortunately, the sleeping medicine we use is extremely expensive, so we save it for the palace Shimmerlings."

I might as well attempt to unravel every Triumvirate Hall mystery, so I ask, "Why are there more girl Shimmerlings than boys? Do boys really have unstable cagic?"

"Maybe, maybe not, but that's not the real concern." Drae Devorla momentarily lets go of me to open a door. "We don't bring boys into the courtyard because we don't want pregnancies. Labor pains turn Shimmerlings into Shimmercasters too. And as for why girls are preferable to boys, I'm not entirely sure. I suspect it's because women are thought to be calmer, less ambitious, and more likely to sacrifice themselves for the greater good." Her tone has soured.

I think we're now in one of the long corridors I followed Drae Devorla and Matron Isme through. My head still hurts, but the sharp pain has dissolved into a fussy ache. It's my heart that hurts more now.

"I'm sure you're angry," Drae Devorla continues. "I was upset when I first learned all this too. It doesn't seem fair. But I hope if you think about it, *really* think about it, you'll realize that no system of government is perfect and ours is better than most."

She releases my blindfold when we reach the passage connecting her wing of Triumvirate Hall to the Courtyard of Youth—the corridor that runs beneath the Maternals' dorm. "If the other Conduits hear what's happened, they'll want you incapacitated until your downleveling's complete, and they might even want you killed. So please, will you cooperate from now on?"

I nod, although I don't really have a choice. "Will you drug me for my downleveling?" I'm not sure whether I want that or not. I'd like to avoid any pain, but I also don't want to be that vulnerable.

Drae Devorla shakes her head. "There's too much cagic in you now for that. Shimmercasters have to willingly surrender their energy. I'm sorry. It's not easy."

She leaves me alone in my small room but doesn't lock the door. I suppose she knows locks don't work on me anymore. I collapse on the bed, lying face down. My head hurts again, almost as badly as it did after I was shot, and I feel like a thousand unsolvable problems are pinning me down: all Shimmerlings are downleveled, a Cityland Conduit probably tried to murder me, and Drae Devorla won't fight a broken system that makes her miserable.

The responsibility heaped on her is immense and unfair. Why can't she see that? Many Shimmercasters would be a great thing, and surely they would hold each other accountable.

"This system is stupid," I say, my words muffled by bedding. "And cruel."

But it's a cruelty woven into our laws and culture. How can a vast system of injustice change without widespread chaos? And how can I, one person, tackle such a sprawling, multifaceted problem?

I feel overwhelmed and already defeated.

I get the sense that the Great Drae thinks my Shimmercaster transformation was my fault—but it wasn't. My body did what it was meant to do, and it's something all Shimmerlings should experience.

And is shimmerdark truly corrupt energy? Or is that just a lie to make sure Cityland Conduits don't use their power selfishly? Shimmerdark is much easier to shape and control than shimmerlight, and it certainly doesn't seem to be driving me mad. If anything, I'm thinking more clearly. And yes, Aerro was troubled—but is shimmerdark really to blame? He watched his family die and he's been isolated ever since—of course he's struggling.

As for Rutholyn, she's dead because Drae Devorla told the Shieldbearers to keep me out of the city.

Steely certainty solidifies in my otherwise scattered thoughts: I don't want to be downleveled.

I *will not* be downleveled.

I sit up, wincing and rubbing my head, and I say it out loud. "I'm keeping my cagic. It's mine."

And if that's what I want, I can't stay here. I need to leave—now—tonight. I probably should flee Kaverlee City too and maybe even the Periph. But where would I go? Where would I be safe?

I'll need help as well. I consider visiting Clicks and Fedorie, but I've caused them enough trouble—and who knows? They might believe Kaverlee's flawed laws should still be respected. I wish I could talk to Fifsa; I'm sure she'd be just as upset as I am, and she might know what to do, but she's too far away.

Yet then I realize who I really need.

Kary.

And I suppose there's only one way to find him.

"Glowy Pony," I whisper, my voice echoing through the dark, oddly shaped room. The cagic horselet can locate anything: roads in abandoned labor agency camps, hidden entrances into shelters, mittens and rain covers. Surely he can find my dearest friend.

There's no response.

I try again. "Glowy Pony, please come back. I shouldn't have yelled at you or blamed you. I'm so sorry Rutholyn died—and I need your help."

Still nothing.

But I have another idea.

Sitting cross-legged on the polished wood floor, I recreate Glowy Pony's horselet body with shimmerdark—I sculpt his bright eyes, his round belly, his stubby legs, and long mane. Then I call for him again. "Glowy Pony, please, *please* come back."

Oh, shining realms, those gleaming eyes blink and that glimmering tail flicks from side to side, and he's standing in front of me again—my mysterious little helper.

If only I could revive Rutholyn the same way.

"It's really you, isn't it?" I say.

The sparkling horselet nudges my outstretched hand.

I tear up and pull his small body close, hugging him like Rutholyn used to. "I'm so sorry she's gone."

He soberly nuzzles my hand again.

"It was all the snow, wasn't it?" I say, huddling around him. "That's why the senneck surprised you."

Glowy Pony sadly nods, but he also looks at me expectantly. He seems to know I called him here for a reason.

"I'm in danger," I say, "and I need to find my friend, Kary. Do you know where he is?"

I shouldn't be surprised, but I still startle when, amazingly, Glowy Pony nods.

21

Kary

It feels good to have a plan again, even if my plan is a simple one: find Kary.

Since I have no warm clothes, I creep into Drae Devorla's bedroom suite. She isn't there, and I try not to think about what she's doing—surely downleveling Auldora—as I rummage through her closet. For a woman who usually dresses plainly, she has a lot of fine outfits. I pull on a deep green pallacoat. The sleeves are a bit short, but otherwise, it fits me. I also take goggles from the workshop, for it can be windy when I use transference.

Returning to my room and Glowy Pony, I say, "I don't think anyone should see you."

Nodding, he dims the blue light skittering over his shadowy body. I didn't know he could do that.

"Perfect," I say, reaching for the door. I'm still not quite sure how to leave Triumvirate Hall. The Shieldbearers standing guard will want to know where I'm going in the middle of the lunar night. Drae Devorla probably also told them to make sure I stay put.

Yet Glowy Pony doesn't follow me; he trots over to the window instead. He then vanishes and reappears on the rooftop.

"Of course," I say softly. I don't have to worry about locked doors, tall fences, or guards; I can summon shimmerdark.

The window opens easily, and as I climb outside, I'm reminded just how miserably cold the Dark Month is. Because the roof's steep, I hang onto the window ledge as I struggle to draw the curtain and close the sash. I then make the mistake of looking down. From this high up, the trees surrounding Triumvirate Hall look like small clumps of moss, and the shiny chariots gleam like scattered coins.

My heart beats faster.

I stretch out my hand, planning to shape a shimmerdark disc, but before I create anything, I hesitate. Even though shimmerdark is mostly black, the edges shine brightly. I might be spotted.

I think for a long moment and then, thank the realms, come up with a solution. If I create a shimmerdark shape inside my pallacoat, like a hidden breastplate, I can cling to it and carry myself down to the city streets unseen.

Trying not to feel guilty about betraying Drae Devorla's trust, I summon cagic against my chest. Then hugging it tightly, I move out into the windy air. The borrowed pallacoat flaps wildly around me as I hover away from the palace walls and float over the neatly tiled roofs of the Landroot District. Avoiding windows, I lower myself down onto an empty street, and when my feet are on solid ground, I dispel the shimmerdark from inside my pallacoat.

Glowy Pony appears beside me with a staticky pop, and I can see just enough of his silhouette to follow him. As we hurry away from Triumvirate Hall, I'm consumed by a slippery, urgent feeling. I'm not used to challenging authority, and now I'm not just challenging Drae Devorla, I'm challenging all eight Cityland Conduits.

At first, I walk in the long, angled shadows cast by the cagic streetlamps and Landroot houses, but once we reach Upper Topdwell, I'm not as careful. There are plenty of people around, even though it's the middle of the lunar night. Many cauponiums are open, glowing a welcoming yellow, and although the baths and library are closed, they're still well lit. Every so often, hired chariots roll past too, carrying boisterous passengers and trailing cagic sparks.

Whenever I was in a foul mood on the Grimshore, I'd stomp off down the beach and almost always, I'd start feeling better. Today, though, the more I walk, the angrier I am. Kaverlee is too dependent on cagic, and aside from Drae Devorla, all that energy comes from children. I suppose people need charged barriers and star nets, but do they also need brightly lit signs, autochariots, and cagic-powered appliances? I pass one shop selling frivolous gadgets like hair curlers, power games, and chatboxes, and I nearly break the window to destroy them. No one wants to admit it, but our world is powered by sacrifice.

I expect Glowy Pony to stop at some point and trot up to a door, but he keeps darting from shadow to shadow, and eventually he leads me to Lower Topdwell. By then, it's early morning and a different sort of people join us in the chilly streets; washerwomen push laundry carts, servants in crisp pallacoats and palliumcoats walk toward the wealthier neighborhoods, and I nearly collide with an elderly man hauling a wagon full of antique gadgets.

I rarely visited Lower Topdwell when I was the Predrae, and I didn't realize it was in such poor shape. The crowded streets are jammed with old buildings that either need repairs or should simply be torn down. It reminds me of the Outer's Cove shelter, except it's not underground and there are more stray cats.

Glowy Pony finally brings me to a two-story building made of round, river-tumbled stones. Its walls are so crooked it looks like a firm shove could knock the whole place over. I think it's a lodging place, although the sign over the door simply reads, "The Bearcur."

"Stay hidden," I tell the cagic horselet, suddenly feeling nervous. If Kary really is here, how will he react when he sees me? Will he be surprised? Happy? Annoyed that I tracked him down? The last time I saw him, things were strained between us.

Hands clenched, I walk into the Bearcur, entering a stale-smelling room. As I suspected, it seems to be a cauponium. Several people are sitting around tables, eating a simple breakfast of what seems to be gray, grainy mush.

None of these people are Kary, though, so I'm not sure what to do. He could be sleeping somewhere, but I can't exactly search the building. Whoever owns this place wouldn't like that.

I suppose I could ask people if they've seen him, but just as I turn to a greasy-haired man who's either humming or snoring, a chair scrapes nearby. A tall, skinny girl then stands up and walks over to me. She's wearing a simple stola and men's boots and carrying a rusty knife. The blade doesn't seem to have anything to do with me, though. I see a pile of partially peeled sour roots where she was sitting.

"You lost?" she says, eyeing the emerald green pallacoat I took from Drae Devorla's wardrobe. Its luxurious fabric and fine tailoring don't belong in this part of Kaverlee.

"I'm looking for someone named Kary," I tell her.

"Kary, huh?" The girl chews her lip. "Don't know any Karys."

"He's a little older than me," I say. "He has black hair and brown eyes… and only one hand."

Now her eyes flicker, but she continues to chew her lip, saying nothing.

"Look, I know he's here," I say, wondering if I should just start shouting his name.

The girl fiddles with her rusty knife. "I can find anyone—for a price."

I sigh, exasperated. "I don't have money."

The girl eyes my fine pallacoat and raises an eyebrow. "*Sure* you don't."

Just then, a large, bearded man enters the room, and trailing after him is—

"Kary!" I exclaim, relieved.

His eyes meet mine, full of… relief? Dread?

"That's Jemes, not Kary," the big man says. His scratchy, nasal voice sounds like it should belong to someone much smaller.

And Kary, who is most definitely Kary, softly says, "Who are you?" to me, and he's such a terrible liar. I'm sure it's obvious to everyone that we know each other.

"Who am I?" I say impatiently. "Don't be ridiculous. I need to talk to you alone—I need your help." Oh realms, seeing him is doing something to me. Shimmerlight dances beneath my skin. In bright light it wouldn't matter, but in this dark place, I'm glowing.

"Is that shimmerlight?" asks the bearded man.

"Course not." Kary gives me a hard look. "You'd better leave."

I'm not going anywhere until I talk to him. "You don't understand. I—"

"Please go," Kary insists, and then adds in an undertone, "You're not safe here."

At the same time, the big man turns to the skinny girl. "Vivie, go find a Shieldbearer and tell him we've caught a runaway Shimmerling. Ask for a reward."

She sneers at me, nods, and runs off.

This is just getting worse and worse. I don't want to deal with Shieldbearers, but I'm also not leaving until I talk to Kary.

"Rucks, do you really want Shieldbearers in here?" Kary says to the big man.

And Rucks, I suppose that's his name, snorts. "I can manage some shiny boots if there's a payout." He then turns and shouts, "Skedge! Lazzle! C'mere. Might need some backup."

Two young men soon join us. They have Rucks's broad shoulders, unkempt hair, and heavy brows. They must be his sons.

"Who's the stola?" one asks, planting himself between me and the door.

"A runaway Shimmerling who's sweet on Jemes," Rucks says. "Viv's getting the city guard."

I stare at Kary, and he gives me a look that's just as intense. We need to talk, but how and where? Maybe if I create a distraction, we can slip away. A small, hot shimmerdark shape inside Rucks's shirt might work.

"So what's your name, fancy locks?" Rucks asks.

And I ignore him; I'm too focused on placing a small sphere of shimmerdark inside his gaping collar.

"I asked you a question," he snarls, and reaching forward, he gives my right arm a sudden, painful twist.

It's exactly how Golly grabbed me, which makes two terrible things happen.

Kary cries, "Xylia! No!" telling everyone who I am.

And I react. Thank the realms I don't knock Rucks through a wall, but I do hurl a globe of shimmerdark into his chest, shoving him over a table. Bowls shatter and gray, grainy mush splatters everywhere.

There's no point hiding my power now, so I dive for Kary and wrap us in a protective shell of velvety, dark energy. The shimmerdark shuts out the oversized men and the hazy room, just like I hid Rutholyn and myself from nocturnes. Suddenly it's just Kary and me in a very small space, a patch of dimly lit floorboards, and the muffled sound of angry voices.

Kary looks around in amazement. "This isn't shimmerlight."

"No, not quite," I say, and because we're so close, too close maybe, I cross my arms between us. "This power is why I came looking for you. I'm in trouble—big trouble." Somehow telling him about my downleveling discovery is going to make it much more real. I'm not sure I'm ready for that.

"Will this stuff... hurt us?" Kary's still looking up and around, examining the shimmerdark.

"No," I say. "We're safe."

He nods and focuses on me again. "You're hurt." He gently touches my forehead.

I quickly turn away. "I'm fine, but what's happened to you? Why are you here? Why are you calling yourself Jemes, and why did you leave Clicks?"

"Long story," he says softly.

"I have a long story too," I say. "And I've made such a mess of things. I have as much power as Drae Devorla now, but she won't let me keep it. So I ran away." I squeeze my hands together as something wonderful happens; Kary pulls me into a hug. I try not to cry. I didn't realize how much I needed this, someone holding me, comforting me.

Yet it's only a quick embrace. Letting go, Kary exhales heavily and looks around our dark, glittering cocoon. "We need to get out of here. Rucks and his kids are nothing but trouble."

"And I don't want to deal with any Shieldbearers either," I add. If I can force my way through Kaverlee's barrier, surely I can walk out of a rundown cauponium. "Which way is the door?"

Kary points over my shoulder. "At least, I think it is."

So I twist around and move our energy shelter in that direction, and although we collide with a few tables, I soon work the awkward shape through the doorway and over the stone stoop.

Now there's damp mud and gravel beneath us.

"I'm going to make an energy disc," I tell Kary, who's behind me. "We can escape on it."

I feel him shift. "What?"

Realms, I have so much to tell him. Putting on my goggles, I hastily explain my plan. "I'm going to make a flat cagic shape with this dark energy—like a big plate. We'll need to quickly climb on it, and then I can carry us to safety."

"That's possible?" Kary touches the energy shield. Sparks gather around his fingers like metal filings drawn to a magnet. "This isn't anything like shimmerlight."

"It's stronger," I say, "But I still can only make one shape at a time. We'll have to move quickly."

Our energy shelter shudders. The big man and his sons must be trying to break through it. I make a tiny opening and peer through. Rucks and his sons are now hurling chairs at my shimmerdark and a crowd has gathered. So much for not drawing attention to myself.

"Are you ready?" I ask Kary. I once thought angry humans weren't as dangerous as nocturnes, but now I'm not so sure. Humans can be malicious. Nocturnes, as vicious as they are, can't.

"I'm ready," Kary says.

I take a deep breath and rapidly expand the energy shell, hopefully shoving back anyone brandishing a chair. I then release the cagic, much like popping an ink bubble, and quickly create a disc large enough for Kary and I.

We jump on the glittering circle, and I immediately raise us up toward the star net.

"Cagic witch!" Rucks shouts.

I rather like hovering in the air. I feel much safer. But the more time we spend aloft and extremely visible, the sooner Drae Devorla will find me. So I guide the disc over only a few buildings, and then I lower us back down onto a muddy roadway.

"Gods' mercy!" Kary stumbles unsteadily as he climbs off the disc. "That's incredible. You're a lot more powerful. What happened?"

"Soon—I'll tell you everything," I say, proudly aware that I'm about to astound him even more. "Glowy Pony, where are you?"

The cagic horselet appears, and Kary covers his mouth, murmuring an astonished, "Realms!"

"Glowy, we need somewhere to hide," I say. "Somewhere close."

The shimmerdark pony turns and trots off.

"C'mon," I say to Kary.

His mouth opens and closes, and I can tell he desperately wants to slow down, think all this through, and discuss it in detail.

"Come on," I urge again, and thankfully, he begins to move. He also gives me a familiar look, a trusting look, and I hope I don't let him down.

22

Reunion

Glowy Pony leads us into a rickety insulae apartment building and up several staircases. Each flight is wobblier than the last, and then the cagic horselet urges us up a ladder into a musty attic. Kary struggles to climb with his lone hand but manages. And once we've shut the door beneath us, I create a ball of shimmerlight, which reveals a sparsely furnished home.

"Someone lives here." Kary steps over a tattered bedroll. Lying beside it is a crate of dishes and rusted cagic stove.

"I think someone used to," I say, for everything's covered in dust. "Besides, Glowy Pony wouldn't have brought us here if it wasn't safe." Although he did lead me to Aerro, who ended up being very dangerous. The cagic horselet may have a knack for finding things, but he definitely isn't all-knowing.

"So… Glowy Pony, is it?" Kary crouches beside the gleaming creature. "What is he? Where did he come from?"

"I don't know what he is," I say, sitting cross-legged on the bedroll. It may be dusty, but I'm too exhausted to keep standing. "And I may have made him?" I stifle a yawn. When did I last sleep? "I have so much to tell you."

Kary sits down on the other end of the bedroll. "Tell me then."

So I talk, and while I do, he's his usual patient self. He never interrupts, he listens attentively, and he offers all sorts of satisfying reactions: a snort of anger when I describe my confrontation with Golly, an open mouth when I talk about Glowy Pony's first appearance, and a soft hum of caution when I mention Aerro's strange behavior. And when I tearfully tell him about Rutholyn's death, he pulls a clean handkerchief out of his pocket for me. I finish my story by sharing what I learned last night; there's no such thing as winking out. "All Shimmerlings could become Shimmercasters, Kary, every single one of them. Drae Devorla says she's obeying the law, but," and I find this hard to say, "I think the law's wrong."

"Of course it is," Kary says with a certainty I appreciate. "Drae Devorla knows that or she wouldn't keep what she's doing a secret."

"That's true," I say, and my lingering worries—maybe I'm overreacting, maybe I misunderstood something, maybe I'm just being naive—vanish. Kary's always been able to see things clearly, and I missed that. Realizing he's grown quiet, I ask, "What is it?"

"Well, I… I think I was downleveled," he says.

"What?" I lean forward. "Why didn't you tell any of us?"

"I didn't figure it out until just now," he says, shaking his head incredulously. "But what you say happened to that kid… I remember something like that—it's my earliest memory. I remember a woman attaching me to a big machine, and I remember pain. All this time, I thought it was some sort of cagic medical treatment."

"I'm so sorry," I say.

He smiles wistfully. "I've always wondered what it would be like to be cagic-touched."

I've never tried to describe my abilities before, so I think for a moment, and then I say, "Imagine a fire here, deep in your lungs." I nearly put my hand on his chest, but after our kiss-gone-wrong, I'm not brave enough to casually touch him. Will I always feel this awkward when I'm near him? I hope not. "Now imagine that fire sending hot tendrils through your arms and legs."

Kary laughs. "Sounds uncomfortable." I'm about to explain that it usually feels good, but he keeps talking. "I wish you hadn't found me."

Surely he doesn't really mean that. My disappointment must show because his expression softens.

"My problems will only make your problems worse," he explains. "You should be talking to Clicks or Fedorie."

I shake my head. "Drae Devorla knows where to find them, but she doesn't know where you are." Again, I'm tempted to touch him, to take his hand with both of mine. "Why did you leave Clicks's house?"

Kary's head falls to one side. He has the same clouded expression he often had on the Grimshore when we asked him about his missing hand.

"Why?" I press.

He gives me a weighty look that seems full of the 'long story' he hastily mentioned in the Bearcur.

"I told you everything," I say, inching closer. "Now it's your turn. Tell me. Maybe I can help."

Kary is quiet for a while longer, but then he leans back on his good arm, sets his jaw in a determined way, and says, "People are looking for me. Bad people."

"What? Why?" I say. We haven't been back on the mainland for very long, and he couldn't have angered anyone while we were on the Grimshore. Before that, like me, he was a child.

"You know that my father went to prison, yes?"

I nod, and say, "For burglary."

Kary nods too. "He stole a famous jewel, the Vaylark, and no one's seen it since. He said he threw it in a river, but the thieves guild thought I had it. They tried to make me tell them where it was." He lifts his wrist stump and smiles ruefully. "But I didn't know."

"So that's what happened," I say softly.

Kary lowers his damaged arm. "Matreornan soldiers came looking for me too, so I ran. That's why I was on the ferry. That's how I ended up on the Grimshore."

I feel sudden pity for young Kary. I can still remember what he looked like back then, skinny arms and legs, wild hair, and huge dark eyes. "What's so special about the jewel?" I picture it as a brilliant blue gem in a heavy gold setting.

"It's valuable," Kary says. "But that's not just it, it's a symbol of Matreornan. It's even on our cityland flag. People think it once ransomed a Highland Tilber king, and an old thrall apparently cursed it too. Most people, though, blame it for letting nocturnes into our realm." He chuckles softly as if that's preposterous. "I *do* wonder if it's cursed, though. The Vaylark certainly ruined my

Dad's life and…" He lifts his injured arm again. "I don't think it's done with me."

Finally I understand why he wasn't eager to leave the Grimshore. "It's been seven years. Do you really think people are still looking for you?"

"I'm sure they are." Kary folds his injured arm against his chest. "Matreornans are obsessed with the Vaylark. They've been fighting over it for centuries. Seven years is nothing to them."

Kary tells the rest of his story fairly quickly. He left Clicks's house as soon as he had land justification because the newsreaders were running headlines like, "One-Handed Matreornan Boy Among Ferry Survivors." He made his way to Lower Topdwell, where he changed his name and found work at the Bearcur. That was fine at first, but then he learned Rucks was illegally siphoning cagic from the city lines and selling it. "And after he told me, that gut stone burnt my land justification docs and swore he'd hand me over to labor agents if I told anyone else."

I give him a sideways smile. "*You* should have asked Clicks and Fedorie for help too."

He sighs. "I wanted to protect them. Rucks is terrible, and the Matreornans searching for me are worse."

I roll my shoulders. It would be nice to lean against something. "Battling wolievs doesn't seem so bad now," I joke.

Kary laughs but then looks at me gravely. "What are we going to do?"

I love that he says "we," and I wish I had the courage to hold his hand. This feels like the perfect moment to reach for him, but I'm not sure I know how to recognize perfect moments anymore.

When I don't respond, Kary keeps talking. "Let's go see Clicks and Fedorie then. They'd want to help us, and who knows, maybe they can."

I nod. "I think we should wait here for a while, though. The Great Drae probably has Shieldbearers looking for me."

Kary agrees, and because I was awake all lunar night, he encourages me to get some sleep. "I'll keep watch."

So while he sits on a crate, I stretch out on the bedroll. Since Glowy Pony seems to have vanished, I make the shimmerlight ball hovering above us a bit larger and brighter.

I feel better than I have in a long time. Facing trouble with Kary is far better than facing it on my own or with a vulnerable child. Yet now that I'm lying still and no longer trying to explain something or escape something, I realize I've ignored my body's least glamorous needs.

"I'll be right back," I tell Kary, and then I climb down the rickety ladder to find a lavatory. Now that it's mid-morning, a few other people are moving around the insulae, but no one pays attention to me. There are surely about fifty or so apartments in this building, so the people who live here must be used to seeing strangers. Even my expensive pallacoat only raises a few eyebrows. I soon find the third floor's shared lavatory, which is only a few doors down from the ladder. Once I've relieved myself, I look into the scratched mirror on the wall.

My once pretty emerald hair color has faded to a queasy grass green. My forehead is a motley of bruises and so swollen I have a perpetually furrowed brow. And beneath my vivid pallacoat, I'm wearing a rumpled sleeping gown. No wonder Kary never seems as enamored with me as I am with him. Well, I can't do much about my injured head or clothes, but I might be able to coax my hair into a becoming knot. It takes me a while to tame it with my fingers, but I eventually twist the strands into a roll and hold it all in place by using the goggles as a headband.

Just as I'm about to step back out into the corridor, I hear someone say, "Then I saw them climb that ladder."

23
Flight

No, no, no; that voice belongs to the skinny girl from the Bearcur; the girl peeling sour roots.

She keeps talking too. "Pa thought no one could follow their glowing circle, but I'm a fast runner."

I clench my teeth because hitting the wall in frustration would make too much noise. I should have carried us further away.

Then I hear a voice that's even more familiar: Drae Devorla's. "The one-handed young man—you're sure he's in the attic too?"

"Jemes? Yeah," the Bearcur girl says. "He's up there."

I cover my mouth with my fingers, and I have no idea what to do. If I was alone, I'd run, but I can't leave Kary behind.

"Legate, Grould," says a man, probably a Shieldbearer. "You two go up and bring down whoever's there."

"No," Drae Devorla says. "I'll go first. Xylia's dangerous. I may need to restrain her."

I think of how easily she subdued me only a few hours ago. I'm no match for her.

I tense as I hear ladder rungs creak.

I can't leave Kary defenseless. Drae Devorla will probably send him back to Matreornan. I'm so agitated motes of shimmerdark frazzle the air around me. *Drae Devorla and I have the same powers,* I tell myself. *If she can defeat me, I can defeat her.*

I peer into the corridor.

Five armed Shieldbearers stand near the ladder—*five*—as well as the girl from the Bearcur. The Great Drae must be up in the attic. I can't see her, but I do hear her having a muffled conversation. She's probably asking Kary where I am, and I bet he's insisting he doesn't know.

"She's not here," Drae Devorla shouts down seconds later. "Search the building!"

I scurry back into the lavatory. If I run, they'll see me, and if I don't run, they'll soon find me. Somehow, though, I need to save Kary. Yet despite everything I could do, *should* do, I stand paralyzed and uncertain.

Feet shuffle, and I hear the confused voices of insulae dwellers. Then the ladder creaks again, and Kary says, "Don't downlevel her. It's not right. You know it isn't."

"It's for her own good," says Drae Devorla. She then must turn to the Shieldbearers, for she adds, "Take him to the palace."

I can't let that happen. Still without a plan, I step into the corridor.

"There she is!" someone says, maybe the girl from the Bearcur.

By the time I take another breath, both Drae Devorla and I are creating shimmerdark shapes. As I expect, she attacks me like she did beneath Triumvirate Hall, trying to wrap a ring of energy around my head. But I beat her to it; I shape a band of shimmerdark around my eyes first. I then expand my loop, forcing her to widen hers, and after that, I drop down, escaping both. Landing hard on my knees, I send a cagic cube hurtling toward the Great Drae. Yet, ergh! Kary's beside her, and I don't want to hurt him too. With an angry cry, I disperse the energy before it strikes. The air's still glittering as Drae Devorla hurls an energy sphere at me.

I'm knocked backward, and WHAM, I slam against something—a wall probably. I know I have only seconds to react. As soon as Drae Devorla covers my eyes with cagic, the fight will be over.

Well, if she can't see me, she can't catch me. I fling up a shimmerdark barrier, sealing off the corridor just like I blocked the mid-passage of the seg-coach.

I realize I'm crying. What have I pulled Kary into? If I can't rescue him, I need to at least escape so I can help him later.

"I don't want to hurt you, Xylia," Drae Devorla shouts through the zapping, crackling field of energy. "I know you're upset, but you have to trust me."

I laugh bitterly. She has no idea how badly I want to trust her. I just wish this horrible nightmare would end, and I could wake up in a world where I didn't have to question everything I once believed.

I make another quick decision. I take the energy I'm using to block the corridor and rapidly ball it up like crumpled paper. Then I send that poorly shaped mass of energy through the wall at my back, bashing a gaping hole into someone's apartment. I scramble through the jagged gash, rolling to the left so Drae Devorla can't see me.

I nearly collide with a startled family, but I don't stop to apologize; I keep moving. I smash the ball of energy through another wall, and luckily, it's an exterior one. As I race toward the new opening, something hot and not quite solid sweeps past my arm. It's surely another one of Drae Devorla's attempts to capture me, but she's too late. I dive out into the cold air and land on a curved saucer of shimmerdark. Thank the realms I practiced this sort of thing.

Clinging to the energy, I guide it sharply to the right and streak away from the insulae, hoping the Great Drae isn't good at transference.

And I don't think she is, because instead of chasing me, she sends another sphere of shimmerdark my way. She misses, fortunately, but punches a hole in a nearby building. Bricks and wood briefly soar skyward before plunging down into the street.

After a quick look over my shoulder, I keep going. I need to put distance between myself and Drae Devorla, although I wish it didn't mean leaving Kary behind.

I don't stop until I reach Upper Topdwell, where I land on an empty street and duck into a covered doorway. Every Shieldbearer in the city is probably searching for me by now, and I'm sure private citizens will soon join them. I grimly wonder what the reward for finding me will be.

I lean against the wall, breathing heavily and feeling defeated. I didn't want to, but I guess I'm going to put another person I care about in danger.

"Glowy Pony?" I whisper. "Can you hear me?"

Thank the source, he appears.

"I'm looking for someone else," I say. "Sir Calvolin Nelvaso. Do you know where he is?"

The sparkling little creature nods—of course he does.

I should probably find Fedorie; she's tough and fierce. But Clicks owns a huge house. Surely I can hide in some secret passage or forgotten closet. I need rest and food and more than anything else, a safe place to stop and think.

It must be nearing midday now, and the weather's nicer than it was last night. There's still an aggressive breeze rolling off the Silkord Sea, but there isn't a competing northern wind anymore. There are also more people in the streets, so instead of letting Glowy Pony trot from shadow to shadow, I bundle him into my pallacoat. Once there, he nudges my arm to point me in the right direction.

At first, we travel toward the Landroot District, but then Glowy Pony has me turn left at the brightly lit Kaverlee Foundry.

That's puzzling, yet maybe Clicks isn't at home right now.

Glowy Pony then has me walk north, leading me through a cemetery.

Or rather, no, he's led me *into* a cemetery, for when I'm about halfway through the snowcapped headstones, he wriggles and clearly wants to stop. Now my heart's thudding. Clicks shouldn't be here.

"This can't be right," I whisper.

Since no one's nearby and there aren't any windows facing us in the surrounding buildings, I put Glowy Pony down. He immediately trots over to the lone mausoleum, a short building covered in bare, leafless vines. He stops at the entrance and looks back at me.

I'm already tearing up. "So Clicks is dead."

But Glowy Pony shakes his little head, *no*.

"He's alive?" I say, feeling like my heart has just been haphazardly flung around.

The cagic horselet nods.

Well, thank the realms, but then… "Why are we here?"

Glowy Pony passes through the mausoleum's chained wrought iron door and looks expectantly back at me.

He wants me to follow him. "Are you sure? Clicks lives in the Landroot District. He's told me hundreds of times."

Yet Glowy Pony steps further into the shadows and hops impatiently.

It's strange how I no longer trust Drae Devorla, but here I am trusting a being I still know nothing about.

He did lead me to Kary, though.

So I look around again, making sure that there's still no one watching, and then I heat a small triangle of shimmerdark and use it to slice through the chain on the door. As for the door, it doesn't open easily; it's rusty and the bottom's stuck in ice. But I only need to open it partway. As soon as I can fit through, I slip inside and close the door behind me, and then I follow Glowy Pony farther into the crypt.

Once we're well away from the entrance, I create a cagic sphere to light our way. Its blue glow illuminates covered alcoves that surely hold human remains. Now that I think about it, this place is too old for Clicks to be interred here—I should have realized that before. These days most people are buried beyond the spreadfarms during the Bright Month, which means the bodies surrounding me have been here for a long time. A few alcoves are no longer even covered, and I avoid looking into them. I just left Rutholyn in a place like this, and I hate to think about her alone in the dark.

The mausoleum isn't large, but it has two basements. When we reach the lowest one, Glowy Pony stops at a sturdy metal door. It reminds me of the doors in the Haberdine subtrain tunnel.

"Through here?" I say, covering my nose. The mausoleum doesn't smell bad in the way I'd expect, but the air is still musty and stagnant.

Glowy Pony nods.

I still can't imagine we're heading in the right direction. I suppose when I asked Glowy Pony to find me a map in Haberdine, he showed me the train tunnel, which was even more helpful. Maybe he's doing something like that now. So I dutifully cut through the bolt on the door, and when I push it open, a cool breeze greets me. Have I found a much larger space?

But no, it must simply be well-ventilated, for I step into a narrow corridor. I shut the door behind me, happy to leave the mausoleum behind, and then I look around. I'm not in a clean or pleasant passage, but I think it once was much nicer. On the floor are colorful yet dirty tiles, and there are faint flowers painted on the cracked plaster walls. Glowy Pony then leads me forward through various rooms, some of them full of crumbling, forgotten furniture, others empty aside from small piles of debris. I feel like I'm in a basement that's been sealed up and forgotten for centuries.

"This is a Dark Month shelter," I suddenly realize. Kaverlee didn't always have a star net or cagically charged barrier walls. The people here once hid like everyone else.

I still don't understand what these abandoned passages have to do with Clicks, yet with Drae Devorla searching for me, maybe this is simply a safer way to reach his house. This network of chambers and corridors must be underneath the entire city.

Every now and then, I hear deep thrumming whooshes, which are probably subtrains, and I also hear water flowing through the pipes that punch through the walls like tree roots.

I follow Glowy Pony as he turns corners and descends staircases. And before long, I'm thoroughly lost.

Eventually, the sound of subtrains fade, and I stop seeing pipes. The walls change too; they are no longer plaster, brick, or concrete, but made out of huge stone blocks. It's also getting slightly warmer, so I pull off my pallacoat.

"Where are we?" I ask Glowy Pony, but of course he can't answer.

We cross a long, subterranean bridge, and I hear water far below. This time it's not the soft trickle of pipes, but the smash and splatter of waves meeting cave walls. I must be hearing the Silkord Sea. Moments later, we reach a set of ajar, ornate bronze doors, and I gape at the intricate reliefs covering them. I don't think anyone in Kaverlee could make doors like these anymore.

Passing through them, I enter a large chamber.

Rich, blue tiles cover the floor and vaulted ceilings, while white marble carvings line the walls. Not far ahead of me, standing in a sunken circle that must once have been a pool, is a two-story statue of the Hidden Gods.

But what really catches my eye are the large niches in the surrounding walls. Seated inside them, or at least in the ones lit by my shimmerlight, are giant, metal figures.

"Colossi!" I say, stunned.

24
The Antiquities Society

The Colossi I know have simplified heads with round eyes and no other features. These ones have human-like faces with stern expressions. They're also made out of an unfamiliar metal covered in a blue patina, and they're beautifully ornate, decorated with engravings of nocturnes and geometric patterns. Empty sockets also circle their necks and arms. Maybe those once held jewels.

I notice light shining out of a side passage—how strange. Maybe I should hide. I'm still deciding what to do, when a group of about ten people emerge. One of them, a woman holding a lantern, runs toward me, crying, "Xylia!"

"Fedorie?" I call back, squinting.

And it is her, although she's cut her hair short and dyed it bright red. She's also wearing a blue outfit with lots of dangling sashes.

Clicks also hurries toward me, and he looks different too. He now has a large, curled moustache and he's wearing fine clothes: an elegant green tago, striped necktie, satin-lined palliumcoat, and eyeglasses—something he dearly missed on the Grimshore.

For a few moments, we are a disorganized tangle of hugs and relieved sighs, but then Fedorie steps back and says, "What are you doing here?"

I could ask her the same thing. "Well, I was following…" I look around for Glowy Pony, but he's vanished. That's probably for the best since there are other people here. "Where am I?"

"They think this was once a Hidden God temple." Clicks nods at his friends.

"And who are they?" I ask softly. They're all around Clicks's age, with fine wrinkles and silver hair in various shades. They also all wear well-tailored stolas, wrapsuits, and tagos, and a few of them carry canes and fine leather satchels.

"May I introduce the Antiquities Society's advisory council," Clicks says grandly. "And I'm a member of the society too. I officially joined last Bright Month."

"The Antiquities Society? What's that?" I ask.

The nearest man, a stocky gentleman with wild, white hair, steps forward and bows deeply. He then says, "We are a group of historians who archive and protect information so it isn't lost or—" he gives me a dark look "—hidden on purpose. In short, we strive to safeguard Kaverlee's past."

"We were meeting to discuss you, actually," Clicks says.

"Why?" I ask suspiciously. Even though I trust him and Fedorie, I don't know these other people.

"No need to worry, my dear," Clicks says. "My friends simply want to help you. There were rumors you returned to the city beneath some sort of strange black energy mid-Dark-Month! Mid-Dark-Month, Xylia!" He looks both amazed and alarmed. "I also heard rumors you were shot. Is any of that true?"

I nod. "It all is."

Clicks pales. "Whatever happened? I tried to contact you at the palace, but I was turned away."

"So was I," Fedorie adds, putting her hands on her hips. "And then today, Shieldbearers came to my insulae looking for you. I knew you must be in danger, so I went to see Clicks…"

"And I called for help." Clicks nods at the group. "The Antiquities Society knows a lot about cagic and all the former Great Draes."

"I suggested we meet here," an old woman says, stepping forward and smiling at me. "It's a safe place—Triumvirate Hall has forgotten about it."

"Yet after all that trouble, here you are!" Fedorie wraps one of her muscular arms around my shoulders and squeezes. It's as if now that we're together, she thinks I'm completely safe.

I wish that was true.

"How did you find this place, though?" the woman asks.

And I'm not sure how to answer. Should I tell everyone about Glowy Pony? I just met these people.

Yet before I say anything, another woman, one with a tight, steely gray bun steps forward. "You're a Shimmercaster now, aren't you?"

"Yes," I say, surprised she knows the term.

The woman adjusts her spectacles and eyes the man beside her. "Told you so."

"Well go on, tell us what happened," Fedorie says. "Don't keep us in suspense."

I'm torn. I want to tell Fedorie and Clicks everything, but can I trust their friends? Then again, who am I keeping secrets for? The Great Drae?

So I sit down on the edge of the empty pool and share my story, and it's somehow easier this time. The painful parts still hurt, of course, but strangely, I feel like I'm talking about someone else. Fedorie and Clicks are outraged by Golly's behavior and sad about Rutholyn's death, and everyone's shocked by Auldora's downleveling.

"We should have known Shimmerlings never wink out!" cries a tiny, very wrinkled woman. "There's no mention of cagic fading in the old stories."

"How abominable," Clicks says, his voice cracking, and he's even more upset when I tell him that Drae Devorla arrested Kary.

"Maybe she'll let him go," Fedorie says.

"Maybe," I say heavily because we all know how unlikely that is.

After a long silence, Clicks asks, "May we, er, meet the glowing pony?"

"Alright," I say. "If he's willing to show himself." I turn back to the doorway where I last saw him. "Glowy Pony? Are you still here?"

Rather than cantor across the hall, he appears before us in a dramatic shower of sparks, and I'm pretty sure he's showing off. Everyone gasps, which must please him, and Fedorie even claps.

"Amazing," Clicks breathes.

"Does anyone know what he is?" I ask.

The Antiquities Society member with wild, white hair snorts. "Isn't it obvious? He's a cagic guide."

"A cagic guide," I repeat. "What's that?"

"Shimmercasters used to have them as companions," he says. "But that was centuries ago. I wonder why this one came to you."

And I wonder why Flutter came to Aerro.

"Tell me everything you know about Shimmercasters," I say. "Please. I feel like I hardly know anything."

"Tell you?" he huffs. "I might as well show you. Follow me."

He leads us further into the vast chamber, our footsteps echoing loudly and Glowy Pony trotting silently.

A Colossi emerges from the darkness, lying on the floor. It looks like someone attempted to move him and then realized how heavy he was. His arm's also missing, and his head's dented. I wonder if looters tried to pry it off.

The Antiquities Society members move slowly. It's probably because they're older, but it seems very reverent, and I find myself matching their pace. A resonant, gut-deep feeling spreads through me too. I've felt very lost since Rutholyn died. Not only have I been sad, I no longer have a purpose. When I first returned to Kaverlee, I had a clear goal—I wanted to become the Predrae again. Now though, what am I trying to do? I don't want to be downleveled and I want to help Kary, but beyond that, my future seems hazy, shapeless, and well, pointless.

This hall, though, seems steeped in certainty and meaning. Something about the ancient space fills me with confidence and seems to promise that what I do still matters.

We eventually reach cascading stone risers, clearly meant to seat many people. Glowy Pony leaps up them as if he already knows what's at the top. The old man follows the cagic horselet slowly, and when he's about halfway up, he lifts his lantern.

"There," he says. "Shimmercasters."

I'm not quite sure what I'm looking at, so I create a large hovering ball of shimmerlight. It reveals a massive mural covering the wall.

Even though it's faded and water-damaged, the painting is incredible. Seven larger-than-life Shimmercasters battle nocturnes in front of what appears to be Kaverlee City. I'm not sure if they're men or women, but they're dressed like warriors. They're also sending diamonds of red-edged shimmerdark into wolievs, sharecks, and carrows. A few carry shining energy shields, and one even brandishes a cagic sword that seems to have a blazing hot blade and cool grip. Maybe that's something I should try. Another Shimmercaster wears cagic armor, which must be challenging to shape and move. And running among them are two shimmerdark animals much like Glowy Pony: a martin and a small goat. Even more fascinating, behind the warriors are three Colossi, and they seem to be fighting the nocturnes too.

I have the heart-tightening-yet-comforting sense that I'm part of something big and wonderful. "Who are they?" I ask.

"They're the Shimmercasters who used to protect the city during the Dark Month," says the woman with the bun. "Hundreds of years ago, everyone lingerslept, but Shimmercasters stayed awake and stood guard. There's evidence of teams like this across the Connected Lands."

"So there are more murals?" I ask. I'd love to see them.

"There are a few," she says. "As well as some carefully preserved manuscripts and paintings. But if cityland officials find them, they tend to disappear."

It would have been much easier to fight the nocturnes if I'd had help. I wish I could return to the days where cagic-touched people weren't downleveled but useful and celebrated. We wouldn't need as much energy either if we didn't have to power sky nets, barrier walls, lights, and heaters. But I can't imagine modern Kaverleans agreeing to lingersleeping. They love their luxuries and freedoms, and I understand that. When I was on the Grimshore, I missed my easy life here so intensely it was almost like grieving a loved one.

I look up at the seven warriors again. "In those old manuscripts, does anyone say the dark energy damaged people's minds?"

"I don't believe so," the woman with the bun says, and her answer doesn't surprise me. Of course that was a lie, an attempt to stop Shimmercasters from becoming too powerful.

I want to know more. I want to know everything there is to know about cagic, and these Antiquities Society people do seem to have answers. "So where does all this energy come from?"

"I'm afraid that's still a mystery," says a tall, lanky man with dark skin. "There are fanciful stories and myths, though. My favorite is the tale of King Wendler who tried to cut a doorway into the Hidden Gods' realm. When he found other realms in between, he impatiently slashed through them. Unfortunately, the nocturnes lived in one of those realms, and they came pouring into ours. When the Hidden Gods saw what King Wendler had done, they tried to stitch the worlds closed again, but they couldn't. So instead, they gave us a gift to protect ourselves—cagic."

I shiver. It's just a story of course, but in this shadowy, otherworldly chamber, it seems like anything could be true.

I wonder why people stopped believing in the Hidden Gods, and I'm sure like many things, there wasn't any singular reason. The shift probably happened slowly, over many centuries.

"Hold on," I say, thinking of Kary's father. "Did the king cut through the realms using a jewel?"

"You've heard the tale!" the lanky man smiles. "The Matreornans once claimed to have the very stone, the Vaylark. But of course, the Nelbarians insist it was their prized gem, the Vethnal, and I think there's another candidate in Highland Tilber. I forget what that one's called, though."

"The Maderci," someone else chimes in.

"No, it's the Quintel," says another man. "The Maderci is part of the Triad Tales."

As Clicks's friends debate which enchanted stone is part of which myth, Fedorie and I walk back across the hall. "You've been through a lot. Are you all right?" she asks.

"I'm…" The truth seems big and unwieldy, so I just say, "I'm hungry."

She smiles brightly. "It's your lucky day, then. After what we went through on that miserable island, I never go anywhere without food." She chuckles and leads me over to a satchel near the empty pool. And oh, merciful realms, she has a meat pie, two hard-boiled eggs, and cold tea. I eat voraciously, and as I do, Fedorie tells me how she's been. Apparently while we were on the Grimshore, her beloved husband Markos remarried not once but twice, and with nowhere else to go, she moved in with her mother. "It's not ideal," she says.

She also tells me about Clicks, who's adult sons spent our Grimshore years fighting over their inheritance. They were very upset to learn that after all their expensive legal battles, Clicks was still alive.

"Now they're still living in his house and trying to prove he's an impostor." Fedorie sighs, and it would almost be funny if I didn't know how hurt Clicks must be.

He joins us as I finish eating. "I must head back up—my sons might start looking for me. I hate to leave you here, Xylia, but at least it's a safe place. I'll return tomorrow with food and other supplies."

"I'll be alright," I say, although I don't love the idea of sleeping here alone, especially without bedding. "Shieldbearers are probably watching your home, though. I hope they don't question you when you return."

Clicks smiles. "Not to worry, my dear. My house has an entrance to these shelters in the cellar—many old buildings do. The doorway used to be bricked up, but these days… it's not." His eyes twinkle, and then he twitches as if struck with an idea. "Now that I think about it, come with me. There is a good hiding place in my home."

I'd wondered about that before, but now that I'm in this temple, there's no reason to put him in any danger. "I'll stay here. I'll be fine."

"Come now, Xylia. There's a room in my home that no one ever, ever enters." He takes my hand and looks at me earnestly. "You will be safe there, I promise, and comfortable too. There's no need to stay here."

I still hesitate.

Fedorie though, nudges me. "Go on. If ol' Devorla shows up, just run back down here."

"Very well," I say reluctantly.

The Antiquities Society members depart in groups of twos and threes, and Fedorie joins the woman with the gray bun, who apparently lives near her.

"I wish I could do more," Fedorie says before leaving. "I'd love to give that Great Drae a piece of my mind."

"This is even better," I tell her. "Seeing you has…" I trail off, unable to express just how meaningful it's been.

Fedorie pulls me close and says, "Just because we haven't come up with a plan today, doesn't mean we won't think of one tomorrow."

Clicks and I are the last to leave, yet as we pass through the temple's ornate brass doors, I say, "Wait—there's something I want to do."

I head back into the chamber, to the fallen Colossus. I find it so tragic something this grand has been lying in such an undignified position for several centuries. Somehow, putting things right down here feels like the first step to putting things right above.

So I gently fill the metal figure with cagic and ease him onto his feet. His stiff joints screech and protest, but I'm able to shuffle him toward his niche, and I soon have him sitting on the marble bench within. Even though Colossi aren't alive, I still feel like I've done this one a kindness.

I turn to find Clicks standing behind me, smiling.

"Now I'm ready to go," I say.

We travel back through the labyrinth of passages, chambers, and stone staircases, and amazingly, Clicks never seems to take a wrong turn. "I'm impressed you remember the way," I say.

"I almost don't want to tell you my secret." He chuckles and points up at symbols painted on the ceiling. "The Antiquities Society made those. I'd be very lost without them."

As a subtrain passes by, shaking the walls, he adds, "You seem different. More grown-up." He looks at me proudly, and I'm not sure it's a look I deserve.

"Everything seems different now," I say. "Even my memories."

Clicks tilts his head. "What do you mean?"

"Well, I was always terrible at lingersleeping," I say. "But… maybe I was supposed to be. Maybe a part of me knew I should be awake to protect everyone else."

Clicks looks intrigued. "Could be, could be indeed."

When we reach his basement, he sneaks me upstairs using a back stairwell. And even though I've never been in his home before, the tapestries, rugs, and polished wood floors are pleasantly familiar. Maybe it's because Clicks told us so many stories about his life in Kaverlee while we were on the Grimshore.

He brings me into a richly decorated bedroom, which surprises me. I expected to be hidden away in a storage closet or attic. "You're sure no one comes in here?" I ask.

"The servants clean it once a month, but that's it," Clicks says. "Even I haven't been in here since… before."

I notice a portrait of a woman on the wall, and I suddenly know where I am.

"This was Bermy's room."

He nods, gazing at the painting.

My heart twists as I think about how Lady Bermilia didn't escape the ferry.

"I don't have to stay here," I say.

But Clicks shakes his head and smiles tearfully. "Bermy would want to help you." After swallowing a few times, he adds, "I'll bring you some fresh blankets, but I need to be seen downstairs. I don't want my sons asking too many questions."

He leaves, and for a few moments, I continue to examine Bermy's portrait. She's wearing a lovely maroon stola that compliments her brown skin and dark eyes, and there's something so present about her expression. It's as if she'd just ran into the artist's studio to pose and was slightly out of breath. I wonder what our seven years on the Grimshore would have been like if she'd survived.

I should probably rest, but because Kary's still in trouble, I alternate between pacing and watching Glowy Pony explore the room. After a while, I also try to summon the shimmerdark sword I saw in the temple mural. I've never created a cagic shape that has two different temperatures, and unsurprisingly, it's difficult. However, I think I'd like fighting with a cagic sword. It's easier to move energy I'm touching. And although it's tough to maintain the dual temperatures, I enjoy swinging a shimmerdark blade through the air, challenging imaginary beasts.

Watching tiny sparks trail after the sword also makes me feel strangely peaceful. Even though the world is still flawed, Kary's still in danger, and I've lost Rutholyn forever, I know who I am now and what I'm meant to do: protect others.

I try to craft cagic armor next. Like the sword, it's extremely advanced summoning. I create the armor after a few tries, wrapping a single shimmerdark shape around my arms, legs, chest, and head. But I can't move in it. It's as if I've encased myself in warm, glittering stone.

Maybe a cagic helmet would be enough though; it would at least stop Drae Devorla from blindfolding me. Yet just as I begin shaping energy around my head, Clicks returns. He hasn't brought any blankets though, and he's also shaking his head as if there's water in his ears, which is exactly what he did on the Grimshore when he had bad news to share.

"It's Kary, isn't it?" I ask.

Clicks's already fragile expression seems to fracture even more. He pulls a letter from his pocket and hands it to me. "This just arrived," he whispers. "I'm so sorry."

I unfold the note, immediately recognizing the Triumvirate Hall stationary. It reads:

Sir Calvolin Nelvaso,

Xylia Amoreah Selvantez may attempt to contact you. If she does, tell her that to ensure her friend remains in good health, she must submit to downleveling. She is to present herself at the Kaverlee Foundry at ten o'clock tomorrow morning.

- Drae Devorla, the Eighteenth Great Drae of Kaverlee

25

The Cityland Conduits

"Remains in good health," I read that part of Drae Devorla's message out loud.

"She's threatening Kary," Clicks says, trembling. "*Our* Kary."

I nod, but I suppose I shouldn't be surprised. Drae Devorla supports a system that abuses people and sometimes even kills them. Hurting Kary is nothing compared to what she's already done.

"I'll have to go." I crumple up the letter.

Clicks twists his hands together. "There must be another way. I'll send a wire message to Fedorie. Perhaps she can help us think of a solution."

Fedorie arrives before Clicks contacts her, though, for she received a similar message. She joins us in Bermy's room, and for a while, we discuss far-fetched plans to rescue Kary. Yet it quickly becomes clear to me that there isn't a safe way to reach him. I have to turn myself in—I have to let Drae Devorla downlevel me.

"I say you fight her again." Fedorie smacks her hands together. "I bet you're more of a match for her than you think."

Maybe I could defeat her with the dual-temperature sword. I'm sure it's a trick she doesn't know. "It won't just be her, though," I say. "Every Connected Land Conduit will be there. I can't fight them all."

Clicks looks helplessly at the papers spread out across the colorful rug; we'd begun to create an ambitious plan to rescue Kary using the Colossi in the Courtyard of Youth. "I wish there was another way, my dear."

"So do I," I say. Submitting to downleveling will be like lying on subtrain tracks, waiting to be crushed.

"I wish we could send Devorla to the Grimshore," Fedorie says, not only stomping her foot but also grinding it into the carpet. "She should know what it's like to suffer."

But I think she does. She's just gotten really good at ignoring it.

That night, I sleep in Bermy's large, very soft bed. As I stretch out on the blankets, I try not to let my worries overwhelm me, yet I soon feel the cold bite of panic. Where is Kary now? Has anyone hurt him?

Glowy Pony settles next to me, relaxing so completely that if he could make a sound, I think I'd hear a satisfied sigh.

"Why doesn't the Great Drae have a cagic companion?" I ask, and then I think about the time Glowy Pony dropped small items on my head while I recharged the seg-coach reservoir. "You don't like us storing cagic, do you?"

Glowy Pony shakes his head, *no*.

"But why not?"

Of course, unable to speak, he can't give me a detailed answer.

Yet I'm sure I'm on the right track. Aerro certainly had problems, but he didn't hoard energy or take it from children. Whatever the natural order is, the Great Drae and her fellow Conduits have been upsetting it.

I suppose there's another question I should ask, a much bigger one. "Are the Hidden Gods real?"

Glowy Pony gives me an answer, but it seems too slippery to hold in my mind. Moments later, I don't even remember asking the question.

In the morning, with Clicks's permission, I borrow some of Bermy's clothes. I don't take any of her fine, ruffled stolas, though, just a drab gray wrap. It's the sort of outfit I'd wear to a funeral, which seems appropriate for today.

I then have breakfast with Clicks and Fedorie, who also stayed the night so she could say goodbye. We are all so sad we hardly speak or eat, even though the food is delicious: griddle cakes, smoked fish, and shortberries.

As I walk to the front entrance, Clicks's sons finally notice me and trail after us saying all sorts of ugly things:

"Are you inviting strange women into the house now?"

"Isn't that mother's dress? Are you letting this girl steal from us?"

Both Clicks and Fedorie try to quiet them. But when the two young men still don't back off, I lose my patience and create a shimmerdark wall, trapping them on the other side.

"I wish I could do that," Clicks says, admiring the glittering barrier.

I then step out into the damp fog, and Fedorie rushes after me. "Are you sure you don't want us to come with you?"

"Please don't," I say, and as she hugs me, I try to absorb some of her courage. She always seems to have so much of it. "Downleveling isn't a pretty sight, and this way, maybe you won't get into trouble for helping me."

"I don't care if they throw us in prison! I don't care if…" Clicks swallows heavily, too overcome to continue. He then pulls me into a hug too, his curly mustache wet with tears.

When he lets me go, I numbly climb into the chariot and sit behind the driver. Moments later, I'm rolling through the Landroot District, and far sooner than I'd like, I see the Foundry in the distance; a square tower about the size of Kaverlee's central subtrain station if it stood on one end. Brightly lit meters on the tower's walls assure everyone that the city has plenty of energy, and a large month clock gleams at the top. Its longest hand has nearly moved out of the blue Dark Month half and into the yellow Bright Month half. First though, it'll pass through a slim, green wedge, for sometimes the Dark Month is slightly longer than the Bright Month and vice versa. A smaller circle near the center of the clock marks the twenty-four hours of the lunar day.

I wait in the chariot until it's exactly ten. Then, head held high, I climb out and walk toward the many Shieldbearers stationed at the Foundry's entrance. Drae Devorla stands among them, wearing a long, blue stola, a dark pallacoat trimmed with silver embroidery, and a gauzy scarf. Her dense curls are now dark purple rather than steely gray, and she's subdued them with a silver clasp. She's even dusted her eyelids with blue powder.

I suspect she's dressed this way because the other Conduits are here. It was the same when I was a Predrae. She only wore fine clothes when they visited us or we visited them.

My stomach churns as I approach her, freshly furious that she's letting this happen. Yes, Kaverlee has laws, but laws are made by people, and people are flawed.

"I'm sorry about this," Drae Devorla says as I reach her, and I scoff softly. I bet she's truly only feeling sorry for herself. She's surely upset that I reappeared, disrupting her orderly life, and she must also be upset that I'm making her reconsider how unethical downleveling is.

"Where's Kary?" I demand.

She looks shocked that I'd speak so sharply to her, but quickly recovering, she smoothly says, "You'll see him in a moment." She then escorts me past the Shieldbearers and into the tower.

"What will happen to him... after?" I ask. I hate that I'm quivering, and I especially hate that those tremors are shaking my voice. I want to appear brave even if I'm terrified inside.

"Kary's future depends on how cooperative you are," Drae Devorla says, sharpening her threat.

My next question is even harder to ask. "And what about me? After my downleveling, what happens then?"

We've reached the end of the vaulted entrance. Drae Devorla stops and clasps her hands behind her back. "First of all, I hope you'll survive the downleveling process and have no lasting damage."

I open my mouth to speak, but she keeps talking.

"I think you'll be fine so long as we rinse your cagic slowly and steadily—and as long as you willingly release your energy. We'll also downlevel you manually rather than mechanically. It's a longer process, but a gentler one."

"But... after—what happens after?" I say, feeling a wave of nausea because I'm really going to be downleveled, aren't I? I'm not going to come up with a last-minute escape plan. I'm about to lose a piece of myself—a defining piece—and I might also lose my life.

Drae Devorla lifts her shoulders in a stiff, clenched shrug. "I'll try to make the case that enduring a downleveling is enough of a punishment for your defiance. If it's my decision, you'll be free." She gives me a tepid look, which I suppose is better than a cold one.

Maybe there's still a flicker of love for me in her, but I guess a flicker isn't enough.

We enter the Foundry's central hall, which I loved as a child for it has such an interesting assortment of old and new cagic processing equipment. Several two-hundred-year-old cagic reservoirs stretch up to the distant ceiling—elegant monstrosities of glass and copper resting on massive, tiled plinths. And standing alongside those ancient reservoirs are modern, pressurized steel tanks, shiny and bristling with pipes, cables, and valves. All the cagic stored here keeps the building warm, and now that I'm a Shimmercaster, the energy thrumming through this place seems to also hum inside me. I glance at Drae Devorla. She must feel it too.

I remember there always being a lot of engineers bustling around these tanks, but today the first floor of the Foundry is quiet and empty. The other Conduits—and Kary—must be somewhere above.

"Put this on." Drae Devorla takes a small garment off the clerk's desk. It unfolds in her loose grip and appears to be a small jumper with no sleeves and very short leg-coverings. "The process works best if we can directly touch your skin," she explains.

I want to refuse, but for Kary's sake, I bring the tiny, black outfit into a storage room behind the clerk's desk and put it on. It's horribly revealing, and I feel just as uncomfortable as I did when wearing my frilly stola in the labor agency camp. As I pull my ankle boots back on, I whisper, "Glowy Pony."

He immediately appears and brushes against my leg with concern.

"I don't like it either," I whisper. "Am I making a mistake?"

To my surprise, he nods.

"Then what am I supposed to do?" I ask quietly-yet-frantically.

The shiny horselet nudges my leg again as if I should already know.

But I can't think of any other options, and once I've laced my boots, I whisper, "You'd better hide again."

Glowy Pony gives me a sad look.

"And… well…" I kneel and stroke his head, "goodbye." Losing my cagic will probably sever my connection to him. Forcing back tears because I don't want to meet the other Conduits with a red nose and puffy eyes, I return to the clerk's desk and Drae Devorla.

"Leave that here." She nods at the bundle of clothes in my arms. As I put it on the clerk's desk, she pulls a small box out of her pocket. "Now I'm going to give you an injection."

"You said I wouldn't be drugged." I take a quick step away from her. I don't want to feel intense pain, but I also don't want to lose control of this situation—at least not any more than I already have.

"Don't worry." Drae Devorla opens the box, revealing a needle attached to a glass vial. "This won't put you to sleep. As I mentioned, you must willingly release your power, and to do that, you need to be awake." Needle in hand, she reaches for me. "This will simply calm you… and make the process easier for all of us."

I still don't hold out my arm. "Do I have a choice?"

Drae Devorla tightens her jaw. "Not really, no."

So I give in because that's what this is all about—giving in. I wince as the needle punctures my skin, and then I hiss through my teeth as the stinging, burning liquid spreads up into my elbow and shoulder.

It reaches my mind as we enter the cagic lift, and it doesn't calm me. Instead, I feel like I'm being crushed beneath a pillow. The air's thick and unyielding, and my thoughts keep sidling away mischievously.

When Drae Devorla hauls the lift's metal doors to the right, I take several wobbling steps into what I realize is the top floor of the Foundry. I came here often when I was young and Drae Devorla was replacing many of the oversized storage tanks that fill the room. Compressors thump rhythmically, and the air is even hotter.

Ahead of me, the other Cityland Conduits move from a conversational cluster into a more formal semi-circle. There are nine citylands but only eight Conduits. Priffa doesn't have one. That used to mystify me, but now I wonder if they simply downlevel every cagically gifted infant. I know they buy their energy from neighboring lands.

The Conduits watch me closely, their expressions ranging from judgmental to pitying. I recognize a few of them; there's the Thrall of Matreornan, with her chiseled, proud face, and beside her is the plump and pretty Vazor of Ganorine. She always has shimmerlight glowing in her silvery hair. Then there's the Mighty Sharn of Highland Tilber; the Conduit who breeds animals, including Osren's horselets. She and Drae Devorla have always been rivals, which still seems strange to me. They are the only Conduits who seem to value knowledge and innovation over wealth and power. As for the Conduit on the far side of the group, he's the only male Shimmercaster and therefore must be the Nelbar of Midnith. He has extremely large muscles that he seems to be showing off in his sleeveless, finely tailored tago.

All the Conduits have brought portable cagic reservoirs that are just as ornate as their outfits, and the most impressive reservoir belongs to the Vazor of Ganorine. It's covered in enamel flowers and has a large glass tank full of curving gold coils. None of the Conduits have their apprentices with them, and I suppose their Shimmercasters-in-waiting were left behind to care for their citylands.

Just as I'm about to ask where Kary is, I see him, and realms, what's wrong with him? He's lying unconscious beneath the giant Dark Month clock, whose inner workings are also housed on this level of the Foundry. He's surely been drugged, and even though he's motionless, Matron Isme stands over him, awkwardly holding a shockgun. I'm surprised that she's guarding him rather than a Shieldbearer, but maybe I shouldn't be. I suppose the Conduits don't want the average soldier knowing how brutal downleveling really is.

I hoped I'd be able to say goodbye to Kary. Yet Drae Devorla must have thought I'd try to rescue him, and it would definitely be difficult to free an unconscious person. Not that I'm in any state to be heroic, though. The medicine's still moving sluggishly through my veins, and I can hardly put one foot in front of the other.

Drae Devorla guides me across the room, and the Conduits step aside, revealing a steel table behind them. It's just like the one Auldora was lying on, and it's positioned rather dramatically in the center of the spiraling floor tiles and directly beneath the chamber's dangling, globe-shaped lights.

The cagic compressors continue to thump away, making a *shugga shugga* sound, and my heart beats along with them.

Soon, so soon, this will be over.

"Honored Conduits of the Connected Lands," Drae Devorla says. "Before we begin, I remind you to abide by the International Energy Accord. Once you've collected fifty thousand summiunits of cagic, release the girl, and I'll complete her downleveling."

I'm perspiring heavily now, and the floor seems to waver as Conduits begin connecting themselves to their reservoirs with cuffs and wired halos. It's a complicated process and many of them must remove several layers of clothing before they can properly attach all their collection equipment. I thought those wires would be attached to me, but I suppose this is what Drae Devorla meant when she said they'd be downleveling me by hand. As for her, she's tethering herself to one of the twelve Foundry tanks that loom over us like massive, shining pillars.

I'm not ready for this.

Yet how can I delay it? Is there a way to keep my cagic for even a moment longer?

"May I say goodbye to Kary?" I blurt, surprising myself. "I might not survive."

Drae Devorla flushes as if my request is embarrassing.

"Please," I say, struggling with the *s* sound because of the sedative. Perhaps I can wake him up, although I'm not sure how it will help.

Drae Devorla looks as if she's about to say no, but then the Vazor of Ganorine gives me a pitying smile and says in her accented voice, "Let the girl bid farewell to her dear boy. Why not?"

So I stagger across the room alone because all the Conduits are now attached to their reservoirs. I trip twice, which is especially mortifying in my skimpy outfit, and then I kneel beside Kary like we're in one of the fanciful stories Clicks used to tell—stories where princes and princesses would wake each other with kisses.

And maybe I can wake him with a kiss, or rather, with a cagic spark concealed in one.

I lean down, sadly aware that our second kiss will be even less ideal than our first, but I still place my mouth on his and summon shimmerdark to my lips. Hopefully the snapping pain of it will wake him. I wait to feel the energy crackle against his unreceptive skin. Instead, though, I feel nothing. Did he just absorb the cagic?

I blink, confused.

"Hurry up, girl," says the Nelbar.

I don't pull away from Kary as wild thoughts tumble through my medicated mind. Can Kary soak up cagic? It must have something to do with his childhood downleveling.

I send another spark into him, and again I get the sense that the energy is simply flowing through his skin and settling into his muscles.

Perhaps I can store cagic in Kary and then reclaim it later. If so, maybe my downleveling can be undone.

So many maybes. But right now, anything is worth a try.

I deepen my kiss, sending even more energy into Kary. His heart beats faster beneath my splayed fingers. He twitches. His eyes flutter.

"It's time, Xylia," Drae Devorla calls.

I ignore her, and I wish I could transfer cagic into Kary more quickly. They'd surely see it glowing around the edges of my mouth, though.

"Xylia!" Drae Devorla says impatiently. "That's quite enough."

"I love you, you know," I whisper to Kary, tearing up because it's true. I should have told him while we were hiding in the insulae.

Then I limp back to the Conduits, my boots clacking on the tiles, and I climb onto the steel table. I stretch out on the uncomfortable surface—so cold against my bare legs—fighting the urge to cry. At least I tried to save my cagic, and what I'm doing now, I'm doing to save my friend.

"Now remember," Drae Devorla tells me, "relax and don't resist. The more easily cagic flows out of you, the less painful the procedure will be… and the less damaging."

I shudder and nod.

All the Conduits then place their hands on my arms and legs, and oh, I hate the feel of so many unfamiliar fingers. It's like how my family was always giving me unwanted hugs, but of course, this is much worse. I wonder how intense the pain will be. Will I faint? Will I die? And if I die, what will death be like? Maybe I'll travel to the Hidden Realms. Maybe nothing will happen at all.

"Are you ready, Xylia?" Drae Devorla asks softly.

I'll never be ready, so I don't answer.

She puts her hands on my forehead anyway and says, "on the count of three," to the others. "Remember, channel her energy slowly. I don't care if this takes hours. I want her to survive. One…"

I take a deep breath.

"Two…"

I want to look at Kary one last time—I'm doing this to save him—but Drae Devorla's grip on my head is too tight.

"Three."

I'm suddenly plunged into searing, overwhelming agony. It's as if one of those tall pressurized tanks is slowly rolling over me, crushing me. I wail, and it's an ugly sound that seems to scrape its way out of me. The pain is unthinkable, horrible, paralyzing.

"Stop fighting, Xylia!" Drae Devorla says, and she sounds so far away. "It will hurt less!"

Am I fighting? I'm not trying to. I'm just suffering. The pressure pulling on my insides intensifies, and it's almost as if the Conduits are prying my bones out. I scream even louder. How can I bear this?

I can't.

Oh mercy, I want my mind to break. I don't want to feel anything anymore.

The procedure has only begun, though, and Drae Devorla said it might take hours. And what if she doesn't keep her promise? What if she gives Kary to the Matreornans? What if she punishes Clicks and Fedorie for helping me? What if my sacrifice is meaningless?

I need relief—a break. I have to stop the pain, even if it's only briefly.

A thought stomps and kicks through my mind: Glowy Pony. The Conduits don't have cagic guides. If they see him, maybe they'll be distracted—maybe they'll stop torturing me.

My muscles throb and even the ones controlling my mouth are barely responding, but I manage to whisper, "Glowy. Show yourself. Please!"

He must appear because I hear murmurs of surprise. The Conduits' hands drop away from me, and merciful, merciful light, the pain fades.

"What *is* that?" someone asks, maybe the Thrall of Matreornan.

"It's some sort of cagic creature," another Conduit replies, I think the one from Capeldell.

"It's obviously a cagic guide," says the Nelbar of Midnith.

And then there's a rush of voices, and I lose track of who's speaking.

"But there are no guides anymore."

"The girl called for it. Can she do that?"

"Maybe we should delay this—study her, study it."

"No, she's too dangerous."

Then a different voice, a wonderfully familiar voice cuts through all the others. "Let Xylia go."

Kary!

I weakly turn my head, and my eyes first focus on Glowy Pony's prancing, dark shape, then the massive clock gears, and finally, on Kary. He's standing now and holding Matron Isme's shockgun, which he's also pointing at her. "Let her go!" he shouts again.

Isme nurses what looks like an injured arm.

So I did wake Kary, and when he regained consciousness, Matron Isme was probably watching my downleveling so he was able to surprise her, overpower her, and take the shockgun.

Realms, I'm glad I kissed him.

"I'll shoot," Kary warns, unfortunately sounding groggy. He's surely trying to shake off whatever drug the Conduits used on him. I'm sure his threat is empty, for he's not the type to hurt anyone. But the Conduits don't know that.

"I'll take care of this," the Nelbar of Midnith says as he creates a sharp diamond of shimmerdark.

"No!" I cry.

Drae Devorla shouts "No!" too. "No fighting. There's too much energy in these reservoirs. We can't risk an explosion." She begins unbuckling me and says to the others, "Help me."

The Vazor starts freeing my left leg while the Conduit from Capeldell loosens my right.

Yet the Thrall of Matreornan mutters, "This is not a good idea."

As soon as my arms and legs are loose, I climb down from the table, feeling even weaker than before. At least I still have my cagic, though. A feeble yet reassuring spark crackles in my chest.

I can barely make it across the room; I have to crawl part of the way. Glowy Pony trots anxiously at my side.

"You realize there's still no way out of this, Xylia," Drae Devorla calls. "The Foundry is surrounded by Shieldbearers, and the city's sealed for the Dark Month. Even if you leave, we'll find you and make you come back."

Reaching Kary, I collapse at his feet. "Stand up," he whispers. "We need your powers to escape."

I try. I do try, but my body isn't listening. I was just partially downleveled. I need to recover.

Worse, Drae Devorla's right. Kary's courage changes nothing. No matter how far we run, the Conduits will chase after us, and there are so many people that Drae Devorla could threaten to make me do what she wants.

Kary reaches down with his scarred stump. I grip his forearm, and although he's unsteady, he's strong enough to pull me upright.

Yet, while he's distracted, Matron Isme lunges for the shockgun. They struggle briefly, the weapon flashes, and she drops to the floor.

"No," Kary cries, and I'm sure he didn't want to hurt her.

The Nelbar of Midnith responds to the sudden violence by lobbing a shimmerdark orb the size of a chariot at us. We duck, Drae Devorla cries out, and the cagic wrecking ball obliterates the Dark

Month clock. Heavy gears drop, smashing the tiles, while giant, glass shards fly outward. Then I hear shouts of pain and panic from the Shieldbearers below.

"Stop!" Drae Devorla roars, fighting to detach the many tethers connecting her to the storage tank, but the Nelbar doesn't listen. He sends a lethal panel of searing, red-rimmed shimmerdark at us.

Maybe I can block it with a shimmerdark shield.

But something else happens.

Something deeply strange.

A beam of shimmerdark bursts out of *Kary's* chest, wild and strong, just like my explosive attack on Golly. His energy rushes to meet the Nelbar's shimmerdark, and when the two collide, they shatter. Shards, this time of cagic, spray outward. Some knock more glass out of the broken clock. Some spatter the walls, chipping bricks. Yet one slices through the Thrall of Matreornan's chest, and she falls dead, and another punches a hole in one of the towering reservoir tanks.

After that, everything seems to happen very fast.

"No!" Drae Devorla shrieks. "No, no, no!"

Copious amounts of compressed cagic sprays out of the tank's gash. Bolts pop. Cables snap free.

The reservoir is going to explode—the same way that canister did when I killed the wolievs. We have seconds. Less than seconds.

"Out! We have to get out!" I cry to Kary, who's staring around the hall, stunned.

Thankfully, his practical nature overpowers his frantic surprise. Scooping me up, he leaps through the broken Dark Month clock and out into cold, foggy nothingness.

I have one last glimpse of the doomed Conduits, struggling in their straps and buckles, one last look at the Great Drae's expression of regret, resignation, and despair. Then there's a blinding burst of heat and light, and the air fills with purple and blue sparks.

I shape a shimmerdark disc just in time to slow our fall, but I'm too rattled to have much control over it. We slam against the roadway and both grunt in pain. I'm vaguely aware of Shieldbearers rushing past, glass crunching, and of chunks of brick wall and reservoir tank thudding down, often embedding themselves deeply in the road. People nearby yell and scream as more explosions burst above, creating devastating, fiery flowers that bloom for only seconds. I stare in disbelief as the top two floors of the Kaverlee Foundry vanish in an angry blaze of cagic.

Drae Devorla, the Mighty Sharn, the Midnith of Nelbar. All the Conduits are dead—gone.

Kary shakes my arm, and I realize he's been calling my name, trying to get my attention. "I'm like you. Why am I like you?"

"I don't... I'm sorry." I can't make sense of Kary's transformation right now—the city's dark. There are no streetlamps, no window lights, no cagic signs over shops, no *star net*.

The terrible reality of what's just happened strikes me like another exploding reservoir. With the Foundry destroyed, the city has no power. The cagic barriers protecting us have shut off.

"Nocturnes," I say to Kary. "They'll get in."

26

The Expansion District

I stand up, feeling stunned, and because I'm still wearing next to nothing, extremely cold. Shimmerlight sparks drift down around me like glowing snow, sizzling and vanishing on the damp ground. More explosions rumble deep within the Foundry, which must mean the tanks on the lower floors are erupting. And the city is still dark—so dark.

Kary gets to his feet too, and as Glowy Pony canters ahead of us, we stagger away from the collapsing building.

How awful: by trying to save myself, I've put the entire city in danger. "I have to get to the Expansion District," I say. It only has projected energy barriers, and they're surely no longer working. The rest of the city is at least surrounded by solid walls, but if nocturnes enter the Expansion District, they'll soon be everywhere.

"Xylia." Kary puts his hand on my arm, and his touch still crackles with cagic. "What happened to me?"

"I… I don't know…" I say, but that's not the truth. "I tried to store my cagic in you, and it came bursting back out. I think. I'm sorry."

Kary stares at me, his mouth trembling. "What?"

"I have to go. I have to stop the nocturnes." I create a shimmerdark disc large enough to ride on. There's no need to hide my powers now for no one's paying attention. The nearby crowd is transfixed by the burning Foundry.

"I'll help you," Kary says. Tiny particles of shimmerdark form on his fingers. He brushes them off, and they make snapping sounds as they vanish.

I shake my head. "We don't know what's happening to you." This might just be temporary; the power I poured into him burning away.

Undaunted, Kary climbs onto the shimmerdark disc. "I'll risk it. I'm helping. Let's go."

There's no time to argue, so I join him on the disc and raise us upward. "Glowy!" I call. "Lead us to the Expansion District!"

Yet the shiny horselet doesn't appear. That's troubling, but I can't dwell on it. I'll have to find my way without him. Using the still blazing Foundry as a landmark, I head west. I also move slowly to make sure I don't fly into the dark star net or slam into a building. I feel like I've fallen into a nightmare. Every horrible story Aerro told me about Haberdine runs through my mind.

Frightened voices echo up from the city, and I hope Clicks and Fedorie are somewhere safe.

"Find shelter!" Kary shouts down. "Nocturnes are coming!"

I can't see if anyone's listening; it's too dark. I also wonder if Kaverleans truly understand the danger they're in. They've never had to shelter before, and other than the odd owleck or carrow flying over the city, they've probably never seen a live nocturne either.

I swerve sideways, narrowly missing a star net support pillar. "I wish I could see better."

"Maybe I can help," Kary says.

A sputtering ball of shimmerlight appears in front of us but then sails uselessly off into the darkness.

"Summon it into your hand," I suggest.

Kary tries again. A small ball of energy flickers on his palm, and thank the source, stays there. He huffs in a satisfied way, and then asks, "Did you give me some of your powers?"

"I don't know," I say, still mystified. "You summoned shimmerdark before. Could you do it again?"

Kary lets the shimmerlight dissipate and then, after a few tries, creates a small mass of glittering dark energy.

"Realms," I breathe. Is he a Shimmercaster now? If he is, maybe he truly can help me.

So as we fly down the city's sloping west side, I give Kary a rushed cagic lesson. "Shimmerdark is firmer than shimmerlight and easier to shape and move. I use it to hit things, make shields, and travel around… which sometimes just means summoning something to hang onto. Keep your shapes simple—they're easier to manipulate that way. And it takes time, but forcing more energy into a shape without making it larger heats it up. Once hot, shimmerdark can cut through almost anything."

Kary listens attentively, but will it matter? Hundreds of nocturnes are probably entering the city—all the monsters I carried Rutholyn through. I'm sure we're already outnumbered.

My eyes have adjusted to the dark, and I see the gray outlines of the labor agency dormitories. We're nearly there.

"Kary," I say, gripping his arm. "Please don't do this. You can still hide. We won't survive."

"I'm not leaving you," he says. "I'll just help as long as I can."

I want to cry, to hold him, to tell him how much I love him, but there's no time.

We've arrived, and where there should be a gleaming wall of energy, there are only dark energy projection towers standing roughly one hundred paces apart. The star net is still attached to their pointed tops, but it isn't charged and glowing, so it stretches over us like a useless black spiderweb.

And oh realms, we can't even land. Nocturnes are everywhere: sharecks and wolievs mostly, but a few sennecks slither into alleys, bearcurs lumber toward buildings, and owlecks and carrows swoop through the unprotected opening.

I hear frightened voices and see the occasional shockgun flash. There seem to be a few Shieldbearers in the tower lookouts. I see they've already killed an owleck and a woliev, but it hardly matters when so many monsters are pouring into the city.

"What do we do?" Kary says, his voice shaking.

"We have to turn the barrier wall back on," I say, "somehow." For even if Kary and I clear this area of monsters, the cagic wall covers several miles, stretching around the entire western end of the city; our best efforts would be like cleaning only one tile of a large floor.

Fear plucks at me as I float us over to the nearest tower. We climb into the empty lookout, and peering over the railing, I examine the energy projectors. The lenses are connected, so if I pour enough cagic into the cables stringing them together, I could technically turn the barrier wall back on. Yet I'd have to summon an absurd amount of energy; far more cagic than I've ever generated. I doubt it's even possible. Yet without the barrier wall, nocturnes will continue to enter the city until they completely overwhelm us.

"Protect me," I say to Kary as I climb over the railing.

He lifts his good hand and seems about to say something, but then just nods.

I work my way down a metal utility ladder, feeling vulnerable. Not only does icy wind buffet my bare arms and legs, nocturnes could attack from any direction.

There are six cagic projectors on the tower, three on each side. Reaching the nearest one, I find the main power cable, a thick cord the size of my wrist.

Just as I tug back the insulating rubber, exposing the bundled wires inside, there's a burst of cagic nearby, followed by an angry, screeching squawk.

I look up and see an owleck flapping away, shedding feathers.

"I've got you covered!" Kary shouts. "Keep going!"

I take a ragged breath and pour energy into the wires. Blue shimmerlight spirals down my arms and into the cable.

The nearby projector towers crackle, I see sparks spraying, and light flickers in a few lenses.

More. I have to summon more. I reach out with my heart and mind. I reach out with my whole self.

Drae Devorla chose me because of my cagic control, and that talent has never mattered more than right now.

So I ignore how cold and uncomfortable I am, braced against the ladder rungs, and I trust Kary to protect me, and I summon and summon and summon. I pour every bit of cagic I can scrounge and glean into the cable. I pour myself into it, every tiny spark of energy hiding in me, from my hair, to my toenails, to whatever binds me together. Everything.

And the cagic barrier turns on.

I don't just see it, I feel it. A wall of solid blue shimmerlight outlines the Expansion District like a smooth brushstroke.

Turning on the barrier isn't enough, though; I have to sustain it.

Yet oddly, channeling cagic suddenly feels easy because I am the wall. I'm stretching around the battered Lower Topdwell homes and shops. I'm cradling everyone and everything within. I no longer feel ladder rungs digging in behind my knees or the frigid Dark Month chill. Instead, I feel the sturdy network of energy projectors and the occasional zap of a nocturne trying and failing to break through me.

I can still see, yet it's a strange sort of seeing because I'm looking in all directions at once—at the Silkord Sea, at the snowy northern spreadfarms, at the city streets. Focusing on Kary, I see he's helping the Shieldbearers by riding a shimmerdark disc from tower to tower to recharge their shockguns. Every now and then, he looks down at the barrier, and I think he's concerned.

No, I know he's concerned. I feel his worry.

I also sense terror and pain throughout Kaverlee City. I hear nocturnes smash through windows and doors. I feel people's panic and agony as they are dragged into the streets.

Yet then I feel something else; hope. Following the sensation, I'm surprised to find my Colossi lumbering into the Expansion District.

They tower over most buildings and are nearly as tall as the insulaes. Prancing ahead of them, tiny and bright and leading the way, is Glowy Pony.

Maybe I'm losing hold of reality. I'm stretched so thin, and I've drifted so far away from my true self.

But no, the Colossi really do seem to be walking though the city. And each one has several Shimmerlings huddled in their shining mechanical hands, their huge fingers positioned like protective cages. I realize the Shimmerlings are moving the giant figures, working together like they did in the Courtyard of Youth. Most of the girls are cagic blind, but there's one sighted Shimmerling in each group shouting out directions. I feel Tah Roli Miri's presence and Paislene's. They've come to help. They want to defend the city. And they also know they're sacrificing themselves. Their trembling courage shines so brightly, I can't look away.

Thank the realms, they are also being clever. The Shimmerlings spread out along the cagic barrier, and once in position, they have their Colossi place them in projection tower lookouts or on sheltered balconies. I then watch the huge metal figures attack the nocturnes invading the city, crushing them, swatting them against walls, and snapping spines. It's impressive and immensely helpful, and yet the nimbler nocturnes like sennecks and catterns elude them and head deeper into the city.

Kary joins a group of Shimmerlings just in time to protect them from a carrow. His cagic shapes are lop-sided and he moves them awkwardly, but he still bashes the huge, black-feathered bird against a wall, crushing its head.

And something else starts to happen too. I feel it before I understand it; something's stirring, something familiar.

Tah Roli Miri suddenly whirls up into the air, shimmerdark clinging to her legs.

I sense her amazement as she reshapes the energy covering her lower body into huge spike of energy, and she then plunges herself into a nearby monster.

Stumbling free from the dead cattern, she's stunned and afraid something's wrong with her.

No, nothing's wrong, I long to say. *This is what you're meant to be.*

Moments later, Paislene transforms too. Cornered on a ledge, she suddenly wraps a shimmerdark whip around a senneck.

Not long after that, a tall, fair-haired girl encases an owleck's head in shimmerdark, blinding it and causing it to collide with a building. Then another girl's cagic changes and another.

Tury, Aerro, and I became Shimmercasters when we were in danger. The same thing must be happening now.

From my unusual, removed perspective, I experience these Shimmercaster transformations differently than I'm sure I would otherwise. I feel the energy whirling intricately through each girl. It perfectly completes little energy puzzles inside them, closing loops, connecting edges, twining loose threads of their being into firm cords. It's beautiful and satisfying, and if I could cry, I would.

Before long, there are more Shimmercasters than Shimmerlings, and now that my cagic-touched sisters can battle the nocturnes directly, they start hunting down the beasts who've crept deeper into the city. Abandoned, the Colossi sit motionless in the icy streets.

Now that I'm acutely aware of everything, I'm also aware of the huge figures and their hollow cores. I wonder why they weren't built with protected chambers inside for their human puppeteers. It makes no sense.

Unless they were never made for us.

Realization sweeps over me.

I once tried to make Glowy Pony larger, but he couldn't maintain his shape. A Colossus, though, would help him keep his form. It would be like a massive exoskeleton.

Kary! I try to call, even though I have no mouth, no voice. *Kary!*

Thankfully, I seem to be able to press my thoughts into him. Kary twists around, searching for me. He's just carried a Shimmerling too young to transform into a tower guarded by shockgun-wielding Shieldbearers. I sense he's glad I'm still alive but alarmed that I've reached for him in such an unconventional way. I've slipped into another realm, he worries.

Kary, give Glowy Pony more energy, I try to tell him. *Make him larger. He can control a Colossus.*

Thank the realms, Kary seems to understand. Creating a cagic disc, he rides it back into the fray, passing new Shimmercasters and the many monsters still prowling the streets. He soon finds Glowy Pony trotting in impatient circles around Sevensy.

Can Kary add energy to a shape I created? Yes, it seems he can. Perhaps Glowy Pony chooses the energy he accepts. Yet Kary's not an experienced cagic sculptor, and when he makes Glowy Pony larger, he simply turns him into a shapeless, four-limbed mass.

But that doesn't seem to matter. Glowy Pony slides his new form into Sevensy. Then amazingly, Sevensy begins moving again. Yet the

Colossus no longer sways like a marionette; he stands up like a person, using his arms to steady himself. Then, limbs swinging, eyes gleaming, he thuds off into the city, chasing the monsters I know he can find faster than anyone else.

My attention returns to Kary, and I'm not sure why he's cornered Paislene and is waving his arms around. She's baffled; I can feel it. But then her confusion shifts to understanding, and she and Kary create small amounts of shimmerdark.

Kary brings his mass of energy over to Goliah, and Paislene dashes over to Winch with hers, and I realize what they've done. They've summoned—or I suppose requested—cagic guides of their own.

Moments later, Winch and Goliah are back on their huge feet too, looking around for nocturnes.

I've seen this scene before, I realize, in the underground temple's mural—teams of Shimmercasters battling nocturnes alongside Colossi. And although my sense of self is no longer very human, joy still seeps through me. I wish I was fighting with them too, but it's also an honor to protect everyone and watch them work harmoniously together.

I have a dislocated, sad sense that I may never find my way back to myself. But if this is the last thing I ever see, realms, it's magnificent.

27

Recovery

The noise wakes me; a deep, rhythmic, *thud, thud, thud, thud.* I'm cold yet lying on something warm, and that something is bobbing gently up and down. I'm also sore in a non-specific, achy way. And I feel weirdly euphoric, and well, small.

"She's waking up," Kary says.

My eyes don't want to open, they're swollen and gummy, but I manage to squint.

Above me, the star net glows blue. It's back on! I exhale, relieved. I also see several Colossi walking nearby—so that's what the noise is. Two-story and three-story buildings stretch up around me, and maybe they're Upper Topdwell shops; it's hard to tell because they have no lights on. I'm also surrounded by sweaty, bloody, bruised Shimmerlings. They're walking, and I must be lying on a moving shimmerdark disc.

"We did it," Kary says, leaning over me. "You did it."

"I'm... back to normal?" I ask weakly.

He nods, grinning.

And I do seem be myself again. I can feel my arms and legs, and the only emotions inside me are mine.

I look around blearily. "Why is everything still dark?"

"We aren't sure," Kary says. "The city walls and star net are on, but nothing else. The Shimmerlings say when they left the palace, engineers were trying to reconnect Triumvirate Hall's energy reserve to the damaged city grid. Maybe they only powered the essentials? After the barriers came back on, we found you on the ground, shining with cagic."

My head feels unusually cold. I reach up and... "Where's my hair?"

"It was gone when we found you," Kary says gently.

"And you had no clothes on," adds a solemn looking Shimmerling who's probably only about twelve.

Merciful realms. Now that I think about it, I realize I'm wrapped in something but otherwise naked.

"You're alive, though." Kary touches my shoulder.

"And the nocturnes?"

"Dead." He smiles proudly. "At least the ones in the city."

"All of them?" I ask.

Kary nods.

"The Colossi helped us hunt them down," Paislene says, appearing in my line of sight. Her curly hair looks even wilder than usual, and her stola's drenched in blood. "A lot of strange things happened today."

"The cagic guides," I say softly. "Of course—they can find anything. Amazing. You're all amazing."

Nearly everyone smiles at me, which is a little like the Bright Month dawning early.

"Why don't you rest," Kary says. "We'll be there soon."

I nod gratefully, not quite sure where "there" is, but confident that if Kary chose it, we'll be safe.

Yet even though I doze, I'm still mostly aware of what's going on. We arrive at our destination, Clicks's house, but no one's home. Paislene knows how to pick locks though, knowledge from her pre-palace days, so we're soon able to head inside. The cagic guides, still wearing their Colossi suits, remain in the street, keeping watch.

Without power, the house is cold and dark, but several of the new Shimmercasters create cagic shapes to provide light and heat. Whoever's controlling my shimmerdark litter, Kary, I think, carefully places me on a sofa. Everyone else splits up to tend wounds and search for clean clothes and beds to rest in.

After a while, I sense someone at my side. I open my eyes and find Tah Roli Miri kneeling beside me. I used to think she was plain, but grimy clothes and messy hair suits her. She looks like a powerful warrior who just emerged from a glorious battle, and I suppose that's exactly what she is.

"How are you?" she whispers.

"Tired," I say. "Why are we here?"

"I don't know who to trust at Triumvirate Hall." Always slightly distracted, Tah Roli Miri tugs a loose thread out of her tattered stola. "Your friend told us what happened to you at the Foundry and what happened before." She frowns. "After what you did today… powering the barrier… it should be you—you should be the next Great Drae."

The old me would have been thrilled that she thinks that. Instead though, I reach for her hand and say, "Then make me your Predrae."

She smiles, and like her rumpled gown and snarled hair, smiles also look good on her.

After Tah Roli Miri drifts off, Paislene appears. "Alright Xylia, get up. Found you some clothes."

I'd rather rest a little longer, but she hauls me up off the sofa, hardly bothering to keep me draped in what seems to be a Shieldbearer's pallacoat. She then directs me into a nearby, spacious lavatory, lighting our way with a shimmerlight orb. She hands me folded clothes and is about to leave when I say, "Wait; could you help me change?" Now that I'm upright, I'm very dizzy.

She rolls her eyes. "Fine, fine." Not being very gentle, she drapes me in another one of Bermy's stolas.

Once clothed, I peer into the lavatory mirror. My reflection is unfamiliar again. Not only am I bald, my eyebrows and eyelashes are also gone.

"I like this shimmerdark stuff," Paislene says, replacing her shimmerlight orb with the inky-black energy. "It's so interesting and mysterious."

I nod. I thought I understood it, but after today, I'm not sure.

"Wish Auldora was here." Paislene changes her shimmerdark shape from a circle to a cube to a pyramid. "I thought she winked out... but your boy says Drae Devorla downleveled her."

"I tried to stop Devorla," I say. "I'm sorry."

"Don't be sorry," Paislene says grimly. "You did stop her, and now she can't hurt anyone else."

I still don't know how I feel about that. I'm glad Drae Devorla can't keep downleveling people, but I wish she wasn't dead. I guess big problems rarely have solutions that don't require some sort of sacrifice.

I'm able to walk back to the parlor on my own, but it saps my energy and I'm eager to sit back down.

Kary checks on me next, joining me on the sofa. After a short silence, he says, "I think you reversed my downleveling."

I nod. I must have. I suppose if his body once generated cagic, that system simply needed to be restarted. After that, the Midnith of Nelbar attacked, triggering Kary's Shimmercaster transformation.

"Do you think you could… do it again?" Kary asks. "Give other people their power back? Undo more downlevelings?"

I breathe in deeply, yet the air seems to get lost on its way to my lungs. "I suppose so." What an overwhelming realization. The Shalvos said they only authenticated a small number of children and downleveled the rest. A huge number of people in Kaverlee and the Periph and probably throughout the Connected Lands might be potential Shimmercasters.

Kary's mouth twitches sideways. "You'd have to kiss a lot of people, though."

I flush. He remembers? I suddenly wish a nocturne was here to devour me whole. "I had to hide what I was doing from the Conduits, and besides… I know you don't feel that way about me." I say the last part quickly before I'm too embarrassed to speak.

He laughs.

I look at him in dismay. This isn't a laughing matter. "I'm sure I'd simply need to summon cagic into a person. Putting my hands on their back would probably work just as—"

He leans forward. "I do feel that way about you."

I draw back.

Kary gives me a look as warm as red-edged shimmerdark. "I didn't kiss you on the Grimshore because you were the Predrae and I'm a criminal's son, but I *wanted* to. I've always loved you, Xylia, always."

I don't know what to say, but it doesn't seem to matter because Kary kisses me. It's so unexpected and wonderful, pinpricks of shimmerlight dance across my skin. After such an unpredictable day, I'm amazed I can still be surprised.

When we break apart, I say, "Are you angry with me for turning you into a Shimmercaster?" I didn't exactly ask permission.

"No, not at all," he says without hesitation. "I've lost some important things over the years, and you just gave one back."

He reaches over and finds my hand, and I squeeze his in return.

The house is quiet now. Everyone else must have found places to rest, so Kary and I try to do the same thing. We attempt to sleep on the sofa with our arms around each other, which is uncomfortable in a way that's worth the trouble. Yet not much time passes before I hear voices and footsteps. Sitting up, I'm startled to see a crowd of people flowing through Clicks's home like it was a subtrain station: fancy Landroot residents, servants, older people, children. Even more oddly, everyone seems to be leaving the house, not arriving.

I spot a familiar face towering above the others. "Fedorie!" I cry.

Seeing me, she shoves her way past several people and jogs into the parlor. "You're here! And you're alive! And… your hair's gone?" She looks down. "And Kary's alive too!"

Kary sits up groggily. "Fedorie, where were you?"

"Saving the city," she says proudly, brushing dust off her clothes.

Clicks soon appears too, looking disheveled yet energized. His gray hair sticks up enthusiastically, like it often did on the Grimshore. "Starless skies! You're both here, thank the realms! And Xylia... what happened to your hair, my dear?"

"I don't know," I say, half laughing, and realms, we have so much to tell them. "Is your family alright, Clicks?" I ask. "And your mother, Fedorie?"

They both nod.

"My boys are still down in the shelters," Clicks says, with an exasperated shake of his head. "They refuse to come up until a Shieldbearer personally assures them the city's safe."

"That's probably for the best," I say. "Shimmerlings are sleeping in their beds."

"Shimmerlings? Here?" Fedorie's eyes widen. "Was Triumvirate Hall evacuated?"

"No, no," I say, "but..." Where do I begin?

Kary gestures to the parlor chairs. "You should probably sit down."

So Clicks and Fedorie join us, settling wearily into curved chairs that are shaped like seashells. I'm pleasantly reminded of how the four of us often sat around Grimshore cookfires.

"Our story might take a while," I say. "Why don't you tell us what happened to you first?"

"If you wish." Clicks clears his throat. "After we parted ways at the Foundry, Madame Straechos and I couldn't simply sit by while you both were in danger. Therefore, we made our way to the Foundry."

"You didn't," I say, horrified.

"Don't make that face," Fedorie says. "We're sitting in front of you now, aren't we? Anyway, those Shieldbearers wouldn't let anyone get close. But maybe we should have thanked them because not long after we arrived, the big clock broke and the whole building burst apart!"

"We tried to find you two, naturally." Clicks's voice quivers. "But there was so much smoke and fire. We feared the worst."

"And with the city's power off," Fedorie says. "We knew we'd be nocturne food if we stayed where we were."

Clicks leans forward. "Thus, we deployed emergency procedure number three."

"What's that?" Kary asks.

Clicks smiles. "The Antiquities Society doesn't just protect historical documents and architecture; we also vow to save lives. All those shelters? If there are ever nocturnes in the city, our members are prepared to usher as many people below ground as possible. Madame Straechos and I gathered up a good-sized crowd and led them into the Upper Topdwell baths, which has an entrance to the shelters. After that, I made my way back through the tunnels—which were quite crowded by then—and evacuated my household."

"It was dark as shareck's guts down there," Fedorie adds. "But the society members had lanterns and knew their way around. I found my mother's insulae, and we evacuated everyone there too."

So even though nocturnes did enter the city, a lot of people were already hiding. I love that even though we didn't plan to, we Grimshore survivors still worked together.

Kary and I then tell our story; I describe meeting the Cityland Conduits and all the devastation that happened afterward. I also try to explain how I became the barrier wall surrounding the Expansion District, yet it's hard to describe something I don't fully understand. Kary doesn't say much, but he does explain where the Colossi came from. Apparently after the Foundry exploded, Tah Roli Miri and Paislene wanted to use the huge figures defend the city. Most of the Shimmerlings liked the idea, but the Maternals wouldn't let anyone leave the palace. Yet then Glowy Pony mysteriously appeared, and the confused, frightened Maternals relented.

"I suppose there are now far too many Shimmercasters," I say, thinking of the brave Shimmerlings who transformed.

"But there are also no Conduits left to downlevel us," Kary points out.

I nod. "Maybe Kaverlee can change now. We could end downleveling and stop Authenticators from taking children away from their families. I suppose we'll have to convince the King and Queen it's for the best, though."

"I don't think we need to worry about that," Kary says, looking out the window toward the palace's dark silhouette. "Triumvirate Hall should worry. They need to convince a large group of Shimmercasters to keep protecting and powering their city."

I suppose he's right. The emergency reservoirs beneath the palace won't last long now that the Great Drae's gone and half the Shimmerlings have left.

"Perhaps it's time to return to the old ways," Clicks says.

"Yes!" Fedorie curls her hands into fists. "With lingersleeping and teams of Shimmercasters protecting us."

Kary looks hopeful too. "Imagine if we restored cagic to everyone who ever lost it. There would be hundreds of Shimmercasters."

"Maybe more," I say, and it's an exhilarating thought. But trying to dramatically shift how Kaverlee operates won't be easy. People don't like change, and they hate giving up privileges. I know.

"Then there are the dead Conduits." I sink back into the sofa, suddenly tired again, suddenly aware that my body has experienced intense stress and trauma. "The other citylands... they're going to be furious."

No one says anything for a moment.

"They'll think we assassinated their Conduits," Kary says.

"It was an accident, though," I say. "We were defending ourselves."

"Will they believe that?" Kary asks.

They won't, I realize. And even if they did, I still caused the Conduits' deaths by resisting my downleveling. It may be a cruel law, forcing Shimmercasters to give up their cagic, but it's still a law. Have I just started a war? The thought makes me shiver even though the room has warmed up. The Connected Lands have coexisted peacefully for over two-hundred years.

"It seems..." Clicks pauses to yawn. "It seems we have a lot to think about. But before we make any big decisions, I suppose I should attempt to retrieve my sons again." His eyes twinkle. "I must say, it is tempting to leave them where they are."

Once Clicks has left, Fedorie heads to the kitchens, claiming she's "hungry enough to eat a shareck." Then it's just Kary and me.

I look over at his damaged arm. "You might be able to make yourself a cagic hand," I say cautiously because I know Kary hates anyone mentioning his injury.

Sure enough, I feel him tense up, so I don't press the idea.

Instead, we simply sit quietly, side by side. I imagine meeting with King Macreolar and Queen Naradara and attempting to explain that the Foundry explosion was an accident. I also imagine trying to prove to Kaverlee that I'm not a murderer. It all seems impossible. "You know…" I start, my words sounding louder than I expect.

Kary looks over at me.

"I think I need to…" How do I phrase this? I rearrange my thoughts and try again. "I think Kaverlee can become a fairer, better place—but only if I leave."

Kary gives me a questioning look.

"I didn't mean to kill the Conduits or destroy the Foundry, but it will always seem like I did." I take a deep, shaking breath.

"Technically, I killed them," Kary says, and to my surprise, he attempts to create a shimmerdark hand. It looks like a child's attempt to draw a mitten, but he makes it open and close.

"You killed them with power I gave you," I say. "Power you didn't know you had."

"Power you didn't know I'd get." Kary tries to create fingers. He shapes three, but they're odd lengths. He glances over at me. "I can't let you take all the blame."

I love that he's willing to share such a complicated burden, but I'm not sure he fully understands the consequences. "If we seem like leaders, if we ask people to make big changes, the Foundry explosion will seem like it was part of our plan. People will think we killed the Conduits on purpose. King Macreolar and Queen Naradara won't want to work with us either. They'll also think we're murderers. And even if we get a few people to understand what really happened, can we convince all of Kaverlee? What about the other citylands? It won't end well."

Kary sighs and nods. "It would almost be better if we had died in the Foundry."

I look at one of the framed prints on the wall; it's a map of the Connected Lands. "If we leave, though… vanish, then maybe Kaverlee can have a fresh start." After missing Kaverlee for seven years, I can hardly believe I'm suggesting this. "The other new Shimmercasters are innocent, and the King and Queen will know that. They weren't at the Foundry. All they did was save Kaverlee afterward, and that makes them heroes. I'll talk to Tah Roli Miri. She's the new Great Drae. She's the perfect person to make changes."

"She doesn't seem, uh… forceful," Kary says.

"She has other Shimmercasters to support her," I say. "Help her."

"But *vanish*." Kary leans heavily back on the sofa. "How do we do that?"

I smile sadly. "We've done it before."

28

The Grimshore

I hide when I see the boat because it could be anyone. But Glowy Pony doesn't join me. He stands on a tall, sharp rock and watches the cagic-powered vessel putter closer.

Yet as I shade my eyes, I realize I recognize that blue-hulled ship. It's the same boat that whisked Kary and me away from Kaverlee last year, and it belongs to a member of the Antiquities Society.

"They're here!" I call, running across the uneven ground, then leaping onto a shimmerdark disc and riding it up to a small group of newly constructed buildings.

Kary's just where I left him, shimmerdark sparing with a couple of other young people.

"They're here," I repeat, breathing hard.

"Good," Kary says, clapping his hands together—one flesh and bone, and the other dark and glimmering. "I was beginning to worry."

"Me too," I say.

"Shall I call everyone down to the beach to welcome them?" asks a young Finneth potter who's now a Shimmercaster like us.

"Our friends don't know about the rest of you yet," I say. "If they see strangers on the beach, they might think something's wrong."

So it's just me and Kary and his cagic guide, a glittering hare, who hurry back to the water.

Glowy Pony's still there, and the boat's even closer. I can now see people on deck waving to us.

Kary waves back. "Fedorie's hard to miss, and there's Clicks and Tah Roli Miri, but who are the others?"

I squint. We weren't expecting anyone else. Yet then I recognize the passengers. "It's my sister! And Mother and Osren!"

Now it's even harder to wait for the ship to drop anchor and for our visitors to climb into a rowboat and join us. I'd bring them ashore using transference, but I'm not sure how much the crew knows.

Tah Roli Miri sails over on a shimmerdark disc, though.

"Xylia," she says in her absentminded, dreamy way, stepping down onto the rocky beach. "It's good to see you."

"You too," I say, curtsying, for she is the Great Drae now. "How's everything back home?" And what a big question; it contains so many smaller ones, for Kaverlee was in turmoil when we left.

"The cityland is well," Tah Roli Miri says, yet exhaustion laces her words. "Everyone lingersleeps during the Dark Month now and teams of Shimmercasters guard the city and the Periph."

I want to know more, but the rowboat's reached us and Mother's helping Fifsa out of it. I rush over to help. My sister's belly is big and round, just like Theandra Shalvo's was the last time I saw her.

"You're expecting!" I cry as Fifsa gives me an enthusiastic-yet-awkward sideways hug.

"You're going to be an aunt!" she gushes. "And I like your hair! What a daring, short style!"

"Thank you," I say. I suppose she wouldn't know I lost it. My hair finally started growing again two months ago and now it sticks out in unpredictable, startling ways.

Mother hugs me too, and surprisingly, I don't mind. "Look!" She holds out her hand. Cagic sparks swirl up off her palm and coalesce into a bright diamond of light.

"Your powers… they're back," I say.

"She's very talented too," Fifsa tells me.

Mother blushes. "I'm still learning."

"Don't let her fool you. She leads the Outer's Cove Nocturne Guard." Fifsa puts her arm around Mother.

"There's only five of us," Mother says dismissively.

"Which means there's only five of you defending the whole town," I say, impressed. "I'm proud of you." And how strange, to be proud of a parent.

Mother gives me a bright, hopeful look, and although it's the same look that once made me cringe, now it just makes me feel grateful.

Fedorie and Clicks hug me too, and Osren gives me a brief, approving nod. Then Kary and I lead everyone up from the beach. As we walk, Fedorie wants to know where we've traveled over the past year and if we've seen any unique nocturnes. I tell her we've journeyed through Matreornan and Highland Tilber, and that we fought a venomous geckog and something with a furry stomach and webbed wings.

"Must have been a batler!" Fedorie whistles in amazement. "They're rare!"

Clicks politely asks if we've had any luck finding the Vaylark, the jewel Kary's father stole.

"Not yet," Kary says. "But we think it might be somewhere in Ganorine."

Returning the stolen jewel won't solve all of Kary's problems, but it should help. And if that gem once really did open a celestial door and let nocturnes into our world, maybe it can help us get rid of them.

"Well then, I've unearthed even more Vaylark information for you," Clicks says, pulling a dossier out of a leather bag.

"And I've brought you more traveling gear." Fedorie hands me eyeglasses with hinged magnifying lenses, a curious collection of bottled liquids, and a fierce hunting knife. "Here's a book on nocturnes too. Might as well know your enemy."

Osren has a present for us as well: a horselet in a wooden cage. "If you don't like her, you can sell her."

"Sell her?" I cry. "Never!" I'm instantly enchanted by the tiny, dappled horse. She wickers softly as I whisper, "I'll call you Speckle."

"No, you won't," Osren says. "Her name's Clip Clop, and if you change it, you'll ruin her training. Anyway, I'm hungry. I think you should feed us."

"I'll show you to the dining hall," I say.

"No need to be sarcastic," Osren grumbles.

Kary gives me a twinkling glance. "Xylia's not being sarcastic. We do have a dining hall, and well… you'll see."

Just a few moments later, we cross a ridge, and our little village is in view: two dormitories, a supply hut, and the already mentioned dining hall. The buildings are all very simple, but even though they're surrounded by thorny Grimshore trees and jagged rocks, they look welcoming.

As we make our way down the uneven path, a group of people emerge, some old, some young, and a few children too.

"Who are they?" Fifsa asks.

"Shimmercasters and Shimmerlings," I tell her. "They were downleveled people we met while travelling. Once we gave them their cagic back, it wasn't safe for them to stay where they were."

Kary gives everyone a quick tour of our settlement, and Fedorie and Clicks are particularly impressed by our well. It's a luxury they never had while living here. They're also eager to help prepare food, so while Kary leads the others off to check the fishing nets, Fedorie, Clicks, and I cut the thick rinds off pinemelons. As we work, they tell me more about Kaverlee.

Apparently, it's been tough transitioning to lingersleeping, but King Macreolar and Queen Naradara have been supportive. They claim they didn't know how routine downleveling was or that winking out was a lie. Ganorine, our neighbor to the south, has transitioned to lingersleeping too, and there's talk of it in Matreornan as well.

"I'd heard rumors about Ganorine," I say. "How wonderful. I've also heard rumors the new Nelbar of Midnith wants me captured dead or alive—Kary too."

Clicks nods soberly. "I hope you're being careful, my dear."

"Always," I assure him. Kary and I use different names on the mainland, and we don't summon cagic when anyone's nearby. "What about you two? What have you been doing?"

"A little of this and that," Clicks says, and he also explains how he finally dealt with his sons: "I started charging them rent, and by the next Bright Month, they'd both moved out."

That makes all of us chuckle, and then Fedorie happily tells me about her new job, assisting a professor at Peremberie University. "He studies nocturne remains," she tells me, nearly bouncing on her toes. "And what a treasure trove there was after the Expansion District battle—so many complete carcasses to dissect! It's kept us busy all year."

Both Clicks and Fedorie also think that Tah Roli Miri has become an excellent Great Drae.

"I wish I didn't have to use that title, though," Tah Roli Miri tells me later while I'm giving her a transference tour of the island. "There are so many Shimmercasters now, I'd like to have a ruling council. The King and Queen agree with me, but they also think there's been too many changes already. They want me to wait... five years at least."

"They might be right," I say. "But remember, you have just as much authority as they do. They call it a Triumvirate for a reason."

Tah Roli Miri smiles. "I suppose that's true."

She's particularly interested in our old cave shelter. She drifts through it as if her feet don't touch the ground. With her phenomenal cagic skills, maybe they don't. "Is this where you stay during the Dark Month?"

I shake my head. "We travel to the mainland on shimmerdark discs and sleep in an abandoned shelter in Highland Tilber." Remembering all the lonesome Dark Months I once spent here, though, makes me think of Aerro.

"Did anyone ever contact that man in Haberdine?" I'd told her about Aerro before leaving, yet I wouldn't be surprised if she forgot. I'm sure she's been extremely busy since then.

Yet Tah Roli Miri nods, and I'm relieved when she says, "Yes, he's fine," in her relaxed way. Visiting Aerro could have been dangerous. "Paislene and Auldora came with me," she continues, "but no one else. We didn't want to frighten him, and like you said, he wasn't happy to see us." She speaks slowly, thoughtfully. "It took several visits to convince him that I was the Great Drae and that he could keep his powers and that he should move to Kaverlee City. Yet…" She gazes out the cave's entrance. "He might be happier here."

The last time I saw Aerro, he nearly killed me. But I only hesitate slightly before saying, "Then he should come." He needs to heal, and that's probably hard to do in a cityland undergoing so many changes.

"How many Shimmercasters does Kaverlee City have now?" I ask.

"Five hundred or so," Tah Roli Miri says in such a vague way, I can't tell if she thinks that's too many or too few.

I suppose the number makes sense, though. All former Shimmerlings surely wanted their cagic restored, and anyone who was downleveled by Authenticators would be eligible too.

"It's been merry chaos," Clicks tells me that evening. "But we're muddling through."

Part of his muddling, it seems, has been adopting Rutholyn's brother, Vonnet. "That dear boy was delighted to have his cagic returned," Clicks says, and then he tells me that the labor agencies are under strict review.

"What about Theandra Shalvo?" I ask.

"I believe she's been sentenced to three years of house arrest," he says, and maybe that should make me feel happy or at least vindicated, but instead I just feel sorry for her.

"The Antiquities Society has been busy too," Clicks adds. "Triumvirate Hall asked us to oversee the restoration of the old city shelters."

Fedorie joins us. We're sitting on a log overlooking the bay. It was always a favorite spot of ours, and even though it's lightly raining, no one seems to mind. "Who would have imagined," Fedorie says, "that we'd come back to this wretched place willingly!"

We all laugh.

"It's different now, though," I say. This was once a frightening place, a trap, a prison. Now it's a haven; a safe place to plan for a better future.

The next few lunar days are wonderful, full of conversation, laughter, and catching up.

"I'll come again," Mother promises when their boat eventually returns. Instead of waiting for her to hug me, I reach for her. When I let go, she says, "I like that Kary boy, but remember… you're both young—very young."

Ah, even now she's going to say things only a mother would.

Fifsa, who's already in the rowboat, winks at me. "Oh, don't worry Mother, Xylia says they only hold hands."

I say the rest of my goodbyes reluctantly, for even though I'm sure I'll see them again, I don't know when. That lunar evening, Kary and I meet in our usual spot, on a windy ridge overlooking the green-gray sea.

"I'm sad and happy," I say. "It's strange."

"Do you wish you were going with them?" he asks.

To be honest, a part of me will always miss Kaverlee and always wish I was the Great Drae. I wanted it for so long, the desire wore permanent grooves into my heart. But I also know I've made the right choice. Power should be shared, not hoarded, and Kaverlee is now on a path leading to something better. Maybe part of growing up isn't just learning to let things go, but learning to be at peace with still wanting them after they're gone.

So I say, "I'm where I'm meant to be."

"Me too," Kary says. He takes my hand, and cagic sparks swirl around us and then out over the water—ready to light our way.

Acknowledgments

Thank you to my wonderful, encouraging husband Stephen for always being willing to talk about plot, magic systems, and characters, and also always helping me find time to write. I love you. And thank you to my amazing three children; I'm thrilled that you enjoy storytelling and world building too.

Thank you also to the amazing writers who read early versions of Shimmerdark and offered such helpful feedback: Julie Artz, Gerardo Delgadillo, Madeline Dyer, Fred Gambino, Stacey Trombley, and most of all, my close friend, the talented author, Alexis Lantgen. Thank you to my amazing parents and sisters for always being supportive. And thank you to my old, beloved writing group, FDIS, who heard the beginning of this story the night we first met and often asked when I'd finish "that book with the giant robots." I miss you guys.

Finally, a huge thank you to anyone reading this book. I'm always encouraged when one of my stories finds its way onto someone's shelf, or even better, claims a little bit of affection in their heart. I truly appreciate any reviews and ratings on Amazon or Goodreads.

About the Author

Sarah Mensinga grew up in Canada and now lives in Texas with her husband, three kids, and two cats. Recently, she illustrated Heather Avis's picture book, Different: A Great Thing to Be, and in the past, she's contributed to the Flight comic anthologies and worked on films such as The Ant Bully and Escape from Planet Earth, as well as the TV show, The Adventures of Jimmy Neutron. When she's not writing or drawing, she loves playing board games and going for walks with her family. If she could summon shimmerdark, she'd use it to go spelunking.

Find more of Sarah's work at sarahmensinga.com

Other Books by Sarah Mensinga

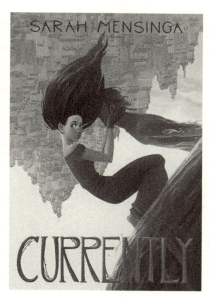

Every year, Nerene's village shelters in Varasay City while the surrounding lands flood. Yet Varasay only protects those who obey its laws, and after Nerene's best friend starts a riot, he's in danger of being cast out. Nerene manages to find Lord Osperacy, a traveling thief with enough power and money to save her friend, but he'll only help her if she agrees to work for him.

Set in a unique fantasy world inspired by the ocean travel of the early 1900's, Currently is a sometimes funny, sometimes gritty exploration of how to survive when you're surrounded by power but have none yourself.

A box just arrived at our house! Hurray, a box! It's addressed to Dad, though, so that means there's probably some boring stuff inside. If only there was something interesting in there, like candy or a robot... or perhaps even a candy-filled robot?

Join three siblings on an adventure of discovery and imagination, well, at least until Dad shows up to open that box and ruin everyone's fun. But is it possible Dad's cooler than his kids think? Maybe, just maybe, he might not spoil their fun after all...

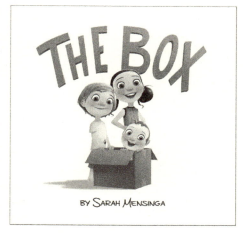

All books available on Amazon

Made in the USA
Monee, IL
28 April 2021